# Chimaera's Copper

TOR BOOKS BY PIERS ANTHONY

*Anthonology*
*But What of Earth?: A Novel Rendered into a Bad Example*
*Ghost*
*Hasan*
*Prostho Plus*
*Race Against Time*
*Shade of the Tree*
*Steppe*
*Triple Detente*

WITH ROBERT E. MARGROFF:

*Dragon's Gold*
*Serpent's Silver*
*The E.S.P. Worm*
*The Ring*

WITH FRANCES HALL:

*Pretender*

# PIERS ANTHONY AND ROBERT E. MARGROFF

# *Chimaera's Copper*

TOR
fantasy

A TOM DOHERTY ASSOCIATES BOOK
NEW YORK

CHIMAERA'S COPPER

A Tor Book
Published by Tom Doherty Associates, Inc.
49 West 24th Street
New York, N.Y. 10010

ISBN 0-312-93213-8

Printed in the United States of America

First edition: May 1990

0  9  8  7  6  5  4  3  2  1

# CONTENTS

# INTRODUCTION

*T*his is the third novel in a fantasy series in which the inhabitants of alternate worlds are distinguished by the shape of their ears. In the first novel, *Dragon's Gold,* young round-eared Kelvin and his point-eared little tomboy sister Jon managed to kill a golden-scaled dragon and later save the kingdom of Rud and their father John Knight from the clutches of evil Queen Zoanna. In the process, Kelvin found love with round-eared Heln, and Jon with Lester Crumb.

In the sequel, *Serpent's Silver,* Kelvin's half brother Kian discovered an alternate world where most folk were round-eared, but it wasn't John Knight's world of origin, Earth. Some folk had flop-ears, and many folk were similar to those of the point-eared world, except that their characters were reversed. Here good King Rufurt was evil King Rowforth, and evil Queen Zoanna was good Queen Zanaan. Instead of golden-scaled dragons there were silver-skinned serpents. Again the forces of evil were finally thwarted—but the mysterious Prophecy of Mouvar had not yet run its full course.

The third novel, *Chimaera's Copper,* covers another stage of that prophecy. But that does not mean the outcome is certain; for one thing, there are those who doubt that the prophecy has any validity. There are many characters, and versions of characters, so it may be best to refer to the following descriptions of characters when there is confusion. They are listed approximately in the order of their appearance or relevance to the story, and of course there is much about them that is not told here. Things are often not quite what they seem, when magic is involved.

# CHARACTERS

*Mouvar*—fabled roundear who made the prophecy and set up a chain of scientific transporters linking the frames

*Queen Zoanna*—beautiful, evil former queen of Rud in the pointear frame; lost in dark nether waters near the Flaw

*Professor Devale*—demon sorcerer and educator

*King Rowforth*—evil king of Hud, deposed. Analogue of good King Rufurt in the pointear frame

*Queen Zanaan*—the good version of Zoanna, in the roundear frame

*Broughtmar*—former aide and torture-master to King Rowforth; a mean man

*Zotannas*—good magician, but little real magic; Queen Zanaan's father. Analogue of *Zatanas,* evil magician of the point-eared frame

*Kelvin Knight Hackleberry*—the unlikely hero of the prophecy, and thus of all the novels of this series

*King Rufurt*—good king of Kelvinia, a gentle and somewhat ineffective man

*Charley Lomax*—one of the king's guards

*John Knight*—traveler from Earth, stranded in the magic realm; father of Kelvin and Kian

*Slatterly*—another guard

*Kian Knight*—Kelvin's half brother, the son of John Knight and Queen Zoanna

*Lonny Burk*—girl of Hud whom Kian loves

*Heln*—Kelvin's roundeared and pregnant wife

*Jon*—Kelvin's younger sister. His ears are round, hers pointed. He sometimes calls her "Brother Wart" because she once posed as a boy

*St. Helens*—familiar name for Sean Reilly, Heln's father from Earth; once a soldier in John Knight's platoon

*Lester "Les" Crumb*—Jon's husband, son of Mor Crumb

*Charlain*—Kelvin and Jon's mother; wife first of John Knight, then of Hal Hackleberry

*Hal Hackleberry*—Charlain's second husband; a good but simple man, whose name Kelvin and Jon took

*Easter Brownberry*—Hal's girlfriend

*Old Man Zed Yokes*—river man who ferries others across

*Phillip Blastmore*—former boy-king of the kingdom of Aratex before it became part of Kelvinia

*Morton "Mor" Crumb*—former leader of a band that helped Kelvin overthrow the evil Queen Zoanna of Rud; now a general

*King Bitler*—king of Hermandy, one of the seven kingdoms

*Chimaera*—with three heads: Mervania, Mertin, and Grumpus

*Dr. Lunox Sterk*—Royal Physician of Kelvinia

*Stapular*—prisoner of the chimaera

*King Kildom*—boy-king of Klingland

*King Kildee*—boy-king of Kance

*Helbah*—old sorceress of Klingland and Kance, good version of *Melbah* of Aratex

*Katbah*—Helbah's houcat familiar

*Bloorg*—Keeper of the Chimaera and official greeter of travelers

*Captain Abileey*—officer in Mor Crumb's army

*Captain Plink*—officer in Mor Crumb's army

*Captain Barnes*—Lester Crumb's second-in-command

*Grool*—Bloorg's second-in-command

*Squirtmuck*—a froogear leader

*General De Gaulic*—Commander of the Army of Kance

*Lieutenant Karl Klumpecker*—mercenary officer from Throod

*King Hoofourth*—monarch of the kingdom of Scud

*Bert*—a guard at the transporter cave

*Scarface Jac*—outlaw of Scud, analogue of *Cheeky Jac* in another frame, and of *Smoothy Jac*

*Queeto*—evil dwarf companion to Zatanas

*Heeto*—saintly dwarf companion to Zotannas

*Smith*—or a man by a similar name, member of Jac's band

*Marvin Loaf*—analogue of Morton Crumb

*Hester*—Marvin's son = *Lester*

*Jillip*—member of Marvin's band, analogue of *Phillip*
*Corporal Hinzer*—soldier in Lomax's camp
*Redleaf*—member of Marvin's band
*Bilger*—member of Marvin's band
*Commander Mac*—in charge of the Recruitment House; similar to *Captain MacKay* and *Captain McFay*
*Trom*—guard
*Mabel Crumb*—Mor Crumb's wife
*Charles Knight*—Kelvin's son
*Merlain Knight*—Kelvin's daughter

# PROLOGUE

## NIGHT

$S$he knew where she was going, if only she could get there. She had prevailed on the foolish John Knight to bring her this far; now she had to go on alone.

She stepped off the raft and sank into the dark water. One arm was useless, but she could still move the other, and her legs. She swam as well as she was able, down, down toward the bottom, not even trying to hold her breath, for it would only buoy her body. The air in her tired chest squeezed out of her nose and mouth and bubbled up in a silvery stream toward the raft and the confused man. Let him go; his usefulness to her was done. The current would carry him into the dread Flaw.

She found the lock, and managed to drag herself into it. In a moment she came up in air, gasping. She sprawled onto a platform, and finally let her consciousness fade.

Sometime later, in the dead of the eternal night that ruled here, a figure came. It was gross and masculine. "You have returned, Zoanna," it rasped.

She roused herself. "I need your help, Professor," she said weakly.

"I see you have broken bones. I can heal them. What will you pay?"

She struggled, and managed to turn over, so that she lay on

her back. She spread her good arm, and her good legs, and smiled despite the pain.

The figure stared down, interested. It reached out to squeeze a breast, as if checking its freshness. "For how long?"

"I want—I want to go to school, this time," she said. "To learn sorcery. For as long as it takes."

"That is long enough." The figure heaved her up and carried her away.

## MORNING

The wide man had once worn a crown. Now he wore only a torn robe and many bruises as he stepped from the transporter into the empty chamber. This was the world they had come from, he was sure. He had watched from concealment as they climbed the ladder to the ledge. Then he had followed, certain of what he would find: their gateway between worlds.

In the otherwise empty chamber on his home world he had not hesitated before using the transporter to follow. What was there for him at home, now, as a usurped king? Nothing but death at the hands of Broughtmar, his former aide, or some other disgruntled soldier. Or possibly at the hands of Zotannas, his queen's treacherous old father. If not death, certainly imprisonment, or life as an outcast. No, there was nothing there for him! Better to plunge boldly into something new, where his chances might be better and could hardly be worse.

Besides, there was something else. It was as if some mysterious impulse drew him along, as if someone were calling him. Someone he wanted very much to meet.

There was a subtle difference between this chamber and the one he had entered. The one on this world had no exit sign. It was cleaner and there were no dusty footprints on the floor. But the smooth sphere-shaped walls were similar, and there was the same magical radiance, that lit the machine and the table holding the parchment.

He hacked, coughed, and rubbed the bruises on his arms, legs, and face. What treachery Broughtmar had shown him! How he would like to go back and destroy the man. Well, someday he might. Meanwhile, he could relax at night by dreaming up torments for his former torture-master. He had thought the man worshiped his master above all men and gods. It showed that no underling could be trusted.

He read the parchment:

*To whom it may concern: if you have found this cell, you are a roundear, because only a roundear could penetrate to it without setting off the self-destruct mechanism.*

*I am Mouvar—and I am a roundear.*

*But because the natives look with disfavor on aliens, I masked my ears so that I could work among them without hindrance. I used the technology of my home frame to set things straight, then retired, for it was lonely. I set up the prophecy of my return, or the appearance of any roundear, to facilitate better acceptance in future centuries. The tools of my frame are here, and you may use them as you find necessary.*

*If you wish to contact me directly, seek me in my home frame, where I will be in suspended animation. Directions for using the Flaw to travel to the frame of your choice are in the book of instructions beside this letter. Please return any artifacts you borrow. Justice be with you.*

The man who had been king looked around and saw no artifacts. There was only the closetlike transporter, the table, the parchment, and the instruction book. He read the book. Phew! There was extraordinary power here! He could change the settings, and—

No, it was better not to tempt fate further. He wanted to leave no evidence of his presence at this time. Later, when he had a better notion of the situation outside the chambers, he might return and do something. All in good time. He was amazed at what he had learned already.

Smiling with satisfaction at the change in his fortune, he crossed the chamber to the big, round metal door. He pushed the lever. The door opened onto a ledge above an underground river—a complete change from the high cliff at the entrance to the chamber on his own world. The surface of the water was eerily lit by luminous lichen on the rock walls. And there, as if specifically placed for him, was waiting one small boat.

Former King Rowforth of Hud, the kingdom in the other frame, smiled his cruelest smile and clapped his big, powerful hands. Again he felt that mysterious influence, as if this had been prearranged. Ordinarily he would be suspicious of such a thing, but in this case he was thankful, because he suspected that it had saved his life and freedom. Maybe it was destined: he was fated to survive and dominate. If that smooth-skinned boy, Kelvin Knight Hackleberry, could claim a prophecy applied to him, why could not he, a legitimate king, have a preordained destiny? All his life he had believed himself destined to conquer, so why not here first, instead of his home world? Might he not eventually conquer all kingdoms in all worlds? The notion was intoxicating!

There came a kind of laughter in his head. Rowforth jumped. It was like his wife's voice, his queen, yet also quite unlike hers. This was the sound of victory and cruelty, while his wife was a submissive and kind creature, fool that she was. Insanity? No, surely not, for he was a king, and a king could not be insane. It had to be some kind of magic.

With rising excitement, the king launched the boat on the somber river, got into it, and applied himself to the oars. The wood handles, though splintery, fit his hands as well as those he had used at home. He put his back into it, eager to see what destiny had in store for him.

Ahead was a black, roaring falls with deep, deep darkness and stars and moving points of light. This was no ordinary night, he knew; it was the dread Flaw! He bypassed it, fighting the current. He knew he didn't want to get swept into that horrendous abyss.

He guided the boat away from the walls and out into the middle of the water as he rounded the bend. He was getting near to something now, and he was feeling it. He believed it would be his aid to destiny. His aid to conquest.

Suddenly he stopped rowing. He seemed to have no choice. What was guiding him?

He gazed down into the water, seeing nothing but his own bruised features. In this world there was a king who looked like him in a country not unlike Hud. That king, unlike himself, had pointed ears. He knew this without knowing how he knew it, or questioning its validity. Here in this world existed a king whose place he might take, if only he hid his ears.

He stood up in the boat, not knowing what he was doing,

and peered deep, deep into the murky water. Nothing, not even fish. Only the dim reflections of himself and the boat, and the rock walls gliding by, illuminated by the lichen.

Yet again he felt that mysterious impulse. He took a deep breath and dived. Swimming competently, conserving his breath and energy, he stroked down. Truly he was in the hands of destiny, now.

He dived deeper, deeper, though his body was growing hungry for air. His arms and legs worked steadily, refusing to be halted by fatigue. Silvery bubbles floated from the corners of his mouth. Into a tunnel, its smooth walls coated with more glowing lichen. He had better be going somewhere, because no way could he turn, let alone reach the boat again before drowning.

Then up, up, and suddenly the water parted. Air! He gasped, his chest working like a bellows, pumping in the air. That had been close! Yet he had been guided, somehow.

As his panting eased and his vision cleared, he realized that he was in a chamber not dissimilar from the one he had recently left. There was a woman here, holding a crystal ball. She had very red hair, and eyes incredibly green. Zanaan, his docile queen!

But there were two things distinctly different about her. This woman had no bruises, and her expression was not at all submissive. Also, her ears were pointed.

Pointed ears? Zanaan?

## AFTERNOON

Rufurt, king of all Kelvinia, rode his favorite mare to the ruins of his old palace. With him were two guards with whom he joked in what was his unkingly yet customary fashion.

Leaving the road, he pulled up by the pile of crumbled, fire-blackened masonry. He dismounted just as if he knew what he was doing. Actually King Rufurt, though a hefty enough man, was the soul of innocuousness, and lacked any real force of decision. That, he realized with a certain mild reflection, might be why they considered him to be a good king. He seldom knew exactly what he was doing, but he depended on good subordinates, and they enabled him to govern the kingdom well.

"Stay here," he ordered his guards, and walked casually away. The whim that had taken him was unusual, but perhaps he wanted to urinate behind a tree in privacy.

Around him were piles of ashes, blackened timbers, and the broken statues of former kings of Rud. Many a piece of once-valued art was buried here, though no one cared to recover it, remembering the history of this place. His evil Queen Zoanna had wrought horrendous evil here, and it would be a long time before that was forgotten.

Almost of their own accord, his feet carried him through the ruins. He went down the three flights of crumbling stairs. There, just as he knew it would be, was the underground river.

Standing there on the final landing, he remembered the words of an ancient prophecy:

> A Roundear there shall surely be
> Born to be Strong, Raised to be Free
> Fighting Dragons in his Youth
> Leading Armies, Nothing Loth
> Ridding his Country of a Sore
> Joining Two, then uniting Four
> Until from Seven there be One
> Only then will his Task be Done
> Honored by Many, Cursed by Few
> All will know what Roundear can do

To think the Roundear had come in his reign, and then in the unlikely form of someone who seemed to be but a boy: Kelvin Knight Hackleberry! Kelvin had saved the kingdom, and then saved it again. As the prophecy had foretold, he had joined two kingdoms. Rufurt still ruled, thanks to Kelvin, whose nature was almost as benign as Rufurt's own, but now he ruled more than twice Rud's former territory. The merged kingdom was called Kelvinia, after the boy, and Rufurt begrudged him none of that credit. But for Kelvin, Rufurt himself would probably be ignominiously dead now.

Why was he thinking of this, and just why had he climbed down all those awful stairs? His legs ached abominably. He needed to rest, but something screamed at him that he must go back or rue the consequence. At the same time he realized that he hadn't really wanted to climb down these stairs. So why had he done it?

Something went "Click." Something that had no business being here.

He half turned. As he did, a sudden chill formed somewhere in the region of his heart. It was uncanny what was happening to him. It was something he was sure had never happened before.

She stood there behind him, holding a crystal ball. Her hair was as red as dragon sheen, and her eyes the green of feline magic with sparks like tiny stars. Her pointed ears identified her with a horrifying certainty.

"Zoanna," he said. "Zoanna, I thought you dead."

"Yes, one-time king, once my feeble husband. I have returned to reclaim all that I once had and all that has since been gained for me. I am back to rule, Sweet Husband. Back to punish the likes of you, and to destroy the likes of that Hackleberry brat."

"No! No! You drowned! I know you drowned, and—"

She made a pass over the crystal ball with her hand. A repellent shade of red immediately suffused the crystal.

King Rufurt clutched his chest in sudden agony.

"Yes, yes," she murmured, her white teeth glistening as she smiled. "Did I ever tell you how pretty your ears are, my erstwhile liege?"

He fell forward, trying vainly to talk. The dock, when he struck it, seemed to be and not to be, while he—

## EVENING

When the king finally emerged from the ruins the sun was setting. His face had somehow gotten bruised, though the bruises had the appearance of those acquired days before. His clothes were now soiled, and he wore a stockelcap pulled all the way down over his ears despite the warmth of the day. He wore an expression that was not at all typical for Rufurt: malevolent.

"Your mare, Your Majesty," said Lomax, the tall guard. Though his voice was controlled, he was upset. *This is not right, not right at all.* What had happened to the king, this past hour?

The king went to place his foot in the stirrup that was being held for him. A hoof came for him, grazing his hip. The king stumbled and fell. When he rose a moment later there was no mistaking his expression: mean, extremely mean. Lomax had thought he might be mistaken before, but now there was no doubt. How could this be?

"What's the matter with you, idiot?" the king demanded. "Can't you control a stupid horse?"

The young guardsman swallowed. "Your Majesty—"

The king drew a riding whip from its harness scabbard and lashed the mare across her face. The horse reared, and Lomax was so startled he let go of the reins. The mare took off, running as though for her life.

The king swore, using an oath Lomax had never even heard. "I can't abide an unruly animal! Catch it and slay it!"

"But Your Majesty—" Lomax started, horrified.

"Do it, idiot!" The whistling lash just missed taking his eye out. Lomax swallowed and ran after the horse. She had stopped some distance away, her white-rimmed eyes as frightened as he himself felt. *What is going on here?*

"Here, girl, here," he said, holding out his hand.

The mare let him take the reins. But as he turned to lead her back he saw that the king had drawn a sword. The king intended to kill this beautiful horse! Unbelievable!

Sensing what the man sensed, the mare yanked hard on the reins. This time Lomax deliberately let them slip. The horse ran off.

The king glowered at him. "Never mind, Your Majesty," Lomax said quickly. "I'll catch her again. She caught me by surprise; she isn't usually like this. It may take a little time. Perhaps—" He strove desperately to think of something. "Perhaps you would prefer not to wait. It's a long ride to the palace. Another horse—"

"Yes," the king said grimly. "Another horse, in any

event." He spoke roughly to Slatterly, the other guard. "Bring me that roan!"

"Yes, Your Majesty," Slattery said, and obeyed with alacrity.

Slatterly held the reins and the king mounted. The guard handed up the reins.

The king raised his whip and brought it down first on Slatterly and then on the horse. "Get on your own horse. You ride ahead of me!" he ordered. "Fast! I want to reach the palace by nightfall!"

"Yes, Your Majesty." Lomax had never seen Slatterly move so fast before. But Lomax himself was moving fast, pretending he was going to catch and possibly slay the king's favorite horse.

Hoofbeats, and the king all but rode him down. The roan whirled, raising dust, and the king turned a terrible face down at him. "You, I want you to get that horse!"

"Yes, Your Majesty. Yes, of course."

"And I want you to ride her."

Hope leaped suddenly in Lomax's boyish chest. "Ride her, Your Majesty?"

"Until she drops! Ride her to her death!"

"Majesty, no—"

The whip caught him across the face, stingingly, telling him more plainly than words that this was not the same man who had entered the ruins. "You will do as I order! If you don't, I'll see you in the torture chamber!"

"But Your Majesty, you haven't—haven't got—" He swallowed, knowing that what he most needed to do was shut up.

"Haven't what?" the king demanded ominously.

"Haven't a torture chamber," Lomax said reluctantly.

"That," the king replied, "will be remedied. Now find that horse, ride her until she drops, then beat her to death. Failure in this will cost you your life in much the same manner!"

Lomax watched the bay whirl as the king rode away after Slatterly. He felt tears welling in his eyes, and knew they weren't entirely from the sting of the whip.

"What's gotten into him? What's gotten into him?" he asked the trees and rocks. He didn't know and wasn't certain he wanted to know. Witchcraft? Magic? Something old and evil and ugly? That ruined palace—who knew what evil spirits lurked in there!

But he was only a guardsman. These were, alas, questions his kind was not authorized to ask. But he knew that this was not his king—not the real king, whatever the body was.

There were tears on his face as he went after the mare. It was as though all the good that the roundear had done were now undone, and the bad was returning with a vengeance. How could this happen, so soon after the great victory of the forces of right?

When he caught up to the horse he discovered without surprise that he simply did not have the heart to hurt her, let alone kill her. She was not at fault; she had reacted to the alien nature of the king, being more forthright than the guardsmen dared be. She was too fine an animal to destroy.

He approached the proprietor of a farm where there were a number of horses. "I will trade you this mare for your worst mare of this color and size," he said. "Provided you keep the transaction secret."

"For how much gold?" the sharp farmer demanded.

"No gold. An even trade."

The man studied the mare. He could see that she was as fine a horse as existed in the kingdom. "You stole her?"

This was getting complicated. The truth was better. "She inadvertently offended the king. He ordered me to kill her. I can't do it. Give me a mare I can kill, and never speak of this."

The farmer nodded. "Now I understand." He brought out a scruffy-looking mare. "This one's ill, and due for slaughter anyway."

"She'll do." Lomax rode off on the new mare. When he reached a suitable place, he dismounted, drew his sword, and stabbed her carefully in the heart, so that she died quickly, without extended suffering. Then he took a whip and lashed the body, leaving stripes all over it. He paid special attention to the head, so that it became unrecognizable. This horse now looked as if it had been cruelly beaten to death. The original scruffiness of the animal only enhanced the effect.

He left the corpse there for others to find, knowing that the news would reach the king soon enough. He walked away, not looking back, thinking that if it were not for a certain lady, and not for his love for his homeland, he would desert for another kingdom. He had no pride in what he had done. He knew he had only reduced the evil somewhat, at great risk to himself. If the living mare were ever recognized—

Late in the day he slunk silently into the royal stable. There he found the groom cursing ceaselessly as he treated the deep welts on the roan.

"Rufurt," Lomax whispered softly to himself. "Rufurt, good king, where are you and who is this impostor who so boldly wears your face?"

# CHAPTER 1

## *Travel*

$K$elvin was not at all happy about returning to the world of silver serpents, but Kian had asked him to please come and be his best man, and their father was after all going to attend. It was, he vowed, going to be the last time he'd travel there. If Kian and Lonny wanted to visit, let them come here, or better yet, let them move here and live here. This world was the way a world should be, without monstrous silver serpents that could swallow a person or capture his soul. Of course in this world there were golden dragons, who had been known to gulp people down, but that was natural.

He was seeing things more clearly as the five of them rode along. His wife Heln was accompanying them as far as the palace ruins, as was his sister Jon. Heln was getting into the later stages of her pregnancy, but she had insisted, to his mixed pleasure and dismay.

"I still say," Jon said in her argumentative way as her horse pulled up alongside his, "that a pointy-eared person could use the transporter."

"Yes, Jon, once," he replied patiently. "Then there'd be no point-eared person and no transporter."

"You can't know that!"

"I know it certainly enough. Look, Brother Wart, has Mouvar ever lied to us? You know what that parchment says."

"Well, it just doesn't seem right," Jon fumed. "And I've asked you not to call me that. It makes people think there's a big mole on my nose or something. It might have been cute when I was little and dressed up like a boy, but now—"

"Right, Sister Wart."

Jon, as was her custom, raised a hand as if to strike him. Kelvin pulled back on his reins so that she rode ahead and he now rode beside his growing wife.

"Teasing Jon again?" Heln asked, flashing him a grin.

"She started it."

"She always does, doesn't she? Why is it you two can't act like adults?"

"Because we're brother and irritant," Kelvin said, proud of having thought of it.

Predictably, Jon turned in her saddle and stuck her tongue out.

"Now that's *really* adult behavior. Ladylike, too."

Jon said some naughty words that drew an immediate frown from Heln and a bit of amused head-shaking on the part of Kelvin's father. "Who's a lady, you—you—" Jon demanded.

"She's got you now, Kel," John Knight interjected. "Ever since St. Helens showed up and talked about Female Liberation she hasn't wanted to be one."

"She never did, Father. You didn't grow up with her as I did. If she could have grown a penis she'd have done it."

"Darn tootin'," Jon said, affecting one of St. Helens' cleaner expressions.

"Somehow I don't think Les would have approved," Kelvin remarked, referring to Jon's absent husband and his own good friend. "But she would have interests appropriate to her anatomy."

"Kelvin, that's enough!" Heln scolded. Jon, seemingly taken aback, merely rode on ahead.

"I'd think she'd get over that," Kelvin said.

"Kelvin, you really have to grow up a little! You and your sister both."

"Yes, Mama," Kelvin said.

For a moment, just a moment, Heln looked as if she'd

stick her tongue out. Little crinkles formed at the corners of her mouth but she managed not to laugh.

Kelvin got her message. She really was annoyed with him and she wanted him to appreciate it. Well, he appreciated. So maybe he'd try not to tease his sister as constantly. He just hoped she was resolving the same about him.

John and Kian had been all but dozing on their horses. Kelvin could imagine that both were thinking of their return to the land of silver serpents and of Lonny. Kian hadn't any doubt he could wed Lonny, and John really seemed smitten with the former queen who so resembled Kian's own mother in outward aspect. But why was he, Kelvin, returning? he had to ask himself. Why when Heln was carrying their baby and might need him, and couldn't use dragonberries to separate her astral self at this time? Why? Because he was John Knight's son and Kian was his half brother. Because each of them had saved the other's life. Because they were roundears on a world where roundears were uncommon, and kin. As his mother Charlain had said repeatedly, claiming it was a saying from John Knight's Earth: "Blood is thicker, Kelvin. Blood is thicker than air, earth, fire, or water. It's stronger than any magic, any witchcraft." So what did that mean? he'd asked, and she had talked about kinship.

John suddenly spoke. "I never knew the ruins were so far away."

"It's the riding," Kian said. "You're not used to it."

"That's for certain," John said. "To ease my backside I'm tempted to use the belt." He referred, of course, to the levitation belt that had been in the Mouvar chamber and was now around Kelvin's waist.

"That wouldn't look right, Father. You know how nervous people get when they see magic." Kian himself had once been nervous about such things.

"Science! Confound it, *science!* Magic is—magic is what that witch had and that the Mouvar weapon put a stop to."

"But then it has to be magic, doesn't it, Father?"

"No! At least I don't think so. It's antimagic, so it can't *be* magic. It has to be science."

"You know," Kelvin said thoughtfully, speaking up and

surprising himself, "it just could be we're in some sort of war. Not a war between armies, exactly, but between science and magic."

"Horse droppings!" Jon said. As happened more and more frequently these days it was a slightly more acceptable version of an expression used by Heln's father.

"Now I don't know there, Jon," John said, easing himself up in the stirrups. "Kelvin just might have something. Back on Earth there was sometimes talk about a war between faith and technology. That was not the same as here, in this frame, or in that frame with the silver serpents, but it's close. Mouvar seems to have science, albeit advanced. The citizens of this world, and the one we're going to, don't. Here or there a sorcerer might fly with a spell, but on Mouvar's world or mine it would be with a mechanical apparatus or belt."

"That's different?" Jon inquired. For once there was no sarcasm. She must really be curious, Kelvin realized.

"Well, I'd say so. But then you have to remember that I'm from a world and a culture where magic wasn't. As a boy I often wished there was magic, but then there were cars and radios and TV sets and airplanes. Unfortunately there were also scientific horrors that I don't like to think about."

"Horseless carriages, talking boxes, glass with moving pictures of sometimes living and sometimes dead people in them," Jon enumerated with satisfaction. "Though why anyone should want to listen to corpses talking I sure don't know! Machines that fly and what you called atomic explosions. Gee, Father, what would life have been for you if you had just called it magic?"

"Only Mouvar knows," John said. Then, fast, as if correcting a blunder, "I mean Mouvar's people, of course. And possibly others who have lived with both."

"Both magic and science? You think that possible?"

"That's what I was asking, Sister Wart," Kelvin said. So much for resolutions, he thought. But the seriousness of the subject seemed to nullify the previous conversation. "I mean, you take these gauntlets, for instance." He raised them high, as if for inspection. "Are they one or are they the other or are they both?"

John gave a sigh that seemed to owe nothing to the chafing

on his backside. "You know I wish I could decide. The gauntlets *seem* magic, but then so do many things that are science."

"I personally don't see what it matters," Jon said. "If something works, why not just accept it? Why did people on Earth have to deny magic anyway?"

"There you've got me," John said. "Magic doesn't follow natural laws, we are told. Magic doesn't follow our logic, so we say it *has* no logic. Magic, simply, unequivocally, can never, ever exist. Why? Because magic is impossible, that's why."

"That sounds stupid," Jon said.

"I agree. Magic does exist here, now. But on Earth where I grew up things were entirely different. To say you believed in magic was to be laughed at, or worse."

"Well I for one don't believe in science!" Jon said stoutly. She was so emphatic that each of them were forced to laugh. When the laughter died down, and her face was flaming, John gave her a most serious look.

"You have to believe in cause and effect, Jon. That's what science basically is. If something happens it has a cause. I still believe that, only today I often don't know the cause and so I accept with other people that the cause is magic. I admit it took me some time to get this far. Beliefs are hard to change."

"Like the transporter," Jon said. "And the spell on it that will destroy it and me if I try to use it."

"If you say so, Jon. To me it's science, but the results are certain to be the same. You and Heln rest overnight and then go home, once we reach the ruins. I know you'd like to follow, but I know too, as you must, that your trying to follow would be disastrous."

"I . . . know," Jon said. Then in a very small, slightly defiant voice: "Magic."

Late that day Jon repeated her now legendary feat of downing a game bird with her sling. They all enjoyed a hearty meal and a good night's sleep. At least Kelvin slept well, he reflected as they approached the site of the old palace, its blackened stones and burned timbers looking ghostly in the morning mist. He wasn't sure about the others.

"I suppose we'll need to get a boat from Old Man Yokes," Kelvin said.

"Where else, dummy?" his sister demanded, as politely as he felt she was capable.

"Of course," John agreed.

So again they met the old river man who had once indirectly saved Jon's life, and through that action the lives of John and Kelvin and possibly even Kian. Yokes was as before pleased at the company and after he and Jon had embraced like fond grandfather and gentle granddaughter, they had to tell everything that had occurred in the interim. This meant that Kelvin had to relive in his memory the experience of almost being killed by a curse and almost swallowed by a serpent. For Jon and Kian it meant telling of days in a dungeon, among other things. Jon sat fidgeting through the recitals until they got to the part about the witch at home and her own very small part in defeating her. Somehow Jon's part became larger than Kelvin remembered it, but the old man's eyes sparkled so that he forbore interrupting and telling it right.

After the stories were all told over steaming mugs of cofea and a plate of mufakes generously spread with aplear jelam, Yokes leaned back in his old rocker and sighed.

"Makes me feel I was right along with you," he said. "And now you're going back?"

"The girl I met," Kian explained. "We're going to be married. At least we are if I have any say."

"Ah, the only one in either frame for you, eh?"

Kian nodded, face flushed but obviously content.

"It was that way for me once," the old man said, and launched into the tale of an improbable courtship with an improbable young woman who later became an improbable wife. The tale took a long time, and Kelvin was surprised to find his emotions stirring as the gentle, aged voice cracked on the sad parts. He hadn't thought of worn old men as having been young and romantic once; he had pictured Old Man Yokes as being old from the moment he was born. It seemed it wasn't so, if the tale was to be believed.

Much later than they had intended, the men of the party

said goodbye to the women of the party and staggered down the long flights of stone stairs with a boat. Before they'd had help, but this was a working day and Yokes had neglected to call in the distant neighbors. By the time they reached the bottom landing and the old dock, Kelvin was sweating. The gauntlets made the lifting easier, but hardly the carrying. The legs that supported the boat's weight were entirely his own, however light it seemed to his arms.

"Look at this!" Kian was pointing. At the dock was an old, worn boat.

"Why that was on the ledge!" Kelvin said, remembering. "The ledge outside Mouvar's chamber!"

"One of those old men probably towed it in," John said. "Now that everyone knows the river is here, there are bound to be people exploring it."

"I hope nobody enters the chamber," Kelvin said. Would any pointy-eared person really be destroyed along with the chamber as the old parchment claimed?

"Anyone who gets down here will have heard about it," John said. "The story's widespread. I wonder that Yokes stood for all our retelling of what even he must have heard."

"He was being polite," Kian said. "Anyway, that's what Jon would have said."

Kelvin smiled, but then he wiped it. Time to think of his sister's annoying ways at another time. Now there was work.

Thus it was that they launched the boat, got into it, and rowed by natural rock walls covered by eerily glowing moss. They bypassed the terrible falls that emptied into a darkness filled with stars, negotiated the bend without difficulty, and were at the ledge. To Kelvin it looked different without that boat there.

He was still thinking about the missing boat as they entered the smooth chamber. He almost expected things to be different here, but things were as before. There was the parchment and the book on the table, and the closet with knobs on its outside that was the transporter.

Something struck Kelvin as the three of them prepared to step together into the adjoining world. Those knobs on the outside of the transporter appeared to him to have slightly changed positions. If the knobs had been moved, that might mean that they would not go to their proper destination and might, for all he knew to the contrary, be unable to return.

His gauntlets began to tingle. That meant danger. In fact—

But even as that thought occurred, he was in motion into the transporter, his body not responding in time.

There was a flash of white that covered all existences. The three of them stood in a transporter in a Mouvar chamber, but not the one they had entered. Nor was it the chamber in the world of silver serpents. This one was rounded like the others, lighted by strange ovoids on the chamber's walls. It was definitely not the same. The open door was the giveaway. That and the orangish daylight filtering in, revealing a grouping of large prickly plants and an assortment of rocks and heaps of red sand just outside.

"This is wrong!" Kian said. "We're not where we should be!"

"Someone changed the settings!" Kelvin said. "I thought those knobs were set differently, but I didn't realize it for sure until—"

"Don't panic," John said. "We'll just step out, step back in, and we should be back where we started."

Kelvin felt a great doubt stirring as the gauntlets tingled on his hands. Could the air here be poisoned? No, Mouvar's people wouldn't have built a transporter on a world like that. Still, there was something. Trembling in spite of himself, he stepped out with the others.

"I wonder," John said, walking to the doorway.

"Father! Don't!" Kelvin cried. He felt ridiculous the moment he said it.

But his father was pushing his head out around the rounded edge of the metal door. Curiosity ruling his actions, he was about to see where they were.

Suddenly John gasped. His shoulders slumped, and he dropped there in the doorway.

"Father!" Kian echoed Kelvin's earlier cry. With a quick leap he was beside John, grabbing his shoulders, seeking to turn his face. Then, with a similar gasp he collapsed on top of his father.

Kelvin stared for one horrified moment. Then he snatched out his Mouvar weapon from the hip-scabbard and leveled it at the doorway. If there was hostile magic being used, this would stop it and send it back to the source.

He squeezed the weapon's trigger. Sparks and a low hissing came from the bell-shaped muzzle. No magic, then. He replaced the weapon in its sheath and drew his sword. He took a step for the doorway and the unmoving bodies of his kin. Too late he saw the small purple fruit lying there. Too late he realized that he could have stepped back into the transporter and been gone.

He breathed a spicy fragrance. He noticed that the sword was slipping from his fingers and that the gauntlet wasn't even trying to hold on. He noticed the floor and the sand and the dust near the doorway. Then he noticed that the fruit was near his face, and—

What a spicy, spicy smell!

# CHAPTER 2

## *Summoned*

*S*ean Reilly, better known as St. Helens, was elated. As the king's own messengers left the cottage's yard he leaped up into the air, waving his arms like a boy. He came down, oof!, on the soles of his aching feet, put his head back until his short black beard pointed skyward, and whooped.

"Did you hear that, Phil?" he asked the pimply faced youth at his side. "Did you hear that?"

"I think all Kelvinia heard it," the former king of Aratex said. He had been staying temporarily with St. Helens while his hereditary palace was reconditioned, to better accommodate the newly appointed government. His position had been reduced to that of figurehead, but that was what he had been all along anyway. Kelvin and King Rufurt had if anything been too generous with him.

"We're going to the palace, boy! To the Kelvinia palace that used to be just Rud's. King Rufurt is finally getting around to honoring me proper! And he wants Kelvin and his brother Kian and John Knight and Les and Mor Crumb there as well! I tell you, there's going to be a place in the new administration for us, just as I always thought there should be! There may be medals for those of us who fought! Maybe a complete pardon for you!"

"I'm not going," Phillip said. He picked at a pimple. "I wasn't included in the royal command."

"Who cares! I'm certain you'll be welcome. You don't know the king! He's the most friendly man in the kingdom!"

"I was pretty friendly," Phillip said. "With you, I mean. I gave you sanctuary, protected you from Melbah, and allowed you to beat me at chess."

"Allowed me! Why you young pupten!" St. Helens bellowed, outraged. Then he got hold of his notoriously volcanic temper as he realized that he had again been had. Phillip was not even trying to hide his smirk.

"All right, all right. So you were a good friend and you resisted that old witch Melbah some, and after I rescued you from defeat—"

"You rescued *me!*" Phillip cried. Then, more calmly. "Oh, I see what you're doing. What you call tit for tat."

"Tat's correct," St. Helens said, in the manner of a long-ago other-world quiz master. "Now we're even." Which of course they were, and had been for some time.

"Another game?" Phillip asked, asking for another game of chess.

"No, no, I've got preparations to make. You've got preparations to make. We've got to get to the Crumbs. We've got to get to Kelvin and the others before they get to the Flaw! What a time for them to take off for a wedding, now that there's something important happening."

"The messengers will get to them," Phillip said. "St. Helens, don't you realize anything about how things are done?"

St. Helens glowered back at him. That was a snottish thing to say, and another time he might have exploded mildly, but now it hardly mattered. The fact was he had never been in the officer class, let alone the governing class. He had always been a common soldier, and proud of it. "I, uh, guess they will. The old man's just a little excited."

"A *little* excited?" Phillip rolled his eyes upward, looking less like the ex-king and more like the young scamp. Looking at him, St. Helens was forced to think that if his wife had borne him a son instead of a daughter, his kid would have been just that impudent.

"I guess we'll all ride together, Phil. I just hope they head off Kelvin and his party in time. I wonder if the girls will ride along. Cursed if I don't think Kelvin's wife, my daughter, should share her husband's and her father's triumph."

Lester and his father were working on a wall when the king's messenger appeared. Les hopped down from the scaffolding, mortar on his hands and the trowel he held, and gazed at them openmouthed.

"Don't get excited, Son," his father said from the top of the ladder. "It may not be anything bad. Maybe something good."

"I knew I shouldn't have let her go," Les said, meaning his wife. As he had found out repeatedly since their marriage, cute little tomboyish Jon had a mind and will that was hers alone.

"You know you couldn't have stopped her," Mor said. "Short of chaining her. And then you'd probably have gotten a lump on your head."

Les unconsciously raised a hand to his sweaty forehead and immediately felt the mortar on it. He would have cursed if the messenger had not been dismounted and there at the gate.

"Lester Crumb. Morton Crumb. You are both summoned to appear before His Majesty King Rufurt, acting king of Kelvinia. You have three days to comply."

Les frowned. "That sounds more like an order than a request."

"I just deliver 'em," the messenger said. "My orders say I'm to tell you three days."

Les looked up to where his father was straddling the wall

and glaring down. They had never been summoned in quite this fashion before. Not by King Rufurt. What did this mean?

Mor held his peace until the messenger had left, then spat. "Danged king! Double his territory, and he treats you like dirt!"

"I wouldn't have thought it," Les said. "But maybe it's an honor, a place in the government or something."

"Maybe," Mor said, scowling.

Jon was the first to see the riders approaching. Instantly her hand was on her sling, rock in place, ready just in case history should repeat. But these were no kidnappers from a foreign nation, she saw with relief. They were two of King Rufurt's finest, their Guardsman Messenger uniforms bearing the winged insignias. Now they were slowing their horses and coming up to them at walking speed.

The messengers pulled up. They glanced down at those in the temporary camp. "Mrs. Hackleberry? Mrs. Crumb?"

Jon found herself nodding, as she saw Heln doing. She'd never been approached by a King's Messenger before, and she knew that Heln had not. She waited, wondering.

"Your husband, Mrs. Hackleberry—has he gone to the Flaw?"

Heln nodded. "He, his brother, and their father."

"Then we're too late. We were to give them a message. They are supposed to be at the palace in three days."

"Why?" Heln asked. "Is there trouble, or—?"

"We're only messengers. You ladies are also summoned. The Crumbs, Lester and Morton, will be there as well. So will the roundear Sean Reilly, alias St. Helens."

"Alias?" Heln asked sharply, not liking this reference to her father.

"All of us at the palace!" Jon exclaimed. "Something must have happened!"

"The messages have been delivered. The king ordered us to stress that you have but three days."

"You know Mrs. Hackleberry is pregnant?" Jon demanded. "Does Rufurt still expect—"

The messengers rode slowly away without answering.

Jon swore.

"Now really, Jon, you shouldn't!" Heln reproved her. "You know—"

"I know those goldbuttoned monkpes weren't polite! What's gotten into Rufurt, sending out creiots like those! Why they're not fit to wear their uniforms! Just wait till Kelvin hears! He'll tell them how to talk to his wife and sister!"

"Hush, Jon, Hush. It doesn't matter."

"Yeah? Then what *did* they mean by 'alias' St. Helens?"

Heln frowned. Her name derived from that of her father, so there was a certain personal as well a familial interest. "I'm sure it was just a misspeaking."

"Sure." Jon whirled her sling and let a rock fly to the rump of the horse bearing the sauciest messenger. Stung, the steed jumped, bucked, and almost threw its rider. Then the big war-horse leaped forward, and the other horse speeded up as well. Horses and riders disappeared in a whirl of dust.

"Jon! You shouldn't have!" Heln exclaimed. But her protest lacked force, and there might even have been the merest trace of a hidden smile.

"Maybe I shouldn't have," Jon said. "But I did." It felt good, she thought, secretly pleased with herself. "Well, come on. We might as well get loaded up and meet the others at the palace."

"But Jon, we haven't good clothes! All we have is our riding togs, and they've been slept in."

"Who cares?" Jon demanded. "If we're invited to a ball, Rufurt neglected to advise us."

Angrier than even she thought she should be, Jon began packing their cooking gear and gathering up their blankets. She knew herself to be a liberated woman. No mere king, let alone king's messenger, had the right to treat her as less.

Charlain laid down a card. "Yes, they need help, Hal," she said. "They are too proud to ask for it, but they need it."

"I'd better go, then," Hal Hackleberry said. "The Brownberry folk have helped us when we needed it."

"Yes. I can manage here well enough for a few days."

He got his things ready, then kissed her goodbye. He set out on foot, walking the two hours' distance to their neighbor's farm. It would have been faster on the horse, but Charlain would need the horse here.

As he walked, he pondered. He had been trying to suppress the awareness, but it was becoming difficult. Charlain's kiss had been perfunctory, without passion. Once she had been more attentive, but never enough actually to bear his children. Well, attentive, maybe, but she was a woman who bore children only when she chose, and she had not so chosen with him.

He knew what it was. He was her second husband, and she had never stopped loving her first husband, the roundeared John Knight. She had thought John dead, and needed a man to support the farm, and he had been there. She was such a lovely, competent woman that he had been thrilled to join her on any basis. Hal knew himself to be a good but simple man, the kind seldom destined for greatness or success with women. He had done his best, and treated Charlain's two children as his own, and indeed, he had come to like both Kelvin and Jon very well. There had been no stepfather problems with them. Now both were married and on their own, but they always welcomed his occasional visits and made him feel at home.

But then John Knight had returned. He had not been dead after all, only imprisoned. John had been scrupulous about staying clear of Charlain, letting their divorce stand. But Charlain—any passion she might have had for Hal had evaporated with the knowledge of John's survival. Oh, she hadn't said so, but he had felt it. Their marriage had become a shadow.

But what could he do? He loved her, and could not bring himself to leave her, selfish as he knew that to be. Also, there was no certainty that John Knight wanted to return to her. Kelvin had been mostly silent on what had gone on in the other frame, but it seemed that there was a beautiful and good queen there who looked like John's first wife, the nefarious Zoanna, and who was in want of a man. If Charlain still carried a torch for her first husband, John might carry one for his first wife. So there was no point in Hal's doing anything; it might only hurt the woman he least wanted to hurt.

If only she loved him *back!*

They gathered together in the second audience room. Wine was brought, and all sipped it except Jon. Of the five, only St. Helens was smiling. Jon had to wonder why. Knowing Heln's natural father, she would have thought he'd arrive still smoldering, ready to blow his top on any pretext. But maybe the messengers had treated him with a little more politeness. Maybe they hadn't called him "alias" to his face. Yes, that was probably it; men like those messengers treated women and absent men with habitual disrespect.

"I'd guess we're about to get our due," St. Helens whispered. "Even you, Jon, for riding with the Roundear."

Jon glared at him. Though he had told her about Female Liberation, she sometimes considered him a chauvinist. No one had helped him more than she. Why if she hadn't grabbed Kelvin's hand and aimed the Mouvar weapon for him, the witch would have won! Maybe she should tell him about the alias bit and see how snug his infamous top was then.

But was this really about that? St. Helens seemed to think they were here for some sort of reward or recognition, but he could be, and usually was, mistaken.

Curtains were pulled open by two lackeys in royal livery. There sat King Rufurt on his throne. Instead of his crown he wore an absurd, tight-fitting stockelcap. He also wore a deep frown, which was even more unusual for him.

"Hackleberry, Crumbs, and Sean Reilly, alias St. Helens, you have been summoned to my presence without explanation. You are wondering why."

This was not, Jon thought, the king's customary way of speaking. But she couldn't ponder that right now; she was too busy trying to look covertly at St. Helens to see how he liked that "alias"!

But the fool hadn't even picked up on it. "Your Majesty," he said, "I suspect the recent conflict with Aratex and its annexing has a little something to do with it."

"Roundear, I did not give you permission to speak," the

king said sharply. "My patience has been severely strained lately. Do not strain it further."

St. Helens looked surprised. In a heartbeat or less he'd realize he'd been insulted and get angry. But even as Jon thought this, the king was standing, glaring at them. Judging from his expression, he was about to order their executions.

Jon found that she was doing what everyone else was doing. All five were trying hard to close unsightly gaping mouths.

"You know of course about Klingland and Kance," Rufurt continued. "Those two related kingdoms ruled by brats Kildom and Kildee. Long have they been a thorn in your kingdom's side."

"But—but Your Majesty!" Mor exclaimed, unable to hold his peace. "There has *never* been trouble between our kingdoms! Never, in all of history!"

"You're a historian, Crumb?"

"N-no, Your Majesty. But it's common knowledge. With other of the seven kingdoms, such as Aratex before we annexed it, there might have been trouble, but never—"

"Silence!" the king shouted. "You will not interrupt again! Not on pain of torture!"

Mor looked as if he were about to choke. After having been treated as an equal by King Rufurt, this was embarrassing in the extreme to him.

"As I was saying," Rufurt continued grimly, "there have always been difficulties. Only recently it has come to my attention that these two kingdoms plan aggressive war. We must take action before they invade our territory. The roundear should have known this. 'Uniting four,' the prophecy says, but just when the 'hero' is needed, he's gone. Probably dallying with wenches in a far foreign land."

"Your Majesty, I protest!" Heln exclaimed, for once not philosophical about a slight.

"Silence!" the king roared. "Do not presume that because you are mated to the roundear and carry his brat that you are above punishment!"

Heln gasped, started to open her mouth, then closed it. Jon, though furious herself, was glad that the woman managed to stifle her reaction. This had gone beyond error or thoughtless affront. This was deliberate insult, by the last person expected to do it.

Something was not right, here. This wasn't the king who had spent all those years in his own dungeon with her father. It couldn't be!

"So they plan aggression, and we must move fast," the king said, as if satisfied with his logic. "Fortunately there is another kingdom willing to be our ally: Hermandy."

"Hermandy!" Les cried. "But Hermandy has always been—"

Again the king's eyes glared around, as if with a hatred of all present and, indeed, of all mankind. It was a look that had never been seen on Rufurt's face, even during imprisonment and humiliation. There was more than hatred there; there was madness.

Jon swallowed. That didn't help, so she swallowed again. Something was starting to form in her mind, something she dared not consider directly right now. But it pushed forward relentlessly.

In the other frame there had been such a king. She had not seen him, and none present had, but Kelvin had, and John Knight, and so had Kian. *Oh, if only they are all right! If only they are safe in that other frame with nothing more serious than flopeared persons and overgrown snakes to worry about!*

Les hung his head. "I'm sorry, Your Majesty. I did not mean to interrupt."

"Do not do so again. As I was saying, the situation is critical. Obviously I will have no help from the Roundear, so I am ordering you male Crumbs to lead troops into Klingland and Kance. And you, Reilly, do you have that belt that allowed you to fly?

"No, Your Majesty. Kelvin has that, as well as the gauntlets and the Mouvar weapon."

"Typical," the king said sourly. "Irresponsible in an agent of prophecy. But never mind that. You are ordered to proceed forthwith to Hermandy, as my personal messenger to King Bitler."

St. Helens looked startled. "Your Majesty, I've never been—"

"Those are your orders. Are you refusing to obey?"

What an attitude! The king seemed to be trying to provoke dissent, so he could claim treason. "No, Your Majesty," St. Helens said. "It's just that I haven't been to Hermandy and I haven't dealt with kings."

"You dealt with Phillip of Aratex."

"Yes, Your Majesty. But—" Then, seeing the way the king was looking at him, St. Helens reverted to his charm, which was a considerable asset because it was normally well hidden. "Though I haven't had the honor to serve you in such a capacity before, I certainly will now."

If the king was charmed, he did a remarkable job of concealing it. He turned brusquely to Mor and Les, as if he had never even spoken to St. Helens. "And you, Crumbs?"

Mor shrugged, perhaps not trusting himself to speak. There was something about the way the king had pronounced their name that made it seem derogatory. Les answered for both of them. "We certainly will follow your orders, Your Majesty. Though neither of us have been in uniform since the recent war, we'll endeavor to serve you as we must."

Again this graciousness was wasted on the king. "You will do that." His dour attention now turned to Heln. "Since your errant husband is not here, you will stay at the palace until he returns or the royal physician delivers you of child. Whichever event occurs first."

Heln had the wit not to show by her expression that this was the last place she preferred to be. The king had not called her a guest, and it might be more like imprisonment.

Jon straightened her shoulders. She was next, she knew.

"And you, Jon Hackleberry, sister to the hero and mate to Lester Crumb—" The way he spoke those words made it sound like a disparagement. He was suddenly very good at sounding bad! "You will stay with her as her companion. Is that acceptable?"

"Very acceptable," Jon said tersely. *As it has to be. But at least I'll have the chance to watch over Heln. She'll need an ally. Until Kelvin's return. Until he's back here, and knocks your lying carcass off the throne you usurped, you impostor!*

"Then this audience is at an end." Uncharacteristically, the king clapped his hands, and retainers who had assuredly not been here during their recent visit took them in charge and led them from his presence.

When they were alone, getting their breath, getting their color back, Jon said what she had been thinking. "He's not."

"Lass, I've thought that myself!" Mor said. "But if he isn't who he looks like, then—"

"That other king, I think. The one Kelvin talked about."

"King—" He paused, his brow furrowing. "Rowforth. Of Hud? King Rowforth of the torture chamber and the serpents?"

"Who else?" she asked, and saw no disagreement in the others.

"But how—?"

"I don't know. I thought they were going to execute him," Jon said.

"Kelvin wouldn't execute anybody in cold blood," Heln said.

Jon nodded. "A pity, maybe. He must have escaped. It has to be. How else?"

Mor nodded. "Uh, I don't know. But it just doesn't make sense. Even if his own people didn't kill him, and he got here, there's Rufurt."

"Which is why we have to play along, Father," Les said. "For the sake of the real king."

"You really think he's not?" St. Helens asked.

"Don't you?" Mor returned.

St. Helens said some volcanic words. Heln turned away, but did not seem to take strong exception. "But kings will be kings, as the saying goes. It could be he's had a lot on his mind. Maybe his imprisonment is catching up with him, a gear loose somewhere. A bad situation coming up, a bad time for it, and—"

"You don't believe that," Jon said.

"No," St. Helens admitted. "We'd better do just as this one says. If he's not the Rufurt we fought for, then it will be out with him."

"And if there's a war started as a result?" Les asked.

"Hm, there is the prophecy."

"St. Helens!" his pregnant daughter said. "You really want

to be fighting again? I thought you'd had enough. After your crossbow wound and after old Melbah—"

"Yes, yes, it was a close thing. But Kelvin did come back in time, didn't he? Just in time. Right, Jon?"

Jon found herself nodding. "We stopped her," she said. In her mind she saw again the moment of the Mouvar's weapon finally going off and sending its antimagic to turn the evil back on its sender. But that seemed almost a lifetime ago. The situation now was not that desperate. But would it become so? She was very much afraid it would.

St. Helens was smiling. He liked the idea of a war that would fulfill that prophecy line. He liked it, though the last two words, "uniting two," had almost cost his life and the lives of Les and Mor.

*You'd better not give me any trouble, St. Helens,* she thought viciously. *I'm a liberated woman, and I'm on to you. You're an opportunist, but you won't opportune your way with tyrants. Try, and I won't wait for Kelvin. Succeed, and I'll rock your charming head off!* And she made a tiny motion with her hand, as if using her sling to hurl a rock at someone's head.

## CHAPTER 3

# *Tribute*

*K*elvin opened his eyes to see a squat, ugly being with a head growing out of its shoulders and no neck at all. The being was crouched down, turning the Mouvar weapon over and over in webbed, long-fingered hands. The creature's arms and legs and webbed toes matched its fingers. On either side of the blunt head were round, flat spots resembling those on the head of a frog. More than anything it seemed like a giant frog with human additions.

As he turned, he could see the others of his party, also conscious. His father looked as bewildered and helpless as he felt. Kian looked, if anything, worse, as though all his buoyancy and confidence were now replaced with despair. Froog men and women were all about them in this steamy swamp. All their weapons were being inspected and chatted over. Kelvin and his companions themselves were bound hand and foot.

"Ohhh, we're not where we should be," John Knight said. "I'm sorry, Kelvin, you were right. The controls on the transporter were tampered with."

But by whom? Kelvin dared not speak the question. There were more immediate matters. One of these squatted directly in front of him and thrust a large, flat thumb of a greenish webbed hand into his face.

"You godhunters go to god," the creature said. Its voice was liquid and bubbling, as if breathed out under water. Throat sacks just beneath its head vibrated as it spoke, obviously with difficulty.

"We're not godhunters," Kelvin said. *Whatever they are.*

"We see," said the being. "We see. God see. God see all."

What god? A god to creatures who looked like these could be evil and multieyed. He imagined a serpent with eyes all along its back and belly and sides: gigantic, looking down at them from concealment in those prickly tree branches, or invisibly from the orangish sky.

"There won't be any wedding," Kian moaned. "I'm sorry, Kelvin, Father."

"You didn't bring us, Son. We came of our own accord." Trust John Knight to try to make them feel better. "We'll get this straightened out and then we'll go to the right place and get you and Lonny married as planned."

"You go to god," the froog-eared creature said reprovingly. "Strangers, tribute. Tribute, strangers."

As it spoke, another of the creatures was poking a stick with sticky needles on it into the Mouvar weapon's bell-shaped muzzle. Its webbed fingers touched and squeezed the trigger. Pretty sparks and a low hissing amused and possibly delighted the meddler, doing no harm. There was no hostile magic so the display was entirely meaningless.

"I'd say these are real primitives," John Knight said. "Not sophisticates like the flopears."

Kelvin knew what he meant. The flopears of the other frame had been extremely savvy and tough creatures. It might be nice if these were their analogues in this strange frame. The beings here seemed to have no inkling. If John had insulted them by calling them primitives, they did not realize it.

The froog-face in front of him repeated, "You go to god. You go to god. All of you together to god."

"Persistent devil," John remarked. "You lads have any idea how to define a godhunter?"

"One who hunts a god," Kelvin said. Stupid talk, but it was necessary to keep their courage up. Where was the levitation belt? He had worn it around his middle and now it was gone. His father-in-law St. Helens had become quite expert with it during the late unpleasantness, and afterward Kelvin had practiced with it and gotten quite good himself.

Where *was* that belt? With it, he could extricate them all from this predicament.

A great cry went up. One of the froogears was strutting about wearing it over its naked loins.

"Oh, boy," John said. "If—but maybe it won't."

Just then it did. Webbed fingers found and pressed the pretty red button. The froogear went sailing up. Froog-faces turned upward, greatly excited or indifferent as suited the individual. Some of the faces made croaking sounds. The biggest of the creatures stretched out an arm and croaked advice.

The fumbler fumbled some more. Off he went, first to the east and then to the west, and finally smack into a prickly tree. While hanging there, not seriously hurt or alarmed, the aeronaut moved the lever at the side of the belt forward and back. The result was that the creature worked itself deeper into the prickly branches.

The big froogear stepped over to John and nudged him with a webbed toe. "Get him down!"

"I'm tied," John said, reasonably.

"Tell how. Get down."

John considered briefly. "Press red button. Move lever to middle position. Climb down tree."

The big froogear turned his face treeward and croaked an evident translation. Almost immediately the adventurer was visible sliding and scrambling among the branches. He fell partway, landed in greenish mud, and got up laughing. A quick roll in a pile of red sand and he approached the leader and held out the soiled but unharmed belt.

"Did we win one, Father?" Kelvin asked. "Are they going to think twice before croaking us in some form of sacrifice?"

"I'd like to think so, Son. These aren't flopears. Maybe they've got something like our dragons, and maybe something like the serpents the flopears sacrificed to. But if they've got the brains of a fleouse they'll be impressed."

The impression seemed to relate only to John Knight. The leader and his followers acted almost as if levitation belts weren't really strange. What was with these creatures, anyway?

After a suitable interval, during which all their gear was examined and reexamined, the leader gave orders. The prisoners were lifted and carried on slippery smooth froogear shoulders. The creatures might look clumsy, but they were quite strong. Behind them, Kelvin managed to discern, other green shoulders carried everything they had brought that was not presently attached to them, including all weapons.

Well, now. If they had any chance to escape, they could grab one of the weapons and make it good. Evidently the froogears didn't really understand the nature of those devices.

Then most of the stuff, including the weapons, was deposited in a hollow tree, and left behind. Kelvin's hope sank; so much for having their things handy!

They were carried an interminable distance. Through vast expanses of swamp. Between prickly tree trunks that looked like something that ought to be growing in a desert. Past huge piles of reddish sand sometimes shading to an orange the color of the sky of this world. Through brush growing in greenish water and up from patches of semiliquid land. Swamp creatures like allidiles splashed out of their way, snapping great toothy snouts, slapping broad tails that made muddy waves.

"Father, do you think one of those?" Kelvin asked, nodding his head at one of the toothy horrors. "Their god?" The thought was revolting, but had to be considered. Allidiles fed most nastily, and these scaled reptilians were the same except bigger.

"Let's just try to wait and be surprised," John said. "And be alert, both of you! Don't give up hope. There just may be—" He broke off to curse as a froogear snatched a wriggling orange serpent from his chest. The snake hissed, bared dripping fangs, and snapped at the face of the froogear—but immediately lost its head in the crunching jaws of the froogear. John's rescuer chewed, spat, then raised the still squirming body and directed the squirting blood into its wide, open mouth.

"Gross!" Kian said, using one of the expressions his father had taught him. "That's worse than anything I've seen on two worlds."

"Or three worlds, for me," John agreed. "Ugh! What must their god be like?"

Kelvin didn't say anything. He was trying not to vomit on himself and his carrier. *Some hero,* he thought again. *Some legendary hero to upchuck just at the sight of blood.*

The froogear squeezed its very fresh lunch. Now other juices escaped through ruptured tissues and mixed with the blood. Yellow, brown, black, and mixtures.

Kelvin lost his battle of the gorge. With no transition at all he was vomiting. The contents of his stomach splashed out across the froogear in front. He was afraid the creature would turn and kill him, or at least drop him in the swamp, but it took no notice at all.

Much later, a year or two by the feel, Kelvin's retching abated. Feeling horribly weak and nauseous, he hardly noticed the slowing of the party. When he did manage to notice, they had come to a complete halt in greenish mud before a flat, still, scum-topped lake. Great prickly trees grew in the water, seemingly out of the scum. An island of some size soaked up orange sunrays and seemed to wait, curiously idle and foreboding. A rock battlement fronted the island and disappeared around the sides.

The froogears repositioned their loads, startling Kelvin and causing his father to give a groan of apprehension. Then the froogears were in the lake itself, wading, and finally swimming with their powerful hind legs. Somehow the froogears kept them above the surface.

*This is where it is,* Kelvin thought. *Now we'll meet their god, or what they think of as a god.* He shivered and felt cold, though the orange sun beat down with fiery waves reminding him of an overheated stove in his mother's kitchen.

They splashed up a ramp. There, concealed until now by the black thorny tree branches, was a huge gate. The froogears put their prisoners down on a dry surface and backed off. Kelvin saw some of them as they dipped back below the scum; bubbles traced their route away from the island.

*Tribute,* he thought. *They've brought their tribute.* It was almost like the time the flopears had tried to sacrifice Lonny. Kian had rescued her, then, and started what turned out to be a significant interaction. He hoped Kian would have the chance to marry her! At the moment that seemed doubtful. He wondered whether Kian appreciated the parallel, and debated breaking the silence to tell him. No, it probably wouldn't be kind.

In an aperture high in the wall there was suddenly a woman's comforting face. She wore a coppery crown on coppery tresses, with coppery rings dangling from two definitely rounded, not pointed ears. She was, Kelvin had to notice, a beauty. But what could such a woman be doing here in this ironically godforsaken place? Or was she another captive, brought here for tribute?

The woman looked down at them from disturbingly coppery eyes. She spoke one word: "Tribute."

*Gods,* Kelvin thought, *she read my mind! But who is she? Is she the froogears' god? If so, she can't be the monster I've expected. She's absolutely lovely!*

"Thank you so much, Kelvin Hackleberry." Her voice tinkled almost in the manner of a bell. She was looking right at him, reading his mind!

Kelvin felt himself blushing. What would Heln think?

But now the beautiful face was gazing at his father. "Oh, and you, John Knight, trying so hard to get that knot untied! What a great pleasure to meet someone whose original home is far down the Flaw! With your son Kelvin, a hero! And your other son, Kian, wanting to wed his truelove in still another frame!"

What was this? Were they supposed to respond? Should he be the one to break their silence? What should he say? Should he ask this queenly woman for their release and her help? For obviously she was a queen, which the froogears took as a goddess.

"Oh, but you mustn't judge by appearances," the woman told him in her musical voice. There was just a hint of reproval. "I am more—very much more—than you imagine."

*But human,* he thought carefully. *A human being who thinks and speaks and has the power of life and death. That is correct, isn't it? You do have the power either to save us or destroy us?*

"Why of course I have those powers, Kelvin!" she agreed brightly. "What do you think I am?"

*A compassionate queen,* he thought with hope.

"Physically," she prompted him.

Kelvin tried not to picture the phenomenal contours he was sure her body had, hidden by the wall.

"Ah, you are married, so you hesitate to conjecture," she said, smiling. "Yet suppose I were to offer you your freedom, in return for that conjecture?"

She was toying with him, he knew. Yet try as he might, he could not stop his mind from picturing that gorgeous body. Was she naked? Was that why she kept all except her face concealed?

She laughed. "Oh, it would be delightful to make you do with me what you so dread! Perhaps I should indeed free you, instead of saving you for a late-night snack."

Kelvin felt the hair prickle at his nape. Her face and tone were beautiful, but the words were teasing to the point of discomfort. A late-night snack? Was that figurative, or—?

"Go on, Kelvin," she said encouragingly. "It is such a pleasure, following your thoughts."

There seemed to be an admixture of cruelty. Beauty and cruelty were not incompatible, he knew. He remembered Queen Zoanna, Kian's lovely but evil mother. But there could be another reason for her to hide her body. Was she something other than she appeared to be, physically, as she had hinted? Perhaps old, as the witch Melbah had been, yet able to assume the semblance of youth and beauty?

The coppery tresses tossed. The laughter was that of a cheerful hostess. "A witch! Me? Shame on you, Kelvin! A hero of your stripe should know better. You have heard of me, or of something like me. Certainly your father has. He told you, too, though you thought he was speaking nonsense. And you as well, Kian. Indeed, I am not like your mother!"

*Insane,* Kelvin thought with a chill. But even as he thought it, there came another voice. This one was gruff and masculine, reminiscent of the toughest of working men:

"Mervania, do you always have to play with our food?"

"Of course I do, Mertin," said the pretty tresses. "And why not? Aren't human females and felines that way? Here I have almost coaxed this innocent young man into lusting after my luscious torso! It can be fun, accomplishing that!"

"GWROOOWOOF!" growled a decidedly unhuman voice. Certainly that dragonlike roar had come from no human throat! The vibrations hurt Kelvin's ears.

"Oh now, Grumpus," Mervania said, "you know it's not really feeding time yet."

"GROOOOWOOF!"

"Yes, yes, I agree. We will have to show ourself. But it's going to be a surprise. Particularly for Kelvin, who is resolutely focusing on my forbidden sex appeal. Kian is thinking of his Lonny, and John of his Charlain and of another named Zanaan. Naughty, naughty John! Only one can be your wife. But you, Kelvin, you are thinking of me, and that is the naughtiest of all."

"That's not entirely true," Kelvin said, embarrassed by the amount that *was* true. "I'm thinking also of Heln."

"Yes, that night you got her pregnant. But now she is gravid, and doesn't look quite like that, whereas I may—"

Mervania's face moved away from the wall opening as if shoved aside. Replacing it was a man's face: coppery eyebrows and copper warrior helmet emphasizing high cheekbones and a bulging forehead. He scowled, and snorted through his nose in the manner of a bull. "Mervania, these aren't even fat!"

"But it will be fun fattening them up," Mervania's voice said. "If I could somehow pose as Kelvin pictures me, voluptuous, almost naked, plying him with succulent grapes—"

*Damn* that mind-reading! And damn his errant mind! She was so infernally good at tuning in on what he most wanted to suppress!

The man's face disappeared. There was a clumping sound, as of something huge and unseen. Then in the opening appeared the snout of a dragon. Its scales were copper rather than a more normal gold, and the eyes it turned down on them were as coppery as its scales. A forked tongue emerged from its terrible mouth, vibrated, then shot down at them. The tip of it dripped coppery saliva and was much too close for comfort.

"Father! Kian!" Kelvin cried. It was quite involuntary. He had been this close to dragons of the golden-scaled variety, but never while bound. The dragon's head drew back. A loud female laughter filled his ears. It was not pretty; rather it was taunting.

It had to be illusion, Kelvin thought. It had to be magic—witchcraft. There couldn't be a dragon here! Not that close to human beings! It would have gobbled them up. Even the sorcerer Zatanas had not been able to control dragons that well. True, Zatanas had ridden one, but that was a treacherous business. No magic could safely handle a magical creature for long.

"I think I know what it is," his father said. "Remember when I was telling you stories about Greek myth? Remem—"

He broke off. With horror, Kelvin realized that his father was helplessly rolling his eyes as if stricken. Magic used against him by Mervania? Magic used so that he would not talk?

The coppery tresses reappeared at the aperture. The coppery eyes that no longer seemed entirely human looked down on him. "You are quite right, Kelvin. I did stop your father from speaking. A simple paralysis hold on his vocal cords. It's wrong for him to want to spoil your surprise. I'd much rather share your naughty vision of me leaning forward to feed you a delicacy, my breasts becoming more visible as my gown falls away, their delightful contours—exactly how does that go, after that?"

Kelvin thought desperately of what his father had been saying. Greek myth, all mixed up with history and therefore partially true. His father had told of such things as the Hydra, a great serpent with nine heads, or was it seven heads; cut off one head and two others grew magically in its place. Then there had been Medusa, a monstrous woman with hair filled with living, hissing snakes. Why did everything he thought of have to involve snakes?

"Keep thinking, Kelvin," Mervania teased. "Keep thinking. There was also Circe, with whom Odysseus dallied for twenty years before returning to his wife. Now *there* was an example for you! Will poor little Heln weave a tapestry by day and unravel it by night, waiting for your return?"

"I think I know!" Kian said. "It's—"

Coppery eyes glanced at his brother. Kian choked and went silent. A spell like a serpent's gaze? Why, oh why couldn't he think!

"You can, Kelvin," Mervania said encouragingly. "You just have to try. You are getting warm, as you used to say in that children's game. Multiple heads. Yes, that's close. But do you recall the particular mythical being that caused you the most terror? I'll give you a clue: it wasn't your wife's namesake, Helen of Troy." She paused, tilting her head prettily. "Oh, excuse me! She was named after her father, a figure of quite another nature!"

He thought hard. Multiple heads. The trinity? Something like that? But something Greek. Something legend. Something that had worked on his boyish imagination and given rise to a nightmare.

"A great hero fought this one, Kelvin. But then they always did, in your father's frame. One of us visited that world back in its infancy, and that's the source."

Kelvin felt as though he were failing a test. All he could think about was the face at the aperture, and whether there was any clothing on what was below it, and his bonds, his father and his brother.

"Dunce!" she snapped at last. "I tire of this. I'll *show* you my fascinating body. I'm coming out."

The gate clicked, then swung wide on creaky hinges. Back

of the opening Kelvin saw a walk, a garden, and a building. Then the face, the beautiful woman's face, was peeking around the gatepost.

"Mervania," he started.

The face kept coming. It was on a long, coppery-scaled neck.

*A serpent woman! I knew it! Gods, she's a snake!*

"Oh, fiddle," Mervania said, and stepped all the way out.

Kelvin drew in a disbelieving breath as he took in the sight.

On clawed feet, a coppery scaled body of immense size. Beside her head, a dragon's head, and beside the dragon's, Mertin's. All three heads were on the front of a body that was all coppery scales, but was otherwise that of a scorpiocrab in all but size. Great pincers reached and clicked in front while at either of the monster's two sides were two human arms: scaly feminine ones on Mervania's, scaly muscle-bulging ones on Mertin's. On the farthest end of the body, coming up last, the tapering crustacean posterior and the long sting, this one of copper.

Kelvin was forced to think, now. The one creature he had been suppressing because of a nightmare. Modified greatly, but recognizable. Instead of a goat's body, the body of a scorpiocrab. Instead of one lion head, one goat head, and one dragon head, two human heads and the dragon. Instead of a serpent's tail, a scorpiocrab's sting. The realization overwhelmed him. To think that he had imagined peeking at the luscious feminine body of *that!*

"Chimera," he whispered.

"Chimaera," she said. "Or Chimæra, if you can fathom it. Get it right, Kelvin."

Chimaera. A monster that had to be far smarter and even more dangerous than the one the ancient Greeks had known.

# CHAPTER 4

# *Amb-assador*

$S$t. Helens rode the big gray war-horse down the country road, musing to himself as he shooed a buzzing insect away from his black beard. It was a sunny, nice day for a ride, but this was to be a long one.

*Damn! Special messenger to King Bitler of Hermandy! Sounds great, but I don't like it. What skills do I have for dealing with kings? Charm, right? But from what I hear, Bitler is about as nice as old Adolf! Sometimes I wish I were back on Earth, I really do. I don't feel like an ambassador for anyone, particularly that guy at the palace. That just can't be Rufurt, it can't! I feel like an ass. Ambassador. Ass. Amb-assador.*

"St. Helens! St. Helens!"

He turned in his saddle to see the former boy-king Phillip Blastmore riding down on him. The boy had evidently been awake after all. Naturally the lad would have followed him, waiting until he was well started on his journey before showing himself.

"Damn!" He pulled up and waited until Phillip's brindled gelding was alongside his mare. "I thought I told you to stay! This is official. Damn it, I don't need a kid along!"

"I'm coming to keep you out of trouble." His mouth smiled, but St. Helens suspected that truth resided in that statement.

"YOU! Keep ME out of trouble?! You, young pupten, have been trouble since you were hatched!"

"I wasn't hatched. I was found under a rock, same as you."

"Probably you were. And old Melbah then took complete charge of you."

The boy's face fell. Immediately St. Helens regretted saying it. Bantering insults were one thing, but real ones were another. There was too much truth in Melbah's early influence over the lad.

"I'm sorry, St. Helens." Phillip's voice trembled. "If you really don't want me along—"

"Now where'd you get a dumb idea like that! Of course I want you along! Glad to have your company. What would I do for trouble without you?"

"But you said—"

"I say a lot of things. Curse of the Irish—one of the curses, anyhow. Haven't I taught you about jokes?"

"Eh, yes. Like when you said 'That girl has nice jugs!' when anyone could see she carried wine bottles."

Ouch! Under Melbah's evil care the young king hadn't gotten out much. A trip or two with the old man might add immeasurably to the lad's education. "You happen to notice anything else about her, lad?"

"She had an excellent figure. I'm surprised you didn't realize that."

Well, maybe there was hope; he was beginning to catch on to the basics. "Maybe next time."

"I can really be a lot of help, you know. I was king once, if only in name. I can tell you the protocol that's expected, and then you won't embarrass us."

"Tell you what, Phil. If you catch the old saint crapping on the carpet, you speak right up."

"Oh I will, St. Helens, I will. Only you didn't do that, even in Aratex. I'd have smelled it if you had."

St. Helens rolled his eyes upward. Smart kid, but sometimes he was a smarty pants. A little dusting of the britches cured that, but royal posteriors presented problems.

"Just let's say that I'll appreciate your help. Whenever and however." *And* if *ever.*

But Phillip was now looking back the way they had come. A horse was approaching with a rider. As the horse drew closer the uniform of a palace guard was evident.

"Now why would one of those fellows be riding after me?" St. Helens asked. "Something new come up?"

The rider was a young guardsman St. Helens had seen at the palace but not spoken to. He could have sworn the fellow rode the king's favorite horse.

"Messenger Reilly," the guardsman gasped. "I'm from the palace detail, but I'm on my own. I've heard a lot about you, how you fought the witch and all. Sir, I'm Charley Lomax."

"I recognize you, close enough. What's the urgency?"

Lomax eyed the boy. "It's for your ears alone, St. Helens."

"You can speak in front of Phil. I trust him."

Charley Lomax, Royal Guardsman, breathed rapidly in and out. His brows knitted as if he were forcing a difficult thought. "Sir, I beg permission to accompany you on your mission to Hermandy."

"The king send you?" This was indeed strange.

"No, sir. As I said, I'm doing this on my own."

St. Helens had heard, but hadn't assimilated it. "You mean you're deserting your post?" He didn't like this. Deserters always had his sympathy, but helping one was trouble.

"I mean I wish to serve the true interest of my king and country. I know that you do too, Messenger Reilly, so—"

"You serve your king by deserting him?" St. Helens asked sharply.

"I don't believe the man at the palace *is* the king."

There it was. "You did right. Very right. Certainly you can accompany me." Then, after a pause: "And call me St. Helens."

"Thank you sir!" Lomax exclaimed, breaking into a grin. "St. Helens, sir!"

The man was in trouble with the man who wore the crown, he thought. If his guess was correct, all of them were about to be in similar trouble. If they couldn't head off that trouble, they would have to prepare to meet it head-on.

They rode on together, the three of them, on Messenger Reilly's mission to Hermandy.

Lester, sweating under the new bronzed helmet with its ostark feather marking him as officer, reviewed the assembled troops. Up and down the columns he rode. From the back of the fine gelding he had been given he looked down into the disciplined faces. Now and then he inspected a sword or crossbow. Briefly he examined the mobile catapults. He felt, he had to admit to himself, and only to himself, like a total fool. Here he was pretending to be an officer when he had never before been one. Serving a king who was probably an impostor, he couldn't have said why. It was one bad, bad situation.

He pulled the reins on his horse's bridle and steered around the huge wheels on the last catapult in line toward his father. Mor, though having been born to fight, looked as uncomfortable in a general's uniform as he felt.

"General Father," Les said in a low voice, "you see anything wrong with these?"

"Top-notch," Mor replied. "The finest mercenaries and equipment Throod had."

Yes, Lester thought, the finest bought fighters. Each trained to kill or die for the cause that pays and never once to question the rightness or the wrongness. Each trained to believe soldiering the highest calling. Good soldiers all, damn it, and not the sort to doubt.

"You want to make the speech, Father? You've got the wind for it."

Mor gave him an almost invisible frown, then stepped his horse around the catapult. He was a big man, on a big war-horse.

"Men," Mor boomed, "we are about to march into Klingland and Kance, the twin kingdoms ruled by twin brothers. Half of you will go to Klingland. Half will go with my son, General Lester Crumb, into Kance. While we are marching, Sean Reilly, whom you know as St. Helens, hero of the war with Aratex, will be on a secret mission to secure Hermandy as an ally. Our armies will meet after victory in the twin capital of Lonris on the Thamesein River. Any questions?"

As Les had expected, there were none. Military commanders normally did not speak that way to troops, and certainly did not ask for questions. The troops might be bemused by this approach. But Mor and Les were not militarily trained except in the fires of revolution. In the war for Rud and then again in the war with Aratex they had served interests they had entirely believed in. It was too bad the same could not be said in this case.

"Then we march. And may the gods smile and bring us united to an easy victory."

Yes, but what victory? To Les, victory was holding Jon lovingly in his arms. That little tomboy could be extremely feminine when she chose! Sticking a sword in a stranger wasn't in the same league. *Oh, if only Kelvin comes to our rescue again! Oh if only, for I fear we are making a mistake.*

Unbidden, a thought came to him. If their king was really an impostor from the frame Kelvin and his brother Kian had visited, then could Kelvin be safe? If the impostor had done something evil to their rightful king, what of the roundear who had bested him? Wouldn't that evil man want revenge?

He was afraid to come too close to an answer. Anyway, it was time to march.

The Brownberries had been in need, all right! The man was struggling to bring in the harvest before the season turned, and the woman was ill with the ten-day fugue. The daughter was just fifteen, and willing and able to work, but could not do enough.

The crux of the problem was this: one man could cut and haul the brownberry plants if he had to, with the help of his good horse. But immediately after cutting they had to be brought inside and the long fibers separated before they hardened. That was a two-person job. If the man took the time to work with his daughter on the separation, he would not have time to complete the arduous cutting and hauling, and much of the crop would be spoiled. But if he did not, the separation could not be done.

Hal's unexpected arrival had been welcomed with something almost like tears. He was not skilled in brownberry farming, but that didn't matter; the girl was.

So now he was seated opposite her in the curing shed, holding the root-end of each plant while she deftly separated each long fiber at the blossom-end, and stretched it out until it came neatly away from the main body of the stem. A good stem could have as many as a dozen of the tough fibers, each of which could in due course be woven into the developing fabric of a new brownberry shirt. Then the squeezed juice of the berries would dye that shirt the traditional brown. Those shirts were the best and cheapest staple of local apparel; almost every rustic wore one.

This also meant that Hal had spent the day doing little except gaze at the young woman opposite him, Easter Brownberry. She had seemed like a plain girl, but now that he saw her in her area of expertise, her hands moving quickly and cleverly, he realized that it was only her shyness. Her hair fell down around her shoulders, the exact color of brownberry, the tresses moving like snakes as her head turned. Easter was well endowed for her age, and her face was attractive as she concentrated. Her breasts shifted slightly within her own brownberry shirt as her arms drew out the fibers. Every so often she glanced at him and smiled, letting him know that she appreciated his help, even though he was only holding. She became even more attractive when she did that.

Then he took a turn, because Easter was tiring. She had to take him through it in pantomime first, standing behind him and reaching around to guide his arms in the necessary motions. The fibers did not just let go; they had to be tweaked just so.

Hal felt her bosom pressed against his back. It was almost as if she were embracing him.

He went a little crazy then. He turned within her arms, coming to face her. He kissed her.

Easter was so surprised she almost fell. "Mr. Hackleberry!" she exclaimed.

Damn! Why had he done that? He was not a man to take advantage of a girl young enough to be his daughter!

"I'm sorry," he said immediately. "I'll leave."

"But—but the job isn't done!" she protested.

True. "Then I will do it. I promise not to touch you again. I don't know what happened."

They resumed the work. But now when Easter glanced at him, she did not smile. Hal felt terrible.

Finally, shyly, she asked, "Mr. Hackleberry, did you mean it?"

"Of course I did! I had no business touching you, and I won't—"

"I mean," she murmured, blushing as she averted her gaze, "when you kissed me?"

"I said I had no business—"

"But did you?" she persisted, still blushing.

"Yes," he said. "You are a most attractive girl. But—"

"You really think so?"

"Of course I do! But that's no excuse to—"

"I guess you want a quiet affair."

"I never intended to—" he began.

"Mr. Hackleberry, I think you're great, the way you came to help us out. Nobody ever thought I was pretty, before. So if you want to go to the loft—"

"No!" he protested.

"I've never done it," she said. "But I'd sure like to do it with you, Mr. Hackleberry."

Hal stared at her, realizing that she was serious. He was helping her, he found her attractive, and she was flattered, so she was ready to jump into the hay with him. The worst of it was, he was so strongly tempted.

Heln was worried and she let Dr. Sterk know it. It wasn't that she had any great faith in the physician as anything other than a doctor, but talk she must.

"Hmmm, young lady," the royal physician said, his eyebrows rising like a crest and making his sharp features even more birdlike. "You say the king is not the king, and—"

"Yes! Yes! He must be that look-alike Kelvin told us about. If he is, he's got round ears like mine and Kelvin's. He can't have pointed ears like you and King Rufurt."

Dr. Lunox Sterk did a little hop from one foot to another, a characteristic that heightened his bird impression. "I think, young lady, that you're imagining. Many women think strange things when they're with child."

"Damn it, Doctor," Heln said, feeling herself getting angry. It was awful to be treated like an unreasonable person, especially when one felt that way already. "You can at least look, can't you? King Rufurt never wore a stockelcap in his life. This king always wears one pulled down around his ears. Isn't that strange?"

"Young Lady, the king is the king. What he wants he does. It is not for you or me or any other subject to question."

"Horse droppings!" Heln said, adopting one of her natural father's crude expressions, slightly edited for decency. "We have to find out if it's the king with the round ears. *You* have to find out!"

"Young lady, you are being most difficult."

"Darned right," Heln said, now trying a pose of Kelvin's sister, again suitably edited. "And I intend to be more difficult. Either you get a look at his ears and tell me that they are pointed, or—or—I'll leave the palace!"

"Leave the palace!" Dr. Sterk was alarmed. "Really, that would never be allowed. I have my orders. Your husband wouldn't want—"

"Wouldn't want me here if the king is the evil impostor!" she retorted smartly.

The doctor held up bony hands. "Calm yourself! It's not good for you to get excited. For the sake of the child, be calm."

"I'll be calm if you'll check his ears. Will you?"

He sighed. She had him over a barrel. If she miscarried or left the palace, he would get much of the blame. "Yes. Yes, I will try to. But the king isn't acting irrationally, for a king. Kings are different. He may be losing his hair, or it may be turning gray, so he's covering it up. Kings can be even more vain than women."

Heln realized that the good doctor thought he was exaggerating for effect. She managed to disregard the insult to women, and fixed him with her eyes. "Forget the hair. Check the ears."

"I—will try. If it's the hair that is disturbing him, I can prescribe a magic ointment."

Victory, maybe! "Now, Doctor," she said in her steeliest tone. She wasn't good at this, preferring normally to be soft and feminine, but she was desperate.

He went to the chamber door as if dismissed by royalty. Without another word, he exited.

Heln lay back on her pillow in the big four-poster bed and

sighed. How totally unlike her! But it was necessary. Why have a sister-in-law like Jon if not to learn from her?

*Yes,* she thought dreamily. *Yes, now we'll all know the truth of this matter.*

But then a dark thought came, unbidden and bothersome. "Suppose it *is* Rowforth?" she whispered to the bust of Rufurt's grandfather. "Suppose it is that evil king Kelvin encountered? What of Kelvin? What of your grandson? What of all Kelvin's gains?"

The bust made no reply. Try as she might, Heln could not make it wink.

"How's she doing, Doctor?" Jon stood outside the chamber and caught the royal physician exiting. She had been standing there throughout his examination, knowing how embarrassed Heln was about her swollen abdomen.

"Delusional, I'm afraid. She has this fear that other-frame folk are coming here. She thinks our king is the one your brother helped defeat in the other frame."

"I think she's right," Jon said. "As a matter of fact, I know it."

Dr. Sterk shivered the full length of his skinny body. Disappointment was on his face. He had wanted agreement. "She wants me to look at the king's ears."

"So do I." Jon felt there was no sense in denying it. If she was to be thrown into a dungeon, too bad. In the meantime, she would hold the sling she had, with the rock that was just the right size for a false king. "There's risk?"

"With royalty, Mrs. Crumb, there's always risk."

"Not with the real King Rufurt. Remember how he laughed? Remember how he enjoyed a joke? This king seems never to enjoy anything."

"I remember his manner. Perhaps some sorcery has brought about a change."

"You will find out?"

"If he'll let me. Yes, yes, I will try."

"When, Doctor?" They had to pin him down. Otherwise he'd be stalling forever. Men were like that, and doctors especially.

"I suppose I must request that he have an examination. If he refuses—"

"Tell him it's his regular examination. He won't know."

"I . . . sup . . . pose." He seemed to speak ineffective volumes in the pauses.

"Now, Doctor."

"Oh, very well." With as much dignity as a man with birdlike beak and ungainly gait could command, he left her for the royal quarters.

Jon sighed. *For worse or much worse. I hope for all our sakes I'm wrong. But if I'm right . . . gods help all of us!*

Dr. Sterk entered the royal bedchamber and stopped. The king stood there wearing his stockelcap and nothing else.

"Well, Doctor? I haven't all day!"

Knowing the king's usual routines, Dr. Sterk doubted that. Nevertheless that was his signal to go to work. He tested the king's muscle tone (excellent), listened to his heart (beating strongly), and tested his breathing (powerful, like that of an athlete). He checked everything that he was supposed to. Except for the ears.

"Well?"

"Your ears, Your Majesty."

"What about my ears?"

"You're wearing a stockelcap. I need to look in your ears for bugs, and—"

"You think I've got bugs in my ears!"

"Check your hearing. It's just the regular checkup, Your Majesty."

"Oh, very well!" The king whipped off the covering.

Dr. Sterk blinked. Those women had been so convincing! But here were two ears as pointed as he had ever seen. A little bit cleaner than he expected, and not quite so hairy, but—

"What are you doing there?"

"Nothing, Your Majesty." He swallowed, trying to remember that he was the doctor. He really had to ask it. "Why, Your Majesty, wear the stockelcap?" Certainly it wasn't because of developing baldness or gray hair.

"Why? Because I want to!"

"Oh." So he wouldn't find out!

"I caught a little head cold in the ruins. Started giving me the sniffles. But they're gone now."

"Y-yes." Now just what was a head cold, and what was sniffles? Some sort of curse? But the king was right about one thing: he was healthy now.

Dr. Sterk was quite relieved when he finally left the royal presence.

# CHAPTER 5

# *Chimaera*

*I*t was strange being picked up and carried by two left scaly human female arms and two right scaly male arms. Kelvin watched the bulge in the male pectoral muscles where they joined the side of the creature. He hardly dared look at the female side where he imagined there was a bit of breast beneath the coppery sheen.

"I hate to disillusion your fond conjectures, but my kind don't have breasts," Mervania told him. There was a slight reproach in her tone, as though he had insulted her, or perhaps disappointed her. "Perhaps if my body was of the goatish nature envisioned by Earth's Greeks, I'd have an udder or two on my chest. But as you can see," she clicked the huge claws that were helping to support his weight, "my main body is of the crustacea."

Yes, he had noticed. Oh, did those pincers feel hard! He was almost disappointed that her body had turned out so unlike his guilty expectation.

"Why thank you, Kelvin!"

He tried to stifle his further thoughts. Now they were

descending a ramp. At the bottom a door was ajar and his father and brother lay still bound hand and foot with the froogears' vines.

There was a third individual, unbound, rather plump, wearing a suit of transparent body-covering armor. Through the armor he could see a body-length undergarment that showed neither seams nor fasteners. The stranger had dark red, wirelike hair, a stern slash of a mouth, and ears that were not quite round as his own, but pear-shaped.

"Why didn't you run out?" Kelvin demanded of the stranger. At that moment the chimaera dumped him on the floor. The scorpiocrab pincers reached past his face, sending a thrill of alarm through him, and neatly snipped the vines. His bonds fell away, and he scrambled to his feet as the monster released the others.

"Because, stupid, it's a chimaera!" the stranger snapped.

Kelvin noted the iron rings set in the stone wall. This place was evidently a dungeon beneath a castle. There were piles of straw for beds. The only other furniture was a trough that stood chest-high and held an assortment of chopped fruits in some sort of gruel. Kelvin could not believe the mouth-watering smell coming from that trough, and he realized that his stomach was really empty. In the far corner he could see an open drain. There was a small stream of water running through a narrow stone depression that entered one side of the cell and exited the opposite. The water looked as inviting as the food, and cool.

"Go ahead, eat, all of you, make yourselves fat!" the stranger said. "If the monster eats you first, that's longer for me!"

"Goodbye for now," the Mervania head said dulcetly.

"Hearty appetites," the Mertin head added.

"GWROOWOOTH!" spat-snarled the dragon head. Huge jaws opened. A forked tongue reached out and just missed licking Kelvin's flinching face.

"Grumpus, no tasting!" Mervania chided.

With astonishing ease the huge mixed-up beast turned, its long copper sting scraping first the wall and then the ceiling as the tail elevated and curled over the back. With a fast scuttling motion the chimaera exited. It turned around its massive

copper crustacean body and its human arms grasped the door's edge. The heads looked in at them as the door swung shut. From outside came the sound of a heavy bar dropped firmly in place.

The cell was not really dark. Light filtered down to them from narrow slits spaced at intervals near the ceiling. By that light, Kelvin could see his father and brother rubbing their arms and legs to restore circulation. The chimaera had not bothered to take the vines. Contemptuous of any plans they might form, it had left their bonds where they had fallen.

"I would have thought there was nothing worse than a golden dragon or a silver serpent," John said, rubbing his feet. "But a chimaera, for god's sake! And copper!"

"Huh," said the stranger. "Where you stupids been? A chimaera could eat your golden dragons and silver serpents for breakfast! Most probably have!"

John Knight gazed at the stranger. "You've encountered them? Other frames?"

"Certainly. You think other worlds don't have transporters?" There was something mechanical and metallic about the stranger's voice. Maybe it was merely its arrogance.

Kelvin watched his father's face. For someone who imagined his own world as far more advanced than others, it was a shock. Kelvin felt a little of the shock himself, and he hadn't his father's illusions.

Kian tiptoed to the door. He listened for a moment, then walked back. "It's gone. I don't think it's listening."

"So we can speak freely now, huh?" The redhead laughed as contemptuously and falsely as could be imagined.

Kelvin found himself looking from stranger to father to half brother. This was a totally incredible situation, even by adventuring standards. Trapped in a chimaera's dungeon with a know-it-all stranger from a different world! That armor had the appearance of glass or plastic, though Kelvin knew of these invisible substances only from his father's description.

"We've never been here before," Kelvin said. "In our frame the chimaera is thought to be only legend."

"You're here by accident?" the man inquired sneeringly.

"Why else?" John Knight demanded, stung by the stranger's manner. "Why else would anyone come here?"

"For the chimaera, of course. Just for the sting of it."
Again that incredible, irritating metallic laugh, as though deep
inside himself the stranger pushed a button. He seemed at
times to be almost as inhuman as the monster.

John's mouth tightened. If the stranger kept irritating
him, there would be trouble. No one made fun of John Knight.

"We're all on the same horse," Kelvin said quickly. It was
an expression he'd learned from his mother, his father having a
similar expression about boats. "We might as well get to know
one another. I'm Kelvin Knight Hackleberry. This is my
father, John Knight. This is my half brother, Kian Knight.
Father came to our frame by accident, and together we came to
this frame by accident. We were hoping to arrive in a world like
ours but with silver serpents instead of golden dragons."

"Real novices, huh? Call me Stapular. I'm a hunter. I'm
here by design. I'm the last of my party that's left."

"The others in your party, they were—"

"Destroyed, of course. Damned locals' fault. They interfered, or we'd have gotten it."

Kelvin felt more and more helpless. Just how had he
gotten to be the mouth for his party? Yet of the three of them
he felt he was best qualified. Stapular was the most irritating
person he had encountered, next to his father-in-law, and he
wasn't certain his father or half brother could endure that long.

"You mean a superior, frame-jumping party came here to
find a chimaera, and was captured by lowly froogears?" Kian
voiced the question before Kelvin thought of it. Kelvin had to
suppress a smirk; his half brother did have a certain talent for
implied sneering, when he chose to exercise it. It was a legacy
from his heartless mother, Zoanna.

Stapular responded to the rudeness as rude people often
do. "You want your nose flattened, roundear?"

"He just wants information," Kelvin said quickly. "We all
do."

"Do, huh?" Stapular's mouth snapped shut as if he
intended to keep all the information he had.

"And exchange. Though there's little we can tell you that
will help."

"Nothing I can tell you that will help either." Stapular
seemed satisfied.

"We were captured by froogears. That fruit they rolled into our chamber—"

"You fell for that, huh? Hah!"

"Yes," Kelvin said evenly. Was this oaf trying to bait them? "We are, I guess you'd have to say, unseasoned in frame travel. We didn't know this world existed, and as I've mentioned, we thought chimaeras a myth."

"Mythstake, wasn't it?"

Kelvin tried not to grind his teeth. Whether Stapular's superior attitude, his repeated use of "huh" or his grating laugh were the most irritating qualities he couldn't have said.

"Well, I'll tell you, Calvin. Unlike your roundear trash, some of us travel freely to any world not proscribed."

"Proscribed?" Ignore the messed-up name and the insult, he told himself. Go for the information. Keep the oaf talking.

"By the green dwarves. You've heard of them?"

"No. Unless Mouvar is one."

"Mouvar is. He visits the Minors. My world is Major."

Kelvin's head whirled. Major, Minor. Minor, Major. How little he knew about things Stapular took for granted.

"The Major worlds—they have more magic?"

Again that irritating laugh, indicating no humor. "Magic! Does this," he tapped his transparent armor so that it gave out a crystalline ring, "look like magic?"

"To us it does. But then we're ignorant."

"Yours must be a science world, then," John Knight said. "Like Earth."

"You claim to be from a science world?"

"More science than magic. As a matter of fact, magic isn't supposed to exist, though some in my frame do believe in it," John said.

"Huh, then you are science."

"Sort of. We were just getting around to discovering frame worlds, perhaps, and—"

"Horseless carriages, flying machines, moving and talking pictures, boxes with little living people imaged inside," Kian offered. It was as though he were intent on reporting all the wonders of his father's birthworld in one breath.

"That's primitive science," Stapular said. "You say you were discovering frame worlds?"

"Not me personally," John said. "My people."

"Then you went from a primitive Major to an even more primitive Minor?"

"If that means science world and magic world, yes. It was all an accident with us. Can't you tell us how you came here?"

Stapular nodded. "It wasn't froogears. It was the squarears. They live here but separate from froogears. They're brighter than froogears, but Minors. They tried to keep us hunters out. When we ignored their ludicrous laws they used magic. They're protecting this last of the chimaera, even bringing it copper. Damn fools! If they realized what that sting is worth on other worlds—"

Stapular broke off. It was as though his flow of speech had been silenced with a switch.

"You're merchants! Traders!" John exclaimed. "Not only hunters but dealers. In fact, from what you say, you're poachers!"

"Hah, you think we'd risk chimaera for the fun of it?"

"No," John said grimly. "I doubt that you'd risk chimaera except for some great profit."

"The squarears don't know the sting's value. No way they can use the transporter and find out. Only roundears and those like us can use the transporter here. The dwarves have the transporters booby-trapped to keep Minors from mixing too much with Majors and vice versa."

"These squarears who live here," Kelvin broke in. "How'd they stop you?"

"Magic, of course. Huh, they used a spell before we could act. We didn't know they were around, and then we were paralyzed, our weapons useless. One of those timelock spells you probably know about."

John interrupted the pregnant silence that developed. "Paralysis we understand, but timelock?"

"Time stoppage in a small area. Gives 'em time. Very unscientific."

"Magic, then," Kelvin said.

"Magic."

"These squarears," John prodded, "they just left you for the chimaera?"

"They left us for the froogears. The froogears delivered us and all our equipment."

"Then it was just the same as for us. Only we didn't encounter squarears."

"Right."

"And the others in your party?"

"Eaten one by one."

"By the chimaera. That doesn't seem possible."

"Huh, a lot you know about it."

"I didn't say it didn't happen. Only it does seem strange. On any world I've ever been on eating something as intelligent as your species is unheard of."

"You're not as intelligent, stupid. Not even I am."

"I, ah, see." John mentally shrugged as he realized that Stapular regarded the chimaera as more intelligent than all of them. Maybe it was true, but the notion took some adjusting to. Was it that those two human heads counted double?

"Could the squarears stop the chimaera?" Kelvin asked. "With their timelock?"

"Magic is magic. Why'd they want to try?"

Kelvin couldn't have answered. It was just a long shot, that they might get help. Long shots seemed to be their best shots, now.

A sudden unbarring of the door drew all of their attention. The door opened enough to admit Mervania's head. She peered in at them, seeming so much the coppery-tressed woman as almost to fool them. She evidently liked doing that! Then the door swung wide and there was Mertin-head and Grumpus-head beside Mervania-head. The scorpiocrab body scuttled inside.

Mervania looked down on them while Mertin added more food to their trough from a large bucket. Deliberately, teasingly, she lifted something large and green to her mouth and sank her pretty white teeth into it.

Kelvin felt his stomach twist. That thing she was eating. Like a giant pickle, but—

It was a forearm. Green, with little seeds stuck to it. Fingers, a thumb. A pickled arm.

Kelvin's stomach heaved, but it was already empty. He was able only to retch without substance.

"Really, Kelvin!" she said reprovingly, licking off her petite lips. "It is as you thought, a pickle. Pickled arm. Very tasty with added copper." She took another bite, her teeth now showing points.

Kelvin retched again.

"And you, Stapular," she continued between bites. "I'm thinking of a new recipe. First I'll dip you in lye while you're alive, and then—"

"Mervania!" Mertin snapped. "Don't give away your recipes!"

"Oh, all right! I'll just leave that for a surprise." She sucked on some now-fleshless fingerbones, then bit them off with a crunch. Those dainty jaws were stronger than they looked!

"This is boring," Mertin complained. "We've slopped the stock; let's go."

Mervania's mouth curved into a frown. "Spoilsport!" she muttered.

Tail raised over its back, the chimaera departed.

"Whew," Kelvin said. "Whew!" Cold sweat beaded his brow in large drops. He felt even sicker than his stomach did.

## CHAPTER 6

# *Dupes by Default*

St. Helens wasn't happy about having Charley Lomax and Phillip Blastmore along. Young bloods were hot bloods and youthful self-control was not ideal. He himself had never had self-control at their ages, and look at all the trouble he'd seen! Yet the young fellows remained as good companions and took his few orders in soldierly fashion. He had been afraid that when they reached the palace in Herlin, capital city of Hermandy, there would be questions. But no guardsman of the dictator bothered the official messenger, and neither did the boys.

King Bitler looked mean. Ornery lock of black hair over his eyes, aggressive black mustache under sharp nose, he was just plain ugly. St. Helens mused on it as he watched the king unseal and read the official letter.

"Sean Reilly," the dictator's slightly mad voice said as his moderately mad eyes gazed down at him. "Kelvinia and Hermandy are now allies."

"Yes, Your Majesty." *And how I wish it wasn't so!*

"Our mutual enemies are the twin kingdoms of Klingland and Kance. By order of Kelvinia's King Rufurt and myself you are to be put in full command of Hermandy's armed forces. Your rank is to be commanding general. Do you accept the commission?"

*I'd better,* St. Helens thought, *or I'll never live to accept or decline another. You'd like that, wouldn't you, pigface!*

"I do, Your Majesty."

"In that case you will proceed against the enemy as soon as you are issued the proper uniform." The tyrant leaned back, a palace flunky bowed to him, and then with a peremptory, sweeping gesture he motioned St. Helens out of the Royal Presence.

The audience with the Hermandy king was at an end. None too soon, by his reckoning! St. Helens knew that like it or not he would be fulfilling the wishes of both Bitner and the king he suspected was Rowforth. He felt his stomach do an experimental turn.

Mor Crumb rode the big horse at the head of the column of the finest troops money could buy, and silently and bitterly chastised himself.

*We're on the way to Klingland, on the way to fight! To destroy boys like my Lester! Lester to destroy other boys in Kance. Damn my weakness! Damn my not standing up to that impostor! Damn, damn, damn!*

Ahead was the border, its location marked by guardhouses

on either side of the road. The guardhouses were empty. Though King Kildom must have received the declaration of war, the border here was wide open.

*Now what,* Mor the old soldier had to ask himself as they crossed, *can that possibly mean?*

Lester did not like generaling. Here he was in fancy uniform approaching the border between Kelvinia and Kance. His father would be at the Klingland border now. St. Helens would be getting fitted for a new black uniform. One way or another they were all going to war. This was not as it should be, kings and prophecies be damned.

Ahead were the wide river and the waiting ferry. An old man with bleary eyes took the pass and poled him and a couple of lieutenants across.

"Something's happening in Kance," the oldster said.

"Yes, what's that?" Les was watching the straining horses pulling the cable as the ferry crossed. He had never ridden a ferry before. The water was high and muddy, so the horses were working hard.

"No one here all morning. Unusual."

"There are usually soldiers on the Kance side?"

The oldster slapped his thigh and cackled. "That's a good one, that is!" he said with a mouth full of rotted teeth. "And you wearing the uniform of a general! With Hermandy for a neighbor and the caps so near the river who'd—" He stopped, aware that his mouth might betray him.

Yes, with the capital city for both Klingland and Kance so near to the river, who would leave the border here unguarded? He knew that there was a witch running things, but he had never heard she was stupid. Witch Melbah had guarded Aratex from Conjurer's Rock, but here there was no high rock overlooking a pass leading to the capital. Why leave the border open? Why not raise the river and a storm such as Melbah would have done?

The log raft dipped and rose with a wave, and the men at the Kance side prepared for its landing. Stolid working types, they had their poles ready.

No problem, but no guards. The raft landed in its berth

and Les and the lieutenant disembarked. They watched the barge go back, the old man bending to his task with the sweeps. No one made comment.

So here they were starting an invasion. So far it was a picnic. Les had imagined there might be rows of archers on their shore. But there were no troops and no one to stop them and demand that they surrender. In a way Lester felt disappointed. He'd almost rather be made a prisoner at the outset than have to lead a fight he didn't believe in. He should have spoken up, but somehow he hadn't.

No soldiers waiting. No resistance mobilized. What did it all mean?

Hal gazed at Easter as they lay in the loft. "You know this is wrong," he said. "I'm married and you're too young."

"I've loved it every time!" she said. "I'm only sorry you have to go now."

So it seemed. He had lost count of the number of times they had done it, these past three days. It seemed she was a lonely girl who had never had this sort of attention before. He could understand her attitude—but what of his own? He was long since old enough to know better! "So have I, Easter," he said. "I think I love you. But—"

"And I love you, Hal! But I know how it is. You're married. You never told me wrong. But will you come again?"

"I shouldn't."

"But you will. I promise, I'll never tell! I just want to be with you, Hal."

Gods help him, he wanted to be with her too. She gave him the love and passion that Charlain lacked. But how could he leave Charlain? She needed someone to run the farm.

"I'll try," he said. And knew that neither storm nor drought could keep him away, wrong as it was.

Jon confronted Dr. Sterk in the hallway. "Well?" she asked with raised eyebrows.

The doctor sighed. "He does indeed have pointed ears."

"So then it is Rufurt, our proper king!" Jon had been so certain!

But the doctor did not look as if he believed what he himself had said.

Kildom faced Kildee in the throne room. Both were lying on the carpet on their bellies. Between them was the playing area for their cards.

"Now you take this one," Kildom said, slapping down a queen. The queen, like all playing-card queens, wore a smirk, as though she and the knave were up to naughtiness.

"No problem," Kildee said. Slap, down went the laughing sorcerer.

"Damn," said Kildom. "I forgot about that."

"You always do. This is the fourth game in which you forgot the sorcerer."

"Better to lose to magic than to might," said Kildee. He studied the face of his twin, so similar to himself that both had identical moles on their cheeks: Kildom on the right cheek, Kildee on the left. That made sense, as Kildom was right-handed, Kildee left-handed. Both faces were quite handsome in childish ways. Today was special because it was the day both rulers turned six.

"Why is it," Kildom inquired, "that we count a birthday only every four years?" Every birthday he had the same question.

"Because," his baby-faced brother replied, "it's Leaping Day, also Monarch Day, a day that comes up on the royal calendar once every four years. If we'd been born on Zebudarry twenty-eighth instead of Zebudarry twenty-ninth we'd be twenty-four."

"True. Quite true." Kildom rolled over and stood up on little pudgy legs. He looked down at his twin, his hands toying with his lace collar. "If only our bodies were grown! Some days I don't think I can wait until I'm a hundred before taking a queen."

"What would you know about *that!*" Kildee retorted. "We're only six and what you have in your royal pants I have in mine."

"Do not! Mine's bigger."

"Bigger butt, maybe."

They tangled, arms and legs and heads. Kildee was on top and blacked his brother's right eye with his left fist. Then Kildom rolled over and blacked Kildee's left eye with his right fist. It was always thus.

"Boys, boys, boys!" Helbah said reprovingly. She was very old, far older than they had reason to think about. She bent over now and picked them up by their lace collars, shook them hard, and sat them down.

Kildom, king of Klingland, looked up at her wrinkled face and tried not to cry. His eye hurt, as it always did when his brother blacked it. "He hit me, Helbah!"

"And you hit him back. You both got what you deserved."

Kildom sighed. So true, so very true.

"You boys are going to have to exercise a little restraint. Your kingdoms have problems."

"They have?" This was news to them both.

"They do. Some people think you are babies. They don't realize that you have the intelligence of grown men."

Kildom wished that his emotions were not those of a six-year-old. He could convince his intellect of almost anything, but his emotions were another matter.

"Now we know," Helbah said, "that Kelvinia has made a pact with your hereditary enemy in Hermandy. We know because old Helbah has her ways."

"Magical," said Kildee.

"Witchy," said Kildom, not to be outdone.

"Yes, yes. Now we mustn't negate the craft by putting false names to it. Helbah has a power that is good and for your protection. She knows you are threatened and by whom."

"We understand, Helbah," Kildom said. He knew his brother would not have to withdraw his suggestion of magic. Magical or witchy, the powers were hers.

Helbah squeezed the boy's tiny hand. She looked into his face as if he were indeed all man.

"Kildom, your kingdom is now being invaded by forces led by Mor Crumb, the former opposition leader in Rud. Kildee, you have his son's invasion on your hands."

"Your magic can stop them, Helbah," Kildee said confidently. "It's more powerful than armies."

"Perhaps. You know that Helbah will try."

Kildom felt more alarm and saw alarm on his brother's face. If Helbah expressed caution, the matter was serious!

"You see," Helbah explained, "Hermandy would not attack you without magical assistance. Bitler wanted help from Zatanas, the sorcerer slain by Kelvin. Now Bitler has found the help he lacked."

"You are certain?" Kildee asked.

"I am certain that there is a power in the newly formed kingdom of Kelvinia. How well controlled and how powerful I can only guess."

"Then you do not know everything," Kildom suggested, disappointed.

"No. My clairvoyance is limited and my precognition all but absent. I know that Melbah, my duplicate from another frame, was killed by Kelvin. I did not know she would be killed or see it happening. There are limits to all abilities, including mine."

"Never mind, Helbah," Kildom said, impulsively grabbing her around the neck. "My brother and I will protect you."

"That's nice," she said, managing to look reassured.

Rowforth, formerly king of Hud in another world, now the imitation king of Kelvinia, looked into the mirror and laughed. His ears looked so preposterous to him. Newly pointed and with no more hair on them than on a baby's rump, they were the proper size and shape for this frame. They had to be, considering where he had obtained them.

Zoanna, his fully pointeared consort here, tweaked his left ear as she massaged it and pulled its point. "They are quite ready to show now, dear Rufurt. The magical ointment has worked its wonders."

"Don't call me Rufurt."

"It's your name now. You have to get used to it. You are after all taking the man's place."

"King's place," he corrected her. Though very bright for a female, she didn't quite seem to recognize the qualitative difference between mere man and godlike king.

"Yes, stoneheart," she said affectionately. She nuzzled the ear, as if liking her handiwork almost as much as him.

Rowforth rubbed his cheek against hers and wished that for all her beauty and her magic she were not so much the local. He had enjoyed punching her counterpart, Zanaan. He couldn't imagine punching Zoanna, since the queen had magic and would retaliate. Too bad, but eventually he would find other women he could beat and pummel and kick and bite with impunity.

"What are you thinking, my lusty king? About destroying those who thwarted me before? About tormenting those who robbed you of your kingdom in that other place?"

"Not exactly," he confessed. In the mirror reflection he did look like the rightful king. It was both reassuring and angering. Round ears, after all, were natural. "I've been thinking of revenge."

"The Roundear of Prophecy? Kelvin, spawn of the roundear John Knight?"

"Sort of. That woman in the palace is his wife. She carries our worst enemy's brat."

"Yes, yes." She seemed delighted with his dialogue.

"I plan on torturing her. Before his eyes."

"Yes, yes, yes." Her eyes were bright, her lips parted and wet. Her queenly robe was falling open, showing more of her intriguing figure. One would hardly have guessed her true age, looking at her body. Magic was wonderful stuff!

"And perhaps a bit of magic. Make pointed ears on them both."

"That would take time. It's not like something you do to extract a confession. Yours was a very special case. They don't have convenient doubles to borrow from."

"You could start now. Get Sterk to ointment her ears. Maybe give her something to affect the cub in her. If she could give birth to something misshapen and revolting before they all are allowed to die . . ."

"Oh yes, yes, yes! Brilliant! You are the greatest, most magnificent consort ever!" She put her hands to his head and turned his face to hers with a ferocity and eagerness that almost scared him. Zanaan had never been like this! She kissed his lips, pressing them hard with hers. Her passions were aroused by what he accidentally said. It seemed that the same sort of thinking aroused them both. He took her in his arms and then to the bed. She looked just like his consort in the other frame, but she was a world different! That malice and savagery lent her phenomenal sex appeal, while Zanaan's disgusting niceness made her appealing only when she was screaming with pain and humiliation.

"It's so early in the day!" she exclaimed. There were golden lights in her greenish eyes. Zanaan had had those too, but they hadn't ever lit up for him.

He enjoyed kingly privileges all morning in a manner he had seldom if ever done before. Thanks, he felt certain, to some magic substance added to his wine that gave him a seemingly indefatigable potency. The queen had done it, surely, but he didn't mind at all. What a lithe and joyfully vicious creature she was! Her rapture was almost like that of pain, which really turned him on.

During and after his exertions he thought not so much of Zoanna, or even of Zanaan. What he most thought about were delightful new means of extending torment in helpless folk, especially in attractive women. How similar the reactions of sex-making seemed to those of agony. Once he got into the real thing . . .

---

# CHAPTER 7

# *Squarears*

*I*t happened so suddenly that Kelvin hadn't time to think. One moment he was trying fruitlessly to sleep on the straw bed the chimaera provided, and the next it was broad daylight and he was looking up at an orange sky with whippy yellow clouds.

His back felt as though a stick was poking in it. He felt around with his hands and recognized the prickle of grass. He was on the ground, outside. But how?

"Greetings, visitors."

Kelvin sat up. The person who had spoken stood beside him: blocky of build, with straw-colored hair and ears that stuck out and were square. There were several similar folk beyond.

Kian and John were sitting beside him. Stapular was nowhere in sight.

"You—you—what?" Kelvin inquired intelligently. He wasn't yet sure whether this or the chimaera's den was reality.

"The squarears," his father supplied. "Remember Stapular telling us?"

Kian was looking past all of them. "We're back at the cave!"

"Very true," the squared individual said. He held a huge copper needle that seemed a duplicate of the chimaera's sting. "You are now free to leave here and continue your journey."

"But—" Kelvin said. Could it all have been a dream? But no, dreams never remained this clear. Besides, he could still taste the mash he had eaten from the chimaera's trough.

"I am Bloorg," said their apparent rescuer. "Official Greeter and Sender, Keeper of the Transporter to Other Worlds, Keeper of the Last Known Existing Chimaera. I'm sorry that we did not check on you in time. We were preoccupied with more deliberate visitors."

"Stapular's people?" Kelvin asked.

"Yes."

"He's still there? In the chimaera's cellar?"

"Yes. He deserves to be, though I doubt the chimaera will find him tasty eating."

Kelvin shivered. Poor Stapular! But why had they been rescued, and that man not?

"That magic Stapular spoke about," John said, almost answering Kelvin's thoughts. "Timelock?"

"Yes," Bloorg said. "We simply took you away without the chimaera's awareness, or yours, or the other captive's."

"But why?" Kelvin demanded. It surprised him that he demanded anything, but the hero's role was gradually growing on him. "Why were we rescued, and not him?"

"Stapular's people were here deliberately. They came to do harm. You, in contrast, arrived by chance."

"You—you know?" *Telepathic?*

"Limited telepathy," Bloorg agreed. "Enough to know your thoughts, though unable to communicate that way."

"And the chimaera is telepathic," Kelvin said. "I know, because—"

"Because it exchanged thoughts with you. Yes, it is a complete telepath, able to receive and send, which is part of what makes it unique. But we have kept it confined for some time. We know how to keep it from our thoughts."

"You're like zookeepers!" John said. "You're a chimaerakeeper!"

"Correct."

"But why?" Now John looked as bewildered as Kelvin felt.

"Uniqueness. In all the frames we know of, this is the last of the chimaera's kind. Should it be destroyed, the victim of genocide, to satisfy an alien's greed?"

"No. No it shouldn't, but—"

"You think of your fellow prisoner and his claim to be from a Major world. Major and Minor are in the eyes of the beholder, as your people say. It was no love of knowledge that brought them here."

"But you did let them be slaughtered, eaten by the chimaera?"

"Of course."

Kelvin looked at his father and brother, and wondered. Were they as appalled by this as he was?

"Your property was also rescued," Bloorg said. He gestured with squared-off fingers. Other squarears stepped forward carrying the levitation belt, the Mouvar weapon, the gauntlets, and the swords.

"So we really are free, then?" Kian asked, seeming hardly to believe it.

"Yes. Go now to your wedding."

Something was not right. Kelvin almost knew, but could not quite pin it down. He buckled on his sword, the Mouvar weapon, and drew on the gauntlets.

"Well I for one am ready to go!" Kian said. "I've had enough of chimaera and poacher. I'm ready to go any time."

Kelvin looked at his father. John was frowning, maybe

disturbed about the same thing that was bothering Kelvin. They had after all been confined in the same place. Driven by hunger, they had eaten from the trough Stapular must have eaten from. Kelvin had felt like a piog, gulping slops, but the stuff had been amazingly tasty.

"Do not waste your sympathies on the hunter," Bloorg said. "He is not quite as he seems, and he knew what he risked."

*But dipped in lye? Cooked alive? Pickled? Eaten?* It seemed all too much. Even the sorcerer Zatanas and the witch Melbah had received kinder fates, and they, more than gruff Stapular, had seemed to be of a different species.

"I repeat, your sympathies are wasted," Bloorg said. "Once you have considered the enormity of what they planned, you will agree that their fate was deserved."

Sympathy then for the chimaera? A creature that mocked them from a feminine face? A monster that munched human limbs with enjoyment? Was that where his sympathy should lie?

"No," Bloorg answered patiently. "You should not feel sympathy for either. They are what they are, and nothing you or we could do would make any difference."

Evil beings deserving nothing more? But Stapular had seemed human. Not likable, certainly, but human. And advanced.

"Advanced by what cosmic standard?"

Yes. Yes, that made sense. A person might think himself advanced, but that was as likely to be vanity as fact. Greed was after all greed, and cruelty was cruelty. But could a monster be said to be cruel? Wasn't its taunting ways simply part of its nature?

"You are remarkably philosophical for one so recently rescued." The squarear was looking at him from blocky pupils in blocky eyes set in a blocky head. Looking, seemingly, into the roundeared, roundeyed, roundheaded depths of him.

"It's my nature," Kelvin said. "I have to question."

"Of course you do."

Kian looked toward the cave. "Any time you're ready, Kelvin, Father."

"All right." John Knight stood. He held out his hand to Bloorg. "In my frame it is the custom to clasp the hand of someone who has saved your life, and say thanks."

"You are most welcome," Bloorg said. They shook, John wincing as he felt the other's hand.

Kian was already on his feet, extending his hand similarly. Kelvin, uneasy for no reason he could quite define, followed their example. When he took Bloorg's six-fingered hand he knew why his father and his brother had acted surprised. It was chilly, like a froogear extremity, but dry rather than clammy. The fingers wrapped around his wrist, showing that they were many-jointed, like little tails. The alien feel of the appendage drove all other thoughts away.

"Come," John said, and Kelvin followed with Kian. It was farther than it had appeared to be, and it seemed to get no closer as they walked. Then suddenly it was much closer, and each step was taking them rapidly forward.

Kelvin looked back. The squarears were gone, vanished.

"Magic!" Kian said, also looking back. "I knew there was something funny about it. We weren't where we seemed to be."

Kelvin had to agree, though he was not elated. Somehow magic and the evident extent of the squarears' powers was depressing. True, the magic of the gauntlets had saved him many times, but it had always seemed to him that having magic was an unfair advantage. What chance did a master swordsman have, for instance, against a bungle-foot like himself, when his sword was clasped by a hand in a magic gauntlet? Kelvin knew himself to be no hero, merely a person whose ordinary abilities were amplified by magic. Now he had encountered creatures who seemed to be far beyond that magic. It was disconcerting.

"Hey, Son, you look glum!" his father said lightly. It was almost a doggerel rhyme, the kind he had done to cheer Kelvin as a child.

"I can't get it out of my head, Father."

"What, that you were rescued? That none of us will be eaten?"

Finally the thing that had been bothering him focused. "No, Father. That Stapular will be eaten." He let that sink, then plunged ahead. "Is that right, Father? Is it?"

"I wondered how long it would take for your conscience to catch up," John said. "You can't let anything be. You always have to work it out to the last degree, so that it makes sense on every level. You are unusual in that, perhaps unique."

"I'm sorry," Kelvin said.

"Sorry! Son, that's what makes you a hero!" His father's friendly hand came around his shoulders. "But look, Son, it's not right by our standards, but this isn't our frame. We shouldn't be here. We're here only by chance. It isn't our business."

"I'm going ahead!" Kian said, and ran on to the cave. He looked inside, looked back, and called, "This is it, all right! Hurry up!"

"He doesn't care," Kelvin said.

"It's his upbringing. It was different from yours. Remember who his mother was."

Kelvin remembered. Evil Queen Zoanna, who had used magic to fascinate John Knight and seduce him and bear his child. Zoanna had evidently liked to play with men in much the way Mervania did, only Zoanna, being human, had been able to take it farther. "Yes, he's seen more cruelty casually applied."

"In the palace he did. His grandfather and his mother were not noticeably kind. Give him credit for turning out as well as he did, given that environment. He did not have Charlain as his mother."

That certainly accounted for the difference! Kelvin's mother was the finest woman he knew, though perhaps Heln approached her.

"Hurry it up, won't you!" Kian called.

"And you can't blame him for wanting to get on with his wedding," John said.

Kelvin abruptly stopped. "Father, I'm going back."

"Of course you are, Son. We all are. First to Kian's wedding, as we planned before getting diverted here, and then—"

"No, Father. I mean back to the island in the lake. Back to rescue Stapular."

"Son, you can't!" But something in John's expression suggested that he wasn't surprised.

"I can. I have the gauntlets now, and the levitation belt, and the Mouvar weapon. I can do it."

"No, wait! The chimaera can stun your mind! Think—"

Kelvin knew better than to think. A man of action he must be, though his nature was far more sedentary. Magic and a prophecy made him heroic despite himself.

He touched the control for "up" on the belt, and suddenly he was floating above his father's head, looking back at Kian's astonished form waving at the cave. It was exactly as it was when he practiced with the belt.

"Goodbye, Father. Wait for me if you will. If not, I'll follow you."

"No, wait, you idiot! What kind of a fool are you!"

"I'm a hero, remember?" And he knew his father understood, despite trying to restrain him. Heroes would be heroes, just as kings would be kings, to the wonder and dismay of others.

Sadly yet determinedly he nudged the control and floated smoothly swampward. A bit of acceleration and the swamp breezed by. Now and then he caught a froogear's surprised face in the greenness below, or sight of one of the swamp monsters. He had no doubt of the proper direction, partly because there was a treeless area that was almost like a road, but mostly because the gauntlets tingled ever so slightly when he started going wrong. Soon the lake and island with its imposing wall were in sight.

*Have to think now. Have to think. Face the chimaera's power? Think to Mervania? Demand that it release the prisoner?*

Down below was the gate where they had waited for the god of the froogears. He drifted over, slowing. Now there was that peculiar walkway bordered by the more peculiar fence. Even while carried by the chimaera he had noticed it. Greenish, tapering, almost thorn-shaped posts. Then there was the ruined castle with openings like vacant eyes. The chimaera, aware of him or not, was nowhere in sight.

He lowered himself cautiously, with a nudge of the belt control. Past moss-grown walls to a spot directly in front of the doorway to the dungeon. Still no chimaera. Was it going to be this easy? Was the monster going to let him get away with this, knowing that he was now magically armed? Or was the chimaera simply asleep?

He approached the barred door. He lifted the bar, grunting from the weight of it, glancing nervously back over his shoulder. The gauntlets felt warm, but the very existence of the chimaera could account for that.

He hesitated, then forced himself to proceed. He swung the door open.

The chimaera waited inside, sting raised on backward-bending abdomen. All three heads had coppery eyes focused on him.

"Welcome back, Kelvin!" Mervania said brightly. A lightning bolt speared from the tip of the sting and sizzled past his head. A warning shot, surely.

He was prepared as he had not been before. The Mouvar weapon was in his hand and properly set to contain any hostile magic. He pressed the trigger and the antimagic weapon emitted a few colorful sparks.

What was this? It wasn't supposed to do that! It was supposed to make a barrier to hostile magic.

The tip of the chimaera's sting moved, almost imperceptibly. Lightning leaped from it to one of the greenish posts. Sizzling, the bolt leaped from post to post. Now Kelvin realized, belatedly, that the posts were copper stings stuck in the ground. The chimaera was emitting lightning, and the stings in the ground received the lightning and made the spectacular display. A stench hit his nostrils that was partly ozone and partly something he had not known before.

"Stupid roundear!" Stapular cried from the cell. He wasn't even trying to attack, but was instead flattened at the very back of the enclosure.

Time to think about Stapular later. Kelvin's hands burned in the gauntlets and he didn't like ignoring their warning. Quickly he adjusted the weapon's control. Now it would not only block hostile magic from reaching him, as perhaps it had just done, but would turn it back on the sender. If it worked as he hoped, the magic lightning would double back on the chimaera itself.

"If you insist," Mervania said.

"Real dumb one, isn't he!" Mertin remarked.

"Groomth," growled Grumpus.

Kelvin pressed the trigger and held it down. Lightning shot from the tip of the chimaera's tail and sizzled right at his feet. He felt it, shockingly, through the soles of his feet and all through his body. His hair seemed to be sparking. The Mouvar weapon, amazingly, did nothing but emit a few colored sparks and get very hot in his hand.

"Really, you must go back inside," Mervania scolded. The chimaera crawled outside as the Mouvar weapon sagged in his tingling fingers. The monster confronted him at close range, and another blue bolt sizzled at his feet.

About this time Kelvin realized one or two things. One was that a species that was near extinction was not necessarily a sweet thing to be near. The other was that he was in real trouble.

Slowly, unsteadily, hardly knowing what he did, he backed away. The chimaera moved after, clicking its pincers before it. He backed into the cell, past the trough, and to the wall beside Stapular.

The lightning stopped. He slid to the floor, as did Stapular. The chimaera closed the door, dropping the bar with what seemed a final crash.

*Thank you for coming back, Kelvin! I know you'll be delicious!*

Oh, the pain! The incredible shaking, tingling all over him. He felt it everywhere, even in the gauntlets. None of his weapons had been any use! Instead of rescuing Stapular, he had made himself prisoner again.

He rolled up his eyes, trying to adjust to the enormity of what had happened. He had tried to play the hero's part, and had only succeeded in playing the fool's part.

"Satisfied, stupid?" Stapular asked.

"It—it should have worked! Mouvar's weapon is antimagic."

"Antimagic!" Stapular laughed his annoying laugh, as nastily as ever. "Dumb, stupid, Minor World creature! The chimaera wasn't using magic."

"The lightning!"

"Electricity. The monster generates it in its body. Copper conducts. Nothing magical about it. Science."

"Science?" Kelvin's morale and hopes plummeted. "Not magic?"

"Now you've got it, Minor World idiot! You've come back to be eaten! Doesn't that make you feel just great?"

"The squarears—"

"They won't help you twice. They have no more tolerance for fools than I do, fool."

"But I have my levitation belt. Once outside, I can—"

"The chimaera can shoot a bolt straight up and cook you in midflight. I've seen it fry passing birds that way. Any that are so stupid as to come within range. Most stay well clear."

"My gauntlets!"

"Won't help a bit. Didn't out there, did they?"

"No, but—"

"But you're back. And you're going to be eaten. Why did you come back anyway?"

"To get you released."

"Me? To rescue me?" The red-haired alien looked astonished. The expression was not typical of the way the good citizens of Kelvinia did it; his eyes widened and his facial lines seemed to click out starkly and then recede in place.

"Yes," Kelvin agreed dully.

"Foolish. Incredibly foolish. Worst possible motive I've ever heard."

"You'd do the same for me."

"I would, huh?" The man emitted his nasty laugh. The laughter boomed louder and bounced around the dungeon, striking one wall and then another. Kelvin had never heard of a building being tumbled by laughter, but it almost seemed possible, now. "Me rescue a dummy like you from a Minor frame? Why should I care whether you're eaten?"

"It's only human," Kelvin said defensively. What was so funny?

Stapular laughed all the harder. With precise control he switched from mocking to insulting to humiliating. He seemed a laugh machine similar to one Kelvin's father had told him about, perhaps jokingly.

"Well gee," Kelvin said wistfully, reverting to a childhood expression, "it sounded right to me."

---

## CHAPTER 8

# *Battles Strange*

General Mor Crumb awoke, dressed, exited his tent and stretched. It was a fine morning; in fact a glorious morning. The sun was shining over Klingland and Klingland was waiting.

He hailed Captains Abileey and Plink, nodded to a second lieutenant, and exchanged perfunctory salutes with a passing private. The horses awaited, as did the mess. As was not customary in any army, he simply got in line. The privates, mostly from Throod, made room for him with haste, while officers tightened their lips at this display of what Mor felt proper. Since when did an officer act like a common man?

"Jerked spameef!" exclaimed one young soldier holding up a twist of reddish meat. His expression and tone suggested anticipation of a bad taste.

"Field rations, soldier!" Captain Abileey said. "What'd you expect, goouck and fish eggs? Be thankful it's not horse manure on a shingle."

The private blanched. Obviously he had not been long in uniform. "Sorry, sir, I guess I was hoping for something else."

"Probably," Captain Abileey said. "But we'll eat well enough later. After victory."

"Yes, sir." The boy brightened at the thought. Klingland was known for its fine shepton and poreef as well as less common cuisine.

"If we don't delay we'll reach Bliston by noon. There's supposed to be only a small garrison, so there shouldn't be much of a fight. Then Gamish and Shucksort and finally the double cap itself. I make it three days."

"I know that, sir. But thank you anyway."

One way or another, they all filled up on dry rations washed down with steaming mugs of cofte from the army pot. In no time at all they were assembled and on their way, riding single file. The officer in official charge rode at the head.

*I don't know why we're doing this,* Mor thought, looking ahead at the blur of green. *Klingland never did anything to us that I know about. Why didn't we just give old Rufurt the thumb in the nose? Maybe it was that wine. Yes, that was probably it. I've never been this complaisant about soldiering before in my life. But he did make me a general. Not that I asked for rank or even wanted to volunteer to fight.*

Prod, prod, prod.

Someone, probably one of the officers, began the "Horse Manure, Horse Manure" song. It felt good to belt out the familiar lyrics, and Mor found himself bellowing jubilantly with the rest: "Makes the giries scream. Horse—" And so it went. All morning went, little by little, unnoticed by man or horse, undisturbed by sniper's arrows or any appearance of armed locals. It was, he had to admit to himself, a dream march. Absolutely nothing was going wrong. Ahead and to the sides the green blurred steadily.

At noon they stopped and rested, ate field rations and drank spring water from canteens while the horses chomped grass. In due course they remounted and proceeded as before.

Prod, prod, prod.

Mor was bothered, perversely, by the ease of this. He didn't trust an easy campaign. Only in dreams was everything perfect—until the dreams turned bad.

"Horse—"

A horse whinnied. It was Mor's own. Then, as though urged by the song, it defecated. Mor, for no particular reason, turned in his saddle and looked at the steaming dung as the horse's hooves pounded the ground.

Prod, prod, prod.

Something was not right. Something definitely was not

right. The horse should have outdistanced its dung in its first stride. Yet the horse walked and the dung remained directly behind. The horse walked but the ground kept pace. So did the smell.

Mor frowned, trying to understand, and to shake the unnatural euphoric mood he was in. All morning it had been this way. Almost as if he had drunk heavily of wine and experienced nothing but its exhilarating effect. He could hardly damp down the feeling, though he knew it was unnatural. He was after all on the way to a fight. Fear was a better emotion than contentment!

There it was, horse dung, steaming and fragrant, gathering flies.

Finally it registered. "Damn!" he swore, appreciating the subtle beauty of it. He knew what was wrong.

"Captain Abileey, Captain Plink," Mor said. "We are in deep manure."

"Why is that, sir?" Captain Abileey's boyish face just missed being ecstatic. Mor knew that this was going to be difficult for him, because he was entirely taken in by the illusion.

"We're making good time, General," Captain Plink said. "No opposition all morning. We must have come a good twenty—"

"Bliston's not that far," Mor pointed out.

"Well, sir?" Captain Abileey inquired. His cheeks were as ruddy as if he'd just stepped from a tavern. Unquestionably this was one of the most contented moments of his life. But Mor, nominal leader, had no choice but to end it.

"Look there," Mor said, pointing.

"Yes sir." The young captain's nose wrinkled. "Horse droppings."

"Watch."

Prod, prod, prod.

"We're not moving, sir!" Captain Abileey was astonished. "We're—something's wrong! What can possibly be wrong?"

"Magic!" Captain Plink said, appreciatively. He was older, and had seen more oddities; he was thus more ready to grasp this insight.

Mor sighed, and said with equal appropriateness, "Horse droppings!"

After that there was nothing to do but call a halt. There was horse manure all around; they could not get away from it. The joy of the advance diminished.

Lester Crumb saw them first: the Kance soldiers riding down on them, poised, swords drawn, in an all-out charge.

"Archers! Crossbowmen! Pick off the leaders first!" It was what his father would have ordered. Sensible and right: officers, after all, had ordered the charge.

Lester's men formed a line, ready to fire at Lester's signal. Les dropped his hand, readying himself for the sight of death. Why was this army charging his own army so suicidally? Like a lot of things lately, it didn't seem to make much sense.

Arrow strings twanged. Crossbows fired. The missiles flew straight for their targets. But the enemy cavalry neither swerved nor slowed in its charge. The arrows and crossbow bolts fell well beyond them. The charge continued, unaffected.

"What? What?" Les couldn't believe it. Not one of the enemy had fallen, or even taken a hit. Every shaft had missed!

The distance between the two forces became smaller. Les imagined that he could see the angered eyes, the set lips, even the sweat on the attackers' foreheads. How could they be immune to arrows?

"Cease firing! Form a phalanx!"

The troops formed the square, spears pointing out protectively on all sides. The enemy riders came closer, closer, while all Les' men waited. There was muted grumbling; they didn't like taking a defensive posture when they plainly outnumbered the opposition.

Damn, he thought, what was there to do?

"Sir," said Captain Barnes, his second in command. "It's magic!"

"I can see that, Captain."

"We need the Mouvar weapon, sir. To turn the magic back on them."

"Agreed, Captain," Les said tightly. "Unfortunately we don't have it." Kelvin had the weapon, and why, oh why wasn't he here, when so much depended on him?

Lester stared gloomily at the ever-charging cavalry. He had to wonder whether they were going to have to squat here and wait indefinitely until Kelvin returned from his brother's wedding.

Then he had a new thought, an alarming one. If King Rufurt had been replaced by the king from another frame, what then had been the rightful king's fate? And if Rufurt had been destroyed or somehow magicked, what then of Kelvin? *What was going on, in that other frame?*

St. Helens should have felt great. Leading troops again— not that he ever had before, exactly. But campaigning was something he knew from the ground up. So why wasn't he happy, now that he was at the head end of it instead of the tail end?

Charley Lomax rode by his left and young Phillip at his right, and behind them stretched the Hermandy army. All seemed to be in order. So what was his problem?

"Sir," the young guardsman whispered, bending near in his saddle. "Have you noticed our well-wishers?"

St. Helens saw what the lad meant. A few sullen faces were staring at them from passing yards and doorways. There were no flowers strewn in their path, no cheers or patriotic cries of well-wishing. The faces were mostly glum and the bodies often ill-fed. The populace of Hermandy reminded him of another. Would the former king of Aratex be reminded? St. Helens turned in his saddle and glanced.

Phillip's face was wreathed in boyish smiles. Taking no notice of anything around them, he appeared as happy as when he was beating St. Helens in chess. After viewing all the death and destruction in Aratex, he still was thinking of glory. St. Helens knew how it was for him because he had once been that way himself.

"I don't think the military is popular in this land," he whispered to Guardsman Lomax. "Considering that the Hermandy government is highly repressive, that's normal. It was that way in Aratex, and, not long ago, before the roundear, in Rud."

"And after this war it will be different here also?"

St. Helens had had a top sergeant once who answered each and every question a private could muster with irrefutable logic. The answer was always the same in St. Helens' experience. He used that sergeant's answer now.

"Shut," he said reasonably, "the hell up!"

They rode on through deeper and deeper gloom brought on by the fact that nothing was as either of them would have wished.

Helbah had to smile as she gazed into the twin crystals. One showed Mor's difficulty, the other his son's.

"Yes," she said aloud, perhaps to Katbah, her houcat friend. "Yes, old Helbah knows a thing or two! Never could defeat my evil frame-sister, but I kept her from invading us long enough! Glad she's gone! She's my malevolent mirror image, you can bet!"

"Meoww," Katbah remarked, arching his slick back. He would rather be battling a leaf or climbing a tree. Instead he was here in her defense headquarters giving her support.

"Now, then," Helbah continued, checking her brewkettle in the fireplace and giving it a stir with its ladle, "here's our plan. Once we've got them stopped we wait until they go back discouraged or until their decent leaders come and surrender to us. No killing. You like that?"

Katbah rubbed his head against her gnarled hand and purred. It was a gentle soothing sound that befitted a feline creature that never, ever killed birds. From the same gentle frame and mold as Helbah, he preferred finding and returning baby birds that had tumbled from their nests. Yet feline was feline, and Katbah, her familiar, responded as only a familiar could.

Helbah looked down at the touch of the velvety smooth tongue on her hand. She ruffled the black fur, tweaked the triangular whiskers, and stared into the oval eyes.

"Katbah, I think we've won. But—" She frowned as she thought of this. "I wonder why? Not just that we've won, but why the invasion. This is utterly unlike pleasant, ineffective King Rufurt of Rud. Or whatever they call that kingdom now. Kelvinia—that's it, after that good lad."

Katbah rubbed against the third crystal on the table. This one was a smoothed square. His paw reached out and tapped it. The crystal was opaque.

"Yes, yes, I'd better. I hate spying, Katbah, but now and then I have to. There is too much of a mystery about this matter."

She drew the square crystal across the rough wooden table to her. She held her clawed fingers above the smooth surface, closed her eyes, and concentrated. In a moment she felt the quiver in her arms and the lightning sparks from her fingertips.

She opened her eyes, staring into a universe of tiny bubbles. Now where? Where? To Kelvinia to find out the cause of the attack. She visualized a man with a big nose, wearing a crown. Yes, there he was, reflected in the crystal as though in a glass box. Rufurt.

Why, she wondered, why? Under her prodding thoughts the view widened. The king was in his bedchamber and he was not alone. Helbah frowned, not wanting to intrude on a private moment between king and—

The woman in the bedchamber turned. As she did, Katbah raised his fur and spat.

Red-as-dragon-sheen hair. Eyes the color of green feline magic with little cometing lights in them. The eyes might have been directed right at her!

*Zoanna!* Zoanna, the evil queen all thought dead. Hadn't she drowned? Yet here she was with the king, whom she had despised in life. Could this be Rufurt, the real Rufurt?

She peered close, moving in on the man with her thoughts. There was a mean look to him, an insane light in his eyes. His ears were tipped, but with a tipping that was new.

*This was not good King Rufurt.*

So, then, it was another paired set, like Melbah and Helbah, from other frames. Similar appearance, dissimilar nature. Only the ears gave such folk away, physically.

And the queen?

Helbah moved in on the queen. The face, just as haughty, just as inhumanly cold and devoid of genuine feeling. The original Zoanna, without a doubt.

So the queen had not died. She had hidden, and now

returned with a look-alike to replace Rufurt. Rufurt had been easygoing and appreciative of life, but Zoanna had manipulated and misled him. When he and John Knight were released from the Rud dungeon, having sprung themselves during the battle, Rufurt had been just the same. She had checked up on him from time to time, not to interfere but to assuage her curiosity and make sure that no mischief was afoot. This, she was now sure, was not he.

Zoanna had been taking something from a wooden stand. She held up a round crystal. Her face a study in suspicion, she closed her eyes.

Now what? The couple had evidently been about to make love, but now seemed to be up to something else. Had Zoanna learned magic? Her father, Zatanas, had known little, though he had faked much. But Zoanna had been absent for some time. Perhaps she had learned. Maybe she had developed a dormant witch-sense.

In the crystal Zoanna held, Helbah's own face appeared. Zoanna's eyes opened as she peered at it.

"Helbah, I thought that was you! Are you so hard up for thrills that you have to spy on the pleasures of your betters?"

Horrors! She *had* learned magic! She had felt Helbah's questing, and challenged it. Only a few selected people, male or female, were able to master sorcery, and even fewer ever made the attempt. Zoanna had evidently discovered that she had the ability, and now had developed it. Here was real mischief!

The king bent forward, also looking. "She the witch?"

Zoanna ignored him. To Helbah she said: "Your time has come, old woman. You won't exist much longer. We're taking over the brat kingdoms. When we complete that chore, you will die. We shall throw you away like the garbage you are."

Katbah leaped at the crystal in sudden fury. Sparkling sharp claws raked the crystal, producing a screech that hurt Helbah's ears. It was the way she herself felt.

"I have stopped the armies," Helbah said. "Just as in years of yore."

"Yes, witchy bonebag, but not for long. I now have means of countering you."

"You can nullify my spells?" Helbah asked skeptically.

"Watch." Zoanna gestured. In the crystal she held was Mor and his army in Klingland. They were paused, looking at a pile of horse droppings. Zoanna took a small vial from a drawer in the stand and sprinkled an orange powder. The crystal flared bright. Zoanna held a finger pointed, and the horse manure lifted from the ground and hovered in midair. A sudden cutting gesture, and the dung fell.

A horse leaped. Mor assumed a startled expression, as did his officers. Then they were riding on, into the target territory.

"No you don't!" Helbah snapped. She made a gesture of her own, and the advance, though it seemed to be going forward, stayed even with a tree.

"That is the last time that will be tolerated," Zoanna said grimly. She made a new gesture, and the movement resumed.

Angered by this insolence, Helbah raised a hand. At that moment Zoanna raised her own hand. There was a loud snapping sound, the smell of ozone, and all three of Helbah's crystals vibrated.

"I can keep this up, bag," Zoanna said. "I can keep this up until they crack."

Helbah reluctantly directed a thought, and all three crystals abruptly turned opaque.

She looked at her familiar, who was now glancing all around, as if fearful that the queen were hiding right in this room.

"Yes, Katbah, she's going to be trouble," Helbah said. "Far more than ever before, I fear."

Katbah spat, angrily and knowingly. Meanwhile, Helbah felt drained.

"Yes, I greatly fear, Katbah, that it is going to be a long, wearying fight. Who could have guessed that that evil queen would return, worse than before?"

The question was rhetorical, but the situation was grim. Helbah wished she wasn't quite so old and tired.

Rowforth looked from the now-opaque crystal to his consort's face. He didn't like what he had just heard. This witch sounded like trouble. "Can you keep her from stopping us?"

Zoanna came as near to smiling as she ever did. The expression she normally used was an artifice that affected only her lips, unlike her tepid analogue in the other frame who smiled with her whole face, on those few occasions she had reason to smile at all. This was one of the things he really liked about Zoanna. "Stop us? You must be mad, lover mine. She'll never stop us. Nothing can."

He wanted to believe her. Then, as he looked into her eyes, he very nearly did.

Torture, torment, pain. With her help, all would be inflicted on their enemies, and especially those treasonous ones who had defeated him in his own frame. That Kelvin, how he would enjoy strapping him up in each newly created torture device! But would the iron maiden, the strappado, and the rack be enough? For that soft young man who yet had caused so much mischief he would devise some special pain.

He began dreaming of the child the roundear's wife was to bear. With Zoanna's help it might come out so hideous as to cause both parents unremitting anguish. Yes, that would be fitting—and fun!

"Zoanna, have you heard of a beast called a chimera?"

"Chimera?" she asked blankly.

"With three heads and a scorpiocrab tail."

She smiled. "Oh, you mean the chimaera! Of course, though it is almost extinct. What a lovely beasti!"

"Could the—could the child of Kelvin be made to resemble that?"

Her artificial smile slowly became genuine. "My dear, you are a genius! Why not?"

So confident, so certain. Surely he would have had to look through all the frames before finding so ideal a consort!

# CHAPTER 9

# Fool's Return

W hat's this armor you're wearing?" Kelvin asked his cellmate.

Stapular, as usual, managed to look as if he were sneering. In a tone just to the right of insulting he said, "What's it to you, Minor World dolt?"

Kelvin sighed. He tried so hard to be polite and Stapular always ruined it. He took another big handful of fruity mash from the trough and munched it, eying the redhead speculatively.

"That's right, go ahead and stuff! Put on some fat so you'll be just what old triple-head wants! You don't see *me* gulping that stuff! But you do what you want. Maybe it'll fry you. Sauté you with a little onlic. Yes, that should be good."

Kelvin shuddered. He had never liked onlic. The other man was obviously trying to nettle him; what made it worse was that he was succeeding. If the chimaera was going to eat him, he almost preferred that it eat him raw.

Still, he was hungry, and he wanted to keep up his health and strength, so as to be ready to escape if any opportunity presented itself. He finished chewing the mixed nuts, fruit, and grain mixture, reflecting that it wasn't bad, in fact it was delicious. He then lay down at the edge of the little stream and sucked up water. Good, crystal-clear spring water, the best. He had to admit that the monster had excellent taste in food and water.

At last he stood and faced Stapular deliberately. *Have to control the body language now,* he thought. *Don't want to appear hostile.*

"I asked, cellmate, about your armor."

"Why should I tell you?"

"I told you about the Mouvar weapon."

"I didn't ask you to. Does that mean I'm obligated?"

"You want to get out. You want to save yourself. Surely you don't want to be eaten."

Stapular hesitated. He was doubtless trying to think of a reason to refuse Kelvin's reasonable request. Even the most unreasonable people liked to appear reasonable, oddly.

Kelvin reached out and touched the transparent plating. It covered all of the hunter except the head and the hands. Just like the armor worn by his Knights of the Roundear and the royalists fighting for the queen. Only this armor was not metal. His father had labeled it "Some sort of glass or plastic." It looked very light, but felt hard.

"The chimaera lets you keep this on. Surely it will take it off you before it dines on you."

"That it will, pale hair. How'd you guess?"

"Seems sensible. I don't think Grumpus could dent this."

"It won't have to. The armor's stout but that's not its value."

"Then—"

"It insulates against the electric bursts. The bolts can climb all over it but not get inside. Particularly when—" He touched something inside his collar with a nudge of his chin. Instantly a transparent hood that covered his entire head sprang up from in back and snapped securely down in front. Similar hoods in the shape of gloves snapped over his hands, and others protected his feet. Stapular was now fully encased.

Kelvin was amazed. "You mean the chimaera couldn't have hurt you at all if you'd done that?"

"Where's your brain? Of course it could. It just couldn't have electrocuted me."

"But—"

"The sting could have pried me right out. Likely Mervania will get me out with lye."

Kelvin shivered. Lye! But he had known that was in the monster's plans, and indeed that had figured largely in his return. Still, it angered him to think that Stapular had remained back in the cell and not attacked the creature's elevated sting from behind, when Kelvin was distracting it. That jointed abdomen must have a weak spot, and if the lightning couldn't strike him . . .

"You think I should have jumped on the tail, right?"

Kelvin nodded, and refrained from saying something nasty like "How'd you ever guess, idiot?"

"Dumb, Minor World imbecile! It would have whacked me against the roof! Maybe flung me over its heads and against you!"

Surely a fate worse than death! But Kelvin refrained from making that sarcastic comment too. "I could have dodged, or even caught you and helped you get your feet."

The man merely glowered at him.

Kelvin tried again. "I once saw a dragon attacked in almost that manner. Of course the heroic knight paid for his bravery with his life, but at least he'd made the gesture, and perhaps saved the lives of his companions."

"You think I should have, don't you?"

*Idiot!* "You were wearing the armor," Kelvin pointed out. "You might have survived. It might have given me a chance to—"

"To what? Attack with your sword and magic gauntlets?" The tone made this seem ludicrous.

"Better than nothing." He didn't like the disparagement and contempt at all, but realized that this was just Stapular's way. Did the man have any love-life? That thought almost made Kelvin laugh.

"You think so, do you? You know how quickly one of the bolts would have shriveled you? If the chimaera hadn't been playing with you, you'd have been charred."

Undoubtedly true! But Kelvin pressed on. "I will be charred later anyway, according to you. Why not in a fight?"

"Because there would *be* no fight! The chimaera controls great quantities of electricity it makes in its body. You'd be no threat at all."

Kelvin tried to consider that, mindful that Stapular was repeating his prior argument. Yet the redhead was after all from a world he called Major.

"Nothing to be done, then?" He remained perplexed by the man's seeming reluctance even to oppose his fate.

"No."

"But you were going to attack it. You and your companions. How?"

"With lasers, of course. Some of us would have been destroyed, but we'd have lopped off the heads and tail."

"That tail means something to you, doesn't it?"

"Yes, profit."

Kelvin wondered about that. Could copper be so valuable where Stapular came from? It didn't seem possible.

"You're confused, aren't you, dolt? Huh, let me tell you those stings are no minor matter. Conductors of electricity while they're growing and attached, and afterward—"

"Yes?" Stapular had shut up, as if catching himself revealing too much. What could be so secret that it couldn't be told even to a companion in death?

"Other," Stapular said. "On Minor Worlds, at least."

Conductors of other on Minor Worlds? Minor Worlds were magic-using worlds. That suggested that the stings were conductors of magic! The revelation made his knees sag.

"What's the matter with you?"

"There's a fence made of those old stings outside. You saw the lightning leap."

"So? A fortune, but not for us. For the next hunters perhaps."

"Magic, Stapular. Magic."

"What are you getting at, Minor brain?"

"Conductors of magic. Magic to fight the chimaera with."

"You're crazy!"

"So you have remarked. I have my levitation belt and my gauntlets now, and I come from a world where magic exists. If I can get outside again, get one of the spikes uprooted, hold it with the gauntlets and channel magic through it—"

"You've got magic?" Stapular seemed less skeptical.

"Y—" Kelvin had never been so tempted to lie before. But deep-grained habits were hard to break. He converted what he had been about to say to the exact truth. "—es. My gauntlets are magic. They often know what to do when I don't."

"Seriously?"

"Yes." But a pang of conscience forced him to add, "Swords, shields, crossbows—they even used a laser."

"But do they know how to *use* magic?"

"M-maybe. Perhaps."

"And perhaps not?"

Kelvin shrugged. "Any chance, it seems to me, is better than none."

"Right, Minor brain. Right. So what are your plans?"

"To get a sting. To confront the chimaera with it."

"While I distract it, I suppose?"

"You'll have to."

"And if it knows your thought? I can keep it out of my head. Can you?"

"I'll have to."

"Easily said. But when it's around, your mind is open to it. You know you can't conceal your plan. Whatever plan."

"Then that is why we must do it now," Kelvin said. In that moment he realized that the only plan he had was for him to get the sting while Stapular interfered with the chimaera. That would be difficult, even if Stapular was effective.

"You could grab hold of the chimaera's sting. Hold on to it. Keep it from directing its bolts."

"I could put my entire weight on it and I don't think I could hold it."

"But you will try?"

"I will try," Stapular said.

Kelvin dared hope. He had finally gotten the man to cooperate. That meant they had a chance, maybe, however small.

Kian looked at his father in astonishment. "What will we do, Father? We can't leave him!"

"No. Of course not. But it's a long way back. We were carried before, remember?"

Kian nodded, looking at the transporter and thinking secret thoughts. Darkly secret thoughts.

Kelvin was his brother. Half brother, anyway. He should not, would not abandon him, especially since Kelvin had followed them to the serpent world. Kelvin had saved them all, several times. He had first saved their homeland of Rud from Kian's own mother. Following the Rud revolution which Kelvin had led, Kian had gone through the transporter searching for his missing father and mother. In the frame-world that was so similar and yet so different from his own, Kian had found his missing father, and the girl he now wanted so desperately to return to. Kelvin had arrived late, defeated the royalists, and gotten Kian and John Knight out of King Rowforth's dungeon. Now Kian had a chance to repay all that.

But damn it all, damn it, Kelvin had been stupid! Going back to that monster-lair to save that—that poacher! No one with any sense would have done that! No one but an idiotic hero!

"Maybe," John said, "we can get help from the squarears. They do want us out of this frame."

"If they'll let a hunter be destroyed, they'll let a fool be destroyed." Immediately he regretted the application. Kelvin *was* at times a fool, but he was also his brother.

"I'm afraid I agree with you," John said. "But if we just start back through the swamp, we'll be caught by the froogears. Then it will be the same as before."

"Will it, Father?" Kian wished there were some other way.

"It will have to be."

Kian scuffed at the floor of the chamber with his toe. "Father, do you think they'd rescue us all over again?"

"I don't think we can count on it."

"Neither do I. Why should they have patience with fools?"

"Why indeed!" John exclaimed with an ironic laugh.

"If only Kelvin had left us with something. He took the levitation belt and the Mouvar weapon. What have we got to fight with?"

"One pair of magic gauntlets and our swords. Plus our wits," John said.

"Lot of good they'll do."

"I'm not so certain. That fruit the froogears rolled in here—do you suppose that grows nearby?"

"Suppose it does? It'd knock us out if we breathed the scent from it."

"Yet the froogears handled it."

"Maybe they're immune. Maybe it just doesn't affect them, Father."

"Hmmm. Possibly. I'm not saying we could use it, just thinking of possibilities."

"The gauntlets, do you suppose they can lead us through the swamp to the island?"

"Possibly. Just barely possibly. They have a wonderful sense of direction, you remember."

"But only the one pair."

"I'll tell you what." John Knight stripped off the right gauntlet and handed it to him. "I'll wear the left and you the right. That way we'll both be protected to some extent."

"Thank you, Father." Kian put on the gauntlet. Though his father's hand was larger than his, the soft dragonskin contracted and made a perfect fit. Had his hand been larger, it would have stretched, magically.

John shrugged. "Why should I let my son be in avoidable danger?"

That was rhetorical, but it made Kian feel warm. He knew that Kelvin was the hero, the son borne of the woman John truly loved, and sometimes he doubted John's feelings for the son of the evil queen. Kian flexed and unflexed his right hand with the gauntlet. He drew his sword, made some experimental slashes at the air, and returned it smoothly to his scabbard. How, he wondered, would his right-handed father handle *his* sword?

John Knight was already adjusting his scabbard on his right side. He drew the sword left-handed, swished it expertly, twirled it, and resheathed it. The glove made *any* hand dextrous!

Kian nodded appreciatively. "That's better than I believe Kelvin could do."

"I'm not so certain. He fought most of the war in Rud with just the left gauntlet. Remember?"

Kian remembered. Lying on the ground in the swirling dust kicked up by the war-horses. His right gauntleted hand locked with Kelvin's left. The two gauntlets wrestling for their wearers, moving their fingers and wrists, pulling their arms and bodies along. It had been a draw. It had been the first indication he had had of the full extent of the power of the gauntlets.

"I'm ready, Father."

"Yes, I thought you would be."

With that they turned their backs on the chamber, and its transporter and all of Kian's waiting dreams. Together they left the cave and walked step by step, never faltering, to the greenish swamp and its incalculable dangers.

There were many, many steps, and many, many wearying days ahead.

*    *    *

Bloorg, the squarear chieftain, scratched his straw-colored hair on his blocky pate and indicated to Grool, his second in command, the crystal. In the crystal were two tired, hungry, insect-bitten roundears, slogging their way through hip-deep greenish water. The roundear known as John Knight suddenly grabbed a serpent in its left hand and flung it far. Kian, the younger roundear, congratulated him.

"Should we let the chimaera have them?" Grool asked. "They are innocent, and intended no harm."

Bloorg shrugged. "Innocent is as innocent does. They are also stupid."

"Stupid. Yes, by our standards. Still—"

"Still they have chosen. They could have gone their way."

"But the other one chose first. If he had not gone back—"

"Yes, as the hunter says, he was very stupid."

"But can we just leave them? Let our cousins the froogears take them again for tribute?"

"It is our ethics not to destroy or allow to be destroyed the purely innocent. Yet once made wise—"

"No longer innocent!" Grool sighed, fluttering her triangular eyelashes above her blue and squarish eyes. "It is an old, old truth, as old as our civilization. They should have learned."

"But it bothers you?"

"Yes, I don't think they intend other than a rescue."

"Unaided? Hardly that."

"Then they are doomed."

"Assuredly. As certainly as the other and the hunter in the chimaera's larder."

"A shame."

"Isn't it."

Bloorg made a magical gesture with entwined fingers and the crystal flickered and went blank.

The chimaera was digging in Mervania's garden. It had a nice assortment of herbs growing for use as condiments. Onlics tossed their purple heads in the breeze blowing over the island, their bulbs waiting below ground.

"I don't know why you bother with this!" Mertin grumbled. What he really meant was that he was not all that enamored with the flavor of onlics, chilards, and musills.

Grumpus' head suddenly snapped upward, and its mouth opened. At the same time the chimaera sting elevated. A bolt of blue sparked from the tip and into the sky above. Sizzling, smoking, still on fire, a foolish swampbird fell into Grumpus' waiting maw. Grumpus crunched, chewed, and swallowed. The chimaera's abdomen unbent and its sting lowered.

"Now, Mertie, you know you like the stew I make," Mervania chided her headmate. "None of us refuses it. Even Grumpus likes it."

"Ain't fittin'," Mertin said. "We, a superior species, eating like our foodstuffs!"

"Nonsense." She patted the dirt lovingly over the bones she had brought from the pantry. Good fungus would grow up out of those eyesockets. It always seemed appropriate that they be buried here. "You know you're just saying that. Fitting and not-fitting has nothing to do with it."

"Groowth," Grumpus agreed, licking singed feathers from his mouth.

"Our kind always used to eat 'em raw, Grumpus. But Mervania had to take up with baking and frying and stewing and pickling."

"Oh, I'm so glad you reminded me!" she exclaimed. "I need some dilber seed. I've decided on pickling that young hero. His arms and legs are so nice and slim."

"Bah!" said Mertin. "Me and Grumpus would just as soon—"

"Yes, yes, I know," she said impatiently. "You've made your point dozens of times."

"Well, it's still true. We would rather eat them au naturel."

"Speaking of the heroic roundear, I wonder what he and his lardermate are up to." Having decided, instantly she reached out with her thoughts. The thoughts she encountered surprised and excited her. "Oh my! Oh, my!"

"What is it?" Mertin asked. "Sneakiness?"

"I'm afraid so. They actually conspire to fight. At least the roundear thinks they do. The pearear's thoughts are impervious, as a pearear's always are."

"Shame to disappoint them," Mertin said.

"Oh, we won't, we won't, Mertin."

"Roast it, Mervania, must you always play with our food!"

"Yes, Mertie. After I do, its taste is delectable!"

---

# CHAPTER 10

# *Sticky, Sticky*

$T$his war was getting to be what St. Helens had once called a bummer, and it hadn't even started. He was just now leaving the border between Hermandy and Kance. Behind him was a file of Hermandy troops. Ahead were forests and lakes and streams almost to the twin capitals. Why didn't he feel great, being a general?

Because this was not a war he liked. Hermandy reminded him too vividly of a country and dictator that had made history on Earth. King Rowforth, if that thing in the palace of Kelvinia were truly he, had really put him in a bind.

"Gee, this is exciting!" Phillip said. Practically in the important general's ear.

"Excitement doesn't start until the arrows fly," remarked young Lomax. "That's what they told me, at least."

"You're right, Charles, only this time it'll be terror. The first time in battle always is. And the tenth time, only you learn not to show it."

St. Helens thought he'd put it right, but the boy was frowning, first at the young man, and then at St. Helens. "Oh, I know it's not a chess game, St. Helens. Real blood will get shed. But gee, just to be leading an army at last!"

"You're not leading it, I am."

"Yes, you're the witch this time."

"Don't say that!" *Brat!* he thought. "I've seen all the

witches I ever want to see. Your Melbah was enough witch to last me for a greatly extended lifetime!"

For a moment there was silence from the boy. *Good!*

Then he popped up again. "St. Helens, you do know that we'll be fighting against a witch?"

"WHAT?" He was momentarily dumbfounded. The dictator had spoken of troops and of two brat rulers, but not a witch. He might have known. And here he was without gauntlets or levitation belt!

"Helbah. A Melbah look-alike."

St. Helens allowed himself a groan. "I suppose she creates floods and fires and earthquakes. Probably throws fireballs as well."

"I haven't heard that she does. But she might. It's what witches do. Melbah didn't like her."

"That's something," St. Helens conceded. Any witch that Melbah hadn't liked couldn't be all bad. Or could she? Maybe one more powerful than Melbah? Melbah, after all, hadn't invaded this other witch's territory.

"I've heard she stops troops cold," Lomax spoke up. "Confuses them with illusions. What's called benign magic."

"Why haven't I heard about it? I'm supposed to be leading this outfit! Even it Bitner didn't tell me, you'd have thought I'd have heard!"

"You never asked," Phillip explained. "And you wouldn't have talked to Melbah even when she was in her guise as General Ashcroft."

St. Helens bit his lip. "This one a general, too?"

"She might be. Melbah never talked about her enemy, and as you know I had few friends."

"I can believe anyone cared for by a witch and manipulated the way you were had few friends," Lomax said. It was a camaraderie he had developed. "St. Helens was your friend, wasn't he?"

"Yes. He was my first real friend."

St. Helens felt uncomfortable. The boy had had playmates, he knew, and as he had grown tired of them the witch had disposed of them like outworn toys. Was the lad still subject to such tantrums? He doubted it, and yet Phillip remained a puzzle. He'd better hope that he didn't attach himself to Melbah's rival.

"I was wondering about those brats," Phillip mused. "Hermandy's king mentioned them and I've heard them mentioned before. Young, aren't they?"

"They are," Lomax said. "Rumor is that the witch keeps them that way."

So she was more powerful! Great! Just what the commanding general needed to hear!

Glumly, General Sean "St. Helens" Reilly resumed his tight lips. He rode on with all the silence he could muster, importantly leading a dictator's brutally trained and brutal troops plus the best mercenary soldiers money could buy.

This was certainly getting to be tiring, General Morton Crumb thought. They were now outdistancing trees and horse droppings, but moving far slower than was natural. Every horse-stride forward carried them only half a stride's distance. It was like moving underwater. Yet the trees and the hills and the silent farm buildings moved slowly, slowly by as they rode the deserted road. They were after all making progress.

"Her magic may be weakening," Captain Abileey said. "Witches too get tired."

"I've heard that," Mor said. Unhappily he was recalling the unequal battle in Deadman's Pass in what was formerly Aratex. That old witch hadn't gotten tired until she'd raised flood, wind, earthquake, and fire. Could this one tire from doing far less?

Captain Plink drew abreast of them. Turning his head, watching the captain's horse, Mor had the impression that the swiftly moving hooves were, though a blur of motion, moving slowly. Something about time-slowing, a trick that was said to be in some witches' repertoire.

"I think we'll get there in a month, General," Captain Plink observed. "We're slow but not stopped."

"Right." Nor would a complete stoppage have bothered him more. If the witch was just playing with them, what would she do when she got mad?

"General Crumb, sir, this may be a little out of place, but

why don't we stop and forage the farms? At the rate we're going we will be out of rations long before we're done."

Mor sighed. True enough. This was after all an invasion. It wasn't stealing, though that was what it felt like.

He called a halt. Watching the horses' legs he saw them drift down to the ground. All were halted in what seemed a normal amount of time, though just how much time he was taking to think he could not actually say. His stomach growled as he gave orders to pillage the closer farms.

"Six men to a farm. Eggs, milk, a chicuck or two. Take nothing but food, no more than necessary, and no liberties with the women. Be quick!"

The soldiers ran off at top speed, drifting on their mounts, as Mor saw it. He shook his head, knowing that even this was taking longer than normal. A roasted chicuck would put a smile in his belly. There had to be something that would help him feel decent. An end to the war might, though he would have had to have been a mercenary to feel that it was right.

How had he gotten into this in the first place? It must have been magic tampering at the Kelvinia audience. Something in the wine that made him receptive to orders he couldn't justify, and made him even a bit eager to fight. King Rufurt using magic? But it was not Rufurt, he felt certain. Rufurt, the rightful king, must have been slain or had something else happen to him. He had known, he did know, but he felt helpless.

"General! General Crumb, sir."

"Yes?" Mor didn't stand on ceremonies with enlisted men.

"We can't get near the buildings, sir. The air holds us back. Neither we nor our horses can enter the driveways."

"Magic again," Abileey observed. "If we run out of rations before she runs out of magic, we'll have to return home."

"I'm certain that's what she's counting on," Mor said. Since he really wanted to return he should have felt elated.

Why did he feel certain that this time the witch's tactics were not sufficient to stop them?

*     *     *

The charging cavalry had long vanished. Lester, searching in vain for some evidence that an enemy had really been there, was forced to consider implications. Arrows, crossbow bolts, and spears were lying spent, beyond an area where there never had been an enemy force.

He gave orders that the various projectiles be recovered. His men fetched them. Thus went the day that could hardly be termed a fighting day.

That night Captain Barnes walked over to him at the camp fire. He saluted smartly as a Throod-trained mercenary naturally would. Les had to think what he was supposed to do, and finally remembered and returned the salute.

"At ease, Captain. What's on your mind?"

"Magic, sir."

"Mine too."

"If every time we encounter the enemy, the enemy turns out to be unreal—"

"We'll end up with no weapons other than swords."

"Yes, sir. But suppose we encounter the enemy and the enemy *is* real? Suppose they have real arrows and crossbow bolts and spears; suppose ours have been lost to the phantoms? I mean, if real ones come right after the phantoms, and we don't know the difference?"

"Good point, Captain. Pass the order, no one to fire as much as one arrow until we determine that our attackers are real."

"Yes, sir. Immediately, sir."

Later that night Lester was trying to sleep and was thinking that one of the mercenaries really should be in charge. The long, mournful howls of wolotes came from all around, chilling human blood with their canine songs. He drew his sword and stepped from his tent, intent on nothing. Outside he blinked in the firelight and breathed a deep breath of cool night air. The wolotes must be in the woods just past the fire.

Suddenly there was a great, gray shadow, with glowing red eyes, leaping at his throat!

He raised the sword and struck, all in one motion.

The animal was gone. In its place, completely in uniform, was a large Kance soldier. Before Lester could recover, the enemy had a sword to his throat and a shield protecting his vitals from a dying commander's retaliation.

Les thought of Jon. His eyes saw starlight and drops of oil on the sword blade. The enemy had only to shove the sword. Les' blood would gush out over the blade and arm and against the armor of the man. His breath would go WHOOSH, and he would fall and everything would turn black.

The soldier smiled, wickedly. A light of triumph sprang up in his eyes, and then—

As suddenly as he had come, he vanished.

Les stood alone in his tent opening. He swallowed, and swallowed again.

This sort of thing could get quite discouraging to an invading army. In the past it must have worked effectively many times.

Why was it, Les wondered, as his knees weakened under him, that this time it wasn't going to?

Zoanna watched as Rowforth, looking so much like the king she had married, rowed the boat with strong pulls of the oars. The eerily luminous lichen on the walls gave a feeling of late in the day. Yet it was early, just before sunup.

She smiled her coldest smile as the swirl of water marked the installation. Such a little thing, so easily missed. No roundear had ever discovered it, and none would if she and others like her had their way. Rowforth was enormously privileged.

Moving carefully so as not to rock the boat, she stripped her soft, velvet robe from her creamy shoulders, and fluffed back her beautiful red-as-dragon-sheen hair. She felt Rowforth studying her naked body, appreciating her soft, round breasts with their firm, rosy nipples. His eyes were traveling down her flat stomach, lingering, enjoying in his lecherously honed way. She was no longer young, but discipline and magic had preserved much of her physical youth, and this was always useful when it came to handling men.

"Now," she said, and slipped over the side. She swam skillfully, like a slick-skinned ottrat, diving deeper, deeper. Carefully she expelled her breath. Above, she knew, her consort would be waiting, leaning on his oars, anticipating the moment when she would again break the surface.

Her eyes saw a fish or two, and then the airlock. Grabbing its edge she pulled up her legs, ducked her head, and somersaulted over and inside.

She gulped air. The interior always had air because of the membrane material that removed it from the water. Here one could breathe and rest and hide a century if need be. Here one could take a transporter and go to a world where magic and witchcraft reigned supreme.

She had been here first as a child, and then later as a young woman. Then there had been a long time when she had not been to this place, or used the transporter. During her last trip, after the defeat of her father's weak magic and her tame guardsmen at the hand of Kelvin's Knights, she had done it right. She had gone back to school and learned what she should have learned as a child. Because of what she had learned, she now had power, more than her pathetic old father and his bloodthirsty dwarf ever dreamed. And what had been the price of this knowledge? Only what she had in infinite store.

She lowered herself onto the waiting platform, rested a moment, smiled contentedly to herself, and then entered the room. The transporter awaited her, and it would be but an easy step, and she would be back at her school. The horned and horny teacher would get her her supplies. How surprised Devale was going to be! Even while they embraced, he had not realized the extent of her ambitions.

She was prepared to offer him a thousand children from defeated kingdoms. In return she was certain he would give her what she needed to defeat Helbah, and the chimaera powder as well. She twisted her mouth as she thought of it: the Roundear of Prophecy's deformed and monstrous child.

She checked the controls on the transporter and then stepped into it. Space-time flashed through her being. Then she was being lifted up in a man's strong arms.

"Professor Devale! Damn your shiny horns, you sensed me!"

Professor Devale did something quite improper for a decent man, that was quite customary for him. "Zoanna," he said, squeezing her close and intensifying his actions. "Of course!"

Heln woke with a startled cry.

"What was it, Heln?" Jon asked. In the days that they had been here, she had become used to Heln's nightmares.

"The monster!" Terror made her voice shrill. "A terrible thing! Three heads! Two of the heads were human, and the other was a dragon!"

Jon took her hand. "That's pretty wild, Heln. I've never heard of such a monster. This one must have been imagination."

"No, Jon, it wasn't!" Heln shook from head to toe under the bedclothes. "Kelvin was with it, and, and—Jon, I think it was going to *eat* him!"

"The dragon head?" Jon was curious, despite the dream's evident horror for Heln.

"No, all of them! It was all one beast!"

"Impossible."

"But it was! And, and that female human head! It had copper tresses, and eyes just the color of copper. It wore a copper tiara and had copper rings in her ears."

"Pretty detailed," Jon said. "I never dream like that."

"Neither do I! That's why I know it wasn't just a dream! It's like the time they were in that frame with the serpents."

"Yes, you did dream accurately then."

"Jon, I'm afraid for Kelvin! I'm afraid for his life!"

"He has to come back," Jon said. "He has a prophecy to fulfill."

"Yes! He must return!" Not really reassured, Heln lay back and closed her eyes.

Kildom pulled Kildee's nose, arousing him from sleep. "You big dunderhead!" Keldee protested.

"Don't hit me, stupid! We need to talk."

"What about, dumbbutt?"

"Helbah. I think she's really worried."

"So?"

"So we should help. Be kings like we're supposed to be."

"Lead an army?"

"Why not? We've lived twenty-four years each. We're as smart as any twenty-four-year-olds."

Kildee scratched his thin red hair and climbed from the bed. He stood in front of the mirror, looking at himself and his brother, both apparent six-year-olds.

"Well, I admit we don't exactly look our age," Kildom said.

"So?" The reflection didn't change.

"Let's ask her to make us big."

"If she could, she'd have done it long ago."

"You think?"

"Yeh. Uh, I don't know."

"Come on, then."

Kildee followed as his brother led him to the witch's private quarters, where they were strictly forbidden ever to go. Naturally they went there all the time, kings being kings and boys boys, and them more than both.

Helbah, her back to them, was talking to her familiar. "Katbah, I don't know if I can. I just don't! If her powers are now greater than mine, and I can't stop her . . ."

Kildom let the door swing back into place. Finger to his cherubic lips he pulled Kildee away from her possible hearing.

"See? It's just like I said. We're going to have to do something!"

"But what?" Kildee was now genuinely and maturely concerned, as indeed he should have been.

Kildom screwed up his face. He pondered the matter, trying hard. "I'm sorry," he said finally. "You and I are just going to have to watch for our chance."

# CHAPTER 11

## *The Berries*

$K$ian and his father were lost. Kian had to admit it to himself the second day when they awoke in their tree-perch beds and saw nothing but swamp below them all around.

"Father," he said, grasping a crawling spider the size of a small bird with his right-gauntleted hand and crushing it, "I do believe it's time."

"I hate to have you do that, Son. It never seems to me to be safe."

"I've done it before, Father. Besides, if we want to save Kelvin—"

"Yes. All right." John climbed down from the tree next to his and stood in ankle-deep slime. "You'd better position yourself there in the bough, because it's too wet here."

"Right, Father." Stoically, but not without apprehension, Kian took the dragonberry from its associates in the armpouch and gulped it down. He could have used a sip of water, he thought, grimacing at the taste. Unfortunately, fresh, safe water was scarce in the swamp, and the hollow gourd they had filled was rapidly emptying.

As usual, he imagined that there would be no effect, that this time it would not work. This business of astral separation was difficult to believe anyway. Then he noticed that his father was noticeably lower than he had been, and that in the next tree there was a body. The body, he realized with his usual surprise, was his own.

The berries had performed as usual, separating his awareness from his body so gently that it seemed it wasn't happening, until it was done. They would kill pointears, but Heln had discovered that roundears suffered only partial death. This had turned out to be an extremely useful thing.

But he had business. There was nothing to do but find their route. To think of Kelvin, and be drawn to him like a needle to a magnetstone. Of course he'd far rather think of Lonny, but Lonny was in another frame and reaching her right now posed difficulties.

He discovered he was going toward the transporter. His thought of Lonny had started him that way! That was the danger in letting one's thoughts wander, when one's mind was in a condition most resembling thought.

He formed a mental picture of his brother's face. Instantly he was going back the other way, over the swamp. The greenery below blurred. Now and then a bird winged past or through his astral form. There was a special exhilaration to this kind of travel; there was no freedom like astral freedom!

Then, abruptly, the blurring stopped. He was over the island. He saw the ancient castle where they had been confined, and the chimaera itself was there, doing something in what seemed to be a garden. Willing himself to join Kelvin, he drifted cautiously down the path that was bordered by the pointed posts. Those posts had green patinas, intriguingly. He floated straight through the barred wooden door.

Kelvin and Stapular were there, both alive and—miracle of miracles—talking to each other. They were hunched side by side at the trough, whispering. Should he eavesdrop, or get out? One berry would not last long, and he needed to return slowly enough to memorize the way.

Another thing: he didn't want to risk getting trapped. He had been snared by a flopear once while in astral form. He had been lucky to survive, and he had vowed never to risk that happening again. The chimaera might be sensitive to the astral form as were dragons and flopears. The fact that the monster had one dragon head meant he could be at risk, for dragons were the original users of dragonberries.

"There's this mental block," Stapular was whispering. "Huh, I can do it but you can't. With my help you can."

Kelvin nodded. "It's what my father would call hypnotism."

"Right. Posthypnotic. You forget until it's time. I don't even show a thought."

"I don't know, Stapular. If I trust you—"

"You have to, if you want to make your play."

"All right. All right." Kelvin seemed determined. "You hypnotize. You make the block."

"Huh. I'll hold up a finger and you focus both eyes on its tip. I'll move the finger back and forth in front of your eyes. All you do is keep your eyes on the fingertip."

"You're certain it will work?"

"It will unless you're an idiot! Now, stupid—"

*So they were planning something!* Kian thought. Hard on the heels of that surprise came another: a startled thought that was not his.

*Another! Another! There shouldn't be! Mertin! Grumpus! HELP!*

Kian wasn't staying around to find out. Instantly he visualized himself going to his father. He envisioned his father's face as he had Kelvin's.

Blurring greenery. He didn't try to slow it. He had to get back, back to his physical body before he was trapped. Once he was in his body he didn't think he'd ever leave it again! He was so panicky that he noticed no details until he saw the froogear staring into his face.

Mervania was shaken. Physically she was standing there in her garden, sting upraised in fright. Never, ever had she thought to—ever!

"What is it, Mervania?" her companion head asked. "You catch a thought you didn't like?"

"Another. Another," Mervania said, awed.

"You said that. Also 'HELP!' Help with what? You losing your wits? Don't do that. I don't want to have to talk with just Grumpus."

"Shut up!" she exclaimed irritably. "I'd thought it legendary. Mythical. But it isn't. It's *real!* What a discovery!"

"What are you blathering about?"

"Grwoom," Grumpus said in turn.

"Shut up, both of you! Can't you see how distracted I am? There was a disembodied human in there!"

"Disembodied food? Doesn't sound appetizing."

She turned on her masculine side and snarled. "Soul-stuff, imbecile! ASTRAL!"

"Ghostly, huh? I thought only humans believed in that."

"It's true. Dragonberries."

"Dragonberries?"

"I should have known! But I thought it was just a myth. Anything that fantastic isn't logical."

"What's logical?"

"Shut up. They take the berries, and then they separate, astral from corporeal. They just move around and they hear and see everything. I should have known when I learned that the young hero was from a world with dragons. That's where dragonberries are supposed to be!"

"How come I don't remember that story?" Mertin demanded.

"Because you're obtuse!"

"Grooomth!"

"That goes double for you, big teeth! Both of you put together haven't the brains of a pickled human!"

"Now see here, Mervania, I resent—"

"Oh shut up! I'm too thrilled to argue with you." Her head darted forward, and she kissed him quickly on the mouth. That startled him into silence. "Listen. With those berries we wouldn't be confined. We could swallow them and go anywhere we wanted. To—"

"Gwroowl!"

"Oh very well!" she said impatiently, and kissed Grumpus too, on the nose.

"Food?" Mertin asked.

"No, not food! We wouldn't eat in that form. But we could see and hear everything!"

"Why would we want to do that?"

"Entertainment, moron! Discovery! Adventure! We could visit distant lands, other worlds, other frames. Astrally we could go and see and hear anything there is!"

"Who cares?"

"I do! And you would too, if you had half the brain of a froogear! I want dragonberries! Listen, Mertin, we might find more of our kind the squarears don't know about! We could visit them astrally, and maybe even—"

"Go to them and mate?"

"Maybe. If the squarears cooperate."

"Would they?"

"I don't know. But think of it. We could be a whole colony. A whole world, perhaps."

"Sounds stupid to me. Why should there be more than two? Two's enough to mate. I could take care of that while you sleep."

"Several would be better. Because that's the way it is. The companionship. The communication."

"One more like you would talk me to death."

"Grwoompth!" Grumpus agreed.

But Mervania refused to be dampened. She wanted those dragonberries, no matter what the cost!

Squirtmuck stared into the roundear's face with puzzlement. He had thought this one dead, but now it was awake and looking back at him. Could it be something like the deep sleep in the mud? He could not be certain, and he did not think more about it now that the surprise was gone. But this roundear was reaching for something under its armpit. A weapon? Quickly he grabbed the ugly creature's pale, knobby wrist. The roundear resisted him and struck at him with its other hand. The gauntlet that had been on that hand had slipped off and dropped into the slime while the creature was unconscious.

Firmly, Squirtmuck placed a webbed hand against the creature's loathsome face and held it while he explored under the disgusting smelly arm. What he found was a bag with a drawstring. He pulled it loose, stood back, opened the sack, and peered inside.

The roundear cried out. "No! No! Father, it's got the—"

"Shut up!" the other roundear said. "You're not helping things."

The creature in the tree bole subsided. But his eyes were big and round as Squirtmuck smelled, prodded with a fingertip, and finally tasted one of the dried berries.

"That will kill you!" the roundear cried. "It's poison! To anyone but roundears. It's magic! Big magic!"

Squirtmuck spat out the bitten berry. His tongue burned and he stuck it out and scrubbed its forked tip with his well-slimed hand. He was not too sensitive to tastes, but this was revolting. He retched and spat. Then, to his great distress, he choked out a perfectly good leech. He took in several deep breaths of good swamp air before recapturing the leech with a quick grab and reswallowing it. Good food was not to be wasted!

The roundear for some peculiar reason was vomiting itself. Squirtmuck looked at the mess in the water but saw nothing wriggling. Roundears probably had peculiar tastes like other eared races; it might be that they ate food not even alive. No wonder it made them sick! The roundear quit heaving and wiped its mouth. Any self-respecting froogear would have licked his own mouth, not used his hand.

"Father," the roundear said, "I think they've got us. Again."

"Tell me something I don't know, Son."

Squirtmuck ignored them. He furrowed his head hard, trying to decide what to do with the dried berries. He wouldn't eat them or give them to another froogear even if it was someone he disliked. Possibly they were magic, as the roundear said; in that case the squarears would be interested. He decided to put the berries with the rest of the loot, and not hide any of it except in the great tree hollow where such forbidden objects were placed. Yes, he'd do that, and the god or the squarears might reward him in this or some other life.

Clearing his throat he looked around at the members of his band busily examining the objects they had taken. One, a brother to one of his wives, had the belt and sword that had been on the big roundear. Another froogear had gathered up the two gauntlets and was sniffing them. Others had the younger roundear's sword and several knives.

"Come!" he said, motioning. Under his watchful eyes certain objects were placed in the bole of the collecting tree and others held out as tribute to the god.

That night, while the foragers feasted and splash-danced, Squirtmuck tried to feed and talk with the captives. He was unsuccessful in both attempts. For some reason the roundears tightened their mouths at the sight of fresh, squirming provender. When all reasonable questions were asked, they answered with foolishness about having great magic and powerful friends.

Long before daylight Squirtmuck considered burying

them deep in the mud and forgetting that they had ever been. Alas, the god had to be served, and the squarears placated.

In the morning they commenced the trek.

Bloorg left his dinner and activated the crystal with a thought. His thought was of the roundears in the swamp. He concentrated on the area between the transporter cavern and the chimaera's island, made a sweep, and found them.

The older man and the younger were both captives of froogears, again. Both on their way back to the chimaera, to be eaten.

He sighed. There was no help for it. They were just too troublesome to save twice.

He scanned back to the collecting tree. Yes, all their things were there, waiting. They would not need them now, but the objects would be re-collected. Sometimes he could wish to give such artifacts to the froogears, but that he knew could be dangerous.

There was no help for it. No help at all. Sighing with regret, he blanked out the crystal. Then, exerting great effort, he strove to erase all memory of the roundears' existence.

Grool asked what he was doing.

"I don't know," he said. "But I think I was successful at it."

Satisfied with himself, now, he sat back down at his table and resumed eating the fire-blackened swampfish and chilled lettuage salad he had interrupted.

The chimaera was really in a troubled state. Mervania kept remembering what she had glimpsed with her mind in the larder room. Mertin, maybe just to be mean, kept pooh-poohing the experience.

"We have to make them show us!" Mervania said. "Even if we don't eat them."

"GRRROOOMTH! WAHH!"

"Oh shut up! You'll get raw meat enough! But this is something we can't ignore! All our life I thought it couldn't be, and now I know it is. We just have to get those berries! Why, with those, Grumpus, we could go see dragons!"

"GWROOMTH?"

"Yes! That's what I've been telling you! And Mertin, try to

think at least as well as Grumpus! All the sights we can see. The chance of finding us a mate!"

That did strike some interest. Mertin had had time to ponder the pleasures of mating, and was working up some urge for them. "If we can get the berries."

"Yes. That's why we have to get these creatures to bring them. We can't get out, but they can if we let them."

"But they won't come back. With or without berries."

"True, but if we can offer them something in exchange, they might."

"What?"

"Our old copper stings. You know how they value those."

"But they're dangerous! Even to us!"

"But if we make a deal—?"

"We'd be risking all our heads. No thanks, Mervania. To toy with food is one thing; to deal with it another."

"GWROOMTH!" Grumpus agreed.

Mervania felt despair. She knew the lesser heads were right, yet she hated to give up. There were so many places she would like to see again and never could in a physical way. There was that beautiful flower world, for instance, where big-headed wizards with greenish skins grew strange crops. How she had relished the meatloaf plants and the maiden's-blood flowers! Grumpus had had his fill of juicy torso trees and gut vines, while Mertin had gone into ecstatic burps after his first feast of rumpkins and chucquash. Those had been great meals and great times, and the wizards had not begrudged them but let them revel. Why had they ever left? Some mischief on the part of the wizards, or just plain wanderlust? She could not recall.

"Mervania, what are you doing, daydreaming again?"

"I thought you said I talked too much," she said curtly.

"You do. You also daydream too much. But they're coming now. They're outside."

"What are you talking about?"

"Use your mind, Mervania. Your supposedly smart mind."

What was she doing, letting Mertin tell her things? She searched past the wall of their island. There she encountered thoughts.

*If I hadn't taken that berry, we wouldn't have gotten*

*caught! That was stupid of me! Stupid as Kelvin!*

Kian Knight, one of the escapees! And—

*I got the boy into this! I should have watched better! Now he'll never see his bride!*

Kian's father! John Knight.

Mervania started their body walking daintily for the big gate. The tribute had been fetched across the swamp and the escapees were back in their power. All was as it should be. Except—

She still wanted those berries. Oh, yes, indeed, she wanted them.

She did not bother with her head-over-the-wall trick. She knew who was there and how they'd be waiting. Such teasing only worked once, unfortunately.

Pushing open the gate she looked after the disappearing row of bubbles and then at the thoroughly bound and helpless Knights.

"Welcome home," she said. "This time it's really no surprise."

"W-what do you mean?" Kian gasped.

"Why, that you were here before, visiting. Did you think I would not know?"

"I deny that! Whoever was here, it wasn't me!"

Poor human foodstuff. So very slow to grasp.

# CHAPTER 12

# *Helbah*

"*H*ere they come!" Phillip was so excited he couldn't contain himself. He was pointing at the Kance cavalry charging down on them. They kept coming faster and faster in overwhelming numbers and still General Reilly, alias St. Helens, did not give the order. At their backs was the open

Kance plain and the Hermandy forest they had left.

"Those horse and riders could be phantoms. Illusions," Lomax said. His voice squeaked boyishly, causing Phillip to look surprised. A very few years older than Phillip, so he might have seemed to the former boy-king to be above fear.

"Back into the forest!" St. Helens ordered. "Take refuge behind trees. Don't fire a shot until you see that these are real!"

The men obeyed, as good soldiers should. St. Helens wasn't certain that these Hermans were good, but he knew they were disciplined. They waited behind the trees, arrows nocked, crossbows cocked, swords, shields, and spears ready should these soldiers turn out to be genuine.

The Kance cavalry halted just out of bowshot. A tall Kance general stood high in his stirrups and waved the Kance flag of blue and white. "Truce!" he called out loudly. "Talk between commanders!"

St. Helens relaxed. His caution in taking cover had been justified; this was a real force, not a phantom one. He was glad to have a truce. Better talk than battle, though battle was probably inevitable.

"Agreed!" he called back. "We meet midway." Then to his men he shouted, "Anyone who breaks the truce dies! Second in Command Lomax, you see that that order is carried out!"

"Yes, sir," Lomax squeaked. If necessary he would die for his general, and St. Helens knew it.

"Phillip—keep the faith."

"What faith is that, General St. Helens?"

Would the kid never learn? "Earth expression. Just do right. Be alert for any truce violation on the part of these regulars."

"Yes, sir, St. Helens. I'll do that." The boy seemed eager, and his old chess-playing self.

"Fine. Then—" St. Helens walked out to meet the Kance officer. The ground was a little wet from yesterday's rain and the smell of damp ground and grass would have been a treat to his nostrils if they had not come through the forest. How did the Kancian know if they'd emerge right here at this particular spot on the border? Reconnaissance, of course. Surveillance by an ancient craft that he'd come fully to believe in. To fight an army was one thing, but a witch? He put the thought out of his mind and walked resolutely ahead.

"General Reilly, Army of Hermandy," he said, approaching the other.

"General De Gaulic, Army of Kance," the other said. The man was big and ugly and had a large nose; the nose was his most impressive feature.

Now there was nothing to do but talk. The Kance general had called the truce, so he would speak first. St. Helens waited.

"General Reilly, also known as St. Helens, you serve a madman. Your people have no quarrel with mine and never have. You should go back."

*Direct. Also depressingly accurate.*

"I serve the interests of he known as the Roundear of Prophecy, Kelvin Knight Hackleberry. It is for the newly formed Republic of Kelvinia that I lead this invasion force."

De Gaulic's dark eyes speared him. "You lie, General Reilly. You serve she who the Roundear fought."

Damn, this man was sharp! "Zoanna?"

"None other."

*I might have known! That temptress wouldn't just have drowned! But why didn't Kian and Kelvin find her? Has she been in a different frame?*

"You are surprised, and yet not surprised, General Reilly."

"Yes, I—"

"Do you want to serve her? Her interests?"

"No. No, of course not. But—" He hesitated, unsure what he should say.

"You do not wish to serve her? You do not want to attack in her name?"

"Not in her name," St. Helens said. He felt more confused about this than he dared admit. "I'm a soldier and I serve a king."

"A false king."

*Damn! De Gaulic must know everything! The witch must have spied it out. Does he know, then, that we can't help ourselves?* "It is not the place of the servant to question the master."

De Gaulic smiled. "Yet you hesitate, General Reilly. Do you ask yourself why?"

St. Helens pulled himself together. It was most uncomfortable, standing here like this, having the truth rammed repeatedly into his unwilling mind. "I serve an ideal. A purpose. A good purpose. I have to invade.

"There will be dying. Much slaughter."

"I know. I'm sorry about that. Surrender to me now. Then when the roundear comes he'll make everything right."

"Will he?"

*I hope.* "He made things right for the people of Aratex."

"Will he with Kance? With Klingland?"

"Both. There shouldn't be fighting."

"And where is the Roundear of Prophecy now?"

"Otherwise occupied at the moment."

The general's expression showed that he knew that there was no certainty of Kelvin's ever returning, but he did not challenge the statement directly. "And yet there will be an evil man in control."

"The Roundear isn't evil!"

"Kelvin Knight isn't in control of Kelvinia. Another person is. He whom the Roundear once defeated in another place. That king and Zoanna, the queen you thought gone forever. Zoanna with more magic at her command than that possessed by her father."

St. Helens felt as if he had been punched. The big-nosed general had better information than he did, and was using it as he might a superior deployment of troops. De Gaulic had just informed him that the worst two people were in control. St. Helens had known it without daring to acknowledge it. Now the truth was undeniable, and pain was in his gut. "Damn!" he muttered.

"I see you will not turn back, General Reilly. You have made up your mind."

St. Helens wanted to say something different. He wanted to explain that he was just a tool, a pawn. The prophecy might compel his son-in-law, with a little help. Yes, it was like a chess game. Kelvin had the power, but others had to make the moves and the sacrifices. Others like St. Helens. He was locked into his slot, unable to escape it.

"I wish there were some other way." He started to turn away, knowing that he was on the wrong side, hating it, but stuck.

A feathered projectile whistled through the air and struck the Kancian general. It made an ugly whacking sound and spun him half around. He cried out, an aged woman's cry, and grasped the crossbow bolt stuck high in his chest.

His chest? No, for on the instant the general was an aged woman. *Melbah!* his mind told him, but he knew that though she had the features, it could not be that one. Melbah was dead.

So the general was the witch! Someone on St. Helens' side had disobeyed his order and the disobedience might mean a victory. Might.

Horses and soldiery raced across the plain. Bowstrings snapped. Shields caught projectiles and bounced them away. The Kance cavalry was charging his force of Hermans.

The woman wavered, then resumed the appearance of General De Gaulic in blood-spattered uniform. His voice was hers, aged and whispery. "Is this how you keep your word, Reilly? Is this the truce of an honorable man?"

"I had nothing to do with it! I swear!" But how could she believe that? He was the man in charge; he was responsible. His side had committed the treachery.

*But it was also smart. It was smart of someone back there to realize. Anything against a witch was justified. Take her out and they had a chance!*

A chance to win a campaign he might do better to lose. What a mess this was!

Rough hands grabbed him on either side. He did not try to resist, though for him that was difficult. He expected to be slain immediately, but instead his hands were bound and he was put on a horse. Two Kancian soldiers rode on either side of him. Two others rode with the general. The witch-general.

Looking back he heard cries of wounded and dying men and boys, and the screams of horses. Dying because he had led them here. How quickly it had dissolved into carnage! He hoped Phillip and young Lomax would survive. The Hermans hardly had his sympathy, but those two boys were enough like him to be his sons.

They arrived at the caps and the joint palace in what seemed like a remarkably short time. The witch was being helped by a soldier to stay on her horse. Then they were at the palace itself: half blue, half white, the color division running right through the big gate and the drive.

They dismounted, and as they did the general turned completely witch and collapsed. She did not move, lying across equally divided blue and white flagstones. She could be dead. St. Helens watched with the Kancians for any sign of life.

Two very young boys ran from the palace. One was dressed in blue, the other in white. Both had large lace collars. Both ran to the witch and dropped down by her, grasping her, holding her, crying.

*Poor kids!* St. Helens thought. *She was all they had.*

Suddenly the boy in blue was on his feet, pointing, face twisted and red. A golden crown on his head pronounced him ruler.

"Kill him!" the child shrieked. "Slay us that man!"

The childish finger pointed at St. Helens.

Charlain looked up from her cards. "She's pregnant," she said.

Hal froze in his tracks. "What?"

"Easter Brownberry. I think you had better marry her, Hal."

"But—"

"The cards told me. I know I haven't been what I should to you, Hal. It was only natural that you find someone else. We had better divorce, so you can marry her before her condition shows."

"But you—the farm here—"

Charlain nodded. "It is true. The farm won't run itself. But I can handle it for a time. Perhaps we can work something out. But first things first. We shall divorce, and you shall marry her. She's young, so really needs your support."

"You are a generous woman, Charlain," he said, amazed.

"You are a good man, Hal, and I haven't treated you fairly. I hope this makes it up for you."

Soon he was gone. Charlain knew she had done the right thing. But even so it had come as a shock. She had put on a businesslike front, but now that she was alone the pain overwhelmed her. She put her face down on her arms and wept.

Lomax drew back a bloody sword from the chest of a Kancian soldier. He hadn't time to question it now or to feel shock at what was happening. With blood on him and fighting going on every side, all he could do was act continually to save his own life.

He ducked around the tree, narrowly missing getting chopped. An arrow from a Herman took the new attacker in the throat and toppled him from his mount, the sword burying its point in the ground. He looked at the young Kance soldier's terror-filled eyes and he wanted to feel sorry for him and he wanted to be thankful that his own life had been spared.

A voice screamed pain. A young voice. Phillip's? He hoped not, but there was no chance to look. He battled another soldier and just when he should be feeling the blade in his innards the handsome young Kancian folded over as though made of rags. Not his doing; another's blade had darted in to take the Kancian's life.

"Lomax!"

"Phillip!" The former boy-king had blood on his face and clothing and on the sword he had just used on Lomax's attacker. The boy looked happy, as if he were having the time of his life.

"Lomax, we've got to retreat! We're outnumbered!"

Yes they were, obviously. What had happened, anyway? He hadn't seen who fired the crossbow. St. Helens had warned them, had trusted him. He was in charge, like it or not.

"We've got to get!" Phillip insisted. "Give the order, Lomax! Now!"

Lomax, lacking a signaling horn, shouted *"RETREAT!"* He charged through the brush, hoping others would take the hint. Around him he saw Hermans backing, retreating little by little into their home territory.

After a long, long time—probably several whole minutes, subjectively distorted by the pressure of the situation—he determined that the Kancians were not following. Around them was the supposed safety of Hermandy trees and bushes.

Through the bushes he could see the road down which they had marched. Defeated and driven back, but not all killed.

St. Helens had trusted him and left him in charge. He would have to find out who had fired the crossbow bolt at the Kancian general. If the man was still alive, he'd have him executed. After that, taste for it or not, he'd order the Hermans back into Kance by a roundabout way.

*St. Helens,* Lomax thought savagely, *you will be avenged!*

General Mor Crumb was eating a handful of bright yellow, exceedingly tart appleberries when Klinglanders descended on their camp. Phantoms, he thought. Wasn't the witch going to learn?

A Throod mercenary screamed and fell back, a short-shafted arrow protruding from his throat. Blood stained the ground and the arrow shaft.

*Damn! Real this time!*

Mor shouted orders, climbing upon his horse, drawing his sword. In a moment they were battling for their lives. A Klinglander raced for him on a big bay mare, spear leveled at his chest. It was like a dragon spear, Mor thought, positioning his shield to take the point. He braced himself for impact, knowing it would be the last thing he ever felt. The point was at the shield, ready to shatter it and take his life.

Then spear, spearsman, and charger vanished, leaving him alive and shaken.

Damn! Another phantom! Mixed right in with the real combatants! Thank the gods, this time.

"Watch out, General!"

He moved his head aside and caught a sword low on his mailed sleeve that almost dislocated his arm. This one *was* real! Damn!

"Fight for victory, men! Fight!" He hoped his words would do some good.

Swords and shields clanged steadily. Bowstrings twanged. Men and horses screamed and both died. Blood bubbled in crimson puddles from torn throats and pierced chests.

On and on into an increasingly weary day. Whoever had thought that war was glorious should be here now!

\* \* \*

General Lester Crumb positioned his army for the big charge at the oncoming cavalry. He did not know why he felt so certain about it, but he knew the Kancians were real this time. Real with death and the means to deliver it.

An arrow narrowly missed him and thunked into a rock. That one was real, at least.

Then they were met on the plain behind the row of hills. Ignorant armies, as John Knight would have said. Ignorant armies clashing just before the fall of night.

He had his sword out and was clanging it with a Kancian. The enemy soldier was very good, and he did his best not to lose to him. A second Kancian came in fast and cut him on the arm above the left elbow. He winced, sickened and weakened all in a heartbeat. He opened his mouth to shout, and then the first Kancian lunged hard.

He barely managed a grunt as the blade skidded off good mail and then penetrated, going deep into his chest. He fell, and his thought, strangely enough, was of his father and what he must be experiencing in the adjoining kingdom.

"Commander! Commander!" a voice shouted in his ear.

But by then he was hearing everything as though it were far, far away. Horses' hooves, poundings, screams, swords clanging against sword, shouts—all changed for him, as if to a babbling of a crowd or a murmuring of a brook.

Faint, fainter, faintest.

Jon could hardly give the war a thought. She was too concerned with Heln and what was happening to her. What *was* happening to her? Jon wished she knew. Every single morning Kelvin's wife was sick and vomiting, and it was no innocent morning sickness. It was so violent that sometimes there was blood speckling it, and that didn't seem to her to be right.

Jon, watching Heln's pale face as she picked at her tray of fancy palace food, wished that she had been a girl. She hadn't been, really, until she got together with Les. Growing up she'd avoided girl things. Climbing trees, slinging rocks at targets she moved farther and farther away, angling for fish in a way her foster father enjoyed—these had been her things. Soft girlish interests and especially those having to do with a girl's interest in boys she had dismissed with contempt. She had never worn dresses if she could help it, and her interest in infants had been nil. Now as an adult, as a woman, she had to feel a lack.

Was there a difference between roundears and pointears when it came to birthing? Jon had no way of knowing. How many roundear women had there been in this frame? Heln was the only one she had known, though there had been two females in John Knight's small band of roundears. Two females with round ears somewhere in this frame, maybe having babies in the natural way. Jon wished she had known one.

Heln gave a gasp, rose from her chair, and ran for the bathroom. Sick again, and not gently so. If this was natural pregnancy, Jon wanted no part of it for herself!

Jon picked up the orangmon fruit from Heln's plate and sniffed it. The fruit smelled fine. She didn't believe it was this that was making Heln sick. But just in case it might be—she ate the fruit, finding it good and taut and satisfying. She was wiping the yellow juice from her mouth when Heln returned, looking pale and worn.

"Heln, I'm worried about you," Jon said as her brother's wife resumed her chair. "You've been sick every morning lately. I don't think it's the food; I just tried some."

"It will pass," Heln said almost disinterestedly.

"Yes, but when? You have to think of the baby, Heln. This may not be good for it."

Heln looked impassively out the window at the gardener working on the tulppies and poplics. The flowers were really beautiful this time of year, their red and white, and blue and white blossoms a solace for their eyes. She didn't answer Jon.

*That does it! I'm going to get Dr. Sterk to prescribe for her vomiting.*

But then a troubling thought: did she trust Dr. Sterk and his medicine! Considering the way he was acting she wasn't sure.

She wondered about it as the sunlight crept over the flower beds and brightened the windows as the birds began to sing. She worried all that morning, and worrying was not like her. Then before she knew it, it was the next day. The oddest thing was that Heln herself did not seem to be worrying; in fact she seemed to have very little interest in anything. What was the matter with her?

There was of course no answer.

Heln was in the royal bathroom, vomiting.

# CHAPTER 13

# *Stapular*

*F*ather! Kian!"

They all embraced there in the chimaera's larder while the alien hunter looked on. As Kelvin had gradually come to accept, looking on was what Stapular did best.

"You've got your belt, Son! And the Mouvar weapon! And your gauntlets! Even your sword!"

"I have, Father." *And a lot of good they've done me so far!* "I've tried the Mouvar weapon but it had no effect. The chimaera could have taken everything from me, but it seems contemptuous and didn't bother."

John Knight heaved a big sigh. "It's something, being prisoners of a creature that doesn't fear our weapons, apparently with reason."

Kian jerked a thumb at Stapular. "The chimaera must fear his kind. They came here to kill it."

"Did, perhaps." *And probably never will again.* "How'd you get caught?"

"Coming back for you," Kian said, seeming annoyed. "We guessed you'd run into difficulties." Politely he did not mention that it had been Kelvin's own choice.

"You were right," Kelvin acknowledged. "The chimaera's too much for me."

"Too much for anyone," Kian said. He did not quite say that that should have been obvious.

"Too much for anyone from an inferior frame," Stapular sneered. The alien had moved away from the wall. One of his hands reached into the trough, picked up a luscious nectorfruit and squeezed it. Pulp and juice squirted from between Stapular's fingers. His hands had to be quite as strong as the gauntlets, yet he had launched no attacks on the chimaera. Kelvin hadn't seen him actually eat, either, though probably he sneaked that in when Kelvin was asleep. Didn't want an inferior observing a superior taking nourishment like any other person, no doubt.

Distracted by Stapular's actions and his own thoughts, Kelvin tried to think of something the two of them had talked about. But had they ever really talked? He remembered trying to interest Stapular in doing something to save their lives, but the hunter had been as adamant then as now.

His father slapped him across the back in a friendly fashion he knew was calculated to build his courage. "Well, Son, we're in trouble!"

"Father, when were we not?" The awkwardness of the situation, and his father's attempt to make light of it were hardly lost on him.

"Say, Stapular, you old phony," Kian said, turning to their cellmate. "You ready to break out of here?" It was a return dig for the hunter's taunt about inferior life-forms.

"Stupid inferior being!" Stapular snapped. As usual his thinking seemed centered on that. Maybe it was because he feared that he himself was mentally deficient?

"Well, we have to do something, don't we, Father?" Kelvin asked. Desperation made his voice squeak. He hadn't felt so unsure of himself since Mor Crumb had propelled him into his first sword fight. The single gauntlet he had then worn had saved him then and many times afterward. Would that it and its mate would do so again!

"I could wish for a laser," his father said. "Unfortunately your father-in-law lost the last one before we fought the final battle for Aratex."

Kelvin remembered. According to St. Helens it was either drop the laser over the Aratex courtyard or let Heln tumble to her death. Although his father-in-law had done many things of which Kelvin didn't approve—in fact, the man had been downright aggravating at times—he had to feel that this was one time he had made the right decision. Now Heln was back home, quietly preparing to have their baby. How glad he was that she wasn't in any of this horror with the chimaera!

Kian spoke up. "A pair of magic gauntlets once propelled me to the top of a huge silver serpent. Once I was up there they knew how to keep me there and how to fight. Kelvin, do you suppose that if you got on top of the chimaera behind the sting—"

Stapular laughed bitterly. "Dumb, inferior life-form!"

"The sting can send out blue lightning bolts," Kelvin said, cutting through his brother's annoyance. "It shot them at me, and—" He launched into his tale.

"Electricity!" John said when he had finished. "It has to be! Like the electric eels we had back on Earth! That's why an antimagic weapon had no effect! Electricity is science!"

"Brilliant!" Stapular said. "For a dumb inferior life-form."

"Listen, Stapular, I'm getting tired of that!" John said, whirling on him. "If you're so brilliant and superior, why don't you tell us how to save ourselves?"

"Because there isn't any way," Stapular said. "You either kill the chimaera with laser bursts or you get caught by squarears and eaten by it. After you're caught you're finished. All you can do is enjoy the food, until you become food."

"You were planning something," Kian said. "You and Kelvin."

"When was that?" Kelvin asked. Never before had he been so puzzled by anything his brother had said. With the puzzle came a lancing pain through his head. This business must be wearing him down more than he thought!

"When I was here before. Not physically. I mean when I returned in my astral form."

"You were here? Astrally?" Now Kelvin understood it, or almost did. His head continued to hurt, as though protesting something. Why was Stapular making that mechanical frown and motioning as if for silence?

"I was. I had those dragonberries we brought, and—"

"Shut up, all of you!" Stapular said.

"Why?" Kian glared at the red-haired, glass-armored

cellmate. His expression suggested that he didn't want Stapular ordering them to do anything.

"Because the chimaera reads minds that don't know how to block and compensate."

Oh. They all fell silent.

It was the nearest Stapular had come to admitting that there might actually be a plan.

Mervania tugged at her copper earrings and considered the matter carefully. They had been planning something, Stapular and Kelvin. Probably they intended some ruse, some trick. Stapular, being a hunter, would have controlled his thoughts. But Kelvin—impossible. She considered what she needed to do.

What she wanted was those dragonberries. They would work on her kind, if the legend was correct. They worked for roundears and dragons; thus she, Mertin, and Grumpus all qualified. Together or singly they could search this frame for interesting sights.

What a release that would be! Their body might remain prisoner here on the isle, but their minds would range everywhere! They could spy on squarears who were their keepers. They could watch the froogears at their yearly secret rituals. It would be such a relief to the boredom they suffered here.

Then, too, there was the possibility of visiting other frames, of seeing even more entertaining sights, of listening in on the talk and thoughts of strangers, humans and their superiors. Oh what fun, what incredible fun they could have! As well as, just maybe, finding a potential mate, somewhere.

All of it dependent on dragonberries. There was the treasure beyond reckoning!

"You thinking of that trade plan again?" Mertin grumbled.

"Yes, Mertin, I am." She felt pleased that Mertin was actually asking her thoughts. Maybe she had succeeded in interesting him in something other than food or sex. Of course he would probably just want to use the astral travel to spy on the matings of assorted creatures. Still, if that made him cooperate with her effort, it would be worth it.

"Offer them freedom," Mertin advised. "Let the older

roundear go with the one who had the berries. Tell them to find the berries for us, get them back, and bring them here. Then when they don't come back, we eat those who are left."

"Mertin, that's perfect!" she exclaimed, thrilled as much by his support as the notion itself.

"That's logical, Mervania, as you should be."

"Grrrromph," Grumpus added, clicking his mouth as if sampling the tender flesh of a captive.

Mervania sighed. Neither of them had much use for feeling; that was her department. Nothing to do now but go to the larder. She could take along some of the fruit they liked so much, and then she could ask. She did hope they would be open to reason. They should be, but human foodstuffs were notorious for being less than smart about certain matters. Suppose they said no? She tried not to think about that. Maybe if they said no and she butchered one and she and her companion heads ate it while the others watched, that would help them see reason. Yes, if they said no, that indeed might be necessary. Just so long as at least one survived to fetch the berries.

She touched the companion minds and they flipped up their tail and scuttled across the ground to the orchard. She and Mertin filled their joined arms with nectarfruit, and Grumpus pinched a cantemellon from a vine with their pincers and stuffed it inelegantly into his own mouth.

Properly loaded with fruit and plans, they scuttled for the larder.

Squirtmuck could not get the collecting tree out of his mind. The objects taken from strangers had never interested him greatly, but those berries were tempting. The one he had sampled had made him embarrassingly sick, but if a roundear's stomach could handle them, then so should his. It was so intriguing, the thought of dying as the young roundear had done, then coming back to life. Squirtmuck had never thought much about it before, but now that he did, the thought of what existed after dying was intriguing.

Irresistibly, bit by bit, he toyed with the notion. Late during the day, while searching for squiggle worms, he managed to get back to the area of the tree. He looked around, saw none of his mates, and made a splashing run for it. Soon he was there, looking into the cavity and its collection of visitor artifacts.

If he took just one of the berries, would anyone know? Suppose it killed him, and he did not return to life. He wasn't quite old enough to want to die. True, he was tired of a lot of what made life, but not tired enough to give it up yet.

He thought about it for a moment more, while the sun started setting and dappling the trees and the greenish water with orange. Why not, he thought, why not indeed? He might not have another chance.

Reaching into the tree's cavity, he drew forth the bag.

Bloorg scratched a square ear and remembered that he had not used his viewing crystal yesterday. As leader of his people and official greeter of visitors he should check the transporter. As usual there would be nothing, but then again there might. There was always that hope.

Sighing, he picked up the squarish crystal from its stand, held it before his eyes, and concentrated.

At first, as was usual, he saw nothing but his own square pupils in his own square eyes. Then he could see into the pupils that expanded and expanded, and then he was seeing back at the transporter cave. It was as he had last seen it, with a drying narcofruit left by the froogears near the exit.

Why was he here? Oh, yes, to check for possible visitors. There were none, as he had expected.

So he would direct his thoughts elsewhere. He should check briefly on the froogears, and then maybe the chimaera's island. It was a chore, but his job. Work, work, work, always the same boring necessities.

He drifted his sight across the swamp, finding the froogears at a camp on a platform of floater weeds. They were doing froogear things. Here one froogear dived off the platform and crawled along the bottom, finally surfacing with a wriggling stinkfish firm in his jaws. There a female covered her breasts and stomach with greenish muck, the better to attract a lover. There child froogears splashed joyfully at the edge of the platform and took turns diving under. The male with the stinkfish in its jaw swam up to the platform and the female. The female took the fish from his jaws, bit its head, and oogled his form. The male climbed up beside her. In a moment the two would be joining. At such moments Bloorg, bored, moved his viewing elsewhere.

He had almost brought his sight back to the crystal when he remembered the froogear leader. Where was Squirtmuck, anyway? Efficiently he moved his sight in circles, checking froogears. Squirtmuck was not there.

What an irritation! He had to search until he located the missing creature, or was assured that it was dead. Wider and wider he viewed, until finally he thought to check the collecting tree.

Squirtmuck was there. He held a bag in his webbed fingers and from it he took a berry. He held it poised in front of his mouth.

Berry? What berry? As from a great distance—which of course it was—it leaped at him: *dragonberry!*

"No, Squirtmuck, no!"

But it was already too late. Squirtmuck, propelled by some incomprehensible flight of froogear fancy, had suddenly and forcefully thrown away the entire bag.

The bar dropped outside the door. All stood back as the chimaera entered, carrying fruit. Kelvin felt strange, watching it. The head called Mervania still seemed to him to be that of a beautiful coppery-haired woman, a roundear at that.

*Thank you, Kelvin.*

The male head, Mertin, could have been on the shoulders of any of the soldiers he had directed against Rowforth in the silver-serpent frame.

*Forget it, foodstuff!*

The dragon head reminded him all too clearly of the dragons with golden scales that he himself had slaughtered.

*GWROOOOF!!*

While the beast as a whole reminded him of nothing so much as a—

The chimaera had entered, while he was thinking. Now it elevated its deadly tail. Kelvin hastily suppressed his thoughts.

The monster dumped its load of nectarfruit into the trough. It smelled lusciously good. Even though he knew it was fattening, he could hardly wait to start eating!

He edged away from the wall, his feet seeming to have a mind of their own. Suddenly he was running, right past the chimaera to the open doorway.

Mervania's pretty head dipped toward his as he passed. "Going somewhere, little toothsome?" she inquired sweetly.

He put on the skids, without knowing why. Now he was standing right beside the monster, with the female human face almost near enough to kiss.

"Well, if you feel that way, Kelvin—" she started, amused.

Kelvin, astonished, realized that she *would* kiss him, even though she intended to eat his flesh later. Because she liked to play with her food.

Suddenly Stapular acted. "Go!" he shouted, and grabbed the tip of the sting, which was now pointed at the ceiling.

There was a flash, as from a close lightning bolt. Kelvin found himself weak and gasping and tingling all over, just outside the door. His feet must have carried him here! Inside the cellar his brother and father lay sprawled, unconscious or dead.

Amazingly, the chimaera too was down. Only Stapular was alive and moving. "Quickly, before it comes to!"

"What?" Kelvin struggled with the thought. His feet wanted to carry him, but he could hardly stand.

"The electricity in this confined space took them all out. But I'm not certain how long before they wake! Hurry!"

Abruptly he was remembering. Stapular waving his fingers at him, implanting a course of action deep within his head.

Kelvin ran to the fence and grabbed a post. The post, slippery and solid, resisted his strength, but he was determined. Then the gauntlets took over and wrenched it from the ground.

"Come on! Get your posterior in motion!" Stapular cried.

He was to run with it back to the chimaera. He was to raise it like a great dragonspear and drive it deep into every living eyesocket the monster possessed! He—

He stood there, his weapon poised before Mervania's fallen face. She looked almost angelic, her eyes closed, her features relaxed. She had been about to kiss him. Drive the point into one of those lovely eyes?

How could he? The chimaera was helpless. It might be a monster, but Mervania was as womanly as any woman he had known, with the possible exception of his own mother. And his wife. Yet here he stood, feet wide apart, tip of the greenish-tinged sting raised above her face, his eyes and muscles concentrating hard on her coppery—

"Now, stupid, now!" Stapular ordered.

Something snapped. Kelvin trembled and pointed the sting away from the lovely face.

"Ineffective Minor World fool!" Stapular screamed. He charged across and took hold of the shaft. "I'll do it myself! I should have known better than to trust a lesser creature to do something important!" He pulled.

Kelvin resisted, pulling back with the strength of the gauntlets.

"You fool, you idiot, you brainless nothing!" Stapular yelled. "Can't you see that it's about to wake?"

True, surely. Yet Kelvin did not yield. "No, Stapular! I can't do it this way! We only want to escape."

"That's all *you* want, maybe, you imbecile! I want more!" Stapular exerted considerable strength, and it was as if he wore magic gauntlets of his own. Kelvin was pulled off balance, but his gauntlets maintained their grip.

"Let go! Let go! Let go!" They fell together, struggling over possession of the copper sting. They rolled over and over on the floor, with Stapular's unexpectedly heavy weight and the armor pressing hard against his simple rustic body coverings.

Then they were up against the trough, and Stapular was bending him back. The edge of the trough struck his head and he saw stars. Then—

Stapular had the sting! He held it poised above the Grumpus head, searching out the dragon's eyeball and its path to the brain. Kelvin had killed dragons that way, and Stapular had learned from his telling, if he hadn't known it before.

"Die, beast!" Stapular said. His body tensed.

Without realizing how he did it, Kelvin was upon him. One incredible leap propelled somehow by his gauntlets; then he and the hunter were going over on the floor. Again they were rolling, fighting for control.

"You fool! You moron! You Minor World trash!"

Kelvin paid no attention to the words. He saved his breath for the combat. It was almost as though the gauntlets had taken weird control over the whole of him. To destroy the monster should be his greatest desire, yet now it was as if his greatest wish were to save the chimaera.

The great beast stirred. An arm with a man's hand on it reached out and grabbed the shaft of the sting where Kelvin and Stapular held it.

"Let go that!" Mertin said. The scorpiocrab claws clicked warningly.

Stapular did not let go. Thus he remained in place as the huge claws reached out, took him around the middle, and lifted him into the air.

"Now see what you've done!" Stapular cried. "Minor World idiot!"

Kelvin released the sting. With a quick motion he brought out his sword. He swished it at the pincer and then struck. Copper gleamed brightly where his blade bit. The pincer would have a scar, but that was as deeply as his blade penetrated. At the same time he felt the shock of impact from wrist to shoulder. Ouch! His arm felt numb!

"You really must not fight!" Mervania said. "You really must not." Her head was awake now, staring at him.

Suddenly the hunter had hold of his own left wrist. He pulled at the transparent gauntlet. It came off—*along with the entire hand.*

Kelvin blinked, but the sight remained. Where the man's wrist should have been was a metallic something that could hardly be bone.

From the foreshortened arm a ruby laser flashed out. It cut through one of the pincers. The pincer and Stapular hit the floor simultaneously.

"Now you'll see!" Stapular said, rising and pointing the stump. "I came prepared! It was planned that I be the last, and hide this until the last moment! I didn't want to have to reveal my nature, but this Minor World scum forced my hand." He glanced briefly at the hand he had removed. "Now, Chimaera—"

Mervania screamed. Mertin made an exclamation of dismay. Grumpus growled. If a monster could tremble, this one was doing so.

Casually Stapular lanced off the second pincer. With his back against the wall, immune from being grabbed, he could proceed to cut off every arm and head.

"Listen, Minor World being," Stapular said. "You wouldn't have it the conventional way! You had to make me ruin my cover! Now listen to the death cries of the last known surviving chimaera in all the frames!"

"No, no!" Mervania cried. It sounded very much like a woman's pleading, and indeed there were tears in her eyes.

Kelvin could not have said how it happened. Suddenly he raised, reversed, and flung his sword forward. It was the gauntlets' doing. For the moment the gauntlets appeared to have chosen a strange side.

The sword turned in the air, the point coming to the fore. The blade penetrated Stapular's throat precisely in the middle. Stapular looked surprised. Then he raised his intact hand and yanked the sword partway out.

Something black gushed forth. Alien blood? No, not blood at all, Kelvin realized. Oil! Stapular was what his father called a robot!

Whatever it was, the fluid was necessary for the thing's functioning. As it poured out, Stapular collapsed. He could not function without oil pressure any better than a living creature could function without blood pressure.

"You have saved us! You have saved us!" Mervania exclaimed, and even Grumpus growled something that sounded appreciative. Monsters valued their lives as much as other folk did.

Now John Knight and Kian were opening their eyes, returning to bewildered consciousness.

"It was all a trick!" Mervania babbled indignantly. "A trick of the hunters!"

"That thing never would have tasted right!" Mertin said with disgust. "It would have given Grumpus indigestion."

"GROOOOMTH!" the dragon head agreed with a disgusted expression.

Kelvin looked quickly to his father and brother, and back to the faces of their captor. Now they were in for it, he thought. Now they were all going to be rewarded in the worst possible way for his colossal stupidity and for the gauntlets' interference. Now they had no way to escape being eaten by the chimaera.

Grumpus snapped his big jaws and darted forth his forked tongue as if hungry already.

## CHAPTER 14

# *Turnings*

St. Helens prepared himself for death, as well as he was able. He expected a spear to be rammed through him or a knife slitting his throat. Yet even as this child-king who was not a child screamed "Kill him!" the witch opened her eyes and stared piercingly at the men holding him.

"No, precious," she said, her eyes flicking back to the child. "He must be a prisoner."

"He killed you!" the child shrilled.

"Not yet, precious. Not yet. Please, darlings, humor me. My kind are hard to kill." With those words the old woman ceased speaking and closed her eyes as though for death.

St. Helens heard a sword snick out of a scabbard. She had spoken too late, or died too early, he thought. Now the brat-king would have his understandable revenge.

"No!" the little guy ordered. "Don't kill him! Put him in the dungeon! As for Helbah, take her in!"

"But—"

At that moment a large houcat, very black, ferocious of eye, leaped from behind the second young king and ran to Helbah's apparent corpse. For one moment St. Helens felt the sharp yellow eyes, and heard the wickedest, deepest, longest-drawn hiss he'd ever heard from anything feline. Then the houcat was on the corpse, breathing in and out against Helbah's worn mouth.

Suddenly the houcat stiffened all over. Then it collapsed like a black, empty bag. The blackness stayed there and seemed even to be melting as a soldier jerked St. Helens' arm.

*Now there were two corpses,* he thought. *Witch's and witch's familiar.* But whatever else he might think of her, he knew that the witch had saved his life.

The soldiers rushed him away.

Lomax steadied his young resolve as he looked up and down the line of survivors of the recent fight. They had lost only about a dozen men in addition to St. Helens, but twenty more were wounded seriously enough to be sent home. The remainder, Lomax determined, were going to cross that border again. But first there was this other matter.

"All right! Who did it! Who fired that crossbow bolt! Who violated the truce?"

No one spoke. All the Hermans remained impassive, while the mercenaries were interested rather than apprehensive. Judging from appearances, none here were guilty.

"You, Phillip, did you—"

He was going to say "see someone do it?" but the boy interrupted him.

"Yes, I did it! I did it! I'm the one!"

"YOU! But why?" His head swam even as he asked it.

"St. Helens plays chess! He knows you have to take out the dark queen!"

"You've killed him! You're responsible for his death!"

"He's my greatest friend! Oh, Lomax, please, please hang me as he asked!"

Lomax shivered. "You really—"

"Please. I did it for him. I did it for all of us. So that we could win. The same as when Kelvin destroyed Melbah in Aratex."

"Damn!" Lomax said, pained and unenthusiastic. The kid really did think it a game! Doubtless he thought that afterward the dead simply woke up and resumed living, ready to play the game again. Kids!

"Please," Phillip repeated. "It was my dearest friend's last request. He was not only my dearest friend, he was my *only* friend!"

Lomax shook all over, unable to stop himself. "You really want me to give that order? You really want to hang by your neck and choke, your eyeballs bugging out? You want to die?"

"Yes."

He considered it. He liked Phillip in spite of himself. Would St. Helens really want him dead? St. Helens had saved the former figurehead king of Aratex from death, and had treated him as a friend. Should he, could he now follow what had been St. Helens' command?

"NO!" he said forcefully. "That'd be too easy on you! You have to go back with us into Kance! You have to fight the enemy and make up for what you've done!"

"Oh, thank you, thank you, kind, gentle friend!"

Was that for refusing to hang him, or for visiting on him presumably worse punishment? There were tears in the boy's eyes, but his voice was not devoid of sneaky triumph. What game was he really playing?

Well, the reality of battle would sweat that out of him, if it didn't kill him first.

*St. Helens,* Lomax thought in what was almost a prayer, *I promise you will be avenged even if it costs every one of our lives!*

The phantoms were not coming now, Mor thought. They'd quit appearing and disappearing in midbattle. Yet his men were losing, losing badly, and not to witchcraft.

He finished off the Klinglander he was fighting and then wheeled his horse. Dead and dying men lay everywhere, and yes, the tide of battle had definitely turned.

It galled him to do it, but there was no alternative. He lifted the horn to his lips and blew the signal for retreat.

Their only consolation, he thought, was that in the forests grew bloodfruit for the treatment of the wounded. Before this war was over, the magical fruit would save a lot of lives.

Thinking grimly of the surgery that would have to be set up, Mor turned his horse. A forest with bloodfruit was reasonably close behind.

Zoanna stared into her crystal and laughed a most unbeautiful laugh that Rowforth found deliciously chilling.

"Look! Look!" she ordered.

He was looking. He saw the witch who controlled the kingdoms of Klingland and Kance lying motionless without a visible sign of life. There was that black houcat lying on her face, melting into it. There were the Kancian soldiers dragging a bewildered St. Helens away.

"Does this mean we've won?" he asked. He felt stupid asking a woman about anything, even Zoanna. He felt particularly stupid now, knowing that he had done nothing to direct the battles or secure the triumph.

"We will have won if she never recovers," Zoanna said. "We must see that she doesn't."

"You will use more magic?"

"Magic won't be needed in the war. Of course my not helping our side will mean many more casualties. Some of those will be our former enemies."

"A shame," he said smugly. "They'll fight their hearts out and never know why."

"Yes, they'll die for us, one way or another. Those who survive the battles may have to die later."

"Slowly, with our help, and with much pain."

"Of course. That is what we both want."

They embraced, the battles revealed by the crystals fading from their minds. Soon, he thought, there was going to commence the fulfillment of all his dreams. It would be brutally, bloodily, ghastlily glorious.

Lester Crumb imagined that he was back fighting the Queen's Guardsmen, with Kelvin's Knights of the Roundear. Then he opened his eyes and found that the man bending over him wore a different uniform. He strove to think, to reorient, and then it came, the pain of the wound high in his chest. Where was Jon? Jon had saved his life and then gone on to become his wife. What had happened?

Different war. Different battle. Different circumstances. Jon was far away. Safe. Oh, he hoped she was safe!

A gnarled hand mopped at his brow. He felt the sweat that was all over his face, soaking his undergarments, the blanket he lay upon. Overhead was the roof of a tent. The tent was flapping dismally in a wind that howled like disembodied souls slain in battle.

"We were fighting Kance soldiers," he said. "I fell. Someone saved me. It was almost like another battle when I was unhorsed."

"Save your strength, Commander."

Commander? Him? He could hardly remember. His head hurt and pounded like a drum beaten to announce someone's death. Oh, if only Jon were here to hold him! He tried remembering the officer's name. Klumpecker, that was it! Lieutenant Karl Klumpecker from Throod.

He looked into the deep blue eyes, noting the blond hair and the smile so typical of Throod mercenaries. Big shoulders, too, and a strong frame, though not quite as great in these departments as his father.

"Did we win the battle?"

"No, Commander, we lost."

Somehow he thought he'd say that. "Many casualties?"

"I'm afraid so, Commander. On both sides."

"Can we win the war?"

"Eventually, Commander. When Commander Reilly and the Hermans and your father and his troops and ours all reach the caps."

"Yes, the caps." Insane business, two capitals in one. Governed, theoretically, by two very slowly maturing boys. Governed in fact by a witch identical in appearance to the one Kelvin had destroyed in Aratex. Would Kelvin soon return? Would he return as in Aratex to put everything right? When he had started this adventure he had been certain. Now wounded, now defeated in battle, he was no longer certain of anything.

"Commander, your wound is so serious that—" The lieutenant paused, seemingly searching for words.

"If I cannot command, you must, Lieutenant. We must not surrender! We must fight on! My father and St. Helens are depending on us!"

"Yes, Commander Crumb. We will fight our way into the caps and into glory."

*With me or without me,* Les added in his own troubled thoughts. He wanted to pass out, even to die, but thoughts of Jon would not allow it. Then it seemed that he was but a little boy, that he was lost, and that all others were gone.

Charlain moved her copper locks out of her violet eyes with a quick sweep of her slender hand. The cards she was laying out on the kitchen table had come out the same as before. Every time the Blind Fool headed Kelvin's file, designating great danger and uncertainty for him.

"Does the prophecy still apply?" she whispered to herself. "Can it still?"

She tweaked her right pointed ear to keep herself awake. John Knight had been intrigued by that habit of hers. Strange man, John. She had once thought of him only as a way of fulfilling the prophecy. He, a roundear, would mate with her, a pointed-ear person, and their son would be the one mentioned in the Book of Prophecy. It had all seemed so simple when she was young. John had come straight from the queen's dungeon, torn, lonely, and confess it now, handsome. She had wanted him from the start, and they had married quickly and without attracting attention. They had had their son, and then a daughter. Only roundeared Kelvin could relate to the prophecy, but pointeared Jon had supported him loyally.

In time Kelvin had indeed slain dragons, and freed their kingdom of Rud from the tyrannous Queen Zoanna. The prophecy was being fulfilled, as she had foreseen.

Then things had changed, and nothing was as she had expected. Perhaps her action in implementing the prophecy had caused the fabric of the situation to change. Kelvin had left this frame and returned to it just in time to save Rud and Aratex by uniting them, just as in the prophecy—but that had been by the skin of his fingernails! Now "joining four" were the next words in the verse that applied to him. He was supposed to join four kingdoms. But how could he? Kelvin wasn't even here! He was in another frame, and the prophecy that he would rid his homeland of a sore was rapidly being nullified. Sometimes she almost thought that John Knight had been right.

"Nonsense, this prophecy business! Nonsense!" John had said, sometimes sitting at this very table. She had soothed him, calmed him, knowing even then that he would not always be hers. He had suffered himself to be soothed, not because he accepted magic, but because she was beautiful in his eyes (and perhaps in others' eyes too), and he liked to be close to her. So his contempt of magic had been muted at times, until finally he began to believe. Then she had lost him, through no choice of either of theirs, in the necessary tragedy of the times.

Now things were changing again, becoming even less settled than before, and the cards reflected it. "John," she whispered, pretending that he was there. Oh, how she loved him! Her second husband was a good man, taken as the law allowed on the extended disappearance and assumed death of her first. But John, John had been the stuff of story. Round ears, for sorcery's sake! And from another frame, a world too strange for comprehension. Moving pictures, talking boxes, horseless carriages, and more, much more. Strangest of all was John's insistence that none of those were magic.

"Well, John, I know you are alive now," she murmured through her tears. "I never would have remarried had I known. I know now that somehow the cards lied, or I misread them, and that you survived what seemed a certain death. I know that I was not your first woman, or your last, and you were not my last man, but I love you and want you, and hope that you will still want me." But there had been others to consider, including the man she had married. Hal Hackleberry—she hated to admit it, but she was relieved that things had fallen out with Hal as they had. Perhaps she had suspected what would happen; the cards might have informed her, but she had resolutely avoided reading them with respect to the Brownberry family, after that first crisis. Even so, she had known that they had a buxom and lonely daughter . . .

Hal was good but fallible. Most men were. She had wept when she lost him, as much for her own complicity as for the loss. She had never been able to love him properly. "But you, John . . ."

She found herself weeping, and this annoyed her. Witchy people who read cards and tried to foretell events were not supposed to be soft and blubbery. She had to remember that.

She forced herself to face the truth. She was dissembling when she told herself she had not loved Hal completely. She knew now that she had never loved Hal at all. She had told him she did, and tried to believe it herself, but it had always been John. So she was as much at fault as Hal for what had happened. Maybe he had known, and so had suffered, and been vulnerable. Certainly she hardly blamed him. She had said that before; now she believed it.

When in doubt, deal some cards.

She dealt them out, asking in her mind, *Where is John? Where is John Knight who was my husband?*

John was with Kelvin. Both in another frame. Both separated from her as though by death's gates. The Blind Fool leered and danced, promising naught. They might or might not return.

She turned a card. There it was again: the Coupling card. Kelvin was already married, to a nice girl named Heln, a roundear like himself. The Coupling card was an unmistakable reference. She placed it on file and turned the following card.

The Birthing card. So they were going to have a baby, a fact she had already learned. But then a third card, to follow the Birthing card—and it came up, yet again:

The Twister card. Meaning grave danger and an uncertainty of outcome.

*Poor Heln! Poor frightened little mother-to-be. You are in for great difficulties.*

But would it be just the birth, or something happening to the child during the birth? Afterward? Stubbornly the cards would not say. Actually, it was wrong to blame the cards for being perverse; they were perverse only when the situation made them helpless. For example, when something they might reveal would be changed when they revealed it. If they told her she would stub her toe when she left the table, she would be careful to avoid that, making the cards wrong. Paradox incapacitated them. So they compromised by presenting the Twister. They weren't willfully difficult.

Maybe she should be with her daughter-in-law for the delivery? Usually that was not a mother-in-law's place, but under the circumstance . . .

Yes, she would go to Heln and try to help her. With the Blind Fool dominating Kelvin's fate and the Twister twirling in to link hers more closely with his, there was no alternative.

"I don't like to interfere," she said aloud, "but what else is a mother to do? Heln, I'm going to come visiting!"

Jon did not like the way Heln looked! It seemed less like a healthy pregnancy every day. Not only was Heln disgustingly sick at frequent intervals, she was now having bad dreams.

"Jon, oh Jon!" Heln sat up in bed, her face pasty, her eyes wild and glassy. "I saw it again, the thing with three heads! Two of them baby heads and the other a dragon's. The baby heads were crying, and—"

*That settles it!* Jon thought. *I'm going to get something for her from the doctor. Dr. Sterk has to know something! He was royal physician before I was born!*

"Where are you going, Jon?"

"I'll be back."

She met Dr. Sterk in the hallway. He looked straight ahead with his birdlike eyes and pressed a small decanter into her hands. "Three drops twice a day in her tefee," he said, and passed on.

Well, she thought, at least she hadn't had to press him. Evidently he'd noticed it too. But did she dare trust his medicine, considering his evident toadyism?

She reentered their room. Heln gazed at her with eyes seemingly reflecting horror. That was not the way a young mother-to-be should look!

*That settles it!* Jon thought again. *Enough torment is enough! I just have to trust. Who after all would want to harm an infant?* Aside from certain royal figures . . .

"Heln, it's time for your tefee." She pulled on the cord to signal the servant. In a moment the servant was there with a big steaming pot of the beverage and a plate with a selection of bite-sized cooakes.

Jon poured the tefee into the cups and carefully added

three greenish thick drops to Heln's. She stirred it with a spoon and the syrupy medicine blended into the dark greenish hue of the beverage.

"Here you are, Heln."

She watched as Kelvin's pretty dark-haired wife took the cup listlessly, and slowly sipped.

Heln's eyes widened. She raised the cup again, in both hands. Eagerly she sucked down every drop.

That was good, Jon hoped.

## CHAPTER 15

# *Disappearance*

$M$ervania's head moved close to Kelvin's and spoke in that disturbingly seductive tone she affected: "Kelvin, since you saved us by destroying the cruel hunter, we will not eat you or your companions."

"You are letting us go?" Was she toying with him again? Playing with her food, as her fellow head put it? Kelvin did not in the least trust her.

"Yes, yes, but there is a price." It was prettily said, her face almost touching his. Even her breath was sweet as she said it.

"What price?" They were already in its power. Anything Kelvin or his companions had, the chimaera could take away, for reason or whim. Surely she wasn't bargaining for a kiss!

"Those dragonberries Kian used—I want some." Very plainly spoken, no artifice showing.

Kelvin looked unhappily to Kian. He hated speaking for him and he hated not to.

"Lost," Kian said, helping John to his feet. "Froogears."

"Unfortunate," Mervania said. This time there was just a

touch of sadness. If the dragonberries were lost, then they were lost, and there was nothing to be done about it. Which meant that the human party had nothing with which to bargain.

"Groompth," remarked Grumpus. He opened his dragon's mouth wide enough to display his swordlike teeth.

"Now we eat!" Mertin said, making a superfluous translation. He didn't sound at all sorry. If dragonberries were of great importance to Mervania, they were less so to him.

"Wait! Wait!" Kelvin cried. He had never felt so panicky in his life. To fail to say the right thing now would be to condemn himself and his companions to being eaten. "Suppose—suppose we get you some? Maybe we can bring you some seed so you can grow them here on your island. Then you'll always have a supply."

Mervania's head tipped coyly to one side. "That would be nice, Kelvin."

*Yes,* Kelvin thought. *If we can get the seeds back home, and if the squarears will let us.*

"I read your thoughts, Kelvin," Mervania said reprovingly. "the squarears will let you. But you must tell them first."

"We will," Kelvin said. Unconsciously he picked up the old copper sting with its green patina scratched from being dropped on the floor. Then he looked over at Stapular, now silent and unarrogant, the oil no longer flowing from his pierced throat.

"You may take back your weapon," Mervania said, "but you must not touch the hunter's."

"Fair enough," Kelvin said. He crossed the cell to Stapular's pinned body, and without his willing it his right gauntlet reached for the sword haft. Fascinated he watched his arm lift the sword from the oil. The blade was covered with a thick dark grease that probably would help preserve its metal. The gauntlet wiped off most of the stuff on a clean section of the body, then sheathed the sword in its scabbard. Kelvin's arm was his own again.

"You must tell the squarears about this," Mervania cautioned. "They must know what was planned. They will come to get this robot and its weapon and guard against this ever happening again."

"I'm glad to have been of service," Kelvin said. He looked into the open blue eyes of the robot he had believed to be a person and was forced to think *Junk, nothing but junk. Not flesh and blood at all.*

"Yes," Mervania said. "An excellent imitation."

Yet he had felt that Stapular was living. Had he been, or was that magic?

"It is what your father calls science," Mervania said. "You are now free to go. Do not forget, though, what you have agreed to do."

"We'll talk to the squarears," Kelvin said. "If they will permit us, we'll get your dragonberry seeds." Unconsciously he hefted the sting in his left hand.

"You may take that with you," Mervania said. "To me it is of no more importance than your hair and nail clippings are to you."

"Thank you," Kelvin said. "Thank you for—"

"Come!" his father said. "Before it changes its mind!"

"Minds," Kian corrected.

Kelvin had only one objection: they didn't have a boat, and he doubted that they could swim all the way back to the swamp.

"You will be met," Mervania said, knowing his thought. "Froogears will come."

"They—know?"

"Some are quite near. Their minds, like yours, are always open."

"Oh." That was all he could manage. He looked at his father and brother, but they were already on their way out of the larder and into the gloriously warm and mild sunshine beyond.

Kelvin looked once more at the dead robot. Why did he persist in thinking of it as a once-living man, though now he knew better?

"You have a quaint human way of anthropomorphizing," Mervania said. "You want to believe that thing was human because it seemed so, even though all it did was insult you in order to keep you from getting too well acquainted and perhaps fathoming its secret prematurely."

That must be it. He looked at the Mervania head. "I—"

"Just as you persist in thinking of me as a pretty woman, though you know even better that I am nothing of the kind. Your human capacity for willful self-delusion is amazing."

Just so. Kelvin turned and walked after John and Kian.

"I like you too, Kelvin, perhaps as foolishly," she murmured almost inaudibly. "I would have missed you, after we ate you."

Bloorg withdrew his mind from his viewing crystal and considered the implications. He had just seen and overheard the conversation of Mervania Chimaera and the visitors. So they had agreed to return with dragonberry seeds for the chimaera. That should be fine, so long as they thereafter stayed away. If those berries kept the chimaera entertained, better yet, and should it actually manage to fulfill its dream and discover some other creature of its kind, making a mating unit, that would be wonderful. How interesting that the man's magic gauntlets had fathomed all that, and acted correctly despite temptation to do otherwise.

Yes, he thought, rubbing his square ears with his usual afterviewing massage, that should work out very well. They would meet the human party at the transporter cave and make certain the visitors got their correct transporter setting. After that there would be an end to commerce. Who would ever have suspected that the foolish visitors would not only survive, but benefit the situation!

Think-whistling an inspiring song, Bloorg stepped outside his dwelling and prepared to summon his underlings for the start of a new day.

The trip away from the island and back through the swamp was one Kelvin had not expected to make. He looked over at his father and Kian as the froogears carried them, wondering whether they were as amazed as he at the turn of events. If they survived this journey in good order, he planned to give up this life of involuntary adventure. Nothing was going to pry him away from Heln and his home again! Froogears, squarears, chimaera . . . just too much! Back home things were sensible with only a bit of magic and sorcery and golden-scaled dragons to break the monotony of everyday life. It was so much better to be among normal things, instead of out among exotic and unnatural things like robots and laser weapons!

"I can't believe it," Kian said. "I'm actually going to see Lonny again!"

That was right! All this had started when they headed out to attend Kian's wedding! But Kelvin was ready to skip that event at this point, not wanting to risk another journey through the transporter. He just wanted to stay with safe, normal Heln and their safe, normal baby on the way.

John Knight said nothing, and the froogears splashed away, transferring them from the lake to the swamp and then, by infinitely slow progress, to the edge of the swamp and finally the transporter cave.

Squarears were waiting there. The big squarear with the chimaera's sting greeted them. "I am Bloorg, the Official Greeter and Sender, Keeper of the Transporter to Other Worlds, Keeper of the Last Known Existing Chimaera, Chief."

That had been his ritual greeting before. Kelvin wondered if Bloorg wondered why they had not left.

"I know," Bloorg said, "where you have been. I know you were to have been eaten but I would not have interfered, after freeing you the first time. You are forbidden to go to the chimaera's island again."

"Mervania wants—" Kelvin gulped and started over. "Dragonberries. They are the price of our release."

"I know." Bloorg lifted a squarecut crystal of smoky color in his hand. "The Chief of the squarears tries to know all. Watch!"

With a wave of his boneless fingers Bloorg changed the flat smoky surface into a living picture. In the picture was a chimaera, a now-animate Stapular, and Kian, John, and Kelvin.

Kelvin gulped. "That's in the larder. Where we were kept. And—is this television?" That was another unnatural wonder he could live without!

"Watch!" Bloorg commanded.

In the crystal a tiny chimaera was attacked by an even tinier Stapular. As Stapular hung on the sting there was a flash of blue light. The chimaera, John, and Kian fell unconscious. The tiny Kelvin staggered outside, struggling to tear up the sting from the ground. He pulled the sting out of its row and ran back with it. Stapular mouthed at him, and he was over the Mervania head with the sting positioned above a very feminine eye.

"No! No!" Kelvin cried, reaching for the crystal. He would not do it! He would not, though it happened over and over in a countless number of crystals a countless number of times. No crystal was going to make him do what he refused to do!

"Watch!" Bloorg said for the third time.

Kelvin controlled himself as well as he could. The miniature Kelvin did not destroy the chimaera with the sting. Instead it happened the way it had in life. Now he and Stapular were fighting, rolling over and over. Now Stapular was pulling off his own left hand, and the ruby light declawed the chimaera. Now the creature was at the mercy of Stapular.

"No! No!" Kelvin protested again, but the crystal merely showed what had happened. Gradually he realized that the image was not a separate thing, but an actual rendering of what had occurred, and could not change the outcome. The miniature Kelvin had out his sword, threw it, and Stapular appeared to die. Now the Mervania head and Kelvin were talking.

At the wave of a strange hand the picture vanished and there was only a smoky crystal in which the tendrils of smoke gradually stopped swirling. There was nothing there anymore except stone.

Kelvin's heart had been beating hard. He felt breathless, as though he had been running. The picture-show was over and he was back, though he had never left. Again he wished he were back in his old familiar, normal world with Heln and his mother Charlain and even his irritating sister Jon, who were surely leading a dull and safe existence.

"What will happen to the oil-blooded man?" he asked.

"The robot will be returned to its makers," Bloorg said. "They may or may not repair it."

"So Stapular may live again?" Did robots actually live? What was living? Stapular had spoken of them as though the living folk were inferior to it in every way.

"It may again be activated, but such a construct will never again deceive us, and none will get close to the chimaera. We owe you our thanks for discovering and nullifying that threat, which would surely otherwise have destroyed the last member of a unique species. We had been aware that Stapular was artificial, but not that he had a built-in laser. As for those doubts of yours about the nature of living, who is to say? There are scientists and sorcerers who hold that there is only thought and that all else is thought's product."

"I—I don't think I can absorb—"

"Never mind. It is only philosophical and abstract. What is important to us is what we perceive. What we accept as real, is real, and what we know to be illusion is generally illusion."

"I . . . see," Kelvin said, not seeing. Ask a simple question, get a lecture in metaphysics with particular emphasis on epistemology. From near infancy he had thought he had more sense.

"That is correct," Bloorg said. "He survives best who does not question too vigorously."

"Stapular won't be back to bother the chimaera again?" He wanted to be quite sure he had understood that correctly.

"Never."

Good enough. He was more than ready to go home.

"But you will return with the seeds," Bloorg reminded him.

"But you said—"

"Correct. You will not go to the island. You will bring the seeds here. They will be carried there by a froogear I designate."

Oh. "You will be waiting? I won't have to—"

Bloorg tapped the crystal. "I will keep watch."

"We will find the same setting? On the transporter?"

Bloorg seemed to have infinite patience. "You will if you look. Come."

They followed Bloorg to the transporter cave and inside. Bloorg showed them the dial on the transporter and where it was set. "Remember this mark. Turn the arrow until it points here exactly. This is where you will need to set the control in order to return. Remember this, all of you."

John nodded. "I don't think I could possibly forget."

"Now you wish to return home. Here is your home marking. Place the dial exactly, or you may go to a world that is not the one you left, such as the serpent world, here." He indicated another setting.

Kelvin reached out and twisted the dial until it clicked at the &, a symbol that reminded him of a coiling dragon but might stand for something else. He had seen his father make a symbol like that while writing. The other setting Bloorg had indicated had a ~ symbol, obviously a serpent.

"You will return now," Bloorg said, and disappeared with a definite pop and a slight scent of ozone.

"Well, Father, Kian—" Kelvin hated to do this, but had to ask. "We had been about to go to the serpent world—"

"I want to see Lonny first," Kian said. "Maybe we can get married right away, and then—"

Kelvin had been afraid he would say that. "Bloorg wanted us to return to our own world now. Maybe we should go there first, and then—" Then Kelvin could make an excuse to stay in his own frame.

"Bloorg doesn't know Lonny."

"Boys," their father interposed. "Can't we compromise? We brought dragonberries with us, but the jar of seeds labeled 'Astral Berries' was left in the installation by Mouvar. I suspect the seeds are still there. Kelvin, you could go back and get them while Kian and I wait here."

Kelvin frowned. Were "astral berries" and "dragon-berries" really the same, as his father assumed? Was the jar still there? It seemed to him now that he hadn't noticed it. Someone had changed the setting on the transporter or the three of them would not have ended up here. Whoever had used the transporter could have taken the seeds. Could it, he wondered, have been Mouvar? If so, what did it mean?

"Well, Kelvin?"

But if the jar remained there, this would be the easiest way to settle things. He could bring it back, give it to Bloorg, then explain that he was worried about Heln, and beg off the trip to the serpent world. "All right."

He took a firm grip on his resolve and stepped into the closet with all the clocks on the outside.

The usual things happened. He stepped out of the closet into the familiar chamber. Things looked the same. Nothing had changed a bit since he and his father and brother had left. Still, he was nervous. Any slight oversight could land him in serious trouble, as the recent adventure had shown.

He checked the table. As he had feared, the jar of seeds was missing.

Well, then, he would have to check to see if the boat was still on its ledge. He crossed the chamber, ducked his head out, saw the boat, and sniffed at the underground river. Time to return.

He checked to make certain the setting was for the chimaera's world—the # mark, surely for squarears—and stepped back into the closet. When he stepped out, nothing had changed in the chimaera's world except one thing:

His father and brother were gone.

Kian had no difficulty in persuading his father. "We'll just hop over and make certain we remember this setting. If we're wrong, we'll hop right back. Bloorg can almost certainly set the control right if I misremember." Kelvin had been standing before the control when Bloorg discussed it, so they hadn't seen the actual settings he had indicated to Kelvin.

"I think it was just before this mark." His father pointed at the & mark.

"I think, Father, that it was just one of the five intervening clicks short." He set it on the % mark.

"You want to try it that way?"

"Yes." Kian was so eager to reach Lonny that he was sure it was right.

"All right. Just be prepared to step out and then back if it's not the right world. That's what we should have done last time." John wasn't worried, because he knew they could check several settings if they had to, until they got the right one. Just so long as they didn't smell any spice!

"Yes, Father." Together they stepped into the closet.

They did not see the same display they had a moment ago

when Kelvin exited, but then they were in a slightly more familiar chamber with a soft bluish curtain of light at its far end and a large glowing EXIT sign.

"Come on, Father!" Kian said eagerly, starting across the smooth floor.

"Wait, Kian! You agreed we'd go right back."

"We will. I just want to step outside and make certain!"

There was no stopping him! Talk about your anxious bridegrooms! John started after him  and noticed something.

"There was dust on the floor before. We left our footprints in it. This chamber is clean! Either this is a different chamber, or someone's been here." John wasn't easy with either explanation; both meant trouble.

But Kian was already ducking through the shimmering curtain. He was as unconcerned as though it were sunshine. Not for the first time John had to marvel at how quickly they all adjusted to the unfamiliar and utterly strange. Still, the boy needed to learn proper caution.

"It's here, Father! The ledge, the ladder, and the tree! This *has* to be right!"

But John had doubts. "Come back inside!"

"All right. Just let me get a breath of—"

John waited for him to finish. When he did not, he grew alarmed. Fearful now, yet determined, he crossed to the glowing curtain and stepped through.

Outside. Fresh air. Beautiful day. High on a cliffside. He looked back. The illusion of a solid rock wall just behind was perfect. If this was technology, and he felt it was, the scientists responsible deserved congratulations.

But where was Kian? He advanced to the edge of the cliff. The ladder was there, made of something unfamiliar on Earth, a woven metallic substance he suspected would never age.

"Kian? Kian?" He was really worried now.

There was no answer. Had the lad climbed down into the tree below? Then why wasn't the ladder over the edge of the cliff and dangling down into the branches?

Fear prickled at him, raising the hairs on the back of his neck. He didn't want to leave Kian but his every instinct told him to return. Better to fetch Kelvin and come back for an organized search than to risk getting caught by whatever had happened to Kian.

He started around, ready to duck through the curtain. At that moment human hands reached from apparently solid rock and laid hold of his arms.

For an instant he thought the hands were Kian's. Then he saw that they were larger, and had dark hairs on their backs. This was someone else!

He had only time to grasp this before he was pulled forward, against a rock face that vanished to become a blue curtain of shimmering light at a spot he knew he had not left.

## CHAPTER 16

# *Charlain*

*C*harlain arrived at the palace at noon. In her bag on the dappled gray plowhorse were only her fortune cards and the remains of the lunch she had prepared. She had thought about bringing herbs in case Heln had nausea or other child-carrying complaints. Then she had realized that the doctor here was the best and that she wasn't versed in anything other than amateur prophecy.

How grateful she should be for that one lone skill, she thought, dismounting from her horse and turning the reins over to the stable groom. True, it had deceived her at times. She had known she would lose Hal after a time and she had feared it would be by death. Better to another woman, she had tried to believe. Better to have him happy than to have him destroyed. But what would John think of it? What would his decision be, should he ever return? The cards so far had revealed nothing.

"Mama! Mama! I'm so glad to see you!"

A sudden tattoo of feet and the shock of collision. A slim boyish figure was suddenly in her arms, hugging her as though life had trickled to its inevitable end.

"Not so hard, Jon, not so hard! Goodness, I can hardly breathe! Only boys are supposed to hug this hard, you roughneck!" She held her daughter back at arm's length. Long yellow hair, greenish eyes, properly filled bosom—she had produced a beauty! She and John. To think that when the children had left on their great adventure with the dragon, really not that long ago, Jon had more resembled the tow-haired skinny boy than the rapidly maturing girl she had actually been. Now Jon was satisfied to be all girl, and that was just as well.

Without knowing why she did so, Charlain reached out and tweaked her daughter's pointy ears. She had done that years ago, mostly from affection. Jon had always resented it because her big brother hadn't ear tips that could be tweaked as effectively.

"How's Heln?" *No sense in delaying it. Get right to the problem.*

"She's . . . doing well." Jon's tone nullified her words, just as they had when as a child she'd tried to conceal the full truth.

"You're hiding something." Just sharp enough to make her answer.

"Mother, why would I do that? You're the one who reads cards. You know everything."

*Yes, Jon would still think that.* Charlain permitted herself a smile. She walked meekly with her daughter into the royal palace holding her hand. Not long ago it had been she who had led her daughter.

Into the guest wing and down the hall, through a door, and they were there. Heln was sitting up in bed. Brown eyes gleaming, black hair shining as she brushed. She appeared well. Considering what the cards had shown, Charlain wondered.

"Heln." Simple, careful greeting to a daughter-in-law.

"Mother-in-law!" Heln put down the hairbrush on the comforter. Her tone was right but her action seemed mechanical.

They embraced. Heln seemed rigid, not at all the warm

girl Charlain had met when she and Kelvin and his bride visited. Something was definitely wrong. She wished that she had been a little less mortal and had studied witchcraft. The cards actually told her very little, however much they suggested.

"You are feeling well, Heln?" A direct question seemed indicated.

"Yes." Almost mechanical, as had been her careful setting down of the hairbrush. Not at all as Charlain would have expected Kelvin's expectant wife to answer.

"She had sickness in the mornings," Jon said. As usual, she was volunteering information when she had the chance. "Dr. Sterk gave me something for her. I put it in her tefee."

"It helped?" Morning sickness was not unusual. She had experienced it while carrying both Kelvin and Jon.

"Cleaned it right up. She hasn't heaved since."

No smile from Heln. Yet Jon's words should have evoked one. Her daughter was a lady, but she did not always use a lady's words.

"We've got a lot of catching up to do," Charlain said, taking the chair Jon brought. "All the news, family and general."

"But Mother, you know everything!" Jon said, and laughed. Still no smile from Heln. She seemed as humorless now as when Jon had found her in Franklin's notorious Girl Market, where she had been raped. Indeed, her attempted suicide by eating dragonberries, then, had opened up the whole new world of astral separation, and given her reason to live after all.

"I'm really not too clear on this war situation. How'd we get into it? My cards won't tell."

"Well, Mother," Jon said, heaving a sigh. She was being quite formal, now, for her, in contrast to her private greeting. That was another signal of trouble. "The situation is complicated."

"Many situations are. Are you implying, Daughter, that your mother can't understand?"

"I can't understand it myself, Mother. Why Kelvin's away or why Lester's fighting. In many ways it doesn't make sense."

"Start from the beginning." Charlain took Jon's hand in

hers, in much the way she had when she had wanted her to tell about some school fight.

"All right, Mother. We were all of us summoned to the palace and briefed by . . . by the king."

"King Rufurt?"

"Y-yes."

A lie. The tremble in Jon's hands said it clearly. Jon was not a trembler by nature except when she lied. For some reason Jon wished to conceal something about their king. Could it be that their king was not who he seemed? If this was true it explained the uncertainty card. Charlain felt a prickle on the back of her neck.

Later, when she was alone, Charlain laid out the cards again, checking on the things that had disturbed her most about her daughter's narration. Rather than ease her concern, this made the prickling much worse. Heln was in terrible trouble, about which Charlain could do nothing. But Lester, Jon's husband, was also in dire straits, and about this she could do something.

In the morning Charlain surprised Jon if not Heln by saying goodbye. "I have to get back to the farm. Hal's a dear, taking care of the livestock, and I know Easter will keep the garden weeded, but I don't want to impose on them."

"Mother," Jon said, taking her arm and leading her aside, "how can you—?"

"Because I'm not angry with them. Either of them."

"But—"

"I always knew I'd lose Hal, but the cards didn't explain. When the romance card came up, I knew. It was a relief! Better that he live a happy life than that he die. He was a good father to you and Kelvin and he worked hard. He never intended to do what he did; it was fated."

"But Mother, if Lester ever did such a thing, I'd—"

"Yes, of course you would, dear. But your foster father isn't Lester. It was in the cards. He really couldn't help it."

"But to start a child with that woman! That wasn't right!"

"No, of course it wasn't. But then your natural father succumbed to the queen of Rud and had a son named Kian. The marriage wasn't dissolved when he met me."

"But Mother, Zoanna betrayed her vows! You—"

"It's not the same, Jon. Easter is a good woman. Simple, young, but good. Hal loves her and she him. I declared us divorced for their sakes. My marriage to Hal is now over. His marriage to her is valid. They have a difficult enough course, setting up a homestead, without my making it worse."

"So you let them use *your* homestead!" Jon said bitterly. "How nice for them!" Her tone said that she would never have been that generous. "You're helping them get set up, by giving them free board, and even paying them for taking care of your farm!"

"Hush, hush. You mustn't sound that way. He was a good husband to me, and a good father to you, when we thought your real father dead."

Jon's eyes lighted with a sudden fathoming. "So you think you and my real father might—"

"I don't know, dear. We'll see. The cards don't show me quite enough."

"It seems to me they never did. Until afterward."

"Your father would say that. Well—" She hugged Jon one final time. "Take good care of Heln and the babe. We'll have a much longer visit another time."

"I'll take care of her," Jon said. "But I'm scared for her! Mother, can't you stay?"

"No. I told you why. Now don't pester." With that small lie she was off to the stable and her horse. She did not look back to Jon, who was not following. Jon pretended not to have sentiment, but her mother knew that her outrageous daughter would be secretly wiping at her eyes. Reunions had a way of bringing pain, and this one did especially. Since Jon had turned fourteen and gone off adventuring with Kelvin, they had seen one another only on brief visits.

She rode away from the palace to the crossroads. There she turned resolutely toward Kance. Her son-in-law was in grave peril. The cards had revealed as much, though she had not revealed this to Jon. Had she told her daughter, she knew Jon would be with her, carrying her sling. Charlain couldn't have that. Jon had to stay with Heln. Because it was obvious that something was seriously amiss with Heln, and she suspected hostile magic. Until she could get the cards to be more specific, she had to pretend ignorance, so as not to tip her hand. She could not help Heln directly, the cards said, but might be able to help indirectly, if she found out exactly what was wrong, and if she could find Kelvin and tell him privately. Since she had no idea where Kelvin was, she had to follow up on another course in the interim.

If she could save Lester, maybe then she could find the good witch Helbah, or let the witch find her. It would take a witch to save Heln and the baby, she felt certain. She just hoped that she could do something to benefit both Jon and Heln, and that she would be able to do it in time.

"Cursed cards!" Charlain muttered. "Why is it you can never really tell me anything?" But she knew she was blaming them falsely. The cards could do only what they could do, no more.

She rode on, past the road marker, and into the forbidden territory of Kance.

St. Helens rolled over on the prickly straw and looked up through the bars of his dungeon cell. He rubbed dust from his eyes. The two boyish faces were still there. Two child heads, each wearing a crown of gold.

"Stupid-looking, ain't he, Kildee?"

"Yah. What you think we should do with him, Kildom?"

"Torture. Bend back his thumbs. Tweak his big nose. Put cream on his feet and get Katbah to lick it off. Shove a washcloth in his ears the way Helbah does to us!"

"That's good! That's very good! Let's!"

"Boys," St. Helens managed to say, "the witch, is she—"

"Wouldn't you like to know, blowtop!" Kildee said, and both kings chortled at his cleverness. He dropped a pebble down that bounced off St. Helens' face, and they chortled again.

St. Helens permitted himself a glare. *Damn Katzenjammer kids! Those two need a good hiding! Best thing for bad behavior ever invented. Royal brats or not!*

"Look, he's maaaad!"

"Yah, let's get some more stones!"

"Stones? How about darts?"

The boys rushed away, giggling. St. Helens lay on the dank straw, anticipating more mischief.

Then there was a dark, furry face where the boys' faces had been. Dark yellow eyes and a tail forming a question mark. The witch's familiar! He had thought it dead. According to lore, a witch's familiar was a part of her in a real sense, so that when one died the other died soon after. This probably meant that Helbah was alive.

But why was the houcat here? It did not look healthy. Why should it waste its energy spying on him?

The day wore on. The boys did not return. St. Helens, turning the matter over and over in his mind, saw no reason to regret their absence.

Lomax drew back his sword from yet another unfortunate Kance soldier and watched him topple from the saddle. They were winning the battle, mainly because they had come upon a small force. Then he saw the real reason. Coming down the hill behind the Kance forces were other fighters dressed in the Kelvinian uniform. He strained his eyes to see through the dust. It was Lester's troops, it had to be! But where was Lester?

A scream took his attention. Turning round in the saddle he saw one of his men finishing off a Kance swordsman as young Phillip's horse shied and the boy pulled the reins.

The Kance soldiery retreated, pursued by the Kelvinian troops. Lomax rode over to check on Aratex's one-time king.

Phillip had an ugly open sword wound on his left arm. Blood stained the boy's clothing and dripped onto the shield he had dropped. Phillip stared wild-eyed at him, as if he couldn't have imagined that he might get wounded.

"It—it hurts!" Phillip said.

"That is the nature of a battle wound," Lomax said. He felt some sympathy, but dared not show it. *After all,* he thought, hardening his heart, *he's responsible for what happened to St. Helens.*

"I'm not ready to die!" Phillip wailed. "I'm not ready!"

With that the boy who had been a king and more recently had shed blood and even more recently bled his own, shuddered as if he had plunged into snow. His face turned white as flour and then, like a sack of that substance, he swayed and toppled from the saddle.

Lomax drew in a sharp breath. Phillip had said he wanted to be hanged, but hadn't meant it. Now he might have died after all.

Mor was worried. The fighting was going just too well lately. What had happened to the phantoms that had plagued them? What about the magical slowing of time? Was the witch running out of magic? Was she dead?

Ahead, a great shout. "General! General! General Crumb!"

"Yes?" He waited for the excited scout to reach him and get his breath.

"General! General, sir! Ahead—"

"Yes, yes, out with it!"

"The caps, General! The caps are just over that rise! We've arrived, General! Arrived at last at the seat of our enemies!"

Mor, though he felt he should do otherwise, heaved a great sigh.

Zoanna looked into her crystal and smiled. The war was going so much better than she had anticipated. Here the Mor forces were already at the caps and the Hermans and the Lester forces less than half a day from joining them. It would soon be all up for the witch and the brats. The brats would look nice in a cage, while Helbah might even teach her a few things before Rowforth stopped torturing her. It had been a stroke of lucky genius to prod that foolish boy into breaking the truce and wounding the witch! The St. Helens commander had seemed about to back away from battle, but that had precipitated immediate combat.

She frowned. Would it be wise to keep the witch alive at all? Witches, while they lived, could always be dangerous. How well she knew, from her own experience! The traditional fate of the defeated witch was burning, because that usually killed her thoroughly enough to make her stay dead.

She studied Helbah through the crystal. The old woman didn't look as though she had power. Lying in bed, turning, tossing, covered in sweat. Her gaunt familiar sitting by her on a

chair, staring at her from wild yellow eyes. Only the interces-
sion of that familiar had saved her life on the battlefield; the
houcat had lent her enough of its life force to sustain her until
she was brought back to the palace doctor.

"I could destroy you right now, Helbah! I know enough
now, and if need be I can always return to college." She smiled
reminiscently at the thought of her horned instructor. She had
but one coin with which to pay that horny one, but he was
always ready for more of that. "But I don't think I have to,
now. I don't think you're a menace."

Contentedly Zoanna blanked the crystal with a directed
thought. The tiny bubbles swirled like a confined section of the
creamy way in the night sky.

"Helbah, I'll keep you alive until I defeat you. And maybe
for a short time after. I need to learn, and Rowforth needs his
amusements. Maybe I can make you seem young and pretty, so
that he'll enjoy your screams even more. Sadism is always
better with an attractive and innocent-seeming subject."

Seldom had Zoanna felt so thoroughly content and so
superbly confident.

Lester gasped as he stood holding on to the slim tree trunk
and watched his men ride over the rise. A scout rode back
accompanied by his second in command, Lieutenant
Klumpecker.

"We've driven them off, Commander," Lieutenant
Klumpecker said. "And St. Helens' Hermans are meeting our
own men."

"The caps?"

"Less than a day's march away."

"St. Helens?"

"I haven't seen him. But the boy who is his friend—the
former king of Aratex—is wounded."

"Bad?"

"I can't say. I wasn't that near."

Probably bad. Lester couldn't imagine St. Helens deserting his troops, so probably he too was dead. That left his father
Mor and himself in charge of Kelvinia's forces. He wondered
how far away his father was. Had he come all the way through
Klingland? Was he still alive?

"We can take the caps in two days?"

"Probably, Commander."

"Good." There was a chance, just a chance, he thought, that he might live to see it accomplished.

Holding that thought he gradually loosened his grip on the sapling and let his knees buckle with him all the way down to the sweet, green grass.

"Commander! Commander Crumb!" he heard, but the voice was uninteresting and far, far away.

## CHAPTER 17

# New Old Enemies

John found himself in a lighted chamber surrounded by men in uniforms. The uniforms were familiar because they had the same cut if not the color of the uniforms worn by the soldiers of Hud. But was this really the same world? Or was it an almost-the-same world? Would he face gigantic silver serpents again? Was there an evil King Rowforth here, or a duplicate king almost the same?

He looked at Kian, held by two of the soldiers, disarmed. His own arms were similarly taken. With regret he watched the soldiers go through his pack.

"King Hoofourth will be interested," said the craggy-faced Lieutenant.

"King Hoofourth of what country?" John asked.

"Silence, prisoner!" The slap stung his face, as he knew the lieutenant intended. "You will speak when spoken to!"

Exactly as it had been in Hud! Only of course this could not be the frame where there was a kingdom named Hud or a kingdom named Rud. It would have a name that would be similar and much else would be similar, but not identical.

Obviously the bad guys were in control here; there had been no hero of prophecy to set things right. It was almost like a movie that kept subtly changing every time it was watched. Only this was no movie, and like it or not he was a participant.

Movie—now there was one of the few things he missed in his home world. How nice it would be to go into a theater and have a vicarious experience! There was a lot to be said for vicarious experience; it didn't lock a person in a cell for months or years, it didn't threaten the person with death. He could break it off at any point and go home to the familiar. That would be nice, right now! If he got out of this, maybe he would see about finding his way to his true home. It wasn't as if there were a lot to hold him in the magic worlds, now that his children were grown, and he had lost the one woman he really cared for. The last thing he intended to do was interfere with Charlain's second marriage, and his mere presence in her frame would do that. So it behooved him to go elsewhere and find his own woman, and try to forget.

"We'll take them to the capital. King Hoofourth will put them in a dungeon, torture them a little, and get answers from them before throwing them away."

"Answers?" the fellow officer asked.

"Like why are they here? What are they doing at the secret cave? Are they planning on invading us?"

"Oh, you mean routine stuff." The officer pulled his right earlobe. It was a round ear, similar to the others here. Once it had seemed that round ears were a sign of special qualities, but now it was apparent that their shape was all that distinguished them. There were truly special pointeared folk—he thought of Charlain again—and ignoble roundeared folk, such as evil King Rowforth of Hud. Unfortunately, King Hoofourth sounded similar.

"Now, out!" Pushing Kian and himself ahead of them the soldiers emerged from the wall of rock. John had to shake himself mentally. That chamber they'd been in was identical to the other except that it had no transporter. Did the bad guys in this frame know about the network of transporters? If they did, why didn't they use theirs? If they didn't, why did they stay here, watching?

"You and you stay. Watch," the main officer commanded, using the celebrated army volunteer system to select two men. "You, down the tree. You, you guide the prisoners."

Without hesitation Kian moved ahead to the cliff and the ladder and descended after the two soldiers. John followed, feeling the unnecessary prod the man behind gave to his buttocks. The descent into the tree was one he had not actually made before, though he had climbed an identical tree and ladder in the frame of the silver serpents.

He wondered, as he carefully made his way down, branch by branch, if this time there would be a rescue. Maybe, just maybe, it was foreordained that he and his son were to die here. That would certainly simplify Kelvin's life, allowing him to complete the prophecy without interference.

*Now I'm thinking like Charlain,* he thought. *Next I'll be reading her Book of Prophecy and studying her predicting cards!*

*But will there ever be a chance? Will I ever see Kelvin's mother again? Will I ever even see her duplicate?*

He sighed soundlessly. Obviously his heart wasn't in his resolution to stay out of Charlain's life. But if he should encounter one of her alternates in another frame, and not an evil one, what then? Actually there had been another woman in his life, evil Queen Zoanna. In the serpent frame he had encountered her good version, Queen Zanaan. Now there was a prospect to conjure with! If Kian could marry in that frame, why not John himself?

His feet touched the ground, bringing his mind to reality. What use were dreams, when he wasn't free to do anything about them? There were more troops and horses waiting here. There was no chance for escape.

At the commander's orders they mounted horses and rode what seemed a very familiar path. Would they meet flopears, he wondered? Maybe Smoothy Jac's duplicate? What about Lonny? Would her duplicate appear? And Zanaan—suppose she was here, too? That could really complicate things!

They rode on, through what became a very tiring day.

Kelvin stepped out of the transporter closet into an empty chamber. Kian and his father were nowhere in sight. Yet they must have come here. Should he stay and search? Or go back and ask the squarear's advice?

He decided to have a look outside. This seemed to be the frame of the silver serpents, but wasn't quite right. There wasn't the dust he remembered. Of course that could mean that this was the right frame and that others had since been here.

He crossed the chamber and walked through the shimmering golden curtain under the glowing EXIT sign. Outside, the cliff behind his back, he saw the tree and the ladder he expected. Only the ladder was down into the tree now, and it had been pulled up. He frowned, wondering, and then his gauntlets began to tingle.

If there was one thing he would never do again, he had promised himself, it was to ignore the gauntlets' warning. Obeying them as much as his own thoughts, he drew his sword and whirled.

A uniformed man, half in and half out of what appeared to be solid rock, was about to strike him on the head with a short club. His sword confronted the man, and at the same time he found his voice, letting the gauntlets somehow choose his words and rap it out as a command.

"Freeze! How many of you in there?" he demanded.

The man was evidently startled to have the tables so abruptly turned. "J-just two. Me and Bert."

"Tell him to come out. Slowly, without a weapon."

"You hear that, Bert? He's got a sword against my gullet. Don't be a hero, Bert. I'm your friend and the commanding officer isn't."

Bert came through the rock, unarmed.

Kelvin sighed with relief. He had been afraid the hidden man would fire an arrow from cover. Give the gauntlets a chance and they took control!

"Where are my friends? Do you have them?"

Bert spoke, looking scared. "Those two men? On the way to the king's dungeon."

"King? What king?"

"King Hoofourth, of course!"

So it was a different frame! He had thought so, when he

saw the setting at %, but was taking nothing for granted now. "King of what country?"

"King of the Kingdom of Scud," the crafty-faced roundear said.

So it was a frame not too different from the silver serpent one, but not identical. "Tell me, is there an outlaw somewhere in the desert by the name of Jac?"

"Jac? You mean Scarface Jac?"

Why not? "Enemy to the king?"

"What else? An outlaw has to be, no matter what else."

"Skin thief?"

The soldiers looked puzzled. "Skin? I don't know what—"

"Silver!" Kelvin said impatiently. Not that it mattered, but the silver skins of serpents had proven to be of great importance.

Both men shrugged. Bert said, "I know he's robbed, but—"

"Doesn't matter." Kelvin decided he'd pay the local Jac a visit before planning his rescue of his father and brother. Even with his gauntlets and the Mouvar weapon and the levitation belt he was just one person. This frame, like every frame he had visited, probably contained some surprises.

"Tell me, can anyone in this frame levitate?"

"You mean fly? Mouvar is said to have flown."

"Good enough," Kelvin said briskly. "Turn your backs."

The two men obeyed him and he wasted no time in activating the levitation belt. Silently he rose above their heads and above the cliffs that towered higher than he remembered, then moved out over the tree and the river. The river was much broader than the rivers in the other frames. He looked back and saw the two soldiers still standing with their backs turned. Good, no arrows would be following him!

He settled down to the business of flying. It wasn't nearly as hard as he had once imagined. His father said he had a natural ability, as he did himself. He gathered that some people couldn't get used to the ground sliding away beneath their feet, the clouds rolling in front of their faces. It wasn't anything to do with bravery, for he certainly wasn't brave. Nor could he credit the gauntlets for his acceptance of flying. It was just a case of being lucky in one thing and unlucky in others.

As he drifted dreamlike over the rolling hills of the kingdom of Scud, he found himself thinking about luck. He had been lucky. Time after time he had been saved from impossible situations by what seemed chance. The silver serpents that could have swallowed him, for instance. The chimaera that could have cooked him with tail-lightning and eaten him steaming hot. Was that the effect of the prophecy, as his mother would say? Was that what was protecting him? To him it felt like mere fortune, that could reverse at any time. He really didn't have a lot of confidence in the accuracy of the prophecy, at least not as it might relate to him. It might be talking about some other roundear entirely.

But that line of thinking led only to mischief. It was better to believe that his mother was right. That the prophecy applied to him, and that he would prevail. So he would do his best to believe that, so that he could rescue his father and brother.

Down below was the first of the connected valleys. Serpent's Valley, home of great silver serpents and their spiritual brothers the dwarf flopears. He looked close but saw no serpents. No holes in cliffs that could be serpent tunnels. Sad to think that they were not here. What would Hud have been without its serpents and flopears? What would Scud be like? Whatever dangers he faced here he hoped—no, *knew* now that he could handle them. With his levitation belt and his gauntlets and his antimagic weapon there just couldn't be anything against which he couldn't triumph. Unless there was another chimaera here, which seemed highly unlikely. Like it or not he was a hero, uncertain nature and weak stomach aside.

He left the valley, passing over the cliff where Kian had once fought a flopear and, almost miraculously, survived. The flopear had also survived, he remembered, falling with his club off the cliff and down, down, to land with a probable splatting sound. As Kian had told it the tough little warrior had not only survived the fall, but had a short time later intercepted him and Lonny at the base of the cliff! Obviously Kian too had lived through great dangers, but so too had that murderous flopear. If it was really the same one.

How familiar the country looked! How very familiar. He flew at near minimum speed into the desert. At home they called this land the Sadlands, while in Hud it was the Barrens. In Scud it would be called something equally appropriate. Strange, though near duplication in people and geography prevailed in related frames the names always changed. Fortunately, perhaps, otherwise the confusion for a frame-hopper would be even worse. Suppose he were to meet his mother's duplicate in this frame, and she not only looked like his mother and acted like her, but had his mother's name? Or suppose his wife? If he met Heln here and she looked the same as the Heln he had left at home, and had the same name, he'd think of her as the same person. That could be very bad, and he was thankful that duplicate individuals bore separate identification. For one thing, the only way a local Heln could have the same name was if she had married a local Kelvin. Was he ready to meet himself?

He shook his head, trying to free it of burgeoning concepts that threatened to make it explode. Flying along at a little over a good running speed he began some unaccustomed philosophizing. It was what he had warned himself against. The squarear had said it was bad to think about such things, but now he did. The thought was, which was real? Was it home or was it the silver-serpent world, or the chimaera world, or his father's Earth? Bad question, and quite senseless, maybe. For of course all realities were real in equal proportion. It depended where a person was, and when. Thus the warriors of the past, and ancestors he had never seen or known existed— they seemed unreal, yet were the very substance of reality, for who would exist without that ancestry? Likewise every possibility, every slight change with infinite variations was, by the very nature of things, real and leading to real realities somewhere else. When such realities mixed, as when folk used the Mouvar network to travel between them, or when John Knight and his band accidentally crossed over—

And there was an answer to one riddle! There would be no Kelvin here, no Heln, because they were the children of the members of that group. They would exist only in the particular world to which that band had come. There might be a Charlain here, but she could never have married John Knight. Maybe Hal Hackleberry, or his equivalent, but not—

Head buzzing, as it always did when he tried to think about such things, Kelvin looked down and spied what had to be Scud's outlaw camp. He would land boldly, and—

But suppose it was the bad Jac who had stolen the dragon scale and kidnapped Jon? That was in his home frame, but couldn't a Jac of that nature exist here instead of the Jac he had more recently known? He hoped the answer was no, but he couldn't be certain. An evil Jac and an evil king in the same frame was more than he thought he could manage. Would Lonny be here? And another dwarf either as evil as Queeto or as saintly as Heeto? These thoughts were making his head more than just swim. The height did not make him dizzy, but the thinking it engendered did. He had to get down and put an end to this.

Since he did not want to be pierced with crossbow bolts or arrows, he would land a short distance away and walk in to the camp. Probably he should have been thinking about that instead of those other things.

Moving his fingers carefully on the control levers on the belt's buckle he came to a stop in midair and descended until his feet touched sand. Nothing moving now, as it had been while he was aloft. He was once more on solid earth, and so his thoughts were grounded too.

Ahead was the camp. Horses, men moving. If they had not seen him in the air, they would spy him now.

Even as he thought this, two horses approached. As they came nearer he recognized the riders and men he had known, though of course these were not the same.

"Stranger, who be you? Quick, or die!"

That was poor unfortunate Smith, who had died such a ghastly death! Kelvin strove to get his thoughts in order, knowing that the threat was real and so were their weapons.

"I have business with your leader."

*"My leader?"* The man was incredulous.

"Scarface Jac. He is your leader, isn't he?"

This Smith seemed to hesitate as if trying to decide whether to use the crossbow he had leveled at Kelvin, or merely cut him down with a sword. Then, deciding it could do no harm, he circled his horse behind the stranger and said, "Walk into camp. I'll be watching you."

Kelvin wished he had landed closer. By the time he was among the tents he was sweating from exertion under the desert sun. A scorpiocrab scuttled out of his way, reminding him of the chimaera. Other than that and a couple of thorny plants he saw no sign of desert life.

They emerged from tents almost as though by magic, Jac among them. He really was a scarface, with a scar that was twice the size and ugliness of Cheeky Jac's, the onetime bandit of the Sadlands. He waited for Kelvin to speak.

"I'm Kelvin Knight Hackleberry," Kelvin said. "I need your help to rescue some friends of mine."

"Why?" Jac asked. It was a challenge as much as a question.

"Their captors are the king's men. My friends and I can help you defeat the king's men. You see, we're from a different frame."

"From a different frame and you want to help us defeat King Hoofourth, Scud's good and proper king? Just why do you want to do that and why do you think I'd be interested?"

Oh-oh, Kelvin thought. This wasn't quite as he had anticipated.

"In the other frame your king was a tyrant and had to be replaced. Isn't he a tyrant here as well?"

At that moment the first woman Kelvin had seen came from a tent and walked straight to Jac. She put her face against the bandit's brawny arm and looked up adoringly. It was Lonny, or at least her duplicate. The girl Kian wanted to marry.

But this wasn't the same frame! Here Lonny could marry the bandit, who had indeed been attracted to her in the serpent frame. There, she could marry Kian. There was no conflict. Just so long as Kelvin managed to rescue Kian and get him there.

"You call our king a tyrant?" the outlaw demanded. "You want him overthrown?"

Kelvin tried to tell himself that it wasn't genuine anger in the bandit's voice. Carefully he said, "It may be that I do not understand. In a world nearly like this one there was a king who was very bad. In that world an outlaw named Jac fought and conquered him."

"You would have me commit treason?" Jac's face was very red, and the scar tissue in the star-shaped mark on his cheek stood out ghastly white.

"I'm not here to start trouble," Kelvin said. "But if your sovereign resembles this other, you must want to be rid of him."

"I must, must I?" This was spoken very agressively.

This had to be a mistake, Kelvin thought. Time to rectify it. He fingered the controls on his belt and instantly was high above the bandits' heads.

"You come down here!" Jac the bandit ordered.

Kelvin ignored the order. He climbed to a suitable elevation, then moved the lever forward for full speed. He was just in time. Even at this rate of motion, he saw the arrows and crossbow bolts come perilously close.

He heard shouted orders and looked back to see men mounting horses. Fortunately the belt could outrun any horse, even the oversized battle steeds.

He sped away across blank desert, then swung to the east. He would catch up with the king's party himself. Even if the gauntlets and the Mouvar weapon couldn't handle the situation, he'd still have to try. If the prophecy his mother believed were true, he'd have to survive this frame and get back home to fulfill it at what he hoped would be some far future time.

But then, as the green hills appeared, a disturbing thought intruded itself. Just maybe the prophecy had no effect in other frames. He always had believed himself capable of getting killed, prophecy or no prophecy, and in a different frame death might be likely. He remembered unpleasantly almost dying when he first arrived in the frame so much like this one. If it hadn't been for Heeto, the heroic dwarf in that frame, he knew he *would* have died. No, no, the prophecy might or might not be real, but it was nothing to stake one's life on.

Down below the road that led, if the geography of this frame did not diverge too far from the frames he remembered, to the royal palace, there was a big cloud of dust. He slowed, hovered, and tried to make out what was happening.

There were horses prancing. Swords were flashing. Men were dying. Gods, he realized belatedly, it was a battle!

He lowered himself silently, trusting that the combatants would be too involved to look up. In the swirling dust he saw his father and brother kept back by guards wearing the Scud uniform. More uniformed soldiers were battling men who wore no uniforms at all but were clad much as were the bandits in the desert. Those who fought the soldiers must be the good guys. But were they? Uncomfortably, he thought of the encounter he had just had. Similar frames were deceptive in their dissimilarities.

*I can't take anything for granted,* he thought. *Just because they are taking Father and Kian to the palace doesn't necessarily mean harm to them.*

But he was almost sure it did. Something about the way the soldiers had acted at the cliffs convinced him that the royal side just couldn't be the right side.

Having convinced himself, he acted. Skillfully he moved the lever. When he was at precisely the right spot he cut off the belt power completely.

He dropped, sword in gauntleted hand, like a heavy stone. He was about to join the fray.

# CHAPTER 18

## *Healings*

*C*harlain saw the dust clouds ahead and heard the drumming of horses' hooves, the clang of swords, and the screams of men. Battle. Men seemed to take such foolish joy in combat! It seemed to her that the very knowledge lent wings to her horse's feet. Not away from danger, but toward it. Toward Lester and whatever danger threatened his life, that the cards had shown her.

*Why,* she wondered, bouncing uphill on horseback, *am I doing this? I haven't any magical witch's fire! I haven't any laser weapon! I haven't even a sword! What's to prevent some mighty thewed swordsman from swinging down on me?*

A moment later she was at the crest of the hill, and saw just such a swordsman as she had feared. His sword blade was raised high and caught the bright rays of the sun here above the dust clouds. In a moment he would reach her and that blade would lop off her head.

She sat on her horse. She stopped it with a gentle "Whoa, Nellie," and waited with hands on reins. The Kance soldier could see her plainly, could see that she was a woman and unarmed.

Of course there were other things soldiers did besides killing, as Heln had found out . . .

The soldier's horse slowed. The young man, hardly older than Kelvin but more heroically formed, stared at her, mouth agape. The sword hesitated. His blue eyes, cold but still youthful, studied her. Then, as abruptly as he had appeared, he lowered the sword, sheathed it, and rode away. She watched him disappear over the rise and then down into the cloud of battle, and she hoped that he too would be a survivor this day.

What had done it? Certainly not her looks, though she believed she was still attractive. Was it because he saw his own mother in her eyes? She could not be certain, but she knew that an ancient witchery had served her well this day. Soldiers commonly killed soldiers in the heat of battle, but not un-armed, unresisting, and thoroughly helpless innocents. A warrior the young Kance soldier might be, but not a mindless, consciousless slaughterer.

She took a deep breath, and then she simply waited until the battle sound diminished and the dust settled in the valley. Soldiers in Kance uniform sped past her on lathered horses. Below, the color of the uniforms resolved themselves into Hermandy's muddy clay and Kelvinia's forest-green. The side that she had expected to win this battle had in fact won.

She was still waiting when the Hermandy soldier approached on horseback. Following after fleeing Kance warriors he had spotted her and turned. Now he rode forward deliberately. He was a big man with hair on his face and a cruel set to his mouth. When he stared into her eyes she knew instinctively that he would not be dissuaded as easily as the first had been.

Should she scream? Who would hear her? Should she wheel her horse and try to run? That charger he rode could readily overtake her mare. Should she look seductive and try to buy a little time? The Herman might not be interested. Judging from appearances, his lust might be mainly for causing pain.

She was not certain what she should do, so she merely waited. What would happen would happen. It might be a quick end, or a lingering one.

"Wait, Private!"

The young man wore mail over his uniform of a Kelvinian guardsman. He was covered head to toe with battle dust. The quarter-moon painted on his helmet proclaimed him officer, though she did not know the rank.

"Lomax! You want her first?" The toothy grin on the Herman was at least as disturbing as his drawn sword.

"I don't like your tone, Private! I know this woman."

"Do, huh." The Herman's horse came closer to Lomax's. "I suppose that means you want her all for yourself."

Without warning the Herman's sword swung at the guardsman. But Lomax ducked aside and sustained a bright coppery slash on his left shoulder. The mail he wore protected him, but barely. His own sword snaked out, and with more luck than science he speared the Herman through the throat.

The Herman toppled and crashed to the ground. He lay there on the grass, just another casualty.

Lomax cleaned his sword, then inspected his injury and the damage to his mail. Finally he turned his eyes to her. He studied her face for several long heartbeats. Then he said: "Mrs. Hackleberry? Kelvin's mother?"

"Why yes." She was astonished at being recognized. "But how do you know? We've never met, have we?"

"We have met, but a long time ago. Remember when you read cards for people? You told me I'd be a soldier and do many brave deeds. I thought you were wrong and my mother thought you wrong. But then we had our war for freedom and afterward I became a guardsman for King Rufurt. Today, as you see, I'm a soldier, wearing Hermandy mail."

She shook her head, amazed. Sometimes even she didn't believe in the power of prophecy. "You and your mother. She wanted to know if you'd finish school and I said yes. Then I saw the other, the battle card, and I had to say."

"And you told her my father would die and she'd remarry. You were right."

"The cards were right. The cards that unfortunately can only indicate. They could not have told me how your father was to die or when, or if there was a way of saving him."

"Nothing's perfect. The cards indicated, and they were correct."

"It is always thus. There's nothing truer than prophecy."

There was silence between them, as pregnant as thought. Soldiers came up and dragged away the body of the private; they had seen what had happened. Then Lomax broke it with the logical question: "Why are you here, Mrs. Hackleberry?"

"It isn't Mrs. Hackleberry any longer," she said. "Hal and I are divorced."

"Oh." His face turned grave. "I'm sorry to hear it."

"Don't be. It was in the cards. I feared that he would meet an early death, and I'm happy he didn't. It was only his love for another woman that ended our marriage. It could have been much worse. But as to why I am here—"

"That too was in the cards?"

She smiled. She had been about to say something about Lester, but Lomax had put it correctly. Without the cards' suggestion that she might affect things here, she would not have come. She had no experience in war, but well understood the risk she took coming here.

"We have many wounded," Lomax said, wiping blood. "Our only doctor was killed. Would you—could you possibly help?"

"I'm not skilled," she said. But Lester might be among the wounded. Besides, there would be others like this young guardsman. "I'll do what I can." She would have to trust the cards to guide her correctly.

She followed him, detouring around a horse and a man that were beyond help. She knew a little herbal lore, she knew how to suture and bind up wounds. If nothing else, she could do as her daughter had done at another place, and mop fevered brows and hold chilly hands.

They reached the bottom of the hill as the daylight faded and the sun eased down. The signs of battle were all around: dead men, dead horses, dropped weapons, and the groans and moans of injured and dying.

"This way, Mrs.—eh, Knight."

"Charlain will do." She followed him meekly to an isolated tent. He pulled back the tent flap and there, lying on a blood-soaked blanket, was what appeared to be a schoolboy. The lad's eyes were glassy and filled with terror and suffering.

"A witch! A witch!" the youth cried, pointing feebly at her.

"Not a witch, Phillip," Lomax said. "This is Charlain, Kelvin's mother."

"Don't let her touch me! Don't let her!" He struggled to sit up, blood spurting through knotted bandages. He shrieked at the top of a weakened voice: "Go Way! Burn her, Lomax! Burn—" His eyes rolled up until only the whites showed. He stiffened and fell back.

Hurriedly Charlain grabbed his wrist. There was still a heartbeat, but it was faint. A lot of his blood was missing.

"Why is he here?" she asked. She couldn't help but rage that such a young boy had been allowed to fight. It was her motherly instinct.

"He's St. Helens' friend. Former king of Aratex."

"Ah." Formerly the enemy, though it had really been Melbah who governed that country. Kings did get their way, ex or current. "Is there bloodfruit around?"

"There is, back a way in the forest."

"I'm not sure he can swallow the juice, but—"

"We'll make him. St. Helens wouldn't like it if he died."

"St. Helens is—" She wanted to avoid the word, but found no way. "Captured?"

"Yes. Or dead. He could be in the same state as this." His eyes flicked down to the boy. "Phillip here killed the witch."

"Helbah? Killed?" she asked, appalled.

"Yes. He wasn't supposed to."

"But Helbah is a good witch!"

"But on the other side. That's how the enemy got St. Helens. We broke the truce, and they seized him."

She thought: *Helbah's still alive. I know, I've read her cards. But she may not remain so long.*

"Can you get the bloodfruit?" she asked, turning to the immediate business. "A lot of it? If you have other wounded who have lost blood it could save their lives."

"I'll send some men back. It's a big grove, but a long ride. They might not be able to get the fruit back until daybreak."

"That will have to do." She gave the former boy-king a final check. Unconscious, colorless, he appeared dead. "Are there wounded to whom I can give immediate help?"

"Many. Some not this bad."

"I'll need help setting bones and severing limbs. Get me your doctor's supplies."

Lomax nodded, went outside, and began issuing orders. She joined him, and he took her to more wounded and dying than she had seen before in her life.

Men sought their foolish glory, she thought, but for too many this was the reality. It was a shame, but they never seemed to learn.

It was nearing dawn when the riders Lomax had dispatched arrived back with the bloodfruit. At her direction the fruit was boiled and the red syrup cooled and administered. First young Phillip, then man after man weakly swallowed a spoonful or a cupful depending on his need. In a surprisingly short time pale faces flushed and men were restored to full vigor.

It was magic fruit, the bloodfruit. The doctor had had the foresight to see it gathered, but in the fighting the wagon with the fruit was set ablaze and destroyed. The doctor had died trying to put out the fire. So until this new supply arrived, wounded men had continually died.

At first she did not recognize him. She had only met him twice, and that under better circumstances. But then the pale, big man she was working on gasped a word, and the word caused her astonishment and joy.

"Jon!" the pale lips gasped.

Lester! This was Lester, her daughter's husband! He had lost a lot of blood but he should be all right once the syrup took effect. Revived by the prospect, she held the brimful cup to his lips and massaged his throat to force him to drink.

"You'll be all right, Lester," she murmured. "You will be, for Jon's sake."

He did not respond verbally. His pulse jumped. From his mouth a trickle of blood issued, thicker and darker than the syrup.

Gods, he was dying! Jon's husband was dying, and she didn't know how she could save him. Yet there had to be a way of restoring him. There had to be!

Desperately she checked through the doctor's bag. Containers of herbs, properly labeled, but often a mystery to her. She wished she had absorbed more herbal lore. Which herb, properly administered, would seal his internal wound and allow the bloodfruit to do its work? There had to be an herb that would do this, but was it the sealant root or the stitching flower? Desperately she tried to remember. She had never anticipated being in a position like this! Her arms and legs felt weighted down. Fog filled her head. Invisible bees hummed in it. She was in need of reviving herself.

She took out the jar of sealant root. Should she try this? Suppose it was wrong? It just might be that sealant root was for some other use. Yet to do nothing, or to delay doing something, might mean Lester's doom. She had come to help him! If only she knew how!

*When in doubt, ask the cards.* It had been the one thing she had always believed in. Without hesitation she took the deck from her pack, shuffled it, and thought of Lester. Then, head swimming, body protesting more than the disapproving glances of assistants, she dealt out the column.

A single pawn card, representing Lester. A new card representing Lester's fate if she did nothing. It was the death card, skull and crossbones. Tell her something she did not already know!

She dealt again. She laid out the card, there on the bloody canvas. The Lester pawn. Now, administer the sealant root, and his fate would be—the death card.

Her hands shook as she riffled the cards and started the third layout. This time it was the Lester pawn card and the thought of the stitching flower. She held a jar of pink blossoms in her left hand, concentrating. She turned up a card: death card.

*No, no, no!* There had to be a restorative! Back in the palace she had read uncertainty. Here she read death, only death. Was she too late?

She checked the labels on the jars. Here was a jar filled with white flower blossoms, well dried. But this couldn't be the stitching flower! Yet it was! What then were the pink blossoms in the jar she had held as she turned the card? She read the label, her tired eyes squinting hard: "Stretching flower." She had had the wrong jar!

Quickly she tried a fourth layout, holding the jar of white blossoms. Pawn card representing Lester Crumb, her daughter's husband. *Now I will administer the blossoms in this jar, and—*

The sun with a smiling face: recovery card! Lester would recover if she got the herbal medicine inside him in time.

How to administer it? She didn't know, but she had to be swift. Hastily she unscrewed the jar, shook dried blossoms into a cup, added water and a few drops of raspberry wine, stirred it, and held it to Lester's lips.

She massaged his throat, edging up the cup. Slowly, lest he choke, she poured.

He sighed. His color deepened. His eyes blinked. "Jon? Jon? I love you, Jon! I want you close. Please, Jon, come to bed."

"Hush, Son," she said, stroking his forehead. "It's only your old biddy mother-in-law."

His eyes unglazed and focused on her. His color deepened until it was a bright red. "Thank you, Mrs. Hackleberry," he said. Then, exhausted, he closed his eyes.

She had won this one, she thought, and with the thought she realized how tired she actually was. She had worked through the night and into the day, seeing nothing but wounds and blood. She closed her eyes, sank back against the doctor bag, and thoroughly relaxed.

Sleep, sleep, sleep, the natural restorative.

Helbah remained weak, but revived enough to take some of her own medicines, and they restored her greatly. But her hours of injury had put her dangerously out of touch. She fetched her crystal and oriented on the enemy battle camp. Soon she ferreted out the woman with the violet eyes doctoring the Kelvinian and Hermandy wounded.

A witch, that young man had called her. She looked the part, but Helbah had never heard of another practiced in these arts. She frowned, watching the healings, wishing that she were herself well enough to do more. Magic restoratives were wonderful, but at her age they could do only so much.

Later the woman in the crystal was reading cards beside a dying man and an open doctor case. She watched as the woman laid out a file three times and three times took up the cards. So that was how she was doing it! She was not trained in witchcraft or healing magic, only in the cards—but they were guiding her well. On the fourth try she found her answer.

Helbah watched as the woman gave the medication and restored the young man to life. Then, exhausted as only someone practicing the art could be, for it drew from the soul as well as the body, the woman sank to the floor of the tent, closed her eyes, and went instantly to sleep.

*Interesting. She has the talent. Largely untrained, but there. Another enemy? Or could she—dare I think it?—become a colleague? An apprentice, someone to help me fight?*

Without quite willing it, she fell asleep herself, dreaming a witch's dreams.

Sometime next morning Katbah entered the room with tail held straight up above his shiny back. He was lean from his ordeal of lending her his life force, but he had taken restoratives and was strengthening. He walked straight to her and stared into her face.

"Those two in trouble again?" She sighed. "Think what we'd have to put up with if they hadn't the minds of grown men!" Actually she was often in doubt about the maturity of their minds; sometimes they were just so confoundedly juvenile that she wished she could take a switch to their little posteriors.

With difficulty she got to her feet, using her cane, and followed her familiar.

St. Helens kept his eyes barely slitted and pretended to sleep. He had successfully ignored the pebbles and the lumps of dried dirt. Now a feather danced before his nose and threatened to make him sneeze. He considered grabbing the string and breaking it, and would have done so in another moment. But then the feather wafted out of his sight, mercifully.

From above he heard them whispering. Little dickens, what would they try next?

Suddenly moisture trickled down on the back of his neck, the side of his face, and on his beard. Horrified, he rolled over and roared. "You brats! You filthy brats!"

At the window, two young faces with golden crowns above peered down, grinning.

"That got him, Kildom."

"You're right, Kildee. Guess this is where we should come next time we have to pee."

"We can fill up with appleberry juice. Come with a big load. Make him smell sweet."

St. Helens mopped at the back of his neck. If there had been anything in the cell to throw, he would have thrown it. He sniffed at his hand, shook some yellow drops from it, and swore an oath so villainous it threatened to char the walls.

"Oh listen to the bad words, Kildom!"

"He's a bad man, Kildee; what do you expect?"

The two dissolved into giggling. St. Helens felt like showing them just how bad he could be. Instead he fought to control himself. This was most difficult because his inner nature urged him to rave and rant and make a spectacular scene. It wasn't through having a saintly disposition that he was called St. Helens, but because his temper had once been as explosive as a famous Earth volcano.

"You brats are going to be in trouble!" he shouted. "You can't do this to a general! You're going to be punished! When I get out I'll warm your butts!"

"Listen to him, Kildom. He thinks he's getting out."

"Never, Kildee. He'll be here forever! Every day we'll come water him like an ugly weed."

"Until the whole cell fills up with appleberry pee!"

"And him swimming in it like a big fat froog!"

"He's already got a big fat froog-face!"

They dissolved into more giggling, unable to maintain their clever repartee.

*"YOU BRATS! YOU FILTHY BRATS!"* St. Helens exploded. He was repeating himself, but he couldn't help it. They were supposed to have the minds of men, so a little manly profanity couldn't warp them. Just maybe he'd remember that they were men in boys' bodies when he got hold of them, and then—then it would be more than a spanking he'd deliver!

"Do you think, Kildom, that there's another form of elimination! Plants need fertilizer as well as water, don't they?"

"Shit, yes! Let's!"

St. Helens felt his face going purple. He could imagine smoke curling from his ears and his head and body erupting in a geyser of fire. Never had he been more uncontrollably furious in his entire life!

Up in the window he saw that he was being mooned by a plump posterior. Only it wasn't going to stop at that. Oh, for anything to throw, such as a rotten tomato!

"What's going on here?" That sounded like the old witch herself! Unbelievable! Was she going to direct his torment herself? Was her aging anatomy going to replace that of the boys beyond the bars?

Abruptly the bare posterior got covered, but the brat remained standing before the window as if trying to conceal it. "Nothing, Helbah," one of them said with attempted innocence.

"Boys! Boys! You know better than to act like hooligans! You're going to have to apologize." It was evident that she wasn't even slightly fooled.

"We were just having fun, Helbah!"

"I'm sure it wasn't fun for General Reilly. Now come away from there this instant!"

The young faces looked down at his sullenly, then disappeared. He waited, but the witch did not take their place. Apparently she hadn't come here to torment him further, difficult as that was to believe.

The witch's familiar appeared, however. The houcat stared unblinkingly at him and at the interior of the cell, then flicked his tail and left without any sign of mischief.

"Witches!" St. Helens cursed. "How I hate the lot of them!"

Later, though not by much, the guard opened the dungeon door and motioned him out. Meekly, mindful of the drawn sword and the fact that he had virtually no chance to fight his way out of here even if he should manage to overcome this guard and take his sword, he climbed the stairs. On the way up, to his astonishment, the two young kings sped past him on their way down. Both boys carried a big bucket of sudsy water, a scrubbing brush, and a broom.

Outside, warmed by the sun and inviting, was a large tub of soapy water.

"Strip! Bathe! Deflea! Delouse!" the guard ordered.

For once in his life St. Helens was only too happy to obey. There was louse grease and soap and a brush and even a washcloth. With near joy for the relief he made use of all of them.

After a thorough cleansing and soak, he saw the guard motioning him out. The man even tossed him a towel. While he was toweling, the guard brought him loose prisoner clothes to replace the lousy uniform.

He felt remarkably good, he thought while dressing. He turned and there were the two kings, both red in the face. Their heightened color went well with their brickish hair and the plans he was making.

"We apologize, General Reilly, sir," the king on the left said.

"We'll never come to your window again," the king on the right promised.

St. Helens grunted, nodding his head in a curt gesture of acknowledgment. He was alert for a trap that was about to be sprung, but in the meantime he'd gotten what he'd wanted for days: a clean hide and the summary execution of the tenants of that hide. He hated lice almost as much as he hated brats!

The brats disappeared. St. Helens was returned to his cell. He stood and gaped at the door.

The cell had been scrubbed spotless. Fresh straw had been provided. What magic might have done readily, the young kings had evidently done laboriously.

"Good gods," he said. He sank down on the straw, physically more comfortable than he had been since capture. "Good gods, she really *is* a good witch!"

# CHAPTER 19

# *Revolutionaries*

*T*he great war-horse gave a grunt of surprise as Kelvin landed on its broad rump. With his left hand, hardly thinking of what he did but just going with the gauntlet, he pushed the rider from the saddle. Grabbing the horse's mane he took the soldier's place. The reins were loose, but that was no problem to the gauntlet which snatched them up without his thinking. Immediately he was confronted by a burly royalist swinging down at him, and the right gauntlet countered for him and quickly ended the man's life.

Kelvin caught a squirt of blood as the royalist corpse toppled. He felt his stomach heave, but somehow he was learning to ignore it. Assuredly he and the others here were in the midst of a tremendous fight. It was as if he were in a different plane of reality, something that had nothing to do with home and family and human values.

"Kelvin, watch out!" his father shouted. So much for being apart from his family! But already the gauntlets were blurring as they moved, transferring sword to left hand and reins to right. The new attacker ended his life on the point of Kelvin's sword, blood spraying from his throat, his own wild swing breezing Kelvin's right cheek. No time to think! Just swift positions, as the gauntlets acted, and the effort to fight with everything he and the gauntlets had, just to preserve his life. How he hated this!

Now one of the royalists' attackers was before him, his ally. It was a big man dressed in the plainest of clothes. Morton Crumb! No, not his friend and Jon's father-in-law, but this frame's very close look-alike. He focused on the man's round pink ears, neither bearing as much as a scar, and that alone kept him from shouting the name.

"You," the Morton Crumb look-alike rumbled, "fight against the king?"

The last time he had tried to answer that question, he had gotten into trouble. "I fight to save my friends," he said, nodding back at Kian and his father.

"Come!" As abrupt as Crumb would have been.

He maneuvered the horse with sure gauntleted hand and fought his way at the big man's side until they were directly opposite the prisoners. Kian and his father had their hands tied behind their backs, and that could complicate the problem of getting them away. The royalist guards might have been ordered to slay them rather than give them up.

"Father, I think we'd better retreat!"

It was the Lester look-alike who had just pushed in. With him was a younger fighter, the exact look-alike of Phillip, former boy-king of Aratex, except for his round ears. There were two riderless war-horses behind them. On the ground were two more dead royalists. On the Lester's sword was fresh blood.

Kelvin tried to think. *This is not really Lester and Phillip, and this other man is not really my brother-in-law's father.* It was hard to think of anything under the circumstances. He was likely to get himself or them killed if he did anything but concentrate on his business.

He looked around. Indeed they were outnumbered, these revolutionaries. "Help me release them first," Kelvin urged.

"We're losing too many men," the big man protested.

"You help us now, we'll help you later. We have things you may not have. We're from another frame."

"I thought as much! I saw you flying down! But we can't help you if you're dead. If you've got power, use it!"

Kelvin realized he had a point. He nudged the control on his belt and kicked himself free of the saddle. He rose to just over the heads of the combatants. The fighting stopped.

It was only a temporary halt, he knew. In a moment the novelty would be absorbed and the slaughter would resume. He nudged the control forward.

The guards' faces came nearer, and so did those they guarded. They stared openmouthed, amazed at what they had been too busy to see when he arrived. In a moment more someone would think of a crossbow or other projectile weapon that could spell his end. But with surprise to his advantage and the gauntlets on his hands, he had his chance.

Quickly he disarmed the guard who raised his sword at him, then descended and stabbed the remaining guard through the throat. A moment later he was slicing through first his father's and then his brother's bonds, while renewed fighting raged ahead of them.

Now then, how to get out? The gauntlets knew how. Without his quite willing it, the magical grippers captured the reins of a war-horse. At their urging he vaulted into the saddle.

"Father! Kian! Up!"

They extended their hands to him, and the gauntlets pulled them up on the horse. The three of them made a crowded horseback.

"This is going to be difficult!" John said. "We're surrounded."

Kelvin's gauntlets snatched a passing sword and handed it to his father.

"Uh, thanks, but do you think—?"

"I'll clear a path. You follow. Close."

With that Kelvin lifted free of the saddle and just over their heads. The horse eyed him suspiciously, but didn't argue; after all, it was a load off its back. Then he pushed the forward lever and flew to meet a royalist riding down on them.

The attacking royalist died, and so did several others as Kelvin fought horselessly and airborne, to open his side of the crowd. The remaining revolutionaries fought inward, led by

the Crumb look-alikes. The Phillip look-alike shouted encour-
agement.

The royalists, caught between enemies, fought hard, but
still perished. The sword in Kelvin's hand never ceased its
darting and its hacking, ignoring, as Kelvin could not, the cries
of slain and wounded men.

Finally the last of the royalists melted from in front of his
wild flying attack. There was the big fellow and the big fellow's
son and the boy and half a dozen others whose faces had a
familiar look. They looked up at Kelvin.

"Now you can retreat," Kelvin said, "and take us with
you."

"Thank the gods that's over!" the Morton Crumb look-
alike said. "Follow us!"

They raced out of what would have been the pass between
the twin valleys in the world of the silver serpents. Up the
roads and into the hills, and finally, their pursuit lost, to a
familiar-seeming region of farms and villages. Here the big
leader of the far-smaller band raised his hand and drew up.
"Whoa. Time for a talk."

Kelvin descended until his feet once more touched the
ground. He shut off the belt. He waited.

"Marvin Loaf," the big man said. "You strangers have any
trouble with that name?"

"Not a bit," Kelvin said. So this was not Morton Crumb
as at home, or Matthew Biscuit as in the world of the silver
serpents, but Marvin Loaf. It made perfect sense.

"Good. Some think Marvin a peculiar name."

"No more so than mine," Kelvin said, keeping a straight
face. "Kelvin Hackleberry. And this is my father John Knight,
and my brother Kian Knight."

Marvin nodded. "This is my son Hester. And this young
fellow we call Jillip."

As in Lester and Phillip. Good enough. Kelvin held out
his hand politely. The custom of handshaking existed here,
fortunately, as it had in every world he had visited with the
possible exception of the chimaera's. His father and brother
dismounted, along with the others of the band. Everyone
shook hands.

"We call ourselves Loaf's Hopes," Marvin said. "Sometimes Loafers. We haven't been doing much raiding lately." He paused again, but no one found any humor in the nickname. "After two years of trying to force a change, this is all we have."

Kelvin saw what he meant. Eight men in all, two of them with slight wounds. The rest who had been in the fight were dead or had been captured by the royalists.

"Your king is bad?" Again, Kelvin wasn't taking anything for granted.

"The worst. He has to be overthrown. How I can't now imagine."

"With our help," Kelvin said confidently.

Marvin looked doubtful. "That flying harness of yours should help, but I'm not sure it's enough. There's really only us eight."

"There will be more," Kelvin said. "All you have to do is get the word out once you've got your army."

"Army? What army? I tell you we're only eight."

Kelvin sighed. How elementary it all was. It really pained him to have to explain it. His father was looking at him warningly, but he went right on.

"If you haven't got huge serpents here that shed skins of purest silver, you have dragons that have scales of purest gold." *Simple. Logical.*

Marvin Loaf was looking at him with eyes that now bulged. His expression suggested that Kelvin was a lunatic.

"Serpents with silver scales? Dragons with golden skins?"

Kelvin abruptly realized why his father had sent the warning look. His morale plummeted. He had walked into another subtle but critical difference between the frames. Yet he owed these look-alikes something. There was a debt and he could not leave with it unpaid.

"My mistake. I told you we're from another frame."

"It must be a distant one. Silver serpents! Golden dragons! These are legend! Nothing like them can possibly exist!"

Nor should chimaeras with three heads, Kelvin thought. Oh, well, these good folk still had to have some advantage, and he had to provide it.

"Look," he said, unsheathing the Mouvar weapon. "This is something very special. It will nullify hostile magic and even turn the magic back on its sender."

"Magic? Magic is myth!"

Kelvin suppressed a groan. Another disappointment! This world seemed so similar to his own, yet it lacked dragons, serpents, and even magic? How could that last possibly be the case? But the robot Stapular had spoken of Major and Minor frames. Maybe this world was like his father's, where magic didn't exist but where magical results were achieved by something called science.

"All three of us can fly with this," he said, touching the belt. "We can hover still in the air as you saw, or move at the speed of a fast horse. That should be some help. It was back there in the battle we just fought."

"Back there I lost over half my men!" Marvin exclaimed, looking suspicious. "Is that belt all you've got?"

"Father!" Hester said, and it was impossible not to think of him as Lester. "Father, he wants to help."

"Good intentions don't defeat tyrants. Armies defeat tyrants."

Kelvin swallowed a lump. He still hadn't answered the big man's question. He glanced at Kian and he saw that his half brother's face was as pale as though he faced instant death. Then he looked at his father and saw that he could expect little help there. Yet his big mouth had gotten him into this, the same as it had with the chimaera. Somehow his big mouth was going to have to get him out.

"We have experience. We overthrew tyrants in two worlds nearly identical to this. And—" Inspiration finally hit him. "If we need to, we can travel back to those worlds, and get what we need there, to deal with this tyrant."

"You think so, do you?" Marvin looked dangerous.

"If we have to. Bring you weapons you don't have. Maybe an army."

"Listen to him, Father. Listen!" Loaf's son urged.

But the big man was drawing his sword. "You've come here without our asking and now you'd leave and we'd never see you again."

"That's not true!" Why was this version of Morton Crumb so belligerent? But he realized that the question was pointless. Characters were similar in each frame, but also different, and the differences showed up most strongly in their personalities, rather than their bodies. So this Crumb was more aggressive than the others, and probably more dangerous to rile. He also seemed clumsier.

"Listen, Sonny," Marvin said, testing the edge of his sword with a callused thumb. "We have been this route before. We have had visits from other frames so often that the king has men watching the transporter! One thing we've learned: visitors are trouble!"

"But Father," Hester protested. "He can't know!" He was protesting, but there was a certain whine in his voice. He seemed to be more dominated by his father than Lester was.

"No, I don't know," Kelvin said. "I don't know about your prior visitors." He felt much as he had when Stapular pulled off his hand and revealed the laser weapon. His gauntlets tingled, but only moderately.

Well, he would use the gauntlets for guidance. He would keep talking, and change the subject if the gloves got bothered. "You have a kingdom where you can hire mercenaries, haven't you?"

Marvin's glower hardly eased. "We have that, Sonny, but we certainly haven't got golden dragons, silver serpents, or magic. Neither do we have riches!"

"But you do have round ears. You can use the transporter."

"Not for a mountain of gold!"

"I don't mean you personally, but at least one of you. Maybe Hester here?"

"The king's men guard the transporter," Hester protested. "And even if we got there, I couldn't use it."

"With my help?"

"No."

"Why not?" The gauntlets were not getting any warmer, which was not a bad sign, but neither was it necessarily good. He might just not be getting anywhere, good or bad. "Round ears means you can use the transporter." *I hope.*

"No way, Sonny. There's more than the shape of ears involved."

"But—" This was getting confusing! According to the Mouvar parchment, round ears were the tickets to use and other-shaped ears a sentence to destruction. Or was that only in his home frame? Were there other rules elsewhere?

"Let me explain it, Sonny. Whenever any of us natives enter the transporter chamber we feel as if our fool heads will burst. So will you, if you attempt to go back."

"You mean—" He strove desperately to make sense of this, his head already feeling swollen. "Magic?"

"Technology. What's the difference, as far as we're concerned? What it means is that it's a one-way transporter. No one can leave by it."

"No one?" Kelvin's knees began to feel like cooked macaroodles.

"No one. That's why the king's men don't use it."

Kelvin tried to think. To be confined to this dull frame forever. Never to see Heln again. To be, furthermore, in a world where there was no way to raise an army and defeat a tyrant? And what about the chimaera? The chimaera would be waiting for the dragonberries he had promised. He had every intention of fulfilling that promise, and would be mortified to renege on it.

"Perhaps there's a little hope," his father said unexpectedly.

All looked at him, the big stranger who had been mainly silent. Marvin looked hardest.

"Look," John Knight said, spreading his hands. "We're as much victims here as you are. But if the transporter is technology, or even if it's not, there may be a way."

"How?" Marvin demanded, showing some interest. "You going to kill off those headbees?"

"Maybe. The chamber beside the transporter chamber— I'm certain it didn't exist in any of the other frames. Maybe there's something that will make the transporter two-way. Possibly a control."

"The king's men would have found it," one of the men said.

"Maybe not," John said. "Not if they didn't know what to look for. I remember how difficult it was to make a computer work, when you didn't know the codes; you could make random guesses all week and never get anywhere, and the damn machine wouldn't tell you."

"You think you know what to look for?" Marvin demanded.

"I might. If it's technology."

Kelvin's gauntlets twitched. What did that mean?

Marvin put away his sword. His grim face showed acceptance but no real belief in John's words. "There'd better be an army in this," he said. "There'd better be, or that's the end of all of us."

But the gauntlets were cooling. That gave Kelvin hope.

# CHAPTER 20

# A Meeting of Kinds

*C*harlain woke up rested. The camp was quiet now, the wounded up and around. It was—good heavens, it was late in the day!

She met Lomax as she was scrambling out of the tent. He was grinning as he came with arms wide for a hug. She let him embrace her and then tell her how many lives she had saved and how grateful they all were. "But now," he finished, "we'll be making our big drive and it's not fair to you—"

"You want me to leave."

"Before we reengage the enemy. Yes, ma'am. There will be more casualties, but we have a good supply of bloodfruit and you have discovered the mysteries of the doctor bag. We can manage, although—"

"Yes," she said. He wanted her to stay with them, she knew, and she didn't want to. She had after all come here for just one purpose, and that was to save Lester's fading life. She had done that, and now wanted very much to get well away from this mindless carnage.

"Then you—"

"I mean I will return home now, where I will be safe. That is what you were saying?"

He looked astonished, then crestfallen. He had asked from a sense of duty. She knew that the last thing he had expected was that she would comply. She felt guilty for disappointing him, but she did have to go.

"I'm not really a nurse or a magician," she said. "I'm sure you will manage with those who assisted me. My daughter may need me, and then there's my son and his wife. Heln is having my grandson."

"I—see." He was doing his unsuccessful best to mask his disappointment. If he were a very few years younger, he'd have to cry. It was nice that she was going to be missed.

"Keep the bandages changed, administer bloodfruit syrup as needed, and keep that boy out of the fighting."

"You mean Phillip?"

"That's the boy. He's reckless as my Jon was at his age. I read his cards and he's at continued high risk with the uncertainty card. Keep him safe."

"I'll try. But Phillip was a king. He's hard to control."

"No harder, I suspect, than Jon. And Phillip of Aratex doesn't have a big brother with magic gauntlets and a prophecy. If Jon was here you'd know what unmanageable is."

Lomax tried a grin, albeit weak. He motioned to a passing soldier. "Corporal Hinzer, saddle Mrs. Hack—eh, Charlain's horse and bring it to her. Have two unwounded men escort her to the border."

"That won't be necessary," Charlain assured him. "I know the way and there shouldn't be any danger for one old woman."

"Not old!" Lomax protested in a manner that had to be automatic. "But if you're sure—"

"You need *all* your men. The war isn't over."

"Yes. Yes, thank you, Charlain. Thank you for your help. You saved many lives."

*You may not thank me always,* she thought with regret. *When things go against you and I'm not there. Then you may want to curse me for abandoning you.*

With some justice, unfortunately.

She waited patiently while her mount was brought, then climbed up and into the saddle. She was a little stiff from all that kneeling. She was about to ride out when Lomax came running to her, his face flaming red. He handed her up a packet and a jug.

"I forgot you hadn't eaten! Here's traveling biscuit, dried meat, and tuber fruit. Wine's in the jug. You must be famished!"

"Not really," she said. "We witches seldom eat."

"Witches?" His face paled perceptibly. For a moment he looked as though he believed her.

"It's what Phillip said when I got to him. And who knows, if I had had a good teacher he just might have been correct!"

She nudged Nelly with her knee, rode through the camp, and out to the road that led to the border.

It was half a day later at leisurely horse-walking speed that she met the cat. It came from the bushes, tail raised, yellow eyes fixed on her, and she knew instantly that this was why she had left the camp.

She said, "Whoa, Nelly," though the horse was already stopped. The cat came nearer. It was very black, blacker than mortal hide ought to be. It sat down, washed itself carefully, pawed down its whiskers, and then did what Charlain had somehow expected. It turned its back, looked over its shoulder once, flicked its tail, and proceeded up a path.

"Follow that cat, Nelly!" Charlain said to her mount. It was silly and impossible that she do so, but Nelly obeyed. That, she thought, had to be the result of magic!

She held the reins loosely in her hands and let the horse plod on at the cat's pace. She sighed and closed her eyes, resting. Not once did she question herself about why she was here or where they were going. She did not even wonder whether it would be a long or a short trip. Somehow she had known that something like this would happen. That had been part of her urgency to get away from the camp. It was as if she had laid down another card, and it had told her to leave the place where she was needed, to find one where she was needed more.

Eventually the path reached its end and they stopped. Here, in an otherwise empty glade, was a huge gnarled tree. Under the tree, waiting, was an old, bent woman, leaning on a stick. Now who would that be, except—

"Helbah? Helbah the witch?"

"Who else, Charlain?"

She felt a cloud lift from her. "I am here," she said without thinking. "Here, as I know you directed."

"You have done well," Helbah said. "Now you will do even better."

Charlain knew that Helbah spoke only the witching truth.

Heln watched behind half-hooded eyes as Jon added seeds and crumbs to the tray on the windowsill. Her task done, Jon glanced at her, saw her apparently asleep, and tiptoed out.

No sooner was the door closed than Heln was out of bed and scuttling, a way she found natural of late, across the room to the window. She stood stealthily waiting until the dark-headed sparren lit on the tray's rim. Bright-eyed, the little bird regarded her carefully. Heln remained frozen, unblinking.

The bird picked up a corbean from the tray, cracked it, and proceeded to eat. Pleased with the fare, it put its little head back and warbled cheerily.

Instantly Heln's hand shot out like a snake. Her fingers snapped closed like jaws on the tiny bird before it could flutter. She raised it to her mouth, her stomach growling for sustenance. The bird raised its beak desperately.

Heln opened her mouth. Easily, without seeming volition, her head snapped forward. Her teeth closed on the bird and crushed it.

She was just swallowing, and brushing crimson stains from her lips, when Jon entered. Jon stared at her and the tray. There were feathers on the tray. There was blood on Heln's mouth.

"Why, Heln, what—" Jon was too surprised and confused to finish the sentence.

"An eagawk dropped on a sparren. I tried to get here and chase it away, but—"

Jon's eyes were large. She was suspecting if not actually aware that Heln lied. Disbelief fought with another suspicion. The kinder, more logical thought survived.

"Oh, Heln, how terrible for you! I know how you love songbirds, how you enjoy seeing them! To have an eagawk drop on one right on the tray!"

"It was only following its nature," Heln said. Stealthily she wiped blood from her mouth and lips, sweeping her hand as if brushing away a crumb.

"Yes, I know, but—Heln, did you hurt yourself?"

"Bit my tongue when I tried to shout at the preybird." She turned all the way from the window. She forced herself to move slowly, as a pregnant woman should. Without another glance at Jon she got back into bed.

"Don't you want to go for a walk this morning?"

"No!"

"But it's so nice out!"

Heln merely closed her eyes as if bored with Jon's presence, which was hardly an exaggeration.

Jon moved to her side and felt her forehead. "You have no temperature, Heln. You seem cool—cooler than I'd think natural."

"You ever been with child?"

"You know I haven't!"

"That's the way it is. For roundears, at least."

"Oh." Jon never seemed to accept that her ears were different from her brother's and Heln's. It was as if the girl thought they were all of the same species. Little did she know!

"I might take another cup of tefee," Heln said, making another attempt to get rid of her.

"I'll pull the cord for the servant. Would you like something to eat, too, Heln? You hardly touched your groats this morning. You aren't sick again?"

"No. I told you I'm all right." When would this nuisance of a girl go away?

Two of Jon's fingers reached out to the corner of Heln's mouth. They picked out a tiny feather. Jon eyed it, and her.

"I was too close to the kill," Heln said. "Blood and feathers sprayed on me."

"That must have been it," Jon said, sounding unconvinced. She held the feather, then carried it as though to dispose of it. But she walked not to the pullcord but to the door. She hesitated, giving Heln a peculiar look, then exited.

Heln delivered herself of a long, low hiss. So good to be rid of that one, if only momentarily. She'd like to be out in the sun, soaking up its rays, warming herself and the other through and through. But Jon, she knew, would think it strange, and the doctor would find it unacceptable. Later, after the other was born, she might go with it into the sunny desert and bask in the warming light and practice—what? She had lost the thought, frustratingly.

A mosqfly buzzed near her mouth, attracted by the stains. It lit on her upper lip, the foolish thing. Instantly her tongue darted out and rolled it into her mouth. The insect buzzed as she swallowed it.

At the same moment she felt the scuttling inside. Reaching down she patted her bulging stomach. *Don't fret, Little Three Heads! Mama will feed you well.*

There was no coherent answer, just a mental growl. It was too soon for the human minds to manifest. But soon that would change. All she had to do was find proper food.

Another mosqfly buzzed through the open window. She waited, rock-still, ready to capture it.

Dr. Sterk listened quietly as Jon described Heln's recent behavior. It was unfortunately evident what was happening to her. "And you're certain she ate it?" he asked.

"She must have! Blood all over her mouth, and this feather." She held up the tiny feather to show him.

"The mind comports itself strangely in pregnant women. Her behavior may seem abnormal, even bizarre, but I assure you it's all part of the process."

"Really, Doctor?" The girl had understandable skepticism.

"Really. Just keep watch and report anything that seems different. If necessary, I can always administer a stronger medicine."

"Oh, Doctor, you've made me feel so much better! You don't know how concerned I've been!"

"I can imagine. But even pointeared women develop strange appetites and behave oddly while carrying. Just go on as you have been, and everything should be all right."

He ushered her to the door and out. Then he allowed himself the grimace he had been suppressing.

Everything would *not* be all right, he thought dismally. Everything pointed to the chimaera syndrome. If that was what it was, and he was sickly certain this was the case, nothing would save that girl and her child except a certain powder.

*And for that,* he thought bitterly, *I'd have to go to a dealer in such powders.* Alas, he knew full well that any dealers who existed had to operate in some far-removed universe.

St. Helens heard them talking through the thick door. Then their jailer had the door open, and they were coming inside. He stood, reminding himself that they were royalty and that, as the saying went, brats would be brats.

They stood there with their golden crowns on their heads, two identical and apparent young boys.

"I'm Kildee, General Reilly," said the one on the right. "I'm Klingland's monarch."

"I'm Kildom," said the other boy. "I'm king of Kance."

St. Helens permitted himself a slight bow. *In name only,* he thought. *In name only are you the rulers.* And in his home world of Earth, any royalty that still existed in England and France was purely nominal. No two frames were quite the same, but certain trends did seem to carry through.

"It is our hope," said Kildee, "that you will agree to come over to us."

"You mean—" St. Helens could hardly believe this, "switch sides?"

"That would be appropriate, General Reilly," said Kildom. The boy reached up and took off his crown; he held it down at his side as though respectfully. His twin brother duplicated his actions.

"In what way would it be appropriate? I'm a soldier and I do what's required of me." Strange little tykes. Did they really think as men did?

"General Reilly, you are not a bad man," Kildee said.

"Thank you. I try not to be, though with imperfect success." If this was a game, it was better than their pee game, so he was willing to play along.

"But your side is bad."

*I've suspected that. But you can't know about the prophecy.*

"There is a prophecy," Kildee said. "We know of it from Helbah."

He should have known! Witches had their infernal sources. "You know about a prophecy? The one concerning a roundear?"

"Yes. Concerning Kelvin of Kelvinia."

"Then you know," he said, sighing, "that there is little to be done to alter it."

"Perhaps in reality but not in truth."

This was puzzling. He hardly expected obscure philosophy from these kids.

"'Uniting four,'" said Kildom, "may not mean uniting through warfare the kingdom of Kelvinia with those of Klingland, Kance, and Hermandy."

"No? Well, what then does it mean?"

The boy frowned. "Prophecies can be devious, Helbah says, and subject to interpretation."

"You don't think it would mean uniting Kelvinia with the remaining three kingdoms? Throod is where every warring kingdom goes for mercenaries and weapons, while Ophal and Rotternik haven't even been penetrated since before Mouvar's visit! As far as latecomers like me are concerned those kingdoms might not even exist!"

"Nevertheless," the boy said pedantically, "Kelvinia may not have to conquer us."

"Don't tell me you want to surrender!" St. Helens found himself hard put to conceal his mirth. These two were really just what they seemed to be: children.

Kildom looked at Kildee and shrugged. Kildee returned the shrug. They both looked back at him. They waited.

"Well, is that what you want?" St. Helens demanded rhetorically. The punch line of their joke was about due.

"It is, General Reilly," Kildom said.

St. Helens started to laugh, but his mouth froze partway into it. Could it be that they were serious?

"We have discussed the matter out of Helbah's hearing and we are prepared to raise the surrender flags," Kildee said.

St. Helens felt floored. In his wildest dreams he had never anticipated this! They were playacting. They had to be. But suppose they weren't?

Better to play it serious, at least until one of them burst out laughing. "You really want to surrender? Why?"

"To save us," said Kildee. "To end the fighting."

"And to save our Helbah," Kildom added.

Whoa! This was more than just interesting. "Those would be your terms? Your only terms?"

The two boys looked at each other again. "Yes, General Reilly," they said together.

St. Helens let out a breath. This was incredible. It seemed he had won the war single-handed! This was even better than he could have imagined!

If it was true.

But if it was true, then for whom had he won it? For what? For the usurper in Kelvinia?

"Will you take our surrenders, General Reilly?" Kildom asked.

Would he? Could he? He didn't want the winner to be those two back in Kelvinia's capital. And would the prophecy be said to hold if Kelvin himself were absent? Kelvin, off in some other frame, doing the gods knew what, and unaware of what was happening here?

"I'll have to think about it, Your Majesties. I'll have to think things over."

Now they were gaping. It seemed that they had never imagined that he would demur!

He swallowed, wanting nothing quite so much as to sink down on the pile of straw. "Please close the door tightly as you leave. I don't want to escape, and I don't want anyone rescuing me."

The two exchanged another glance. Maybe they did understand. Certainly they knew that he was on the wrong side.

They left, leaving him with his chaotic thoughts.

## CHAPTER 21

# *Return Journey*

*K*elvin hung suspended above the ledge, watching for the king's guardsmen. The updraft from the cliff was shockingly strong, much more than there had been in the other frame. He trusted his levitation belt, but this was a balancing act that made him a bit nervous.

He had left just two living men at this site, but more might have come while he was rescuing his father and brother. His gauntlets were tingling a mild warning, and that could mean that he should act while acting was still possible. The others in his party had already begun ascending the tree, certainly a more difficult task than in the world of serpents and flopears. It was time that he and the gauntlets act.

The chamber was to the left of the transporter chamber. No sign of it either from here or the ledge. He would have to just step through the rock face at the right spot, and find himself in either the transporter or up against guardsmen with swords. There was really no choice except to trust the gauntlets.

He landed on the ledge, facing the cliff face. Was he following the guidance of the gauntlets properly?

He drew his sword. *All right, I'm a hero!*

As though annoyed, the gauntlets yanked him forward, into rock that vanished.

He was in a chamber lit by the glow. It was otherwise unoccupied, and sparsely furnished for the comfort of vigil-keeping guardsmen. A couple of blankets, discarded crusts and rinds from lunch, and one broken wine bottle. Some vigilance!

He put his head out the shimmering blue curtain in time to see his father pulling himself up the ladder at the cliff's edge. Below him was Kian and below Kian were the others.

"Guardsmen back there! Six of them!" his father called. The updraft really pulled at him as he struggled the rest of the way up. "Redleaf got 'em with his crossbow! Good man, that! He picked them off so fast and at such a distance that they never knew what happened!"

Kelvin sighed. More dead. That was one reason he knew he was a fraud as a hero: he hated killing. Well, it couldn't be helped. At least his kin and Loaf's Hopes were intact.

Kian came up, followed by Hester. His gauntlets gave them a hand as each arrived at the ledge. Below, Marvin Loaf was having trouble with branches and updraft. Jillip climbed past their leader, grinning broadly and devilishly as only a young rascal could. There was something insulting about the way he hung by one hand and pretended, only pretended, to give Marvin a leg up. Was it a joke, or insolence, or was the kid merely a slacker?

"Sort of slow, ain't he?" Redleaf remarked.

"Comes from too much bleer," Bilger cracked. He had to be the thinnest, with the possible exception of Jillip.

"Bleer, you must mean Cross-eyed Jenny at the tavern!"

"Hey, I thought it was the girls who got fat!"

The Hopers chuckled and laughed at their own great wit, and generally acted like fools while Marvin wheezed along, never slowing and never wasting breath. Before he'd quite reached the top and Kelvin's reaching hand he looked up, very red in the face. "How many you get?" he inquired.

"No guardsmen," Kelvin said, giving him the hand. "The two live ones and the dead are both missing. The men you stopped must have been replacements."

"Very likely."

Kelvin heaved on Marvin's arm and he came the rest of the way. As big around in girth as his look-alike, and with all the muscle, he was not built for trees and ladders. He breathed deeply for a moment, then looked down at his ascending men.

"What's the matter?" called Redleaf. "You a little winded, old man?"

"Redleaf, if you weren't the best crossbowman in existence I'd jump down there and kick your butt!"

Jillip tittered, then corked it. The big man's scowl suggested that he showed good sense.

Still grinning until the top rung, Redleaf, Bilger, and the others battled the updraft until all were together on the wide ledge.

"All right, there's no going near that transporter," Marvin said. "But that anteroom where the guardsmen go is another matter. Have you been there, Sonny?"

"It's empty," Kelvin said. "As I told you, no guardsmen. I made certain, just as we agreed."

"Well, let's have a look." John felt about until he located the entrance. He disappeared into the rock face, and Kelvin followed. One by one the others joined them. Jillip picked up the empty wine bottle and stood examining that while everyone else felt the walls.

Every wall felt solid, with the exception of one spot at the far end where there was a flat area with a transparent section at eye level. Looking through this "window" as his father would have called it, Kelvin saw the transporter.

"I don't see any button or lever in here or in there!" John complained. "Give your gauntlets an order, Kelvin. Let them search!"

Kelvin was quick to comply. The gauntlets did search, just as he mentally told them to, but they did not find anything on the flat area or its window. He wanted to go, but the gauntlets were reluctant, and kept his hands and fingers moving and pressing in various patterns.

*Well,* Kelvin thought sadly as he let the gauntlets play, *I suppose I can get used to living here. But I'm going to miss my wife and the chimaera is going to think ill of me. I wanted to get the seeds for it. I'd promised, and I always keep my word.*

*Stupid mortal, relax and let the gauntlets do your work!*

Kelvin jumped. *Mervania—is that you?*

*What other head would it be, stupid? You must have known I'd keep track of you!*

*But you don't have the dragonberries!*

*No, but I do have a mind! The mind is not limited in intelligent species.*

*But if you've found me, and—*

*I have stayed* with *you. If I had let go I would have lost you for good. I must admit I am growing tired of it. You are most boring. You don't like bloodletting at all. You wouldn't even have had the ferocity to attack those guardsmen if the gauntlets and I hadn't urged you on.*

Kelvin glanced around at the others. It seemed impossible to him that they did not know what was going on in his head.

*What do you want me to do, Mervania?* He hated to admit it, but he felt better having her along. His mind did feel inferior at times.

*Why thank you, Kelvin. You are quite correct: your mind requires buttressing. Very well, I will tell you what to do. Bring the entire crew here to my frame. I can help them.*

*You could eat them!* He shuddered, just thinking of it. Then he saw Kian looking at him as if he were crazy. He had been showing his emotions!

*Stupid mortal!* Mervania thought with something almost like affection. *Of course I could! But I won't. I want those seeds you're going to get. Then I won't need to cling to your frail mind in order to travel across the frames.*

*But why help these others?*

*Because I'm a good creature, that's why! You assume I'm evil merely because my dietary habits differ slightly from yours. That is a narrow view. Besides, I don't like tyrants. I've eaten a lot of them, and believe me, every time their minds gave my stomach trouble.*

*You've eaten tyrants?*

*Of course! You don't think I was always confined, do you? All humans are devourable, but some are tastier than others.*

*She likes to play with our food,* her brother head interrupted. *Actually it was only a couple of tyrants. One proclaimed itself a god, and the other built pyramids of human skulls. Delicious thought!*

*Mertin, don't mess with my concentration! It's tedious enough keeping such a tiny mind on line! Grumpus, what is that you're chomping? Spit it out! Do you want to make us sick?*

*Gag, gag, gag. Urp, urp.*

Kelvin felt his own innards twisting and fluttering with the monster's retching. This was a disadvantage of telepathy he hadn't thought of!

Then the gauntlets pressed his fingers against either side of the window. There was a pop, and the flat area slid away, taking the window with it. There was now an open doorway between them and the transporter.

"What did I tell you!" John Knight said. "Holy—YOW!" He clutched first his temples and then the front and back of his head.

Everyone else in the chamber was reacting similarly. Someone screamed. Two of the men dropped to the floor and writhed.

Kelvin knew why. There was a buzzing sound so loud and painful that it seemed to fill every crevice in his head. This was the head-splitting effect they had been warned about!

*Well, I'm certainly not going to put up with this! Get yourself out of it, stupid mortal! I'm leaving!*

*No, no, Mervania, wait!*

Abruptly he felt her absence, but not an end to the pain. She had made good on her threat. The gauntlets, unperturbed, were feeling carefully above the doorway.

"You want to use that transporter? Go ahead!" Marvin charged clumsily toward the front of the chamber. His men quickly followed.

Kelvin was growing faint. But the gauntlets suddenly pressed hard on a round area above his head. It was a flat, dark spot where the top of the door had been.

*CLICK!*

Silence. Sheepish faces turned. There was an end to panic.

"You've done it!" his father exclaimed. "Now we can go!"

"Not without us!" Marvin said. He had stopped just short of the shimmering curtain. "You're going to help us, remember?"

"Of course we'll go together," John said, while Kelvin just

stood there for a moment, supremely gratified by his success. "You'll get your help, Marvin, just as my son promised. My son always comes through."

Marvin nodded, coming back to them. "Got to admit he's doing that! First two of you transport, then my men, and you and I last. Agreed?"

*Spoken like a leader,* Kelvin thought. *A cautious one.*

"It will be a bit startling to see," Kelvin told Hester. "We'll step in, there will be a purple flash, and then we'll be gone."

"What's it like to experience?" Hester asked.

"Uh—"

"Does it hurt?" Jillip interjected.

"No. No, it doesn't hurt," Kelvin assured them. "You'll find out what it's like soon enough. Just—follow me!"

As boldly as though it were just an everyday occurrence, he stepped into the adjoining chamber. His gauntlets didn't tingle, so he walked over to the transporter. There he found the chimaera's sting that he had apparently dropped and left. Oddly, he hadn't thought about it. Could that have been Mervania's doing? She had evidently been in his mind all along, until the awful sound drove her out. She might have made him forget about something like that.

"What's that? Copper?" Marvin seemed more than just curious.

"Yes. There's a lot of it where we're going."

"Copper? Lots of copper?"

"Yes." The revolutionary leader's manner was puzzling. Why should he be concerned about copper, when he could go after gold?

"It's rare here. It's our most valuable metal. One copper coin is worth three gold or two silver."

"We'll get you copper," Kelvin said, a mental dawn breaking. So copper was the most valuable metal, here! "Enough to buy your army. You do want that army?"

"Want it? I'd kill for it!"

Expressions had a way of carrying across the frames, Kelvin thought. His father had spoken that way at least once or twice about matters of lesser importance.

Taking a deep breath and a firm hold on the sting, he stepped with faked confidence into the transporter. He was confident that it would work, but not about the rest of this misadventure.

Bloorg was waiting. In his hand was his copper sting, point on the metal floor. Kelvin nodded to him and waited also, feeling that it was the thing to do. The squarear could pick up from his mind what was going on.

Soon they were all there, with the exception of his father and Marvin. Then John Knight stepped from the transporter, and the group leader.

Marvin's eyes widened as he looked at Bloorg. His hand went to his sword.

Kelvin's right gauntlet grabbed the big revolutionary's wrist. "Don't! The squarears are in control!"

"Copper!" Marvin gasped, straining at the gauntlet.

"Friend." *Maybe. In authority, anyway.*

Bloorg spoke. "You were to bring the chimaera its seeds."

"We reached the wrong frame," John said, pretending not to notice the struggle going on.

"My fault," Kian explained. "I'm sorry. Even after you told us the setting—"

"I told you the setting for your own world. You disobeyed."

"I was there," Kelvin said. "I went to our home world for the seeds. They were not where Mouvar left them. I'm certain we can get the seeds, but it will take time to find the berries and harvest them."

"So you came back empty-handed."

"Yes." Kelvin felt uncomfortably like a schoolboy being scolded. It wasn't as if he hadn't run into difficulties.

"Who," Bloorg suddenly demanded, "are these others?"

Kelvin was sure the squarear already knew. But he answered hastily: "From the world we reached by error. They have a purpose in being here. The chimaera was in touch with me mentally. The chimaera approved their coming."

"The chimaera does not make policy. The chimaera does not make law."

"But—"

"You have disobeyed by returning here without the seeds. You have broken law by bringing others."

"I'm sorry," Kelvin said. He had known of no such law, but realized that ignorance was no excuse. Bloorg was like a teacher about to mete out punishment. But perhaps if he explained—

"The cost of our returning was that we help these people," he said. "You see, they have a tyrant, and—"

"Keep your mind still!"

Kelvin tried to relax. He knew that Bloorg was getting the story from him, and he hoped he was getting it right. There were so many things that he himself did not understand. For instance, why had the transporter been one-way until the gauntlets made it functional?

"Mouvar has his reasons," Bloorg said. "The people of that frame were not and are not ready. The transporter was for others."

"Mouvar watches over us all, doesn't he?" The thought slipped out into speech before he realized it.

Bloorg's eyes glowed. "You too are not ready."

Kelvin did a mental shrug. In time maybe his kind would be considered adults by the like of Bloorg and the chimaera. For now they were children or animals who weren't ready yet to learn.

"Precisely. Animals. Mentally inferior life-forms."

Now Kelvin groaned mentally. He wondered how much of this conversation was being followed by Marvin and his men. It probably didn't matter, but they would be affected by the outcome.

Snick, snick, snick! Marvin and his fellows had their swords drawn. Kelvin had stopped watching them and had released Marvin's wrist as soon as Marvin seemed accepting. Now he realized that either he or the gauntlets had made a mistake.

"No squareheaded foreigner calls me an inferior life-form!" the revolutionary leader boomed.

Bloorg waved a hand. The blades glowed red. The men cursed mightily as their swords clanged to the floor.

"They have powers," Kelvin explained belatedly. "In many ways they are more advanced than we are. They have magic here, while in worlds like yours and my father's there's only technology."

"Do you know what you're talking about?" Marvin snarled. He shook his hand, his eyes narrowed with the lingering pain.

"Not really," Kelvin confessed. "Only that it's well to do what Bloorg says."

Marvin wrung his hand. "It's burned!" he said, looking at the palm. "It's burned bad!"

"Is it, Marvin Loaf?" Bloorg asked. His hands did marvelously strange tricks, the fingers twining and untwining like snakes. One finger snapped out at Marvin and made a circle of all his men.

Marvin looked astonished. "It's stopped! It's not burned anymore!"

"Mine neither," Hester said, amazed.

"Or mine!" Redleaf exclaimed, holding out his hands and staring at them.

Awe held the strangers from the wrong frame transfixed, silencing them.

"Now that that little demonstration is over," Bloorg said, "we can proceed with business. The chimaera had no authority from me to do what it did. The chimaera deserves to be punished."

"More than it has been?" Kelvin demanded. "More than being confined to one little island?" Kelvin was astonished by his own words. He must have had some help from the chimaera in forming them.

"Quite right. The chimaera shaped your thoughts and you spoke them as your own."

The chimaera was getting him and all of them into more trouble!

"Wrong. I am quite aware of the chimaera's reasoning in this matter. But I do not understand why it wants to give up its supply of copper to these simple beings."

"Because," Kelvin said, knowing that this was the chimaera's thought and that Bloorg would recognize it as such, "I am tired of being a target. Every inferior life-form with access to a transporter comes after my shed stings. I don't need them now, especially if I can locate others like myself. All I need is enough copper in my diet to keep from growing pale and weak and unmetallic. These roundears had a one-way transporter and can have it again. Let them take the copper to their own world and keep it there, confined. Whenever I shed an old sting they can have that as well. Then let the inferior life-form poachers go to that world to steal the copper. They will discover that they are as much prisoner as I am!"

*Hoo!* Kelvin thought. *That would serve the poachers right! It would also rid the other frames of them. They would have to settle down to honest work in their primitive prison frame, hating every minute of it. The chimaera had a beautiful notion!*

*Thank you, Kelvin,* Mervania's direct thought came. *I am rather pleased with it myself.*

"That's very commendable, Mervania," Bloorg said. Now Marvin Loaf's face changed, as he caught on to what was happening. Perhaps the chimaera had touched his mind, too, with a bit of explanation. "But what about the sting you now have? Your kind have been slain through the centuries for single stings. Indeed, the robot Stapular would have slain you earlier, had he not been waiting for your latest sting to mature. That was why he was able to deceive me; I assumed that since he allowed his living companions to be slain, he had no weapon sufficient to harm you. Surely there will be other poachers."

"That," Kelvin/Chimaera said with asperity, "is why I am confined to an island and why you guard the transporter! I expect you to do a better job in the future."

Bloorg's eyes closed and opened, their lids making an audible click. It seemed the chimaera had scored tellingly. "That might reduce the number and strength of expeditions, Mervania, once it is widely known."

"It will be," Mervania/Kelvin said. "And if the transporter is kept locked, at Marvin Loaf's outlet, and these inferior life-forms do not use the sting in magic—"

"We won't!" Marvin exclaimed, evidently willing to ignore the remark about inferior life-forms. "We don't even believe in that stuff! Much. All we want is the copper. Any horserear poachers come for it, we'll know what to do with 'em!"

"Agreed," Mervania/Kelvin said.

"Agreed," Bloorg echoed.

Kelvin was surprised and relieved. He had been afraid that all of them, the chimaera included, would be punished. Evidently the chimaera had understood the situation better than he.

*Naturally, Kelvin,* Mervania's thought came.

# CHAPTER 22

# *Apprentice*

G rip my hands tighter," Helbah ordered. "Let your essence and mine mingle."

Charlain tried to do as directed. The glade, the trees, the animals peering on, even the aged face, all blurred. It was the dizzying twirl Helbah had made her do, and that bitter wine. Now her arms and legs felt numb. Her fingers tingled. She was, was . . .

Helbah's hands. Helbah's arms. Helbah. Where did Charlain end and Helbah begin? She could feel her heart beating in Helbah's chest, feel the pain of Helbah's reopened wound, feel the blood seeping, seeping through her black satiny wrapper.

"Helbah! Helbah! I'm you!"

"We're we. Notice which mouth you're speaking from."

Charlain noticed. She had spoken from a nearly toothless mouth with sagging cheeks—Helbah's. But when Helbah spoke it was from a mouth that had all its teeth and was perfect except for a bitter aftertaste.

"We can do it now!" one of the mouths said. "Concentrate!"

Charlain tried to remember. Her legs and arms jerked her. Over to the huge tree. Over to the big crystal sealed in its hollow. Her eyes fixed on its surface, then below. Murky smoke swirled and twirled. Then—

Soldiers fighting. Klingland uniforms against Kelvinian uniforms. In the background, through clouds of dust, the huge dome of the Klingland capital

Swords clashed. Crossbow bolts flew. Men died. More dead lay in the red uniforms of the Klinglanders than the green uniforms of the attackers. Even as she realized this, more died.

"Hurry! Hurry!"

They had to be helped. They had to be given new strength. She could almost feel the weakness in those red-uniformed arms. She wanted them stronger, stronger, stronger, their minds and bodies refreshed.

It was like a great wind blowing through her, out of her, into the crystal, into the bodies and minds of the defending soldiers. A green-uniformed soldier was knocked from his saddle with a broad sweep of a defender's sword. Now another, and another! The green-uniformed men were going down like harvested stalks of grain! Now they were panicking, turning, running. Their horse's hooves raised dust as they rode into their dust, pursuing them, chasing them, forcing them to keep retreating and not turn back.

"Now! Now! Now!"

Dust rose, twirled, and—

Blurring twin capital domes, city, hills, forest, big hills, bigger hills.

Another army. Green uniforms with a few black uniforms. Bigger than the force driven from Klingland's capital. Fighting soldiers wearing the bright orange uniforms of Kance. The green uniforms and the black uniforms were winning. Orange uniforms lay with dead or dying bodies in them in the valleys and across the hills. There was no doubt the orange-clads were being driven back, closer and closer to the twin capitals.

*This must not happen!*

Strength, strength, strength surging through her arms. Out of her arms, to the bodies and minds of the defending warriors.

A green-uniformed soldier dropped his sword and died. A second was cut down in similar manner. Here a black uniform screamed its agony until a great war-horse's hoof crushed the unfortunate Herman's head. More and more, the green- and black-clad died or were unhorsed. More and more the orange-clad struck down their opponents and fought with renewed force.

Now the orange had stopped retreating. Now the armies were facing each other in unyielding lines. Now the spears flew and the swords clanged and the spectacle was increasingly ghastly.

The Kance army was fighting well now, but remained outnumbered. No matter how hard the orange fought, they were certain to be cut down in the end. They had to have help. Magic help. Witch's help.

With an intensity she had not imagined she had, Charlain felt the buildup, the great ballooning of rage. In her body, in her soul. Growing, growing, growing. She believed the mechanism to be good and just, yet the force was so strong she could not begin to control it.

In the crystal, above the armies, there developed a great roaring ball of flame. All fighting stopped. The soldiers of both armies looked up. The blacks and the greens trembled. The orange-clads waved and cheered. For the ball was orange. Orange was on top.

With a sudden swoop the ball shot over the invading army. It descended. Men threw up their arms, trying vainly to ward off its heat. It glowed, and the horses danced, spilling their riders and stampeding in terror. Little tendrils of flame grew out of its sides, reaching down, touching, burning, crisping as it sped. Men cowered and threw away their fire-hot weapons. The horses bolted for elsewhere. There was chaos.

The ball imploded with an earthshaking report. Sparks showered down on the Kelvinian army.

The Kancians charged. Encouraged by the panic in the enemy resulting from the witch's fire, they met little fighting resistance. Their swords swung freely. Their spears darted. Men, good, bad, and indifferent, choked and died.

"Oh Lester," Charlain whimpered, remembering how it

had been with him, knowing that similar horror was now being visited on so many more on his side. But there was no stopping it. The invading army was retreating, racing headlong for safety.

Charlain felt herself falling. She felt her face against the ground. She felt blades of grass in her nose and tickling her ears. She felt that she herself was dying.

"Oh what have I done?" she moaned. "What have I done?"

"You did what had to be done," said her other mouth there above her. "What I had to do and you had to help me do."

"But all that killing! All that death!"

"This is the idiocy of men. We cannot redefine their nature. We can only intercede to enable the right side to prevail."

"Meow!" said Katbah, her other body's familiar. Gently, soothingly, the creature rubbed against her head and sounded a comforting purr.

Zoanna stared at the crystal with disbelief. The Kelvinian fighting men and the pick of Hermandy's fighting men were being routed! They shouldn't be. She had endowed them with special strength through her newly acquired powers and had weakened the enemy with others. Now they were losing, and this was contrary to reason. What had happened?

Then she knew. "Helbah!" she cried aloud. It didn't seem possible, for she had seen the old witch almost dead. She should have known that the only good witch was a dead witch, not an almost dead witch.

In the crystal a burst of witch fire formed above the Kelvinian army. Men fell from their horses, grass browned in places, and the mud from a recent rain dried.

That settled it. It was definitely the witch.

"Damn her! Damn!" Zoanna swore. She would do that literally, as effectively as her powers allowed. First she would have to get the witch's image in the crystal, and then by all the evil in existence she would crisp her to a cinder!

The crystal's image swirled and opaqued without her

willing it. The opacity vanished, leaving a clear crystal with Helbah's grimly wrinkled face inside.

"Helbah, I'll get you! I'll finish you!"

The face smiled grimly. "Will you, Zoanna? Try!"

The challenge was too much! Zoanna raised her hands, spoke the words of power, and sent forth a ball of fire.

It backfired. She was thrown across the room, flat on her back amid a pile of smoking furniture and room furnishings. Behind her there was a large crack in the palace's wall.

She sat up, gasping, feeling her ribs, blinking her eyes. She focused on the crystal. There was Helbah's image, with a pleased expression.

"Helbah," she gasped, amazed. "You're strong!"

"Stronger than you, Zoanna."

"We can become allies. We—"

"You are going to leave this frame forever. You and your impostor of a monarch are to vanish. Leave on your own, or be destroyed."

"You can't threaten me, you old bag of bones!"

"Zoanna, I do not threaten. I, far more than you, have the power to destroy."

"Prove it!" Zoanna screamed, losing all control. "Prove it, you old hag!"

"Certainly, Zoanna."

In the crystal the aged face was replaced by a gnarled hand. The fingers separated, spreading to their maximum. Behind the hand, on a level with it, were two deeply burning feline eyes.

"No! NO! *NO!*" Zoanna cried, panicking.

"Yes, YES, *YES!*" mocked Helbah's voice.

The crystal grew pink, then rosy. Belatedly Zoanna tried to put up some mindscreen to abate what was happening. She had become so enraged that she had neglected to ready her defense.

Suddenly there was a loud splintering sound. The crystal turned black and cindery. Then it imploded with a great whoosh of air. Zoanna, who had climbed to her feet intent on retaliation, was back on the floor. Bits of broken and powdered crystal covered her from head to foot.

"Damn you, Helbah! Damn you!" she cried. The gritty stuff was in her mouth and eyes. She had never felt more frustrated or angry.

"What's the matter, dear?" Rowforth had chosen this moment to come casually strolling into this wing of the palace. He appeared unperturbed by the disorder, and in fact he seemed hardly to have noticed it.

She glared at his pudgy form, seething. How dare he act as if nothing had happened!

"YOU!" she screamed at him. "It's your fault!"

"That it is, dearie," Rowforth said in Helbah's voice.

Zoanna stared at him, appalled.

"Goodbye, wicked woman," Helbah said. Then her projection faded, leaving only Rowforth, standing there with a bewildered expression.

Zoanna gazed for some time at the vacant spot where the crystal had been. This was once, she realized, that she had been outmagicked and bested. She had underestimated Helbah, and thought her dying and finished, and so ignored her. That had been a colossal mistake. The witch had survived and recovered, and gathered her magic for an effective retaliation.

Well, Zoanna could do that too! One more visit to Professor Devale, and she would be ready. But first she had to see what she could do to shore up the crumbling attack forces she had launched. Otherwise the war would be lost before she was ready to finish Helbah.

Needing something to occupy her mind, she rehearsed the brutal tongue-lashing she would give Rowforth the next time he gave her the slightest pretext.

St. Helens listened hard. The sounds that had been growing nearer were now receding like an outgoing wave. Why?

"I wonder, I wonder," he said aloud. There was nobody to hear him except an apparently deaf raouse that went right on nibbling his hunk of bread. Halfheartedly he threw his left boot at the rodent. The boot missed by the length of its tail. He drew off his right boot and threw that with as little effect. He went back to pacing his clean cell.

"Those boys, they said surrender, and I thought it was because they were losing. But now it sounds as if our side has been driven off. More witchcraft?"

A commotion at the dungeon door did not quite startle him. He stood back and waited as another prisoner was brought down the stairs. His cell door opened, and a big Kelvinian was pushed inside.

"Mor!" St. Helens exclaimed incredulously. "Mor Crumb!"

Mor rubbed at a spot of blood on his right cheek. He shook his head as though trying to clear it of cobwebs. "Yah, they got me, big mouth. Me and a hundred or so more they stuck in a stockade. Gods know how many died!"

St. Helens' mouth went slack. "You're blaming me? You're calling me big mouth?"

"That's what you are! You were all for this war. You could hardly wait to get your commission!"

"Mor, I never wanted to fight! But there's the prophecy, and the king—"

"The king you knew is not our beloved Rufurt! He's a nasty imitation from another world! You knew, and yet you approved everything he wanted!"

St. Helens felt his face flushing. At another time he would have exploded like his namesake, but this was a friend. Moreover he knew the man to be right. "We were all of us witched or magicked. It's Zoanna, I'm certain."

"Zoanna?" Mor repeated, with disbelief. "She's dead!"

"I wish she were. We all wish. But she must have escaped John's wrath. She must have gotten away and brought back King Rufurt's impostor from that frame Kelvin visited. It's the only answer."

Mor glared at him, then took his fists out of his ribs and crossed to the straw. He sank down, wearily, as though all his air was out.

"St. Helens, what are we going to do?"

"I fear we are going to lose."

"Can we lose? With the prophecy working?"

"I never believed as completely in that as you pointy-ears do," St. Helens said. "Kelvin isn't in this frame. He might not even be alive."

"That would cancel the prophecy, I suppose." Mor sighed noisily. Clearly he was as much at sea as was St. Helens.

"There may be a way," St. Helens said.

"What way? My men were running as if they'd never stop."

"The boy-kings. They're sort of friends of mine, maybe. Nice little chaps. They even cleaned this cell. They offered me their two countries' surrender."

"WHAT?"

"That's right. Only I'm not sure the witch would let them. Only she's a good witch, not the Zoanna kind."

"Witch's tits! You mean actually surrender?"

"That's what they said. They're afraid for themselves and for Helbah and I think for Helbah's cat. They're only kids, younger than Phillip."

"They're twenty-four," Mor said. "They age one year for each of our four. They only look like six years old."

"So it is said. But they want to surrender, that's the important thing. What should I tell them?"

Mor looked down at the clean floor and scratched a flea he'd brought. "You could tell them yes. Zoanna and her consort we can get rid of once the fighting's over."

"We hope. It was tough going before, wasn't it?"

"Yes. I'd hate to fight a revolution all over again, and this time without a roundear."

"I have round ears," St. Helens reminded him.

"Yah. Yah, you have. But St. Helens, you're no Kelvin."

"It don't look like he and his father and his half brother are coming back. Be nice if they did."

"I don't like to say it, but I figure their disappearing and the evil one appearing may not be coincidence."

They sat in gloomy silence for several long moments. Then Mor spoke his thought: "If they're winning, they won't surrender."

"Probably not. But they're just kids."

"The witch would prevent them."

"I don't know. She bosses them and spanks their butts, but maybe they have the governing decisions."

"You think?"

"Naw. I think they're only kids."

"Difficult situation."

"Yah." Halfheartedly he picked up a boot and threw it at the raouse, missing completely again. The rodent looked up in annoyance, grabbed another bite of bread, and streaked for its hole. St. Helens wished he could do that himself.

"All right. All right. If they'll give the surrender I'll take it. If it's legal it should end the fighting."

The raouse came back out of its hole.

Heln held her tummy and cocked her head to one side as she listened to a conversation in a distant part of the palace. Her hearing was getting more acute than it had been. And something else. Something she hardly dared think about.

"And you really want me, Your Majesty?"

"Of course. Who wouldn't? You're lovely."

"But the queen. Your Mrs., Your Majesty!"

"What Zoanna doesn't know won't hurt her, will it? Now just turn over and I'll unbutton—"

Heln pulled her round ears flat down over her head, pinning them and making them hurt. It didn't drown out the giggly scream of the wench. Yet she wasn't really offended by what she had heard. Once, she knew, she would have been.

*Heh, heh, heh, like old times! Doing a maid while the queen naps. This one's a bit fat, but I'll bet she's got bounce!*

*Oh gods, I wanted to be a good girl! But he's the king! Who can deny the king? Besides, his wife's gone, poor man, and she was bad and threw him in the dungeon. Will he know I've done this before? Ah gods, he's biting me! What is he doing down there? OH! OH! OH!* OH!

Heln knew what her thoughts should be, and these weren't her own. She screamed.

Jon woke up with a start.

"Jon! Jon! I'm hearing voices! And I'm thinking other people's thoughts! I know what other people are thinking!"

*Poor girl, she's demented!* "It's all right. It's all right, Heln. You've just had another bad dream."

"You hypocrite!" Heln exclaimed with sudden helpless fury. "You think I'm crazy!"

"Just a bad dream." *I'm going to have to talk to Dr. Sterk.*

*She's not right! She's all mixed up, and paranoid! But can he help her? Can anyone help? Gods, I wish Kelvin were here!*

Knowing that all was really hopeless now, Heln permitted herself a scream that threatened to collapse the walls of the palace.

# CHAPTER 23

# *Scarebird*

*T*hey stood at the edge of the swamp watching the froogears come laden with copper stings. The Crumb look-alikes and their brethren watched with disbelief as the pile grew higher and higher before the transporter. Finally, late in the day, it was all there and the second stage of the operation was about to begin.

"Will this be enough?" Kelvin asked the big Loaf. "Is this enough copper to buy an army sufficient to overthrow your tyrant?"

"Son," Marvin said, very red in the face, "if we lose with this much copper, we deserve it! I didn't know there was so much anywhere. At home I know there's not. Can we start sending now?"

Kelvin nodded. The Loafers began working in a way that belied their name. Bundle by bundle they reduced the pile, tossing each into the transporter. There was a purple flash as the stings traveled alone to their destination. At the other end the men who had gone back were presumably unloading as fast as the stings arrived.

Suddenly Kelvin had an uncomfortable thought: Could they be certain that the people who were to get the copper were in fact getting it? The guardsmen might have come in force and overwhelmed those they had sent back. Consequently the tyrant king could have the copper, and would remain entrenched in a land that was identical to Kelvin's homeland but with a broader river and higher cliff.

*Kelvin, you're worrying again!*

*I am, Mervania. I can't help myself.*

*Suppose you go back and I stay with you as I did before?*

*If the guardsmen are there they will kill me or capture me. You wouldn't be able to stop that.*

*Yes.* Mervania managed to make the thought disinterested.

*Or can you come to the rescue?* If there was something he had overlooked . . .

*No, I'm confined.*

*I mean, mind-stunning anyone who attacked me, as you did with my father when he—*

*Not at such distant range, Kelvin. I'm only in contact with you, there. It would be like you trying to score on an enemy soldier out of your sight beyond the horizon.*

Kelvin thought that over. He didn't like it. *The squarears will help?*

*They would not interfere with another world's affairs. That might annoy Mouvar.*

*But the copper's an interference!*

*Not to them. Copper's a mineral. Besides, there's no way they can use this transporter.*

"No use—? Oh, I forgot! Wrong ears, right?"

*Your mental deficiencies never cease to amaze me.*

*Yes, really stupid, ain't he?* the chimaera's other human head broke in.

*Then I'm really on my own?* Kelvin asked despairingly.

*You're the hero, Kelvin.*

Kelvin looked at his father and brother and his newfound friends. Was he just scaring himself needlessly? No, the chimaera had as much as assured him that his worries were justified.

"I'm going back," he said abruptly. He drew his sword and flexed his left gauntlet. "If all is not going as it should, I'll return." *I hope.*

"And if it is, you'll stay?" his father asked, catching on.

"Until you join me. The chimaera will warn you if I get there and the king's guardsmen are in control and I get caught and can't return." For Mervania could touch other minds more freely, here in her own frame.

"Why can't we all go?" Marvin asked. "One after the other?"

"Because one after the other we could all be killed or captured. The squarears can't help and neither can the chimaera. So I have to find out."

They were still discussing it as Kelvin forced his feet to carry him into the transporter. His heart skipped—

It seemed to be all right. The four Loafers he had seen into the transporter were there with a big pile of sting bundles behind them. All four of the men were covered with sweat from the work of lifting bundles the froogears had carried with ease. The labor of getting copper to this frame was more than any of them had anticipated.

Kelvin heaved a sigh of relief and exchanged greetings. Redleaf, Bilger, Hester, and of course Jillip. The boy, unlike the three grown men, was sweatless and resting. Why did they let him get away with such laziness?

"King's guardsmen been around?" Considering the mountain of sting bundles, the question seemed unnecessary.

"Uh-uh," Redleaf said. "Just us and the copper. Jillip's supposed to be watching. He's too weak for anything else."

"Says you!" Jillip said.

Redleaf grinned and bent to pick up the just-arrived bundle. It was almost like a farm operation John had once told Kelvin about. A machine transporting bundles of grain or grass that had then to be carried by hand. He doubted that the grain bundles had ever weighed as much as copper.

"When the royalists learn what we've got, they'll want it," Hester said. "We may need an army just to get this to where we can buy one."

"Blrood, you said." *Not Throod, as at home, or Shrood as in the silver-serpent place.*

"Yah." Hester grunted as he helped Redleaf swing the latest bundle onto the stack.

"I guess I'll check outside." *Jillip isn't doing it. He must think he's royalty. The kid's a slacker, all right.*

He stepped outside and discovered that it was now an overcast day. Dark clouds in the sky rather than the white pillows that had been there when he left. A day like this seemed made for worry.

To dispel worry he activated his belt. He lifted slowly, slowly by the rock face. Another ledge, narrower than the one he had left, was between him and the top of the bluff. He settled there.

The gauntlets began to tingle their warning.

Now hypersensitive to their messages, he looked quickly down at the great tree and the broad slash of river. He saw nothing unusual. Why then the warning?

Suddenly it was dark. Not the shadow of a thickening vapor, but a deep darkness that covered the cliffside and the ledge while leaving the more distant landscape unscathed.

He looked up, expecting to see a dense cloud or wind-tossed mass of dust. What he actually saw astonished and terrified him. It was a great dark something hung there on outstretched wings, supported by the cliff's updraft. It blinked great yellow eyes and snapped an improbably large beak. It swooped overhead, darkening the landscape.

What by a god's god was that? It was the size of what his father had described as an airplane. But this was nothing to carry passengers! This—this dragon-sized *thing* was alive!

He stood there trying to shut his mouth. He shivered from head to toe. Birds he knew about, bats he had heard about, but he had never seen or heard of *that!*

The gauntlets had quit tingling as soon as the shadow had passed. They knew the monster hadn't seen him. What if it had? He shivered again, thinking about it. He searched the skies anxiously for some time, actually fearing to move from the cliff face. He looked down at where he had exited from the transporter chamber.

Jillip stood alone on the ledge. He was fumbling with his clothing, intent on relieving himself into the treetop. Fool kid! Didn't he realize that they'd be climbing down that? He could just as well have stood over against the cliff.

The gauntlets resumed tingling, and grew warm. In a heartbeat it got dark again. The great something slid silently down, swooping like an eagawk.

Jillip seemed to sense it. He turned. He screamed. He tried to jump back. But he was too late, too slow. Huge talons plucked him from the ledge.

Men appeared from the rock face. "Scarebird!" Hester exclaimed. "Everybody back!"

They quickly crowded back into the chamber. Everyone except Kelvin and—

"HELLLPPP MEEEEEE!"

Gods, he was still alive! Because the scarebird had gone after Jillip instead of Kelvin. He had to help the boy! He had at least to try.

The gauntlets were ahead of him, activating the belt. He shot up at an angle like a stone from his sister's sling. Before he could draw breath he was up against a leathery neck the size of a tree trunk, breathing the stench of reptile and more terrified than he could remember ever being before.

But the gauntlets, his best friends, knew what to do. They put the belt in neutral. He looked at the unmoving wings carrying him and the creature, at the great beak and strangely shaped, gigantic head. Was this a bird? Even apart from the sheer size of it, it seemed alien. He was here to help Jillip, but maybe it was he, Kelvin, who needed help.

*"SCCCRRRREEEEEE!"* The creature let out a great scream or cry. It turned its beak, blinked its eyes, stretched its neck out farther, and—

Suddenly there was a slipping sideways. Kelvin saw the cliffs and the rockspears thrusting up. He hadn't time to think of Jillip or anything else.

He was tumbling, over and over and over. Quickly he slapped the control. The rocks loomed closer, and he hastily adjusted his course. Now he was flying just above the treetops.

SNAP! SNAP! SNAP!

Kelvin winced in pain and accelerated with a push of the lever. He leaped ahead and was immediately out of the thing's reach. Looking back he saw a great head with a pointed top, dark yellow eyes the size of ponds, and a pointed, saw-toothed bill with something flapping from its hooked tip.

His back smarted. That was where the tip of the bill had scraped. The brown material in the beak was the exact center section of his best brownberry shirt. Kelvin considered that he

now wore two arm coverings and that the fastenings in front
had popped off as the flying thing's beak ripped away the back.

"*SCCCRRRREEEE!*"

"HELLLLLLPPPP!"

Oh shut up! he wanted to say, but didn't. There was no
help for Jillip. Unless, unless—

Kelvin climbed to a higher altitude, leaving the monster's
air current. He circled above it, keeping the distance. *Even
when I fought dragons and serpents I had at least a spear!* No
spear now, and no way of getting one. Besides, if he could
somehow kill this—this scarebird—Jillip would surely be
killed in the fall. That might be inevitable anyway, but Kelvin
didn't want to hasten it.

He shrugged out of the remains of his shirt and let the
wind take away the ragged strips. *Poor Heln, she sewed on that
for a week.* With normal use such a garment would last for
years. There was a brownberry farm not far from the
Hackleberry residence; he remembered that a little girl lived
there. What was her name? Easter. Not that that related to him
in any way, other than as a source for the material for another
shirt. He hated to think of how upset gentle Heln would be
with him when she learned about the shirt. Her life must be
pretty quiet now, while she waited on the arrival of the baby.

Now shirtless, he must resemble those bigger-than-life
cinema heroes his father had once described. Except that his
chest was skinny and not bronzed and muscled the way a
fictional hero's would have been. Had it been his place to pick
a hero, Kelvin would have been at the bottom of the list!

He eased the speed of his flying and fell back, keeping the
scarebird in sight. Oh, if it would only land! Then he might be
able to swoop in and rescue Jillip. But it showed no sign of
doing so.

Below, the terrain looked less and less like that of home. It
was rougher and becoming more so. It was hilly, irregular, and
forested, a lot like the way the fabled kingdoms of Ophal and
Rotternik were said to be. Faint hope for any rescue here!

A tang filled his nose, erasing the memory of the reptile
smell. Salt. The ocean was nearby, just as it would be at home
in this region. Maybe that was good news, and maybe not.

He flew on, marveling at how fast they were traveling. The wind, that was what was making the scarebird soar and sail so effortlessly and so fast. The ocean updrafts, the air currents like sea currents, carrying this great, great winged ship. Sky ship—his father had used that term once in telling a story. That was what the scarebird was, only living. A living sky ship.

Now he saw the ocean, and still the great black kite sailed on. An estuary with great mountains of foam and towering rocks. Up the estuary, following the wild, great river that broadened until it was almost as wide as a sea itself. Then trees, gigantic trees! Trees such as Kelvin at his most imaginative had never dreamed of. The tree they had climbed was big, but compared to these it was scarcely a sapling. These were growing up from the water, reaching to the sky, and into the sky, each huger than its neighbors.

And circling, dipping in and out of enormous branches, were dozens of scarebirds! There was a whole colony of them here!

*Poor Jillip! The kid's done! There's no rescue from this. I can't—*

But somehow he couldn't leave. He circled in the air, like the scarebirds themselves, waiting, watching for the monster carrying Jillip to land. He saw that there were many of the monsters hanging upside down in the trees. Like bats, but big. Bigger than any bats or birds imaginable.

The scarebird flew to the top of a great tree. There, deep in the branches and foliage was a monstrous nest. Beaks the length of swords reached up from the nest, opening wide, waiting. *Mama's coming. Mama's coming with your dinner.*

"KEL . . . VIN! SAVE ME!"

So Jillip was still conscious, and in good voice. That suggested that he had not been seriously hurt, yet. He was looking back, and had spied Kelvin, urging him to do the impossible. Poor kid!

Kelvin accelerated, flew past the nest, curved, and came in low above the tree and just below some clouds. That gave him some cover. He saw ruddy throats, open. Those young were hungry!

The chimaera was telepathic. Could this other monster

also communicate mentally? It seemed unlikely, but maybe worth a try. It wasn't as if he had a wide range of promising options. *BIRD! Put down that man! Put him down unharmed!*

"SCRRRREEEEE!

There was no indication that the scarebird knew his thoughts, or cared if it did. In its talons Jillip was now limp, having fainted or been killed. Those talons could have squeezed him lifeless at any time, unless the monster wanted to feed its nestlings live and squirming food. Kelvin hoped it was death, because to be alive when those ravenous chicks fed—he couldn't bear that thought!

"SCCCRRRREEEE!"

SNAP! SNAP! SNAP! The little rascals were impatient. Would one skinny boy divide enough?

"Bird! Bird!" he called, feeling stupid. "I want to talk! As one rational creature to another!"

Did the monster hesitate? It was probably just deciding how to portion out the morsel. He doubted that the thing could talk. His father had told him of a talking bird in his frame of Earth called a polly, so maybe some did talk, however. What else did he have to try?

Jillip's head lifted. His arms and legs straightened. So he had only been unconscious, not injured. Now the very worst was incipient, and Kelvin saw no good way out.

"SCRRRREEEE! SCRRRREEEE!"

"You already said that," Kelvin muttered with gallows humor. He nudged the acceleration lever and got far closer than he wanted. It wouldn't help Jillip if Kelvin also became a meal for the chicks!

The bird spied him. The saw-toothed beak was more formidable than any sword. It darted at him now, the bird intent on grabbing him. It seemed to be well aware of the value of doubling its investment.

The gauntlets jerked him down. He ducked his head, snapped his feet together, and dived under the incoming head. Below the bird, Jillip's drained face looked at him in startled comprehension as he grabbed a leg the size of a normal tree trunk.

"Kelvin! KELVIN!"

"Shut up!" he said. It was a terrible thing to say to a

desperate boy on the edge of losing his life, but necessary. He needed a moment to think, if the confounded bird gave him a chance.

As he might have expected, the bird turned, swooped, slipped, and dived. They were still well up in the air. Kelvin's position changed as quickly and bewilderingly as it might in a whirlwind. Sometimes he was right side up, sometimes upside down. The belt kept him flattened hard against the scaly surface with more than human strength.

He knew the bird would soon tire of this, and soar up and then in to the nest. He saw water below, and Jillip almost skimming it. Then they were rising again, rising with the air current. Now it would be climb, climb, circle, circle, circle, and in for a landing. What had he gained? He remained as clumsy a hero as ever.

As the bird straightened in flight he let go of its leg, and made a grab for the talons. He got hold, nearly upside down, and tried to will his gauntlets to pull up the great, powerful toes. The gauntlets tried; he felt his shoulders and arms take up the strain. But it was not enough. He tried kicking himself back from the foot with all his strength, but still the talon would not budge from the boy.

"Save yourself, Kelvin!" Jillip gasped. "My life is finished. My life's not worth your life!"

Sensible talk, but unfortunately late. Suddenly they were bouncing. Up and down, up and down. Branches the girth of a man's legs were slapping on either side of his face. They had come to a landing at last, on the rim of the scarebird's nest.

*"CREEEE! EEEEEE! EEEE!"* SNAP, SNAP, SNAP!

The chicks were eager for dinner. Their hungry cries were deafening. In a moment they would have their desire.

Kelvin slapped a branch out of his face and drew his sword.

A great beaked head with huge yellow eyes was looking at him under the gray belly. It was mama's beak and mama's eyes. She would snatch him from her foot like a scared rodent, and some lucky chick would be the recipient. As for Jillip, who was costing Kelvin his life—

"NO!" Kelvin shouted, and jabbed his sword into the fleshy part of her left foot.

The bird's head shot back out of sight, her talons opened suddenly, and she let out a screech which made the prior ones seem faint. Kelvin wasn't waiting, nor were his gauntlets. With one clumsy lunge he grabbed Jillip and tumbled with him into space.

Wind whistled by their ears and brush slapped by their faces. Bits of bone and rotting animal carcasses were strewn on branches they passed. Somehow the gauntlets managed to hold the boy, yet also activate the belt. Upside down scarebirds hung from branches bigger than normal tree trunks. He glimpsed these briefly, peripherally, hoping they got even lesser glimpses of him, and then he was flying.

Below them were hard rocks in deep water. Past them, so close she almost touched, passed the angrily screaming big mama.

Kelvin adjusted their acceleration as the bird caught the air again, ending her dive. They were soon speeding up the river, back the way they had come. When he knew the bird was far outdistanced, he took a more comfortable grip on Jillip, who was now returning again to consciousness. He had fainted somewhere during that mind-numbing scream, which was perhaps just as well.

"Jillip, your leader assured me that there were no dragons, no giant silver serpents, no magic in this frame! What by all the gods is that creature back there?"

"Scarebird," Jillip said, puzzled. "Don't you have scarebirds in your frame?"

"Never heard of them! Never want to see one of them again!"

"Must be a placid existence you have," the boy remarked.

# CHAPTER 24

# *Army*

*T*he journey to Blrood was surprisingly uneventful. For a full day Kelvin labored with the belt transporting the copper from atop the cliff to the ground. Constantly he broke off in his labors to reconnaissance for guardsmen or scarebirds. The guardsmen never came, nor did the wings of the great bird again darken the cliff.

Getting packhorses for the copper proved to be easy. The Loafers knew the farmers they could count on, most of whom had suffered at the hands of guardsmen. Help for them now was not in short supply.

Disguised as merchants, they made their journey and met the Blrood soldiers who had been dispatched to see them on their way. The territory, the fruit they ate along the way, even the people they saw all seemed a rerun. Once a large violet and light-rose bird flew over calling from a long beak "Pry-Mary! Pry-Mary!"

"Primary bird!" Kelvin guessed. He was certain it couldn't be the purgatory bird, though except for plumage they did seem much the same.

"Political bird," Hester explained. "Also termed beginning bird."

Kelvin nodded and let his eyes wander on to the expected monument. The cairn appeared almost identical to those he had seen on similar missions in two related frames. About the only difference was the inscription which here dedicated the cairn to the memory of Blrood's soldiers, rather than Shrood's or Throod's. Again it seemed they had perished in a two-hundred-year-old war, but not against Hud or Rud. Though he had forgotten to inquire, the kingdom he was now attempting to free was the kingdom of Fud.

"Recruitment House!" Bilger called. This time the fruit juice dripping from the revolutionary's mouth was definitely red rather than orange or yellow. More packhorses more heavily laden, more local armed men accompanying them.

This time it was not a Captain MacKay with pointed ears or a Captain McFay with round, but a Commander Mac. The commander had round ears as did the last such individual, and his facial and body conformations had similar outlines. But in Throod the big gray-haired, gray-eyed man had lost an arm. His equivalent in Shrood had been slightly balding, had had two good arms and one peg leg. Commander Mac had all his hair but was missing half his teeth, a fact that became evident as soon as he spoke. He had all his extremities, but his back was bent more than the others and his right shoulder sloped. In addition to all the other differences, Mac wore a patch over his left eye.

The commander held out his hand. Talk and drinking and card playing ceased. Veterans and recruits alike turned their attentions. "Marvin Loaf. You've got the copper?"

"Some. More back in Fud. Safe, I hope."

Mac and two veterans went out and checked the packs. The stings had worn through their coverings in places and the copper was drawing attention from those who dared not touch. A path cleared for the commander. He cut open a couple of bundles, scratched the copper with a knife, smiled, and felt the other bundles with his hands.

"With what you have here you can buy our finest and best fighting men, all equipment, horses, and catapults. Gods, I didn't know there was that much copper! You've got your army."

"Actually there is a catch to our generosity," John said quickly.

They all looked at him inquiringly. Particularly Marvin Loaf.

"Let's go back in and discuss it," Commander Mac suggested.

They did. On the way in John explained: "The catch is that when all of this is over my boys and I leave this frame forever. We're here by mistake. Marvin's help makes us indebted to him, and we pay our debts. Besides, we had much the same situation back home until we did what Marvin's doing. Only our land is called Rud and its tyrant was a woman."

"Either sex, an army's an investment!" Mac said. "A tyrant is a tyrant is a tyrant until it's dead."

"I like that," Marvin Loaf said.

They found a table, mugs of bleer, and soon had a large assemblage of onlookers. As in similar situations two times before in two different frames, Kelvin was pressed to talk. He did so now with pleasure. But long before he had recited their adventures skepticism reared its monster head.

"Do you really expect," one grizzled oldster demanded, "that we believe that? Dragons are impossible enough, but dragons with golden scales?"

Annoyed, Kelvin broke off his narrative to explain. "They swallow golden nuggets from the streams. Since dragons live until they are slain and many have lived for centuries and possibly for thousands of years, the gold migrates to the scales."

A young man there for recruitment shook his head, studying Kelvin with a skeptical expression. "I've heard of migrating metals in the bodies and shells of shellfish. That's science. But dragons aren't. Dragons are myth."

"Different worlds, different rules," John broke in. "Go on, Kelvin."

He wanted to, but to his astonishment he was losing his audience. None of these tough fighting men wanted to believe this junk. He was hardly into his tale of how they'd had a people's revolution in Rud and the prophecy had made him important, particularly after the dragons.

"And these posters you put up, they really did get you men?"

Kelvin stared at the commander with disbelief. He sounded as skeptical as the recruit.

"Untrained ones. Volunteers. Farmers and others who had had enough of oppression."

"Go on."

He did, but it wasn't fun. Everything he said convinced

them that he lied. The painful thing was that lying was one skill he had never cultivated, and one talent that he lacked. He could no more have exaggerated his own part than Jon's.

"That's blood transfusion!" the young warrior snapped. Kelvin had been giving a graphic description of what befell Jon and himself at the hands of the sorcerer.

"Uh, if you say so. Now the dwarf Queeto was catching her blood, and—"

"Science."

"Magic where I come from. Zatanas was using sympathetic magic, the only magic he was skilled in. Rather than using a doll with my fingernail parings or hairs in it, he used my sister. Same blood, so as she weakened, I weakened."

"That's bunk! I don't believe that one."

Kelvin felt exasperated. How could he get through to this clod?

"You have scarebirds here. I'd say they are sometimes as big as dragons, and fully as dangerous."

"Scarebirds are natural! They have been a part of the natural world since before men! What you're talking about is unnatural."

"Here, maybe. Not at home. At home scarebirds would be unnatural." He did not mention the chimaera; he saw no need to stretch their incredulity that far.

"I can vouch for everything he says," Kian offered. "You see, Zatanas was my grandpa, and Zoanna my mother."

There was instant silence. Someone slurped bleer. Then a big veteran with a craggy face and bulging muscles laughed. In a moment all the Blroodians were laughing. Kian's apparently ridiculous statement had convinced them that it was all a joke.

Kelvin felt alarm at the look on his brother's face. In a moment, if he did not act, Kian would. That would mean trouble—big trouble—and he had had more than enough of that! Kian might have better self-control than his father-in-law, but barely.

Though it pained him to do it, he started to get up. If he challenged the big man right there and the gauntlets helped him in the fight, that would at least end the laughter.

His father came to their rescue. "It's something to laugh at here," he said calmly, addressing the bleer, "but back then it wasn't. Remember I originated in a world where it would all have sounded ridiculous. We didn't believe in magic there. But let me tell you what we did believe in: we believed in the scarebird."

Silence. Every eye turned to John, diverted from the promise of immediate action.

"Father," Kelvin broke in, "you never said you had scarebirds!" Immediately he wished he had kept his mouth shut. Now everyone was looking at him.

"I didn't mean they were there when I left! But Earth had them before I was born. Way, way back in my planet's history. They were around before any humans were. Every now and then some of their bones were found, sometimes a complete skeleton. They weren't as big as the ones here, but they were similar. The scientists in my time called them pterodactyls. They existed, let's see, approximately one hundred and twenty million of our years before my birth."

"How did you know that, Father?" Kelvin had to ask. When his father started talking about Earth stuff Kelvin almost reverted to child stage. He'd been a question box, his father had said, and Kelvin wasn't certain he'd changed.

"Well, Kelvin, it wasn't magic. My people mostly didn't believe in magic, you see, and certainly the scientists didn't. There were scientific ways of determining the ages of bones and other things. The pterodactyls, what you call the scarebirds, flew Earth's skies long, long before there were men, but their bones proved their existence."

"No humans to see them at all, Father?"

"Not on Earth. In other frames, perhaps. Earth didn't have humans and pterodactyls living at the same time. In other existences, such as this one—yes. These are a lot larger than those we had, however; they've had more time to evolve."

The faces had all grown serious. Now Marvin, looking so much as Morton Crumb would have looked back home, spoke:

"I don't know about what these fellows say, but there are mighty strange things in other frames. Tell them, Hester. Tell them what we saw."

Lester's look-alike said: "Short fellows made all of squares. Crystals that they saw things in—things at a great distance. Some big creature we don't even have legends about that ingests copper and produces the copper stings we brought. People that seem descended from froogs, with the ear patches of froogs and a froog's habits."

"All that's true," Marvin said. "We were all of us there. So do you want our copper or don't you?"

Commander Mac swallowed. "Those stings were produced by some monster? Grown on it?"

"You calling us liars?" There was danger in the big man's voice, as though he would risk his beloved revolution on it.

Commander Mac took a swig of bleer, lifted his eyepatch, and rubbed a nasty scar where an eye had been. He contemplated, as a soldier had to, then spoke in a very reasonable voice. "I believe copper's copper." He looked around at his friends and associates. No-nonsense types, all of them more concerned with their skills and their work of killing than with the wild fantasies of others.

"Maybe that's all we need to know," the grizzled old fellow said. "The rest, that's none of our concern. Copper, after all, is copper."

Having pronounced a verdict, the unofficial judge retreated to a distant chair. Others joined him, and someone dealt cards. Left was only the young mercenary.

"Well, I think we really need to proceed on that assumption," said Commander Mac.

Kelvin looked at his father and brother and felt his own mouth gaping. It was all over then—all his story telling. It didn't seem to him to be right.

"Yes, I quite agree," Marvin said. "Why don't you visitors go out and see the Flaw. Quite a sight! You've probably never heard of it."

They had of course heard of it, but didn't say so. "Come along," John Knight said. So they trooped out together, one collection of male kin. Left behind were the locals, who had an important matter pertaining to the revolution to decide.

"Why, Father?" Kelvin wanted to know. "Why leave, when there's so much that's so fascinating to tell?"

John checked to make certain no one else was following. "We have to give them a chance to hash things out alone. As for their incredulity—well, people were that way on Earth, too,

Kelvin. Not all folk, but some. If they don't want to believe, they don't want to know. Something like magic."

Kelvin wondered, and thought he understood. His father hadn't wanted to believe in magic for the longest time. He had denied that there was magic until it was impossible to doubt it anymore. He still tended to think in a nonmagical way.

"I want to see that Flaw, boys," John said. "You know I've heard about it, and I've been through it, but I've never actually seen it. Not when I had my wits with me."

Kelvin remembered the first time he had seen the Flaw. That had been at the beginning of his warring experience. He and the Crumbs had been buying an army to use against Kian's evil mom. Jon had tried to shoot a star with her sling, and she had been frustrated. Like people who refused to believe in magic even while experiencing it, Jon hadn't believed in the inefficiency of her sling or the distance of stars.

When they reached the wooden barrier it looked just the same as it had in the other two frames, except that some of the graffiti were different. His father stood, openmouthed, staring through the observation hole and into the velvety-black, star-filled depths.

"It's—it's the womb of creation!" His voice carried awe. "Gods, it's a crack through Earth, Earth's worlds! An opening through all worlds, all possible worlds, all alternatives!"

"You had it on Earth, Father?"

"I . . . don't know. I don't think we did. But maybe another part? Maybe in the Arctic—or maybe another time."

The afternoon passed while John gradually built acceptance for something he hadn't quite believed in. Another day passed while a message was sent to the Fud palace. Another day drinking bleer, playing cards, and waiting for an unanticipated reply to the ultimatum. Still another day while Kelvin worried. Then finally they set out.

At the border a delegation of uniformed guardsmen met them with the Fud flag and a surrender flag. An enormous cheer went up and down the ranks of mercenaries, though many might have experienced regrets. An adventure too soon over. A war not fought. Bonus pay but not fighting pay. No spoils, no captive wenches. Back home to the Recruitment House to wait unemployed for possibly many more months.

"And so," the guardsman spokesman was saying, "His Majesty surrenders unconditionally to overwhelming numbers. In anticipation of a change in government he has abdicated his throne."

Amazing! Evidently the despot of this frame was relatively cowardly. They would have to make sure he didn't have some treachery in store.

"Well, now that that little matter is settled—" Kian said, looking happy.

Kelvin knew that this entire adventure had been just a little matter delaying a wedding, in Kian's view. Well, maybe so.

## CHAPTER 25

# *True Love Runneth*

*H*eeto the dwarf met them first. They had been traveling their weary way from the transporter by foot, Kelvin now and then soaring overhead to see if he could spot someone. They bypassed Serpent's Valley, not wanting to get involved with the flopears and their reptile ancestors this trip. The gauntlets had been very faintly tingling, not really signaling danger but suggesting that he should move right along to avoid it. In fact, they had been tingling that way for the past day or so, as if they, too, wanted to get this matter over and done with. Finally when their party was on a good road with maybe half a day's hiking ahead, there was the dwarf.

"Heeto! What are you doing here?" Kelvin asked, dropping down out of the sky and landing right in front of him. Was this another wrong frame? He had set the indicator carefully, but there had been so many nasty surprises! Would they never get back to the frame of good Queen Zanaan and lovely good girl Lonny Burk?

The dwarf jumped, startled, then stared at Kelvin incredulously. "You can *fly!*"

"Yes, I can fly, but only with this belt. It's nothing to get worried about. I'm Kelvin, the same Kelvin whose life you saved."

"You saved us all," Heeto said. "From an evil king and his attempted alliance with flopears. Now, thanks to you, we live in a decent kingdom."

"My father and brother and I have come back. But we won't all stay. Kian wants badly to see his Lonny."

"Yes, Lonny Burk. She is to marry Jac."

"WHAT?" Kelvin felt nearly as devastated as he knew Kian would be. To have gone through so much and to have got here finally at long last and to find her marrying Jac! Not that Jac wasn't a fine fellow, a good skin-thief as his fellows had proclaimed, and a capable revolutionary when helped as required. No, Jac was fine, *but not marrying Lonny!*

"Your brother has returned to her?"

"Yes."

"She did not think he would, ever."

Kelvin looked at the sky. It was early morning now; only a short time since they had risen. But how long had they actually been gone from this reality? He could feel the sun warming his skin, and he knew that this reality felt like the only one, and certainly it was now for him. But they had been weeks away by their reckoning. Suppose time here was different, and instead of weeks it had been months, possibly even years?

"She missed your brother, but she thought him gone," the dwarf explained. "She faced the prospect of life as an old maid. Jac believed this too, and asked her to marry him."

"Right, I understand." *I just hope Kian does.*

"Jac would not have asked if he had known Kian would be back. Jac is an honorable man."

"He is." *Here,* he thought. *In other frames he's a villain. But here, yes, as honorable a person as ever comes.*

"You will attend the wedding? You and your brother and father?"

"It's today?"

"Yes. The Grand Ballroom is in the official Hud palace. The ceremony is to take place at noon."

"We'll be there," Kelvin said, knowing now that they were in the right frame and much nearer the palace than he had thought. Now he understood the quiet urgency of the gauntlets: it wasn't a physical danger, but an emotional one. They must have known what was about to happen here, and urged him to get here before it was too late. "Where's your horse?"

"Being shod," the dwarf replied. "I was going to get a silver ring."

"Silver ring? Why?"

"For the wedding. For Jac to slip on his bride's finger."

Kelvin felt stunned. But then he remembered his father telling him of a similar custom on Earth. When his mother and father had wed they had simply declared before witnesses that they were married, and after that they were. People wishing to end a marriage divorced in similar fashion.

"May I come with you?"

"Of course. Can you fly with two?"

"You want to fly? Yes, my belt should support your weight too. But you will have to hold on tightly, because—"

"Don't worry! I don't know how to fly, but I know what a fall can do!"

Thus it was that Kelvin went with the dwarf to the jeweler. The jeweler was an elderly, wizened man who seemingly dwelt in his shop. In addition to accessories to his daily life, there was a fine display of clocks, rings, silver plate, and assorted jewelry. He reached under a counter to a secret place and brought out a polished, highly decorated silver band.

Heeto took the ring and examined it. He held it up for inspection in the morning sunbeam coming through the shop's window, then handed it to Kelvin.

Kelvin looked at the workmanship. Flopear without a doubt. In the narrow silver band, just the right size for Lonny's finger, were incised tiny figures. Held to the light the figures seemed to be those of children, and as Kelvin squinted it seemed that the children were running and tossing a ball.

"I never get over what the flopears can do with silver," the oldster wheezed, leaning over the counter. "Those old folk, strolling hand in hand through flowers. How do they do that?"

"Magic," Kelvin answered, remembering his problem with the skeptical men of the other frame who refused to believe in magic. He did not tell the old man that his eyes saw something entirely different. That artistry was twice as special as it seemed! The old man needed all the comforting illusions he could get. Did the picture change for every viewer? Kelvin had more than a suspicion that it did, and that each would find pleasure in what he or she saw. Heeto did not have to worry whether Lonny would like the ring; it would make her like it!

They left the shop, Heeto carefully putting the ring in a small bag he hung over his shoulder. As they emerged into the bright glare of early day Kelvin had an idea. It was a foolish one, but maybe he was ready to be foolish for a change.

"Heeto, would you like to fly yourself?"

"With you hanging on to me, Kelvin? I don't think that would work very well."

"Well, by yourself, then, if you don't go far or fast. Just to feel what it's like." The gauntlets gave no warning, so this seemed safe.

The dwarf's eyes lighted. "Not far or fast!" he agreed.

So Kelvin squatted and put the belt on Heeto and instructed him in the handling of the lever. When he was certain Heeto understood, he stood back and let the dwarf try it.

Heeto nudged the lever ever so gently. Suddenly he shot up high. "Slow!" Kelvin cried, alarmed.

"I did it slow!" Heeto cried.

"Then even slower on the reverse!"

The dwarf's progress slowed, then he hovered, and finally he came slowly down. "I know what happened," he said, breathless. "I was too light for it."

That made sense. Kelvin caught him as he came within range, so that there could be no further misjudgment. They both agreed that they had had enough experimentation. Yet despite his scare, Heeto was flushed and happy. He had had an experience he would never forget. So it had been the right thing to do, risk and all.

Kelvin donned the belt again. Then he held Heeto, and they flew at a comfortable walking speed the short distance down the road to where John and Kian Knight were still plodding.

"Kelvin, what's that you've got?" Kian demanded.

"Come see for yourself," he replied as he landed.

Kian came forward, squinting his eyes against the far too bright sunlight. He paused, and his eyes widened. He held out his arms. "Heeto! Heeto, my friend! What are you doing here?"

"I was on a mission," Heeto explained, and rushed forward on short little legs that nevertheless were quite swift. He grabbed Kian around the waist as a child might. Kian hugged the dwarf with just as much affection.

Kelvin stood back, eying them and his father speculatively. Kian was the happiest he had ever seen him, so how would he react to the news Heeto brought?

"Lonny—she's all right?" Kian wondered.

"She's . . . in health," Heeto said.

"But—?" Kian obviously sensed something.

"She thought you were never coming back. She thought you didn't want her."

"I want her! Gods, I want her!"

"She's marrying Jac."

Kian clutched his heart region. His face slackened. His mouth gaped. It was exactly as though he had received a sword thrust.

Kelvin watched his brother settle down into the dust of the road, place his head in his hands, and shake. He wasn't crying, exactly, but his reactions were those of a man on the verge of dying. Kelvin knew he had to do something for his brother.

"The wedding's today, Kian. At noon. We have time to get there. My gauntlets have been tingling; they know it's not too late."

Kian looked up, brightening. "Yes, yes! We must go! We must be there!"

"Kian," said their father, "Jac was good to us, and saved all our lives more than once. Hers too. If they want each other, you won't interfere?"

"No, Father," Kian said bravely. "No, of course not."

But Kelvin wondered. His brother, unlike himself, had been brought up and spoiled rotten by a ruthless and evil woman. Kelvin had seen far more of his father and himself in Kian than Zoanna and her evil father Zatanas, yet there was a heritage. When Kian was frustrated beyond sanity, would his mother's side come out? Would he pull his sword against Jac? That, Kelvin decided, must not happen.

"The bride and groom won't arrive until the wedding," Heeto said. "You can take time to clean up from your travels, and Queen Zanaan will get you better attire. I see, Kelvin, that you have lost your shirt."

"Zanaan, she's still queen?" John Knight asked.

"Yes, still queen. The people all love her."

"The people have great sense." John Knight spoke with conviction, as though this were a sentiment he had long needed to express.

"What of Rowforth, her husband?" Kelvin asked.

"Rowforth hasn't been found," Heeto said. "He managed to get a knife into Sergeant Broughtmar, his former lackey. We found the sergeant dying on the roof. The king somehow got away, and hasn't been seen since."

"He's still alive, then?" This was bad news!

"Until he's caught. Everyone wants him taken alive so he can be publicly executed."

"The poor queen," Kelvin said.

"No, no. Not poor queen at all," Heeto protested. "She was a prisoner, a hostage to him. She suffered more than any of us. If she could have, she would have divorced him long ago."

"Yes, I suppose that's true." Kelvin looked at his father's face and thought he saw something there that he did not entirely like. He remembered how evil Zoanna had bewitched him, using her magic to keep him enthralled so that she was able to have a child by him. Was it possible that there had been more to it than that? Perhaps a really good copy of Queen Zoanna without her evil ways was what his father really wanted, and certainly Zanaan was that. Certainly she was beautiful. But did he want his father with that woman? Childhood memories of seeing John so content with his own mother Charlain cried a loud if irrational protest.

His father, for his part, had a look of positive eagerness on his face.

They were almost to the gates, the same gates that had once gone down to permit a charge of flopears on war-horses directed against the Freedom Fighters' troops. Kelvin was recalling that war in all its hideousness and the glory of their triumph, as they approached.

Suddenly a horseman wearing a worn uniform of the Freedom Fighters clattered around the corner. "They got him! They got the king!"

"Alive? Alive?" someone shouted.

"Alive! They found him hiding out near serpent territory! Just barely surviving! They're bringing him now!"

Kelvin and his party waited. Kian and John, a bit more anxious to enter the palace than Kelvin was, were partway up the walk. Kelvin turned back to the street.

Soon horsemen came trundling a cart. Looking out of a cage on the cart, ragged, dirty, sunken-eyed, big nose sunburned and peeled, was the figure of the king. What a relief to have captured him!

But as the cart drew even with him, the face behind the bars spotted them, and the wretched creature called out: "Kelvin! John! Kian! Thank the gods!"

Kelvin blinked. The supposed King Rowforth had filthy, round ears. But if this was not Rowforth—if the ears were not the positive identification they seemed—then it had to be good King Rufurt of his homeland!

Unless the evil king was trying to fool him. Rowforth was capable of anything, to save his evil hide.

"John, remember those days in the royal dungeon? You and I together—remember?"

The cart trundled past. The shouts of angry, enraged, and rejoicing people who had served under the Rowforth yoke followed and drowned out whatever else the prisoner was saying. The face looked back at them, pitifully, and Kelvin wondered. Could it be, was it possible that this was King Rufurt?

He hurried to catch up. "Father, do you think—?"

But his father was looking eagerly toward the palace.

Kelvin wasn't sure that he had ever heard the prisoner. He wasn't quite certain he had heard correctly himself.

Was it King Rufurt? Impossible, but also impossible to ignore. Rufurt was pointeared, and so could not use the transporter. But that reference to the dungeon—had Rowforth known about that? How could he be sure?

Things moved so rapidly the rest of the morning that Kelvin hardly thought again about the man in the cage. All he could think about as they entered the great ballroom at noon was his brother and what his brother's reactions to immediate events might be. They had been briefed about how the bride and groom would enter by opposite doors, and how the queen herself would conduct a little ceremony. At the end of some ritualized questioning Jac was to slip the ring on Lonny's finger and the queen would pronounce them wed. Was it Kelvin's imagination, or did she sound a little sad when she explained about her part in it? Was he missing something?

All three of them—Kelvin, Kian, and John—were there to witness but not to make their presence known to others until the ceremony's end. All were dressed in stiff, heavily laced clothing that Kelvin, for his part, would be only too happy to shed. Later they would get new traveling clothes, the queen had promised. She was solicitous and helpful in forming their plans. Kelvin had to hope that his father was not going to stay here and marry her, though he knew this was a bad attitude on his part. John's marriage to Kelvin's mother had been sundered long ago, and Hal Hackleberry was a good man. The past was over and done with.

Someone was playing music. It sounded loud and had the effect of drowning thought. A beautiful woman sat at a piangan and stroked its red and yellow keys. The music changed as soon as everyone was in place, and from an oceanic swelling of sound it went to triumphant march. It was time for the bride and groom to enter by the opposite doors and stand before the queen.

The facing doors opened. Kelvin immediately focused all his attention on his brother's face. Kian did not look angry or enraged, he looked sad, even heartbroken. It was pitiful to see anyone, especially a brother, in such condition.

Lonny and Jac came forward until they met, joined hands, and turned to face the queen. Their audience had a side view of bride and groom while bride and groom were unable to see their unanticipated guests from another frame. No matter, as local custom decreed, bride and groom simply gazed each into the other's face.

Jac, dressed up and clean, was handsome despite his scar, and older than Kelvin had realized, really of John's generation. He looked somehow grim rather than happy, though that was probably because of the gravity of the occasion. Kelvin remembered how he had suffered buttersects in the stomach when he married Heln, even though it was exactly what he wanted to do.

Lonny was beautiful, with her hair garlanded with flowers and her bridal outfit enhancing a body that had at the worst of times been quite attractive. She too was unsmiling, perhaps maintaining her composure by sheer willpower, for she was normally a cheerful girl. Kelvin remembered that she had at one time used the gauntlets, and evidently gotten along with them well. The gauntlets served whoever wore them, but he liked to think that they liked some wearers better than others.

"Lonny Burk," the queen intoned, as serious as the two of them, "do you wish to marry Jac Smite, also known as Smoothy Jac, also known as Savior of our Land?"

"I do," Lonny murmured faintly.

"And you, Jac Smite, also known as Smoothy Jac and Savior of our Land, do you wish to marry Lonny Burk?"

Jac seemed to hesitate. His eyes darted in the direction of the properly attired roughnecks who had been with him in a skin-stealing operation and then a revolution. Possibly, though not certainly, he was having second thoughts. He looked at the queen as if appealing for some recourse, but found none.

"I do," Jac said at last, clearly and unmistakably.

Kelvin's pity for his brother intensified. It seemed that the girl he loved really did mean to marry his friend. Had it been a mistake to keep quiet? Yet what kind of a situation would it have made, if Kian had dashed up and told her of his presence and his love just before she was to be married to another man?

But the ceremony was not finished. The queen now

addressed the guests, asking simply, "Is there anyone here who objects?"

Kelvin looked at his brother, hoping he would speak. He had been afraid Kian would lose control, but now was sorry he hadn't. Lonny just didn't look that eager for the union. Neither, surprisingly, did Jac. Was it just a marriage of convenience? In that case—

The queen turned back to the couple. "Since there are no objections, I therefore declare—"

The gauntlets gave Kelvin a sharp jolt. "Wait!" It was out of his mouth before he realized it.

The queen seemed almost relieved for the distraction. "You? You object, Kelvin Knight Hackleberry. Why?"

Kelvin hesitated. The gauntlets jolted him again. "My brother wants to wed her!" he blurted. He was conscious of a roomful of eyes orienting on him. "He's come back from his native frame for that purpose. We were delayed, we couldn't help it, but all the time he intended—" He stalled.

There were murmurings and whispers and some outright exclamations. But it wasn't Kelvin's words that raised the most excitement, it was Lonny Burk's reactions.

Lonny stared at them, focusing on Kian. Her normal rosy complexion turned white, and with one little cry of "Kian!" she sank to the floor, unconscious.

Kelvin had to move fast to keep up with his brother. Already the former princeling was at his truelove's side. Kian knelt by her, taking her hand. "Lonny, Lonny, don't die!"

Her eyes opened, blue and achingly beautiful. "Kian, Kian, I thought you gone forever! That girl in your own world . . . I—I—"

"Hush, sweet Lonny," Kian said. "She—wasn't for me. You were. It just took me a while to get my mind straight. It will be all right." Then he looked up to see Jac staring down at them. "That is—"

Jac's big hand came down and clasped Kian's shoulder so hard he winced. "Friend, Companion Closer Than Kin, Kian Who Made Me What I Am, if Lonny chooses you, I will not object."

Kelvin sighed relief. But in a moment Kian, who seemed

to have been rocked by a fist, was saying, "No, no, my friend, I lost my head. Right is right. You deserve her."

"Why do you say that, old friend? We fought the serpents together. We fought the king's minions and warriors. We dared greatly and we won. You deserve everything, including Lonny. I should never have interfered!"

"Well, actually—" Kelvin started, trying to alleviate the colossal awkwardness of the situation.

"I felt I should marry her because it wasn't right to let her grieve any longer," Jac said. "But now you have returned. That changes everything."

"But I left her for Lenore Barley. I—"

"Who," Lonny asked with sudden strength, "is Lenore Barley?"

"The girl in the other frame who looks like you," Kian explained. "But there is more of a difference between you than just her pointed ears. She made love physically with different men, while you and I—"

"Shared a more intimate joining," Lonny said.

"Yes, yes, that's true, but—"

"But it didn't mean anything to you."

"No, no, that's not true! It meant everything!"

"Did it, Kian?" Lonny's face had found its blood supply. Her eyes flared warningly.

"Yes. Yes. And that is why, Lonny, you must marry Jac! He deserves you, while I do not."

"What he means, is—" Kelvin started, realizing that things had gotten completely turned around.

"That's not true!" Jac insisted. "You deserve her while I do not! I have been with many women in a physical sense, while you—"

"Enough!" Lonny exclaimed. "I'm not the least bit interested in marrying either of you! You—you philanderers!"

Kian and Jac displayed openmouthed astonishment, then fell into each other's arms and shook uncontrollably. Lonny stared at them in near incomprehension, then rose to her feet, picked up the train of her wedding dress, and disdainfully swept past everyone to her door and out the way she had come.

Kelvin looked at his father as the door closed behind the

intended bride. John Knight shrugged, obviously as bewildered as Kelvin felt. Had those two jackasses learned their lessons?

"Go after her, Kian, she's yours!"

"No, no, my friend, *you* go after her!"

"Pitiful, isn't it," John Knight remarked. He was looking at the queen, and it was uncertain exactly what he meant.

"It certainly is," she said. "And after all my plans, all the flowers and festivities!" Yet, oddly, she did not seem completely displeased.

The heartbreaking sounds of the prospective grooms' sobbing filled the ballroom and drowned out the sympathetic murmurings of the guests turned spectators.

# CHAPTER 26

# *Over*

*I* tell you, Father, it was him!" Kelvin insisted.

"Nonsense," John replied. "King Rufurt here? With his pointed ears? He couldn't even use the transporter! It's impossible for Rufurt to be here!"

"Maybe his ears were changed, Dad. Or maybe Jon is right and the warning is just to keep pointed-ear persons in their place. Maybe he came some other way, not using the transporter. You did, the first time, and Kian did. Maybe it's dangerous and uncertain and painful, but the Flaw makes it possible. They're going to execute him, so I think we should see. I swear it sounded like Rufurt."

"With all that noise the crowd was making, you thought you heard words you didn't. That's happened to me a number of times. Or maybe Rufurt's using magic."

"Maybe somebody's using magic! Bad magic! Dad, we owe it to Rud's king. We haven't been back there since this business started; something might have happened. If Rufurt somehow got sent here—"

John Knight frowned in a way that meant he was considering. Obviously he had something of a different nature on his mind. "I suppose I can stand one more trip to a dungeon. I hate them, though."

"Just to make certain, Dad. That's all. It would be a terrible thing if that really was King Rufurt and we let him be killed in Rowforth's place."

"Terrible, but unlikely. All right, we'll go get permission from the queen."

How glad he sounded, saying that. But Kelvin doubted that his father's joy was at the prospect of seeing their king.

In her throne room Zanaan looked every bit the queen, John thought admiringly. Her very beauty and regality made him a bit tongue-tied. But in due course, trying unsuccessfully to ignore the fact that he had once made love to a body almost exactly like hers, he got out the story.

"And you say this Rufurt of your homeland is a good man?" Zanaan asked. Obviously it was his story and not him she was most interested in. That could, of course, change. She did not know how intimately he had been involved with her evil look-alike.

"As good as Rowforth is bad!" Kelvin said. He had been standing silently all the time his father talked.

That annoyed John, and he wondered why it should. What was wrong with the hero of the prophecy taking the initiative? Was it because Zanaan so enchanted him?

He pondered, and realized that the aspect of Zoanna, without the evil, really did not fascinate him in the same manner. There had been magic and a cutting edge to Zoanna that compelled him; both were lacking in Zanaan. Unfortunately that made her like bleer without the hops: not of great interest for long. He was surprised to discover this, but had to recognize its truth.

"Then we certainly must leave no doubt in any of our

minds," the queen said. "My husband deserves execution while his look-alike deserves only the best."

She did not believe them, John realized. He couldn't blame her. He himself had thought Kelvin mistaken, but where kings and execution were concerned, there was slight margin for error.

They followed the queen outside the palace and around the palace wall to the dreadfully familiar stairs. It smelled no better than when he and Kian had been prisoners here. Again he remembered far too vividly Sergeant Broughtmar putting the tiny wriggling serpent into that unfortunate revolutionary's ear. What horror!

"You're shuddering, Dad!" Kelvin said. He had not been a prisoner here, so could not understand exactly how terrible it had been.

"Memories, Son, memories." Was there really anything that could be worse? Even the onset of an illness had never hit him this hard.

"I can go down and check, Father. Just so we find out who's here."

"No, I won't shirk my duty. If it is King Rufurt, I'll know him. We became as close as brothers in our imprisonment in Rud. Thank the gods Zoanna kept a more decent dungeon!"

"He'll have pointed ears. Every guard we talked to said he didn't, but he must!"

"If it is Rufurt. But you were right, ears can be changed. The difference between a pointed ear and a round ear is just a slight extension of cartilage."

They reached the landing and the guards who had preceded them and the guards who were already there parted and permitted them to approach the one cell that was occupied. In that cell, sprawled on a pile of straw which had not been changed since their own imprisonment, a short, squat man with a big nose lay with closed eyes. The sunbeam from the high barred window did not quite reach his face but fell short of it, settling on his water dish. As Rowforth had done with others, the prisoner was fed and watered as if he belonged on all fours.

John stared long and hard. His senses said "Rufurt," but

he knew how unreliable senses were. They would have to get him out into the light.

"Rufurt!" he said.

The prisoner sat up. Then he scrambled to his feet and rushed to the bars. He stood there panting, his eyes wild. Truly he now resembled animal more than human being.

"John! Kelvin! Kelvin the Roundear! I knew you would come! When I called to you I knew you would come and rescue me!"

John stared at the ears. They were round. This could not be the man he had spent years with in Rud's dungeon! It could not be, and yet he felt that it was.

The prisoner focused sunken eyes on Zanaan. They widened, reflecting an inner surprise that seemed to border on terror. "Zoanna!"

That did it! This had to be Rufurt. But how?

"I am Zanaan," the queen said. "I am said to look much like Zoanna, but I do not share her personality. But you—you look much like my husband Rowforth."

"I am Rufurt! Rowforth is in my world!"

"Your ears," John said, feeling foolish. "Round."

The prisoner touched those appendages with dirty fingers and scrubbed at caked brown material at their tips. Scars were revealed, healing but visible.

"He cut off my tips! The one who looks like me did it! And Zoanna watched! Then they took me in the boat and they threw me in the water and I went into the Flaw. I came up sputtering by the waterfall, exactly as you did, John! Then I climbed out, and I recognized things from your description and I wandered all around. I found appleberries and other fruits and—and then I reached these valleys, just as you did. I didn't know whether to climb down and meet your flopears or keep going, but then three men came and roped me and tied me up! They called me Rowforth and I knew then what had happened. I knew that I was in trouble and all I could hope for was that you would come back here and get me out. Just as Kelvin got us out before."

"That clinches it," John said. "Your Majesty, let King Rufurt out. He's not the vile man you were married to."

But Zanaan, who also knew her husband well enough to tell him from another of similar appearance, had already instructed the guard to use the key. The key was in the lock and the tumblers falling. With a loud squeak the barred door was opened and good King Rufurt was free at long last.

If this was Rufurt, then what was happening back home? *Oh, Heln!* Kelvin thought with sudden alarm. *Jon! Lester! Mother! What is happening there?*

John woke, unable to sleep, and lay tossing on the bed. Finally he rose, dressed, and left the bedchamber where his two sons, each in a different bed, were sleeping. He walked the halls, uncertain as to why he was being tormented. The statuary and furniture loomed up in the darkened palace, just as it had when he had paced the hallways at night in Rud's palace.

*So this is Hud, and Hud is all. Everything I need to think about. Kian will probably stay here after he and his girl make up their differences. Will I? Zoanna was everything I wanted, I thought, when besotted by her sex appeal. Zanaan has her beauty and not her nature. She has everything good that Zoanna didn't. But Zoanna had something too. The evil creature had an art! She used enchantment on me, or at least doped my wine. I believed her to be my ideal, but I was wrong. Others had been just as wrong. But now here is Zanaan, the good, perfect woman that I longed for. So why this hesitancy? Why is it that I'm still thinking of Charlain?*

And there was the other aspect of it! He *had* been smitten with the queen, but then he had escaped her and found Charlain, and now the aspect of the queen lacked power over him. Charlain was married elsewhere now, so that was over— but his heart refused to admit it. His heart still wanted only that one woman. He never would have left her, had he not expected to die. He had not wanted her to be associated with him then, lest she also be killed. He had stayed with her because he loved her, and he had left her for the same reason. So it really didn't matter whether Zanaan was evil or good; he had lost his fascination for her likeness.

The irony was that Zanaan, freed from her evil husband, was now available, while Charlain was not. He would do better staying here, and away from there. Only mischief could come of his return to that other frame.

His feet had unconsciously taken him to a door. He paused, uncertain. He knew whose door this was—but no longer wished to knock on it.

Then he heard voices beyond it.

Zanaan's voice: "Oh, darling, I know you've given her your word and you don't want to hurt her, but—"

A man's voice: "It is true. I did that. I owed her, and once I thought I loved her, but that changed after I met you. But now that Kian is back, if she wants him—"

"Oh, yes! I know she does! I could see it in her eyes. I thought she loved you, but when she saw him, I knew! But the idiot kept denying her, and it is true that Hades has no fury like that of—"

"And we can marry too. You and I. Mr. and Mrs.—"

"King and queen. I see no reason why I should abdicate. And you'll make a good king, a fair and just king! Do you think you can bear being called 'Your Majesty'?"

"I can stand it, if that's the price of you."

"I rather think it is, Jac."

There was the sound of a kiss.

"Oh Jac, Jac! We'll be so happy, you and I! Not like the usual royal marriage."

"Yes. Happy. The former royalty-hating bandit—"

"Revolutionary!"

"If you prefer. The former revolutionary and the queen!"

"Darling!"

"I thought I came to the palace to conquer, but I was conquered."

"You were everything the king wasn't. It seemed so promising! And then Kian didn't come back, and Lonny was near suicide, so you had to—"

"And you know, I lied about having known many women."

"Liar! Hold me! Hold me tight!"

"Oh Zanaan! Zanaan!"

"Oh Jac! Oh Jac!"

John tiptoed away from the door. They were going to be happy, he thought, and so was the land.

He didn't feel envious. He felt relieved that this was happening. So he let his feet take him away from the door to the royal pantry and back to his bedchamber on the second floor. He was happy for Jac and the queen. He only wished that he had some similar prospect for himself.

When he woke in the morning John thought he had dreamed the episode of the preceding night. Kelvin was getting dressed in his conventional clothes: new brownberry shirt, greenbriar pantaloons, cushiony cotilk stockings, and heavy walking boots.

"Where's Kian?" John asked.

"I don't know, Dad. He woke me up and started talking about Lonny and how he couldn't live without her. About how he was going to go to her and somehow make her understand. I must have drifted off again because I've just now awakened and he's gone."

"What time was that? Early or late?"

"Much too early or much too late. Do you think he'll marry her? We really need to get home. At least I do."

"He will, and I do too. There's something strange about King Rufurt being here. If Zoanna is alive and Rowforth is impersonating Rufurt . . ."

"Kelvinia may be in more trouble than Rud ever was with Aratex!"

"I'm afraid you're right, Son. What in the world can that woman be up to! It seems obvious she's alive. I was so sure she was dead, but maybe that was wishful thinking."

"Can we even be sure of that?" Kelvin wondered aloud. "I mean with so much magic and science around—"

"We can be very certain she's not dead. If zombies exist I don't think they snatch look-alikes from other frames. At least I hope they don't."

"Father, do you think she's really planning a war? Maybe has already started one?"

"That's why we must get back. If Rowforth has taken

Rufurt's place, the two of them will be ruling the country without bloodshed. Unless they are causing it as rulers. And that is an ugly possibility."

"She could be up to anything. Maybe she's trying for revenge?"

"Could be. Son, don't say anything to Kian about this. I really think he'll want to stay here now, and really, considering that Zoanna is his mother, here is the best place for him."

"You don't think he'll fight for Zoanna again?" Kelvin was incredulous.

"No, he wouldn't do that. But if he's here with his bride he won't have the temptation. If Zoanna's alive, I think you know what we shall have to do. We don't want him there for that."

Kelvin shuddered. "No, not for that!"

"I think we'll attend his wedding this day. Maybe he will come to appreciate Zanaan as the mother he should have had. If he doesn't wed Lonny today, you and I and King Rufurt had better go home anyway. I don't think we dare wait longer."

"All right, Father. But will he—"

"He'd better!" John said.

Later in the day they did indeed attend the wedding. With them, cleaned up and fancily dressed as the others, was King Rufurt. In fact, they were the ones conducting the ceremony of the double wedding of Kian to Lonny, and Jac to Zanaan. If the king had any private sentiments about marrying the woman who so resembled his evil wife to another man, he concealed them well, just as John Knight concealed his sentiments well. Kelvin was privately glad it had worked out this way, because of sentiments he too was glad to conceal.

"Kian Knight from our frame," King Rufurt said, "do you wish to marry Lonny Burk of this frame?"

"You know I do," Kian said, gazing into Lonny's eyes. It was more than evident that any misunderstandings the two had had yesterday had been resolved in the intervening night.

"And you, Lonny Burk, do you wish to marry Kian Knight?"

"I do, oh I do!" Lonny agreed, her good nature restored.

"You, Jac Smite, et cetera, do you—"

"I do!" Jac said.

"And you, Queen Zanaan, lovely and good widow or divorcee of absent abdicated discredited reprehensible former King Rowforth of Hud, do you wish to marry Jac?"

"I do indeed want to marry Jac!" She and he exchanged secret smiles. It was evident that the marriage of compassion and convenience between Jac and Lonny would never have worked out; neither of their hearts had been in it.

Now John Knight took the floor. "Does anyone here have objection to either joining?" he asked the onlookers.

There was a stillness in the ballroom reminiscent of what might have existed at the dawn of time in a primeval frame.

Kian and Jac produced silver rings and slipped them on the fingers of the brides.

It was Kelvin's turn. "Then," he said as forcefully as his threatening-to-quaver voice could manage, "you are married. For as long as you wish it, or until time bites its end." The last words were John Knight's contribution to the service, and perhaps to other minds than Kelvin's they made sense.

"Kiss, kiss," Heeto urged, as if fearful they would forget that detail, and the grooms and brides did.

Someone started the applause, and then the music played, as the group that had been organized for yesterday's festivities acted for today's. The piangan and silver pipes sounded beautifully.

"Goodbye, Kian, good luck, long life," Kelvin said, shaking his brother's hand, feeling that it might be for the last time.

"Goodbye? What are you talking about?"

"There may be trouble at home," John said. "We have to find out."

"But—"

"If I'm here, maybe he's there," Rufurt said.

"Rowforth? You mean—I'm coming too!"

"No you're not!" John Knight said. "You're going to stay here with this delightful, beautiful girl and have a proper honeymoon. If there is trouble and we need help, one of us will be back."

"But really, you can't leave like this!"

"We have to," Kelvin said. "You see to your wife; I'll see to mine."

Lonny squeezed Kian's hand. "I think that's a great idea, Husband."

"I have my gauntlets, the Mouvar weapon, the levitation belt, and the chimaera's sting," Kelvin explained. That one sting he had not included in the shipment to the other frame. "I doubt there's any trouble I can't handle with those! Probably Rowforth is in the palace, and—"

"Rowforth! My husband!" the queen exclaimed, overhearing.

"I'm your husband now, dear," Jac reminded her. "You divorced him, if he didn't die first."

"Yes, of course, but—"

"We don't know that he's there," John said. "But there's a chance that he might be."

"You'll bring him back?" Heeto asked. "For punishment?"

"If we can. If we don't have to destroy him ourselves," Rowforth's look-alike said.

"We'll be back in any case," John Knight said. "Not to stay, you understand, but just to visit and let you know what happened."

"When?"

"As soon as our problem is cleared."

"I still think I should come."

"No!"

Kian looked relieved in spite of himself. Jac, who had been fidgeting throughout the exchange, now said: "If need be, we will both go to their rescue, Kian."

"And if need be you can have all of Hud's armed forces and all the fighting men our treasury will buy," Queen Zanaan added.

It seemed a satisfactory solution. Once again, and then several more times, everyone said goodbye.

Then it was time to travel fast, and without mistake in the transporter.

# CHAPTER 27

# *Return*

$K$ elvin sat in the middle of the boat, rowing with the help of the gauntlets while King Rufurt filled the stern seat and John Knight sat at the bow. It was just as well that his brother hadn't returned with them, he thought, or they'd have been overloaded.

They passed the roaring falls into star-filled spaces, the Flaw. The gauntlets rowed through the turbulent water without difficulty. Then around the bend, past eerily glowing walls, their boat and themselves lit by the lichen's radiance. A swirl in the water that Kelvin had noticed on previous trips—a sort of dimple, actually—and then finally the boat landing.

"I think we'd better be cautious," John Knight said. "There could be enemies waiting for us here."

"I'm very cautious," Kelvin agreed, drawing the Mouvar weapon. That would handle magic, and the gauntlets and his sword were ready to tackle anything else. After the adventures he had just undergone, a possible scrap with armed men or even an attack by magic could hold few terrors!

"Perhaps you'd better stay hidden down here," Kelvin suggested to the king. "Until after we see how things are above."

King Rufurt looked up the stairs and a set of stubborn lines appeared at the corners of his mouth. "I'm still ruler."

"Yes, that's why we don't want you to fall into the hands of Rowforth again."

"Rowforth and Zoanna. Damn Zoanna! My former queen!"

"We're all subject to sorcery," John Knight said soothing-ly. "Even those of us who never wanted to believe it possible."

"I'll go check," Kelvin said, touching his belt. He rose above the boat landing. In his right hand was the Mouvar weapon. Strapped on his left side was his sword, while strapped between his shoulder blades was the lightweight sting the chimaera had given him. He was as armed, he thought, as a human being had ever been.

They had brought King Rufurt back here through the transporter. Kelvin had been alert for any warning tingle from the gauntlets, but there had been none. Did that mean that Rufurt's surgically rounded ears made him eligible to use Mouvar's system, or was the prohibition against pointears a bluff? Maybe he should make Jon happy and bring her here, and see whether the gauntlets tingled for her. Her life must have been relatively dull, recently, far from the action, helping Heln prepare for the baby.

He nudged the lever forward with his finger, keeping the Mouvar weapon in his hand. He rose above the first flight, and then the second flight of dusty, ancient stairs. Finally he was at the hole that let in daylight to mingle with the softer radiance of the lichens. He accelerated and shot outside fast, in case someone was waiting there.

He paused in midair. Two men in guardsman uniforms sat at a block of masonry playing cards. One of them looked up with open mouth while the other played a card.

"Kelvin, you can really fly that thing!"

"Practice," Kelvin said. "You are waiting for me?"

"King's orders. You are to go directly to the palace, now that you're back. Your brother get married all right?"

"Yes, after some delays. Nice wedding. Everyone was there."

"Your father return with you?"

Kelvin hesitated. He didn't want to reveal too much to these guardsmen, good men though they were. His brother, he knew, would simply have lied, but somehow lying for him was not natural. "He's not with me," he temporized. That was true, as far as it went. John Knight and the genuine king had remained below, letting Kelvin scout the territory alone.

"We have a horse for you. Do you want to ride?"

"I thought I'd fly and surprise someone," Kelvin said. He reholstered the Mouvar weapon, placed his hand over his central buckle, and accelerated out of their sight.

*What do I do now?* he thought, looking down at blurring farmland. *Do I just go to the palace? I should have asked questions. Why didn't I think of that?*

Because he really wasn't a hero, he knew. He had all kinds of limitations and inadequacies. If it weren't for the magic and science devices he happened to have, he'd be nobody. Others might be fooled about him, but he didn't fool himself.

Down below was a troop of horsemen and men on foot wearing Kelvinia's grass-green uniforms. He lowered and hovered, while shouts went up and fingers pointed at him. No missiles followed, so he was still the Roundear of Prophecy as far as these men were concerned.

Cautiously he descended until his feet touched the ground. Soldiers who had been drooping from fatigue now ran forward with joyous and triumphant cries.

"He's back! He's back! The Roundear's back!"

Kelvin waited. Soon a man with what seemed a bad burn on his arm was pumping his hand and shouting loudly: "General Broughtner! General Broughtner! Someone get the general!"

In due course, after much handshaking and incomprehensible expressions on the part of the soldiers, General Broughtner was there. The pointed-ear general who had fought so valiantly in the war with Aratex drooped in his saddle and looked almost as though he had lost a campaign. Kelvin remembered that he had been a village drunk before the formation of the Knights and the Rud Revolution. It was possible, looking at him now, to think that he had regressed.

But when Broughtner spoke it was not with slurred speech, and no fumes of wine were on his breath. "Kelvin! Thank the gods!"

"I just got back," Kelvin explained. "From my brother's wedding."

"I know. Now we're saved."

"I don't know what has been happening. Has there been fighting?"

"Has there been!" Broughtner dismounted with the help

of a private. He staggered over to Kelvin, shook his hand, and grabbed his shoulders. "Kelvin, we are at war! We've been losing, thanks to that witch! But now that you're back that will change. Now that you're here with that weapon."

Kelvin thought: *So Zoanna is fighting with magic! So she really is a witch that I have to destroy. Thank the gods Kian stayed behind!*

"See these burns?" Broughtner said, pointing. "Witch's fire did that! She's using witch's fire! What chance has an ordinary man against that?"

Kelvin looked at the scorched faces and arms. None had been fatal or even very bad, but maybe others were. The general was right, there was no way the ordinary soldier could fight against witch's fire.

"You'll burn her, won't you? The way you did with that witch in Aratex. Send her damned fire back to her. Burn her up!"

"I'll burn her," Kelvin promised. It seemed a dreadful fate to inflict on anyone. But then all that the Mouvar weapon did was send the magic back on the sender. If Zoanna was burning her one-time subjects then she deserved to burn.

"She's back behind the Klingland and Kance borders, way back to the twin capitals. She's got plenty of men fighting for her—Klinglanders and Kancians. If you don't stop her she'll take over Kelvinia!"

"I'll stop her," Kelvin promised again. His hands went to his belt.

"There's some of our own still fighting near the caps. At least there were. Take care. Witches can be dangerous."

"I know." Kelvin lifted off and cruised toward the border. He wished now that he hadn't slept through history class. He knew that Klingland and Kance bordered what had been the kingdom of Rud on its eastern side. He remembered that there were twin boys born on a once-every-four-years bonus day. The boy rulers were young in body but aged, thanks to a bit of prenatal magic, only one year for a normal person's four. But he had always heard the infants terrible, as they were called, were but mischievous perpetual boys. There was always something about a caretaker who had allegedly administered the calendar spell as they were born. But to the best of his recollection they were not bad boys, and their guardian mostly minded her own business. Certainly Rud had never fought with these lands, or had not fought with any other with the possible exception of Hermandy. If Zoanna had gone there with Rowforth seeking allies to get him a throne, then the situation was at least as serious as had been the affair with Aratex. Everyone seemed to think the witch was simply a guardian, but if Zoanna enlisted her as an ally then it was she who was hurling the fire.

Roads and hills and forests and rivers later he neared the caps. Down below he spied a dust cloud of battle, and in the sky was a ball of fire.

*It's time to act!* he thought, lowering himself to the ground. *It's time to crisp a witch as I crisped Melbah.*

He landed on a knoll, drew the Mouvar weapon from its hip holster, and prepared to intercept and turn back the witch's fire.

Charlain concentrated hard on the crystal as she guided the fireball. It was easier now. She had better control. No longer did she destroy men and horses with the witch's fire, but merely frightened them. If need be, she knew she would do more with it, deliberately.

In the crystal, men wearing the Kelvinian uniform were looking skyward as she danced the ball. Why didn't they give up? Why didn't they leave them alone? Was it because of magic Zoanna commanded, that sent them back? That must be it! They had no choice! It was the only explanation for these suicidal charges.

Below the fireball she knew there were men who were only boys. Perhaps that Phillip lad, and perhaps her own son-in-law. Perhaps big, hearty Mor Crumb who had so cheered her spirits the one time they had met. That had been after the wedding of Kelvin and Heln, and of Jon and Lester. She had been feeling sad because she knew there was so much more to the prophecy than just ridding Rud of its evil ruler. And now, now that evil ruler was back, so what actually had been accomplished?

"Charlain! Watch what you're doing!" Helbah was scolding; she didn't like it when her accomplice's mind wandered. Without intending to, Charlain had let the fireball drift past the invaders and over the forest. Helbah naturally wanted the fireball exploding where it would at least pose a threat.

Carefully, watching the crystal in the tree bole, Charlain brought the ball back over the troops. She knew that Helbah's look-alike, Melbah of Aratex, would have flung it right into their midst. Helbah was like Charlain herself in that she didn't really want to maim and destroy. The invaders had to be stopped, that was all, and if there was a way that would leave all intact, both favored it.

"Meow!" said Katbah, his dark paw touching the crystal over the men. "Meow!"

*Oh, all right!* Charlain thought, and exploded the fireball.

Phillip peeked cautiously out from behind a tree at the edge of the glen. He had stumbled about for days since running from his outfit. It hadn't been that he was scared, exactly, but Lester had been trying to make him go home and then those fireballs had started and all pandemonium had broken loose.

Now, having survived for some days on berries and a few bitter nuts, scared all the time that he would be caught, he had actually reached the glen. He had known something was going on here because he had seen the witch on the road walking slowly with a stick. He had wounded her properly once, he thought, but witches were notorious for surviving almost anything. Thus he had watched her and the cat from the woods, fearful that they would see, yet knowing that they had other things to think about. It had been luck that he had gotten into the woods and luck that he had remained undetected. With more luck still he might yet make up for the trouble he had caused.

There were *two* witches in that glen. He could not see them clearly there in the mist, but he knew there were two. He had been watching them while his belly growled from hunger and his arms and face smarted from their contacts with netishes and poison oavy plants. He would get her, he promised himself. He would get her.

Old witch Helbah was standing to one side of the tree, partially turned. The other witch and the cat were at the crystal. If he was very, very careful how he aimed he'd skewer old Helbah through the heart. After that he'd have to quickly kill the other witch and the cat. He didn't like it, but he knew it was necessary. How much mercy, after all, did a witch have? He remembered too well how Melbah, his nurse and mentor, had cackled gleefully while burning alive someone she had thought troublesome.

He cocked the crossbow carefully. Bolt in place, three others close at hand. Melbah had trained him in the art of crossbowing as well as in wood stealth and survival in the woods. Melbah had taught him well. Lester and St. Helens did not know how very much he had learned.

He rested the crossbow across a log, placed his cheek firmly against the stalk, and took infinitely careful aim. There would be but the one chance. This time he would get her right through the heart.

*Blood! Mama! Blood! Blood!*

Heln stifled a scream. It was the baby demanding that it be fed! That it be fed what was proper food for its growth and development and eventual birth.

"Heln, what's the matter?" Jon asked. She was bending near, almost asking for it.

*Jon is my friend! Jon is my friend!* Heln reminded herself. She thought for herself this time, hoping that the baby would understand.

*Food, Mama, food!*

*HUNGRY! WAHHHHH!* A second thought, different from the other in tone. How many babies drifted in her womb? What kind?

*GRRRRRWWWWW! HUNGER! HUNGER!* Gods, a third, and so unhuman!

"Heln, you're scaring me," Jon said. "Why do you look like that?"

They were only food sources, after all. Hunger of a superior life-form superseded everything else.

"Heln!"

She had to get her teeth into that luscious throat! Nourishment pulsed hot and red just beneath that vein. She was strong, very strong, her teeth would rip and tear into that luscious flesh, her tongue would lap up the steaming blood—

"Heln! Stop it!" The food source pushed at her head, holding her back, challenging her to use her full strength.

*Food, Mama, Food!*

*Hungry, Mama, Hungry!*

*Gwrrrrrowth!*

"Dr. Sterk!" Jon's voice rose suddenly in fear. "DOCTOR STERK! HELP!"

Kildom nudged Kildee in the ribs. "Come on!"

"What?"

"She's gone. Let's do what we said we'd do!"

Kildee followed his brother around the palace wall, worrying. Kildom was always getting him into things! He'd agree out of frustration from Kildom's challenging digs, and then he'd be hooked. This time he was really caught and he didn't like it.

Kildom ran right up to the dungeon guard just as they had planned. "Trom! Trom! They're coming, Trom! We just saw them run into the trees!"

"What are you two up to?"

"It's true, Trom," Kildee said, playing his part. "We saw three of them in the woods. Soldiers, wearing the Hermandy uniforms! I don't know how they got there, but—"

"Damn! If you're lying to me I'll hold you while Helbah soaps your mouths!"

"No, Trom, really. Enemy soldiers! Maybe slipping up to kill Helbah! Maybe to kill us, Trom! Trom, you've got to do something!"

"I can't leave my post," Trom said. "Even if I believed you I couldn't." He looked worried, Kildee thought.

"Trom, you go with my brother and I'll guard. Please, Trom, please."

"Oh, all right," Trom said. "But if anything happens here, you raise a shout!"

"I will, Trom, I will," he promised angelically.

Trom should have been warned by that, but he was distracted by the urgency of their message. "Come," said Kildom, taking off at a run.

Trom hesitated a moment more, then followed him at a brisk walk that became a trot. They rounded the corner of the palace and were out of sight.

Well, there was no helping it now. Kildee took the key he had surreptitiously taken from the guard's key ring and ran with it as fast as he could go. Down the dungeon stairs, to the dark, recently scrubbed cell.

"General Reilly, General Crumb, come quick! My brother and I have begun your escape!"

## CHAPTER 28

# Goodbye Again

$K$ elvin's finger was already tightening on the trigger of the Mouvar weapon when he noticed that his gauntlets were hot. Well, that was natural, wasn't it? The gauntlets warned of danger, and certainly that ball of fire was danger. So why did he hesitate?

He knew what would happen when he pressed the trigger. The witch's fire would return to its sender and destroy her. The Mouvar weapon was antimagic, as his father had deduced. By moving the little fin-shape on the handgrip he would simply counter the magic, wipe it out, as it were.

Was it really Zoanna hurling that fire? Or was it the other witch, the one said to live here?

*No, No, Kelvin! Do not destroy the witch! Do not destroy her!*

It was the chimaera's thought! The monster was still with him! He had thought Mervania long disconnected.

*You think I don't want those berries? Leave it to you and you'll never get back with them! First you'll fool around fighting, then you'll go see your wife, and forget about what's important.*

"But the fireball!"

*Believe me, I know better than you!*

*But—*

The fireball that was now ahead of the advancing army dipped groundward. Now was the time to act!

*No! No, you fool inferior life-form! Don't you feel your gloves heating? You'll kill your mother!*

That got him. He didn't know what the chimaera meant, but he knew a warning. Indeed, the gauntlets were burning; he had been concentrating so hard that he hadn't noticed, or had taken it to be from the radiation of the fireball. Quickly he moved the knob on his weapon so that it would simply counter the magic rather than rebound it on the sender. He started to squeeze the trigger, pointing the weapon skyward.

The fireball exploded spectacularly, sending down to the ground, just ahead of the troops, a golden waterfall of scintillating stars. The knoll shook, and his face hit the grass. He let loose of the weapon and for the moment he felt complete and overwhelming terror.

When he was able to look he could see the Kelvinian troops scattering, responding to the terror he'd felt. Behind them the fireball grew bright, sputtering like a dying fire. The fire hurt his eyes, creating afterimages that disoriented him and made him feel as if he were again in astral form. Then the images faded as the waterfall faded, and there was nothing but littered landscape and fleeing men.

Kelvin swallowed. "It—it could have killed, but it didn't!"

*Now you know,* Mervania said to him in his whirling head.

*You said my mother!* Kelvin thought back, dizzy.

*Would I lie to you, when your mission for me is incomplete? Now you are soon to learn about your mother.*

Phillip startled at the sound of breaking brush. His shot went wild and he heard the bolt thunk hard in the trunk of a tree down in the glen. He hadn't time to turn his head before he was grabbed hard from behind.

*"YOU BRAT!"* St. Helens roared. "You totally senseless nincompoop! Wasn't shooting her once treachery enough for you? Did you have to do it again and mess up our escape?"

Phillip was abashed. "I did it for you!"

St. Helens picked him up in very muscular arms and shook him. The face of this man who had meant so much to him since he had first accepted him as friend was terrifyingly red. St. Helens, he thought with shock, was about to kill him.

"You did it for yourself, you show-off brat! Don't you tell me otherwise! Don't you even think otherwise!"

Phillip bit his tongue, whether deliberately or accidentally he couldn't have said. He tasted salt and felt blood trickling from the far corner of his mouth as St. Helens quit shaking him. Maybe the blood would appease him, he thought. He gazed into those angry eyes and everything he'd thought to say vanished from his mind.

"She's a good witch, Son," Mor Crumb said behind St. Helens. He was as big and rough a man as ever lived, and one who had no reason to love witches. "She's the kind we can deal with."

"A witch is a witch is a witch," Phillip intoned. It was, he'd learned, since his kingship, a common saying.

"Not this witch, Son." Mor spoke firmly, fatherly, with a hint of reproach.

"She's a good woman," St. Helens agreed, the fire in his eyes dampening. "She'd have helped us out of our real difficulties when she and I first met. She's not the enemy. Our enemy's back at our home palace."

"Zoanna?" Phillip managed.

"Zoanna."

"But you—"

"Were bewitched. Had your mind twisted. We all did. Same's the bitch did to John Knight, long time ago. But now we know. We know it's her and we can manage to do something."

Phillip looked at Crumb's face and then back at his former friend. They were both serious. Was it that he had unwittingly let himself be used by Zoanna exactly as he had let himself be used by Melbah? A witch was a witch was a witch. But couldn't there be a good witch?

"You may be right, Generals Reilly and Crumb, but I was going by experience. A witch is treacherous, cruel, and unforgiving. That's how Melbah was. How could I think that this witch would be different?"

"You couldn't, Phillip."

St. Helens opened his hands and dropped him. He hit the

ground and saw both men staring past him. He turned. There, standing before them, apparently unarmed and unprotected, was the witch who to his eyes looked exactly like the one who had raised him. Only not quite. Up close this woman was softer, with more agreeable lines, as if she had been known to smile sincerely.

"You did what you thought right," she said. "You knew that Melbah had always deceived you and that her word was not to be trusted. You assumed I would take advantage of General Reilly's trust. You are a boy; you thought as a boy does. Make a witch harmless and she will not harm you or those you love. It is an old recipe, long believed. To truly follow the recipe calls for the witch's complete destruction. In order to destroy a witch you have to believe in her malevolence."

"I—I did," Phillip agreed.

"And now you don't?" Her voice was soft, not unfriendly.

"I—don't know. I guess if you want to harm us, you can."

"I'm glad that you are not so certain. Come, the three of you. There is someone in the glen you will want to see."

"The other witch," Phillip said.

"Yes, you might say that," Helbah said agreeably. "But she is no stranger to any of you. I think, Phillip, that you are going to be surprised to learn exactly who she is."

Phillip got to his feet, wiped blood from his mouth, and followed Helbah. As his feet found their way he now and then looked over at St. Helens and Mor Crumb. These big men, these strong men, were at least as bewildered as he.

In the glen, near the large tree with the flat crystal set in its big bole, lovely Charlain stretched out her arms as though to long-lost children or her dearest friends.

Charlain? Kelvin's mother? A witch? Now indeed a lot about this mysterious roundear bubbled up from the bottom of his brain and drifted into place. The Roundear of Prophecy had a mother who had powers and was now using them to fulfill her son's destiny! But *against* Kelvinia rather than for? How could that be? Was she too bewitched?

"Phillip, St. Helens, General Crumb," Charlain said, "as you now must realize it is our old enemy that we have to fight. Zoanna and the man who appears to be but isn't King Rufurt now control Kelvinia. Every soldier, whether Kelvinia, Herman, or a mercenary from Throod, has been deceived. Each of you has been tricked similarly. Klingland and Kance are not the enemy, though they are the kingdom you fight."

"I know we were bewitched by her," Mor said. "But you, Charlain—a witch?"

"A necessary recruit, I'm afraid," Helbah said. "Charlain had the talent and I had need for it. Fortunately for all of us she learned quickly and well."

"There's something else," Charlain said, "My son Kelvin is here now, back in this frame and not far from where we stand. I saw him in the crystal."

"Then we're saved!" Mor Crumb said. "The Roundear will make everything right. He'll win this war, and—"

"You forget that the real war is inside Kelvinia," Helbah said.

"Yes, yes, of course," Mor said. "He'll get them out of the palace before you can say scat! Burn wicked Zoanna as she deserves! Burn the impostor king as well!"

"No," Charlain said. "Not immediately, anyhow. There's something more important he has to do."

"More important," Mor asked incredulously, "than destroying the former queen of Rud and the former king from the other place? More important than stopping the fighting?"

"Yes. Far more important. I have consulted the cards and the cards have never lied to me. There's a nodule, a crisis point. Either he fulfills this subsidiary task promptly and without fail or this fighting will not end and the prophecy will never be fulfilled. For the good of all of us and the eventual fulfillment of the prophecy he has to do what his mother tells him. Each of you, understanding or not, must help me to that end."

They stared at her, amazed, but hardly doubting her.

Kelvin, urged on by Mervania Chimaera's thoughts, walked slowly down the road that led to the glen. Ahead of him, prancing, flicking its tail, looking back with a come-along expression every now and then was a huge black houcat.

*I'm getting into trouble,* Kelvin thought. *I really can't trust the chimaera. It's putting me right into the hands of the witch!*

*When have you not been in trouble, stupid mortal!*

Mervania responded almost affectionately. *And why would I want to have you in the hands of a witch?*

*To make a deal, maybe. As you did with me.*

*And that you haven't yet delivered on! Be brave, little hero, and use some sense!*

*That's all right for you to think, Mervania. You don't have to face a witch!*

*You faced me, Kelvin. Do you honestly think a witch could be worse than I am?*

*No! Nothing's worse than a chimaera!*

*I'm glad you realize it. And remember, I'm right here in your thoughts, protecting my interests.*

Kelvin wondered if he could possibly comprehend the chimaera's interests. He tried not to project the thought or call it to the chimaera's attention. The creature was a puzzle! Compared to the chimaera, dragons and witches were quite comprehensible.

*Thank you, Kelvin.*

Ahead he could see five people waiting. Two women, two big men, and one large boy or man like himself. Was one of those witches really his mother?

*Do you doubt me, Kelvin?* The thought had a tinge of menace.

Kelvin felt chastised. Focusing mainly on the houcat's constantly flicking tail he was only gradually becoming aware that the fog was lifting. He could have flown this distance in half the time with less internal agony, but the chimaera had decreed walk.

*You may fly now, if you wish.*

*Thanks a lot!* If the monster caught the irony, fine! He touched the button in his buckle, pressed it in and rose to the height of a horse's back. He nudged the forward lever and floated down the road, the houcat still ahead. He accelerated ever so little and he was there.

*They* were there. St. Helens in prisoner clothes, Mor Crumb in worn and filthy general's uniform. Phillip, the former king of Aratex, in filthy common clothes. A short, smiling woman who looked astonishingly like Melbah, the witch he had caused to burn. And, most surprising of all, a woman who appeared to be his mother.

"Come down, Kelvin," his mother said. "We have to talk."

It was as if she said "Come down from that tree" or "Get off from that woodpile." Could this be his mother, and wasn't there anything he could do that would surprise her?

Kelvin descended to the ground and deactivated his belt. This whole scene was strange, but his mother seemed to be the spokesperson here.

"Kelvin, we're all glad to see you. Come here!" Her arms went wide as he took a step forward.

Could this be some cunning illusion, designed to make him walk blithely into a trap?

*If you don't trust your mother, trust me,* Mervania thought with a certain amused disgust. *I want those dragonberries. Do you think I will allow you to be trapped before I get them?*

That satisfied him. A moment later Charlain was hugging him hard, as a mother long deprived must hug her son. He relaxed, all doubt gone that it was really her.

"What's this?" she asked, touching the copper sting on his back.

"A chimaera's sting, Mother."

"I thought it might be. Good, you hold on to that! Someday it may prove important."

Kelvin swallowed. Mom was so practical sometimes! No questions like "What's a chimaera?" or "How did you ever come by it?" Just instant, practical acceptance.

The other woman spoke—the witch who looked like Melbah. "Charlain, you must show him."

"Yes, I suppose I ought to. Come, Son, over to this tree, over to this crystal. Now what I'm going to show you may be a shock. Please be brave, Son; I know you can be."

"Mom, I just want to get rid of Zoanna and return home to my wife!" Kelvin protested.

*Listen to her, you idiot!* Mervania snapped. *You won't like this.*

Again, Kelvin found himself placing more credence in the monster than in his mother. He went with Charlain to the tree. What was going on?

Charlain's fingers stretched out and there was a tiny spark that danced between her fingers and then from her fingertips to the crystal. Suddenly the crystal was a window on a distant scene, as other magic crystals had been.

A madwoman stared and gibbered, crouching in a corner. On her wrists and ankles were chains. She was naked and grotesquely pregnant, as though she were set to deliver not a child but a colt. Her skin had a coppery sheen. Her dark, sunken eyes stared right at him. She screamed.

Why was this madwoman being shown to him? Why was she screaming like that, as though she saw him?

"KELVIN!" the imaged woman screamed.

She knew his name! This pathetic, mad, pregnant woman saw him and knew his name!

Suddenly the features of the woman became preternaturally clear. That chin, that nose, those facial contours, those round ears! "Heln!" he said incredulously. "Heln?" For how could such a horror be possible?

"Yes," his mother said. "That is she."

Kelvin felt the ground open under him. It was just too much. He sank down on his knees, his hands reaching out to the crystal. "HELN! HELN! NO, NO, PLEASE!"

In the crystal a raw piece of meat appeared. Impaled on a stick it waved before the face of the woman he tried not to believe was Heln.

The madwoman focused her glassy eyes on the meat. Her fingers curled. She licked her lips. Suddenly her neck shot out, fast, like that of a striking reptile. Her teeth sank into the flesh. Blood squirted, and ran from the corners of her mouth. Her chained wrists lifted and her clawed hands pushed the meat farther and farther into her savagely chomping maw.

"Kelvin!" the madwoman said between bites. "Kelvin!"

It couldn't be her! It couldn't be!

The picture in the crystal seemed to move back. His sister Jon came into view. She was holding the stick that supported the raw meat. It was evident that she did not dare come closer herself, lest her own flesh be attacked. Beside her, steadying her arm, was Dr. Sterk, the royal physician.

Kelvin thought he had seen horrors in the other frames, but none compared to this one in his own frame! "No, no, no," he said.

"Accept it, Son." His mother moved her hand and the

magic scene vanished. It was now just a flat piece of crystal stuck in a tree bole.

"Mother, what can I do? Where is she? How can I—"

"She's in the royal palace."

"Good! I'll go there immediately, and—"

"No, Son. You must not."

"Not?"

"The evil queen is there, and will not be lightly subdued. In any event, there is no time for that. The queen put the spell on Heln, but cannot undo it. There is an antidote, and you must get it for Heln before she gives birth. That could be at any time, and that birthing will kill her."

Kelvin, noting the gross distension of Heln's body, understood. That birthing would rip her apart! "What antidote? Where?"

"Where you got your copper sting, Son. The chimaera has it."

"It has!" Had the chimaera held out on him?

*No. I did not know about this until you entered this frame and contacted your mother.*

"You know about the—?" he asked, amazed.

"The monster who speaks to you in your mind? Yes, the cards told me."

"But I have no idea what the antidote is!"

"Helbah here knows. There's a powder. A powder no chimaera can live without. It has an opposite effect in cases like this."

"What is this powder? How will I know it?"

*I have it,* Mervania thought. *I never thought I would need to give any of it away, but I see I do.*

Kelvin realized that there was a solution to this horror. If only he had known before, he could have gotten the powder and saved Heln before it got to this stage!

# CHAPTER 29

# *Antidote*

John Knight was munching on smoked fish while waiting for Rufurt to make his move.

Rufurt leaned over the board and considered before moving a pawn. It might have been a troop movement or an execution.

"Good move!" Zed Yokes said.

The king nodded. A king's moves had after all to be approved. He took a swig of the appleberry wine and handed it to John. John shook his head and sipped from the water jar instead. That fish the old river man had brought was salty!

"So there's really a war on between Kelvinia and the twin kingdom," John mused.

Zed nodded, smiling his pleasant old man's smile. "The news comes to me on the river. It comes slowly, but it comes."

"So that must be what my son is up to—bringing it to a stop."

"Just so he gets the impostor," Rufurt said. "He and the queen."

"You still call her queen, Rufurt?" John inquired, amused. "After what she did to both of us, and the kingdom?"

"You know what I mean. Villainess is more like it! Witch will do."

John moved a bishop diagonally across the board. "Check."

Rufurt immediately took the bishop with his black queen. "Sorry to do this, John. Particularly with this piece."

John tried to smile, hoping to give the impression that he

had sacrificed the bishop deliberately. Rufurt needed cheering. When Kelvin came back—and he didn't want to admit he was beginning to worry about that—there should be cheering aplenty.

"You think your son's a match for them?" Zed asked.

"He'd better be." John looked around the ruins of the old palace, remembering how the last revolution had been. "There's the prophecy, of course. I'm afraid I really believe in that."

"Now, you mean," Rufurt said. "You didn't believe in it in the old days."

"No, I didn't." How many times had he scolded Charlain for filling the boy's head with nonsense. How little had he known!

"But now you believe in prophecies and magic."

"In this frame I do! Some prophecies, some magic."

"Why is that, John?" The king put a bit of archness into it, knowing very well.

"The chimaera, for one thing. Other things we saw and experienced. I'll never again say with full certainty what can and can't be. In an infinity of frames I suspect anything is possible."

"Right you are, John. It's your move, isn't it?"

John concentrated on the board, difficult as that was for him. Finally he moved his remaining white knight.

Rufurt nudged the black queen onto the knight's square. "Sorry again, John. You're not concentrating."

"While you are." *Damn St. Helens for reinventing this game!*

"It's the experience of governing," Rufurt said. As usual he ignored the fact that he had lost his kingdom to Zoanna once and spent all those years in the royal dungeon.

"Hmmm," John said. If he moved his own queen down now he could take Rufurt's and checkmate his king in the bargain! He made the move. "Check!"

"Can't win them all," Rufurt said. He stood up from the block of masonry and stretched. His eyes scanned the skies. "There! Him, isn't it?"

John strained the eyes he hated to admit were less effective at distances than Rufurt's were. Something definitely was in the sky, and coming at them. It seemed to be the right size. "Yes," he said.

Within moments the figure was right above them. It descended, and hovered. Then, somewhat shrilly, it called: "Dad, Your Majesty, I'm going back to the chimaera's world. Wait here! I'll explain later!"

Kelvin started off again, then paused. "Mother divorced Hal. She's single now, and a witch."

With that John's surprising offspring dived rather than flew through the ruins and out of sight.

"Those young folk sure are in a hurry!" Tommy Yokes' grandfather remarked.

But John hardly cared about that. Charlain was single? Suddenly a wonderful new horizon lay before him.

Kelvin could hardly wait to reach the transporter. Very skilled now in how to hold his body while flying, he barely slowed before reaching the river ledge. Now was not the time to ponder the mysteries of the Flaw or of being. He opened the huge metal door with the help of the gauntlets and leaped inside. He barely took time to set the control for the chimaera's world, and was off.

After what his father had termed "special effects" he found himself in a somewhat more dusty chamber facing a froogear.

The froogear held out a small packet composed of one large folded leaf. Kelvin took it.

*This is it?* he demanded of the chimaera.

*It is in there, Kelvin,* Mervania's thought came. *Three little grains that will expand to a powder. Be careful you don't sneeze on them.*

*Thanks, Mervania. I'll get back with those dragonberry seeds when I can!*

*I'll let you know about that, mortal! Hurry—you haven't much time.*

*Right!* Clutching the packet, Kelvin leaped back into the transporter.

Mervania sighed. The sky was orange and cloud-filled and it was a good day to be working in the garden. Fortunately she could weed around the pumash and squakin plants while keeping a small bit of mind tuned to Kelvin.

Why was she helping this inferior life-form? Hadn't she paid her debt to it when she let it and its fellows go? An inferior life-form was after all an inferior life-form.

*That's what I've been telling you, Mervania!*

*Mertin, you know that isn't nice, scanning my thoughts that way!*

*You're doing it with Kelvin and his kind!*

*Of course! They're inferior life-forms!*

*Foodstuffs.*

*If you will.*

*I knew we should have eaten them.*

*Groowmth!* Grumpus added, tossing their dragon head.

*What I don't understand, Mervania, is why you gave him the powder.*

*You know, Mertin. You know if you think about it.*

*You think about it for me.*

*I don't want to.*

*Do it anyway.*

*Oh, very well!* Mertin was so vexing sometimes! Without giving it great attention she recalled the egg clutch they had laid just after dining on a stringy old wizard. There had been something wrong with it, as she soon realized. The eggs didn't have coppery shells, but were soft, and inside there was no more mind activity than from insects. Concentrating ever so little, she had gleaned that soft, single-headed beings were being formed that would closely resemble foodstuffs. The horror of producing monsters was too much, and the antidote, had it been available, had to be taken before the laying. There had been only one thing to do, and her body had a head for it.

*Groowmth!* Grumpus agreed, smacking his mouth. The memory of the eggs was still strong with it.

*There. Satisfied, Mertin?*

*Not quite. The offspring of the foodstuff female will be like us, if she delivers while under the influence of the chimaeradrake root. It will have three heads and copper in its blood. In time it will grow a sting. Why destroy our own, Mervania? Why prevent its birth?*

*Dunderhead! Consider the horror! One of us raised by*

*mortals! Cared for by the very inferior life-forms that are our food! Assuming they care for it at all; they might instead imprison or destroy it. No, any chimaera who comes into being must be here with us, in proper society, so as not to be stunted by regressive influences.*

*I understand, Mervania. Don't get so excited—you're making us ill.*

*I don't care if I do! Kelvin had to have the antidote, and I provided it! After she takes it the female won't lay an egg containing a superior life-form!*

*It'll be dead. The hatchling and the female. An inferior life-form won't adjust.*

*Possibly. I hadn't considered that.* Mervania remedied that by considering it now.

*At least there won't be a living superior life-form among inferiors,* Mertin thought, satisfied.

*If the antidote reaches the female in time.*

*Yes. But if that inferior female dies too, he may reconsider about fetching our dragonberry seeds.*

*But he made a deal!*

*He did. But inferior life-forms sometimes forget things when under stress.* She pondered further, troubled. What could she do to ensure that Kelvin would not be distracted from his true mission of fetching the seeds?

Then she had it. She would have to be there, mentally, when the antidote was administered. Then, with a little guidance of precisely the right nature—yes.

A sound impinged on her thoughts. Someone ringing the bell at the gate.

She reached out mentally. A froogear was there, and in its arms was something that caused Mervania to start with surprise. This—why this changed everything!

As the sun was setting, Kelvin found his mother and Helbah waiting where they had promised outside the palace. He cut the speed of his belt, lowered his feet, and landed before them.

"You get it, Kelvin?" his mother asked worriedly.

"Right here," Kelvin said, holding up the packet. "The chimaera sent a froogear to meet me at the transporter."

"That's nice, dear. Now Zoanna and the false king have fled the palace. Helbah is trying to locate them with her crystal. She's stronger now; she says I've been a big help to her. Come now!"

"But—" Kelvin protested as he followed her. "The queen—"

"Oh, Helbah can counter her fireballs! Once it was two witches against one, the queen was done for, and knew it. She won't want to give herself away, but if she does, Helbah will be ready. Can you hurry?"

"Good idea," Kelvin agreed, and activated his belt. Scooping his mother up in his arms—she weighed less than he did, now, which surprised him somewhere in the background of his mind—he hopped-flew the remaining distance. Actually the gauntlets made her seem even lighter, and they knew how to support her; he would have bungled the job on his own, he was sure. He carried her through the wall blasted open by Helbah. Through the twilight-lit throne room and the ballroom and down the halls.

"Here, this is it!" Charlain exclaimed, indicating the guest room that Kelvin and Heln had once shared.

Kelvin never paused. With all the strength of his left gauntlet he shoved in the door and paused, hovering in midair.

Dr. Sterk looked up birdlike and agitated at the bedside. Jon turned, her mouth an O of surprise. On the bed, limbs chained to the bedposts, was a bloated, misshapen thing of pure horror. This couldn't be Heln! His gentle, lovely, loving wife! It couldn't be—yet it was.

"Kelvin! Mother!" Jon cried, gladness and horror mixing.

"She's having her contractions," Dr. Sterk said grimly. "But there's no way she can birth it without destroying herself! I could cut, but—"

Kelvin swallowed. He thought he had come prepared, but his mind had gone blank.

Charlain struggled in the grip of the gauntlets. "Let me down! Let me down this instant!"

Oh. He touched down his feet and shut off his belt. He lowered his mother to the floor. She started across the room.

Night fell in an instant. Lightning cracked outside, lighting the windows. The oil lamps blew out. They were now in deepest darkness with Heln's unhuman screams.

"Darn!" Kelvin heard his mother say. She snapped her fingers. Immediately a little ball of fire appeared near the ceiling and stayed there, brightening until it gave off more light than there had been from the lamps.

"Mother—?" Kelvin asked, his heart pounding. "What—?"

"That's my fireball," Charlain said. "The darkness is Zoanna's mischief. She gave Heln the poison potion. Helbah may need a little help dealing with the queen, and I'm going to be busy here. Why don't you go outside and find her?"

"Mother, the powder!"

"Yes, and fast! Give it to me!"

He handed her the leaf packet. She held it near Heln's face. Heln drew in a breath to scream. Charlain touched the packet with a fingernail. The packet went POOF! and a cloud of pinkish smoke obscured Heln's face and head. From the midst of the smoke came an unhuman coughing and then a gasping, wheezing sound. The wheezing became a shrill whistle, as of an escaping gas. A heartbeat after that there was a choking from the midst of the pink cloud.

"Mother, she's—she's—"

Charlain raised a finger. POOF! and the cloud was gone. Heln lay there, sickly and pale, her eyes shocked and unbelieving. "Kelvin, Dr. Sterk, Mother Charlain—it's gone!"

"I know it is, dear. But your baby isn't."

"But—"

Then both froze for a moment, as if listening.

"What—?" Kelvin started.

*Will you give over, oaf?* Mervania's thought came. *The job is only half done. Let me concentrate on them; the situation is critical.*

Kelvin shut his mouth. Oddly, he felt better, knowing that the chimaera was present. He trusted Mervania's motive; she wanted this finished so he could go fetch her dragonberries.

"This is no ordinary delivery, Heln," Charlain said. "Now you know what is entailed. Are you strong enough?"

"I'll have to be," Heln said weakly.

"Then focus on the first, and bear down."

Heln's eyes rolled. Faintly she said, "I'll try." Then she lapsed into unconsciousness.

"Darn!" Charlain said. "Sorry, Kelvin, you shouldn't hear your mother swear."

"Is she—dead?"

"No, of course not. But we're all going to be if you don't get moving!"

"What should I do?" Kelvin had never felt more helpless. All he could think about was the stories of expectant fathers boiling water while the wife was in childbirth.

"How should I know?" his mother snapped in exasperation. "Go find Helbah!"

"But—"

"Your life and Heln's and all the others depend on it! Now go!"

Heln's eyes flickered open. "Go, Kel," she gasped. "You wouldn't like what happens here." She sagged down again.

*Believe her, inferior form,* Mervania thought.

Hardly realizing what he did, Kelvin left the palace. He knew that birthing a baby was difficult, but something more than that seemed to be in the offing. What was going on?

Outside a gust of wind struck him in the face and almost drove him back. Rain spattered, hot and smelling of sulfur. Lightning cracked, luridly illuminating everything with an unnatural cast.

Where was Helbah?

"Over here!" her voice cracked.

There she was, hanging on to the gatepost. He activated his belt and flew over to her.

"Kelvin," she gasped weakly. "I need your help. I can't do it without you or Charlain, and your mother has her hands more than full. So it has to be you. I can't contain them."

"I—I'll do what I can." Kelvin knew that he was an inadequate substitute. "What can I do? Tell me, Helbah, tell me!"

A great ball of fire looped across the sky. Helbah raised her hands, and a smaller ball formed at her fingertips. The small fireball shaped itself into an arrow and shot skyward as though from a bow. Witch's fire collided above them, and there was a shocking thunderclap as both magically generated missiles imploded into nothingness.

"I'm getting weaker and she's getting stronger!" Helbah said. "With Charlain's help I had her beaten, but now I am alone, and her fireballs are getting closer before I can nullify them. I was shooting them down at the horizon, but now it's almost overhead, and soon I won't be able to stop them at all. I never thought Zoanna would recover so rapidly and well! If Charlain doesn't finish quickly with that chimaera so she can add her power to mine—"

"What?" Was Mervania attacking instead of assisting?

"Get that thing off your back!"

"The sting?"

"Of course the sting! What else have you got on your back? Get its butt down on the ground, way down, in contact with the dirt. Point the point east, where that fireball came from."

Numbly, Kelvin did as directed. He hardly understood any of what was happening, inside or outside. Some hero he was!

"There." Now Helbah's fingers lightly touched the sting and moved up and down its copper surface. Lightning flashes came from her fingers and were reflected by the copper.

"What?" he asked dazedly. "What?"

"Shut up! I've got to locate her and I can't use the crystal. When a fireball comes, you zap it. This is a case where science can counter magic, as with the Mouvar weapon."

"But I don't know how to—"

Helbah made a gesture. There was a poof of magic, and smoke. Lightning flashed in the sky. Where Helbah had been there was a large white bird resembling a dovgen.

Kelvin blinked, and then the bird—symbol of gentleness and peacefulness—was in the sky, flying, darting from side to side.

Another fireball appeared from the east. This one was smaller than the last, not much larger than the bird. It streaked for the bird, and Kelvin stared with opened mouth as his gauntlets tingled.

He grasped the top of the sting's shaft with his left hand

and put his right hand farther down as far as he could reach. He tried to will lightning to stop the fireball.

Blue lightning crackled and snapped. A long, thin bolt shot from the tip of the sting and stretched out and upward. Above him the fireball sent by Zoanna was intercepted, pierced as if by an arrow. There was an improbable sizzling sound, a whiff of pure ozone, and the fireball vanished.

"I did it!" he exclaimed, astounded. "I shot down a fireball!"

Below where the fireball had been, a bird fluttered groundward in the fading light.

Kelvin's joy turned to horror. "No! No! No!" Without Helbah all was lost!

"Meow?" A blackness detached itself from the dark and reached up a paw.

The houcat! Helbah's familiar! Was it trying to tell him something?

Another fireball appeared. This one was larger than the last. Obviously Zoanna *was* gaining strength! Angry, determined, Kelvin put his hands on the copper sting and made the lightning jump. The bolt hit the fireball and the implosions all but deafened him. He gasped, almost knocked off his feet. Hot rain struck his face.

"Meow!"

He was getting weaker. He could feel it in his legs and arms. It seemed that it was his own life-energy that powered the shots. He was generating electricity from his body, just as the chimaera did, but his body was only a fraction the mass, and not adapted to this. How many bolts could he get from this sting? How many before he collapsed? Now he understood why Helbah had needed help!

He had to keep knocking out those fireballs. He thought the houcat was telling him as much. The familiar might be all that existed of Helbah, and that but for a time. If one of those fireballs hit the palace, it would be destroyed. It was up to him, then; he and the gauntlets and the chimaera's sting.

The chimaera! He tried thinking to Mervania, but got no answer; there was no indication that she was tuning him in now. What was going on within the palace?

"Meow!" Looking down in the moment of a lightning flash he saw every black hair standing up on Katbah's back. The animal's tail looked like a sharply bristled brush.

A phenomenally large fireball rushed with blurring speed across the sky. The queen was determined to finish them off now!

Concentrating hard, he threw the lightning. The ball seemed to accept the lightning and swallow it. There was an uncomfortable crackling that made his teeth ache and the blue lightning bolt snapped and cracked its full unnatural length from sting-tip to fireball.

Was this going to be the one that would destroy them?

"Meow!"

The little paw touch on the copper shaft felt like the blow of a hammer. The sting tipped. Remembering that Helbah had said the butt should make contact with the ground, he pushed down on it. Still the tip tipped, pointing more visibly, more directly at the fireball that was lighting the sky.

Lightning sizzled and there was a pop that might and might not have been in his ear. Streamers of fire faded rapidly. The lightning bolt vanished. Katbah, mewling as from singed pawpads, backed away.

How much longer could this go on? How much strength did Zoanna the witch now have? Was he going to weaken right out of the fight? Was it going to be the gauntlets and Katbah left to defend the palace?

No, he'd stay conscious, and he'd keep doing this, whatever it was. Eventually the wicked witch would have to weaken. Eventually there would have to come an end to night!

There was a horrendous roar from the palace. Katbah hissed. Kelvin turned, and saw a long low shape charge from the palace into the night. It looked a lot like a small dragon, but of course that couldn't be.

PLOP! A white bird, singed and sooty and apparently almost dead, fell beside Katbah. It lay there in the lightning's flash. Katbah sniffed it as all went dark.

"That was some trip!" Helbah groaned.

Kelvin swallowed. "You're—back?"

"Of course I'm back! For a dimwitted boy you ask the dumbest questions!"

"I—I'm sorry, Helbah. I thought—"

"You thought that fireball got me. That's what you were supposed to think! That's what Zoanna was supposed to think!"

"Meow."

"Yes, Katbah, you did right. Can't depend on a hero for everything. Particularly one as inexperienced as this."

Considering all the adventures he had had in his relatively short life span, Kelvin did not feel he was inexperienced. But the need to get on with this was great.

"Helbah, what did you—?"

"Found them. Cave in the mountainside. Now it's up to you, me, and Charlain. Get that fireball, will you?"

Almost absently Kelvin directed the chimaera's sting to lightning out another approaching fire-bolus. The ground shook.

"But Mother is—"

"Here," Charlain said behind him. "And congratulations, hero, you are now the husband of a relatively healthy, loving wife, and the father of a healthy, squalling baby boy."

Kelvin's mouth dropped open.

"And a rather pretty baby girl," Jon said, emerging with a bundle.

The enormity of the change in his life hit him then, as did the ground before he had half realized.

## CHAPTER 30

# *Defeat?*

"Wake up, hero! Wake up!"

He felt her slapping him. Helbah. Then he felt the cat's tail under his nose and he wanted to sneeze.

"Does he do this often, Charlain?"

"I wouldn't know, Helbah. We'll have to ask his wife."

*Wife! Heln! The baby!*

*Babies!*

Kelvin sat up, then stood up. He was dizzy. There were stars in the sky, not all of his making. A moon, bright and coppery as a chimaera's haunch, lighting the grounds of the Kelvinian palace.

He made his way unsteadily to where Jon stood, holding his daughter. The baby's face seemed oddly familiar. The eyes were dark, almost coppery—

He froze. That face, after allowing for the difference in age—

*Don't be concerned,* Mervania thought. *All foodstuffs look alike to us too. She favors me only slightly.*

Kelvin reeled.

"What's the matter, Kel?" Jon asked, alarmed. "She's not ugly, she's remarkably pretty for a newborn baby, and so's her brother, Mother says. Nothing wrong with either of them."

"But—"

*What your mother doesn't want to tell you,* Mervania thought, *is that there were three. The dragon fled.*

But—"

*It was a very tricky disenchantment, Kelvin. You can't undo in a minute something that has developed for weeks. We saved your wife's life by breaking the chimaera into three: boy, girl, and dragon. You may keep the first two. That's fair, isn't it?*

Kelvin's mouth was stuck halfway open.

*Now go in there and see your wife, and be brave when they tell you about the third. It was the best that could be done, Kelvin. The two are completely human, except—*

*Except?* he thought numbly.

*They will be telepathic. Sorry about that; it just couldn't be helped. Now be on your way. I'll be on mine; I have business at home to hold me for a while.* He felt her presence fade; she was gone.

Kelvin shut his mouth and started toward the palace.

"Uh, I know she wants to see you, but not just yet," Jon said. "It was a difficult delivery, and there's blood, and she's sleeping—"

"True," Charlain said. "And we do have other business out here. Stand by, Kelvin."

He stood by. Jon turned and walked into the palace with the baby girl. *They didn't know the whole story!* he thought. *They didn't know Mervania's part in it.*

"Later we must talk, Kelvin," Charlain said. "But right now we must deal with the queen, or all can still be lost."

Kelvin finally found his voice. "Yes. I'll help here."

"We have to get to work," Helbah agreed.

"The fireballs!" Kelvin said. "Are you watching? I forgot to—"

"She has quit sending them for the time being. It takes as much energy to generate them as to abolish them. I must admit I'm surprised at her strength. If you hadn't come out when you did we'd have been finished."

Kelvin refocused on the problem. He had managed, with the help of the chimaera's sting, to make witchfire arrows! Or at least the lightning to shoot them down. But indeed the battle was not over; not until Zoanna was gone. He stared into the sky. He'd never expected to see the moon out tonight; it had been so dark. But of course the storm had not been natural.

"Do you think they're trying to escape?" Charlain asked.

"I think they're planning something," Helbah said. "Zoanna swore she'd never give up. If that's so, we'll have to finish her."

"She'll come back if we don't, won't she?" Kelvin asked.

"Probably. One thing you can say for her, she's not a quitter."

"Nor is Rowforth. He's just as bad!"

"Fortunately Rowforth hasn't her magic. Let's go get them."

"To that cave?"

"As I told you, for a slow boy you ask the dumbest questions! Of course to the cave!"

"How will we—?" Helbah was clearly the general, he thought.

"Charlain and I may not need you there. Hand your mother the antimagic weapon. It won't crack Zoanna's barrier, but it just might help. You stay here with the sting and Katbah

and watch for fireballs. Your former queen is just mean enough
to try one final attack on the palace."

"I—I'll watch." He handed his mother the Mouvar
weapon. Then he thought again and handed her the belt and
short scabbard. She took these with as little surprise as though
he had handed her a pot in her own kitchen. She strapped on
the weapon, seeming not in the least curious about it.

"I'm sure you will," Helbah said. "Charlain, hop on my
back!"

With astonishment that seemed lately never to cease,
Kelvin watched his mother climb piggyback on Helbah's aging
shoulders. Then, as the moon hid under clouds and it was as
dark as the inside of a serpent, there was a whooshing sound.
The moon came back and there was a white dovgen climbing
into the sky with what looked like a small gray shrewouse
clinging with tiny paws to its feathers.

The bird disappeared into the dark sky. There were no
lightnings. No flaming balls of witch's fire.

"Meow." Absently he reached down and stroked the cat.
He was back to the little-boy stage, he thought, waiting
patiently for adults to accomplish adult business. All in all it
wasn't too bad a place to be.

Katbah rubbed against him and purred contentment and
wordless understanding. He was beginning to understand why
witches had familiars; they could be a lot of comfort on dark
nights.

No, not too bad a place for someone who had never
wanted the hero mantle in the first place.


"Ohhh," Rowforth moaned. "Zoanna, you're taking too
much of my life-force. It's flowing out and nothing is replacing
it. Zoanna, you're draining me!"

"Can't be helped. You want to win, don't you? Quit your
whining."

"But Zoanna, if you kill me in order to destroy them,
where's my triumph? You don't want me dead." Then he
paused, a new and not entirely pleasant thought occurring.
"You don't, do you, Zoanna?"

Zoanna, now the complete witch, did not answer. She
merely smiled in ever so enigmatic a fashion.

Rowforth, who had been merely uncomfortable, now found that he was thoroughly scared. He resolved that he would find some way of being useful to her other than at the expense of his life-force. To fail to do this, he strongly suspected, would cost him dear. It could, he knew in the depths of him, cost him his life.

John and Rufurt had ridden the plowhorse double half the way to the palace. John for his part was having second thoughts. True, the lights in the sky meant big things afoot, and probably danger to those he loved. But, and the thought jolted him worse than the plowhorse, the intelligent thing would have been to go back to Kian and get his help.

"Curse it," Rufurt said with disgust, "there's never an army around when you need one!"

Looking at the dancing lights in the sky and having his senses beset by implosive blasts, John had to agree with the former king's estimate. But he had to go on. Somewhere ahead there was Charlain!

Jon watched Heln nursing her firstborn and felt a stirring inside her that she had never honestly felt before. Possibly, just possibly, she herself was not completely devoid of maternal instinct. She looked down at the secondborn she held. She certainly was a cute baby! She had her grandma's coppery hair. But how were they going to tell Kelvin about the horrible third one?

Well, maybe they wouldn't have to. The thing had gained its feet immediately and scampered out before they could do more than stare. Heln, lapsing into unconsciousness again, hadn't seen it at all. Maybe nobody but Jon, Charlain, and Dr. Sterk ever needed to know of the horror that had been the remnant of the evil enchantment. It was safely gone.

"I'm sure they'll be all right," Dr. Sterk said, putting his beak of a nose almost in her face. "I wasn't certain. We physicians have so little training in magic."

"I'm sure that can change," Jon said.

"It will. It will have to. After all, magic is the basis of all healing."

"I've heard that all my life. From Mother, mostly." Jon

looked at the window and was surprised how light it had become. The ball of fire Charlain had left had gradually grown dimmer until now it was about as bright as that of twin oil lamps.

"I'll light the lamps again, Doctor. I'm not certain how long my mother's light will last."

"Probably almost until morning," Dr. Sterk said.

Jon busied herself with the lamps. She hadn't a coal to apply to the wicks so she simply held them near the witch's fire and—not surprisingly, to her at least—they lit.

"Good girl, Jon."

"Doctor, do you mind if I go out and see what Kelvin and our mother are about? It has been a while."

"No indeed, Jon. I'm wondering about that myself." He took the baby from her.

Heln stirred, weak and wan in the bed. "Please Jon, find out about Kelvin."

"Don't worry about him," Jon said, patting the new mother's hand. How wonderful it was to have Heln back, instead of the monster she had become under the enchantment! "He's our hero and nothing bad will happen to him. He didn't come in before because I asked him not to. There was blood, and you were just about unconscious." *And we had to clean up the gory tracks of that horrible third birth!*

Heln sighed. "Of course. You're right, Jon. You almost always are." She closed her eyes. *And we didn't want to rouse you until that was done either,* Jon's thought finished.

Jon left the palace, sling in hand. She was wondering if what she'd told Heln was true. Prophecy or no prophecy, she knew she had on more than one occasion saved her brother's life.

Kelvin stood at the gatepost in the moonlight. His hands were on a copper something that looked a little like a dragon spear that she hadn't noticed before, in the mixed excitement of the birthings. The point of the spear thing was pointed skyward; was it some sort of new weapon? Why would he need anything different if he had the Mouvar weapon that had won the war with Aratex? And there, next to his leg, rubbing up against him, was a large, black houcat.

"Kelvin?"

"Jon!" he exclaimed, as if seeing her for the first time. "Is Heln all right? Are the babies—?"

"Calm yourself," she said with a tired smile. "They're all fine. Heln's asking for you. As soon as you finish here, you can go see her." What a boy Kelvin was, actually, she realized. How much more grown-up she and Heln were, and even her own Lester.

"I have to watch the sky for fireballs," he said. "Mother and our—" He paused, swallowed, and then went on: "Our ally, have gone to finish something."

"You mean the witch from the twin cities, don't you?" How naive did he think she was? Who else had been defending them from Zoanna and the false king these past days?

"Yes—yes, that's what I mean. Helbah thinks they're licked and that she can finish them."

"Isn't that a job for a hero?"

"I'm not complaining," Kelvin said.

Jon lightly touched his hand. "You've sent back Zoanna's fireballs, Kel?"

"This stopped them," he said, touching the copper spear.

"Why stop them? Why not send them back?"

"Witches erect magic barriers when they expect magical attack or counterattack. The returned fireballs might have bothered Zoanna but they wouldn't have crisped her unless she'd dropped her guard. She might even have been poised to bounce them back again, and that could have made it worse for us."

"She maintained that through magic?"

"Yes."

"Kelvin, why don't you go after them?"

"I'm supposed to guard the palace. If I neglect my post, and the queen sends one more fireball, we'll lose even if we kill Zoanna. Anyway, Helbah can handle it."

"Are you certain?"

He frowned. "Why?"

She bit her lower lip and tried to see off into the darkness, past the forest, to the mountainside. There was just the faintest of flashes there, first high up and then low down.

"Look, Kelvin," she said, directing his gaze, "isn't that a battle? Aren't the witches going at it hard?"

Kelvin's eyes squinted. "I don't see . . . I can't see past the forest."

"It is," she said. "The witches battling. Kelvin, I think you should go and help."

"They've got the Mouvar weapon."

"But it may not be enough. Zoanna can't take time to throw a fireball at the palace. Helbah and Mother have her occupied."

Kelvin frowned. "You really think I should—"

"Yes." She was really worried now.

"All right, then." He took up the copper spear and strapped it to his back. He did something to his belt and his feet left the ground, and he soared like an untethered cloud. He looked back once, and then he was flying through the moonlight in the direction of the mountainside.

Jon sighed. She hoped she had done the right thing. Her brother seemed so helpless sometimes!

"Meow?" The black houcat seemed almost to question her.

"Yes, kitty," she said. "Kelvin's off to be a hero, and I know that someway he'll save the day. Because he is guarded by the prophecy, while the others aren't. I wish I was going with him. I wish you and I could fly."

"Meow." Something stung her legs, like a jolt of what her father called static electricity but which she had always thought magic. The stars grew smaller and somehow the grass and the gatepost grew high. Ozone was in the air and there was a taste in her mouth that surely she had never tasted before.

She flexed her white wings. A black creature the size of a shrewouse climbed up between her shoulders and gently gripped her feathers with claws.

Jon flapped her dovgen wings and flew after Kelvin.

*I'm off to join the witches!* she thought as the fields and the trees slid by. Somehow she wasn't at all surprised.

Helbah sweated and strained to keep the barrier erected. She could feel it bulging inward, pushing at them, wanting to break. The heat from the steadily roaring flames was getting to her, and worse still, to her apprentice.

"Now, Charlain!" she said. With all their strength they pushed together, back, back. Who would have thought Zoanna commanded such power?

There was only one thing left to try, and she tried it. Hate technology though she might, there was such a thing as a mixture of technology and magic. She raised Kelvin's Mouvar weapon to point at the cliff, though where it pointed hardly mattered. She pressed its trigger.

The fireball receded from before them. It retreated to the cliffside and the entrance to a cave. It stopped there, held in check by Zoanna's barrier. If Zoanna should drop the barrier she would be consumed by her own bolide. If Helbah could now add her own witch's fire the barrier would surely disintegrate.

Unfortunately the Mouvar weapon recognized no distinction between Zoanna's fireball and her own. Should Helbah try a magical counterattack, it would rebound on her and Charlain.

She was weakening alarmingly fast. That treacherous injury she had taken on the battlefield still vitiated her strength; she needed far more recuperation time than she had gotten. She didn't know how long she could go on. If only Zoanna would weaken before Helbah weakened further. The Mouvar weapon held her in check for a breathing spell and then its power weakened and Zoanna's fireball was drifting back.

Now she regretted telling Kelvin to remain at the palace. She needed him here, with his copper sting! With that he might throw a nonmagical electrical bolt through the barrier. That would be the end of Zoanna and the worst of her many consorts.

THUNK!

The feathered crossbow bolt, definitely not magic, protruded from her arm. Blood started from around the shaft. She had only heartbeats left, if that, to maintain consciousness. Heartbeats to contain the barrier protecting them from the witch's fire!

She could deal with the wound, by focusing her magic on it, for it was not a critical one. But if she did that, there would be no barrier to Zoanna's magical attack. She had to maintain that barrier!

The wound burned horribly. Her arm seemed to swell to twice its normal size. She lost feeling in the extremity. Her finger loosened on the Mouvar's trigger. The weapon dropped, and she after it.

"Helbah! Helbah!" her apprentice cried.

*Poor Charlain,* Helbah thought as her senses faded. *I've failed you and the rest.*

"Good shot, Rowforth!"

"Nothing to it, my love." Despite his faking it, he could hardly stand. How he had gotten to his feet and aimed the crossbow was a mystery proving once again his remarkable endurance. "Better get them now, love, while you have the chance."

"I'm going to, sweetie. But I intend to savor my victory. Look who's there! Can you see him in the morning light?"

Rowforth squinted. "Kelvin!"

"That's right. We've got the entire bunch! At our mercy, only we have no mercy."

"Burn them! Burn them!"

"In good time." She sharpened her eyesight, a trick she had only recently learned. The thin, tawny-haired trouble-maker and prophesied curse was definitely there. He was trying to help Helbah and at the same time he was looking up at them. Helbah was almost finished—and he was almost finished.

She began forming a fireball in front of the ledge. Slowly, slowly, slowly. No need to hurry. Big, big. Hot, hot. Oh, it was nice!

Rowforth gasped weakly and sat down. He was being drained beyond his tolerable threshold, but it couldn't be helped. This was the fire that counted!

Rowforth picked up his crossbow, tried to put another bolt in it, and tried to crank it taut. He fumbled with the cocking mechanism, then dropped it, too weak. "For the gods' sake, Zoanna, you're weakening me too much!"

"How much is too much?" she inquired indifferently.

"This will be the fullest revenge, Rowforth. You didn't know I knew about the maid, did you?"

Even in the hot glow from the fireball, Rowforth's face was white. "I thought—"

"You thought you could be unfaithful. That was an error on your part."

"You were unfaithful!"

"Zoanna is Zoanna. My consorts are my consorts. You were only a consort, my sweet."

"Was?" Realization made his voice weak.

"Was, sweet," she said firmly.

Rowforth's eyes bulged above his big ruddy nose until his very face looked obscene. "Zoanna, you're draining me completely! You're killing me!"

"I am, Your Unfaithfulness. It's all part of my triumph. For my next consort I think I'll take a young and inexperienced boy. That guardsman who stole your prize mare and ran off and joined with that fool St. Helens, what's-his-name— Lomax. Yes, for a time he might be quite pleasant. With what I know now I can make him come to me. Come and perform, delightfully."

"ZOANNA! ZOANNA!" He could not even move his hand to draw the dagger he carried. All of what energy he retained went into his pleading, accusing shouts.

Feeling a bit smug about it she moved the fireball to where Helbah's barrier had been. Past the spot, to where Kelvin could feel the heat and not quite fry. The boy was now trying desperately to get the chimaera sting from his back. *Excellent, Kelvin! With that you really could destroy me!* Now his mother was helping him, pulling at a thong, guiding it off his shoulder with her fingertips.

"That's too easy for you!" Zoanna said. She nudged the fireball closer. Now they were burning their dainty fingers on the sting, as they tried, but failed, to point it at her. Like houcat and shrewous, this game!

One more little nudge and it would be all over. She was almost reluctant. Wait until they nearly had the sting grounded, almost pointing at her. Wait until the very last microsecond. Wait, wait, wait, savoring.

She glanced down at Rowforth's inert body. Too bad he was already out of it. He would have enjoyed seeing Kelvin die. It was appropriate: it was Rowforth's remaining life-force that was in the fireball, doing the deed.

She nudged the fireball just a tiny bit closer. There, let them fry, let them cook and steam before she burned them. Let their lungs burst, their hearts explode, their eyeballs melt. When she was done only their charred bones would remain.

Now, now, now was the moment! Now her triumph when all her enemies burned.

Throwing back her head, she vented a vengeful laugh of complete and final triumph.

Kelvin felt his skin blister. The stench of his own burning hair was in his nostrils. His hands and the leathery gauntlets protecting them were cooking on the copper surface of the chimaera's sting. Waves of continuous pain were making him nauseous. His mother was beside him but he had almost forgotten her. What magic she and Helbah had had was vanquished. There was no way, no way at all that they could survive.

Klunk! It seemed to be an irrelevant, meaningless sound to accompany their dying. The fire around them was somehow fainter. Then, remarkably, the fireball vanished and his eyes flashed with pain.

Was this death? No, it hurt too much!

"KELVIN! CRISP THEM!"

His sister's voice? It couldn't be! Delusion before death? He couldn't think.

The fire was gone now. Through streaming eyes he could see the cave above them. Two bodies were lying there. Zoanna's and Rowforth's. Were they dead?

"HURRY, KELVIN! HURRY!"

It *was* Jon's voice!

"Kelvin, I can't find another rock!" Her voice was close and unmistakably hers. "She's going to wake! Hurry!"

No time to question. He placed his hands on the copper, heard the sizzle, smelled the burning flesh. He was screaming, though hardly aware of it. He ignored the agony ballooning bigger and bigger and threatening momentarily to explode his heart. Only one thing to think about: lightning. Pure, sizzling lightning to cleanse and destroy . . .

"Kelvin, she's awake! She getting up! She's—"

CRACK! It was his bolt, scoring.

In the blue afterimage he saw two skeletons on the cave ledge. One stood upright with raised hands, but now all flesh was gone from it. Yet it remained vertical, unwilling to fall down. The very bones were shapely, retaining the outline of a beautiful woman.

Magical beings died hard. Maybe witches died hardest. Almost entirely destroyed, they could yet somehow return to life. Or so it seemed possible to believe, right now.

The figure moved. It didn't fall. Its arms came together over its head, as if shaping something between the bone-fingers. Something like another fireball.

"Kelvin!"

Again he willed the lightning.

CRACK!

The standing skeleton crumbled, yet it remained intact. It landed on hands and knees, trying to break its fall.

CRACK! SIZZLE! CRACK! Lightning bolt after lightning bolt. He felt himself being drained, but he gave it his all. The bolts blasted the skeleton apart, and blasted the individual bones, and blasted the fragments.

Now nothing remained on the ledge or in the cave but ash. As he stared upward the ash stirred in a morning breeze and slowly lost all shape.

He tottered himself. Now he could die. It was done.

"Kelvin, did you get them?" Whispery and dry, it was Helbah. He had thought her dead.

"They're gone," Kelvin gasped. "Forever, I think."

"Good. Your mother—?"

He looked down at the crumpled heap that had been she who had borne him. "I—I don't know."

"She may survive. You may. I may."

"Yes." But unlikely, he thought.

"The war—will you surrender to me?"

War? Surrender? What was she talking about?

"Do it, Son. *Please!*" It was his mother, reviving, still able to speak!

"I'll do what you ask," he said, hardly aware of what he was promising. "Your side won. Kelvinia stands defeated."

*It was never my war in the first place!* he thought. *Never Kelvinia's. Never mine.*

"In that case, I'm sure we will survive," Helbah said more briskly. "Charlain, hands!"

Charlain lifted her arms with difficulty and placed burned palms against Helbah's. There was a sizzle and the blackness disappeared from their hands. Both women grew rosy and visibly stronger. Burns and scorch marks disappeared. Fire-frizzed hair lost tips of ash and became all dark and healthy. Helbah's shoulder wound stopped bleeding and she removed one hand from Charlain to start to pull out the arrow's head.

"Kelvin!"

Hands touched, gripped, firmed. Helbah held his right, his mother his left.

The agony faded. His heart resumed beating normally. Strength came back in waves that were positively exhilarating.

"There," Helbah said, dropping his hand. "We are now whole again, thanks to some help from a friend."

That was an overstatement, for she still had a crossbow wound in her arm. But now she was able to attend to it.

Jon appeared suddenly, breaking through some brush. In her arms was Katbah. Over her left shoulder hung the sling that had saved all of them.

"Kelvin, we did it!"

"We did, Sister," he agreed. He was thankful that Jon hadn't arrived a moment earlier, for then she would have seen what pitiful shape they were all in. How had she gotten here, anyhow?

"She inherited some of her mother's latent talent," Helbah said. "Katbah recognized it. Smart Katbah."

"It was awful!" Jon said, looking happy. "I looked for another rock after I changed, but I never found one. I knew all the time she'd only stay down so long. If you hadn't lightning'd her, Kel . . ."

Katbah, who had been contentedly snuggling in her arms,

suddenly stiffened and jumped down. Every hair on the familiar's body stood out. The hair on Helbah and Charlain flared as well.

"There's a presence," Helbah whispered. "A presence whose energy I utilized."

Kelvin's heart resumed pounding. Did this mean Zoanna had somehow survived the lightning? Had they been cruelly tricked?

"Calm yourselves," a feminine voice said. It seemed familiar, yet strange. It wasn't Zoanna, or Helbah's or Charlain's or Jon's. Yet he knew that voice! It—

"Mervania?" Kelvin exclaimed.

"Perceptive!" Mertin's voice said. Then there was a growling, as of a dragon.

"But I *hear* you!" Kelvin said. "Why aren't you in my head?"

"Because I'm here outside your head, inferior life-form!" Mervania said. "I came to tell you that you needn't bring those dragonberries. One of you planted some seeds, maybe accidentally. I've now got plenty of them."

The seeds they had carried with them and that Kian had lost? They had somehow come up in the chimaera's frame?

"You catch on eventually, human foodstuff."

"Then I won't need to return to your frame? Ever?"

"Don't say it!" Mertin said.

"No," Mervania said. "You won't have to return, Kelvin."

There was a growl of disappointment. "Damn it, Merv, if you'd kept your mouth shut he might have come, and we could have eaten him."

"I know, Mertin. But leave me my foibles. He's a cute boy."

Kelvin sighed, thankful. "You came all the way here, astrally, just to tell me that?"

"No trouble, Kelvin. Actually I thought I might give you some help, but you seem to have done well enough on your own. Not without the use of my present, though."

"Yes." A horrid thought hit him. "Will you stick around? Do you mean to stay here?"

"Calm yourself again, Kelvin," Mervania said, amused.

"No, you won't see me again unless you come visiting, which I wouldn't advise. I want to find my own kind. In an infinity of frames there has to be one where an intelligent life-form is dominant. Where one of our kind may have hatched and survived in a civilized manner, instead of degraded by savages. Here the only intelligent beings are houcats and dragons."

"I . . . see."

"Unless your wife would like to visit."

"What?"

"Don't be concerned. We wouldn't eat her. But we could give her more of the powder, so she could birth one of our kind in a suitable environment. It's a rare talent, to be able to—"

"No!" Kelvin cried, echoed by Jon.

"Well, I did help her," Mervania said, sounding hurt. "Considering that I already had the dragonberries, I really didn't have to."

"You already had—when you—the birthing—?" he asked, stunned.

"Her and her damn-fool sentiment!" Mertin exclaimed angrily, accompanied by a similarly outraged growl.

Kelvin realized that Mervania had indeed been generous, by chimaera definition. She had no longer needed him for the berries, yet she had done him a singular favor. She had saved his wife's life.

"Well, actually, I did it mostly for the offspring," Mervania said. "This is no frame for a Superior Life-form."

"All the same, Mervania, thanks," he said sincerely.

"Now see what you've done, Merv!" Mertin said accusingly. "You've made him grateful. The mush is so solid you could bite it!" And the dragon growled with similar disgust.

"But he has such a charmingly foolish image of me!" Mervania said defensively.

All too true! Kelvin swallowed, then uttered a difficult truth. "I—I think my daughter *does* look like you, Mervania, and I—I don't mind."

"Why thank you, Kelvin," she replied, sounding genuinely touched.

"Goodbye, Mervania."

There was silence. After a moment he realized that the chimaera was gone.

The others were staring at him, but Kelvin didn't mind that, either.

# EPILOGUE

*I*t was not a big, fancy wedding. Certainly nothing to compare with what Kian's had been. But when John took Charlain's hand, pushed back her copper hair, gazed into her violet eyes, and said, "Charlain, we are again wed. For always, you and I," and she replied, "Yes, John, always, you and I," there was not a dry eye in the ballroom of what had been Kelvinia's palace.

Later, after the formal reception and the shaking of hands of all well-wishers, the bride, groom, their family and closest friends sat together in the lounging room.

Jon still wiped at her eyes. It was apparent that she had been moved even more than she might have wished, and in more ways. Brave, tomboyish Jon, holding Lester's hand and trying valiantly to stem the tide.

"How come Easter's pregnant and I'm not?" she demanded in a whisper of Lester. "She's younger than I am!"

Startled, Lester turned to her. It was evident that a certain attitude had changed somewhere along the way. "We'll discuss that later," he whispered back.

"We'll do more than that!" she muttered. Then she looked around as if fearful that someone had overheard, or had noticed her tears. It seemed that no one had. At least, no one gave any sign.

Kelvin noticed, though. He was tempted to say something brotherly, but then thought better of it. He and his sister were getting on famously these days and he didn't want to wreck it. So instead of telling her that she had a right to weep, or whatever, and that the wedding made it legitimate, he turned to Morton Crumb.

"It was a nice wedding, wasn't it?"

"Yeh, very nice." Beside Mor sat his Mrs., fat and comforting Mabel, whom Kelvin hardly knew.

Kelvin turned to his wife. She had recovered so nicely during the past weeks. No nightmares, though he hardly understood how that was possible. Maybe it was the efficiency of the chimaera's powder. She sat there calmly nursing Charles, whose pink, chubby expression never betrayed what he might have been. Twin Merlain lay sleeping beside her. They were to be Knights, by mutual agreement, now that the marriage of their grandparents had been restored.

"You comfortable, dearest?"

"You ask me that so often! Yes, of course. But I'll be more comfortable once we're home."

Kelvin smiled. There was a type of comfort that he had not had recently that only she could supply.

"Well anyway," Rufurt spoke up from across the room, repositioning the crown on his head, "that's another two words of your prophecy. 'Uniting four' means Kance, Klingland, Hermandy, and Kelvinia. We're one confederation now, each with one vote, with brothers Kildom and Kildee having the power to veto all the rest of us. In all of history there's never been such an arrangement, but Helbah wanted it."

"It's for the best," Kelvin said. "I trust Helbah. Kelvinia never had any difficulties with Klingland and Kance that Zoanna and your look-alike didn't invent. And with those boys in charge you know Hermandy will behave itself."

"They already got rid of their dictator," St. Helens said. "I say hooray for them."

"I'm sure we all do," Kelvin said almost automatically.

"And Kelvin," his father-in-law said, leaning forward, "you know what's next for you. The prophecy says 'Until from Seven there be One / Only then will his Task be Done.' Well, there are still three kingdoms left for you to conquer."

Kelvin considered carefully before he spoke. St. Helens was not an evil man, though he did sometimes talk like what his father called a war hawk. Those two young fellows in the twin caps had many, many years to grow, and he was certain Helbah wouldn't let them declare war yet if ever. All in all, one pleasing solution as far as he was concerned.

"I'm glad it's only old words some people believe in, and that I'm not even nominally in charge," he said.

No one looked disappointed with his answer, not even St. Helens. They were all too polite to speak the obvious: as a hero, he was an inferior life-form.

It was a great, fine time in Kelvinia and the confederation.